The Fairy Comaras

Italian American Fairy Tales

By Angela Sabatino

Satchmo Press

Paperback ISBN 979-8-8054-3807-4

Cover and Book Design by Joseph Ricci. Illustrations from Shutterstock.com.

Printed and bound in the U.S.A.
9 8 7 6 5 4 3 1

Satchmo Press
New York, New York, USA

To Jean, a Fairy Comara and treasured friend

Prologue

Like Adam and Eve, our downfall came from an apple; our apple was a company who changed the dynamic of social interaction; after that, we faded into the sunset. Face-to- face became Face Time and by 2005, the Thursday evening meetings of the Fairy Comaras got smaller and less frequent. This, of course, was not the only reason, most of us are now in our 70's and either moved away or died. Add to that, that our neighborhood was changing; people moving in and people moving out. But, technology definitely diminished the value of the Thursday evening meetings. Today, Fairy Comara meetings are replaced by an APP. There's an app online if you feel depressed, or experiencing grief, there's a I hate my ex-husband group, my dog doesn't love me group, I can't go to sleep group or a I have nothing to say but I'm going to say it anyway group, you name it, they got it online. I'm still waiting for a I want everyone to kiss my ass group, maybe I'll start one myself. Fairy Comaras don't do well online; when we talk to you, we want you to feel the energy between us, not the warmth of an overused cell phone.

Some of you out there had a Fairy Comara in your life; if she is still alive, she's helping you right now. If not, you carry all her wisdom or remember something that she did for you that changed your life and pointed you in the right direction. We don't wear halos, we don't have magic wands but, our determination to help you is a force to be reckoned with! We come in many guises; we're in sweatpants or heels, we're plus-sized or slim, short or tall; we range from stay at home Moms to those running their own business. And, you never know when you're going to meet a Fairy Comara; sometimes they come out of left field. Perhaps a person you only say hello and goodbye to? Sometimes they can actually be a family member like an aunt or an uncle. You only know that this person made an indelible mark in your life one time or, maybe, many times.

And, a Fairy Comara doesn't have to be Italian, either. Comaras can enter your life as white, black, Asian, Irish, Puerto Rican, Russian, you name it, we come in many colors and many cultures. It just happened that we're Italian; except for Irish Marie. We were sent by God to help others overcome the most challenging circumstances in their lives; when they're at their lowest point. We even helped in circumstances where we knew we'll never get a Thank You. This is how we made our brownie points with the big man upstairs.

The word, Comara, sometimes gets a bad reputation because of the Mafia movies, the mistress is always referred to as a Comara. There was only one Fairy Comara, that we knew of, that was a mistress and, she ended that one-way street relationship a long time ago but, she was not a putana. And to be honest, even if she was a putana, she helped a lot of family and friends and that has to count for something. However, that's not really what a Comara is; Comaras are regarded by Italians as someone who either is a godmother through baptism or a friend of the family who is so close that she's like family and well loved. So, when it came time to actually put a name on us, we chose the Fairy Comaras. Each of us helped someone in our family or in the neighborhood. We've pulled more rabbits out of our hats for people than a circus magician.

I want to start off by saying that I am not a writer; Antoinette Fresca put me up to this. She's one of the Fairy Comaras. She asked me to write up a "history" of us so that all the Fairy Comaras that are alive can save it and show it to their children and grandchildren. For almost five years, she kept on asking me, on and on and on, to do this until I finally said basta! OK, and went on my laptop and typed. Don't get me wrong, I have the time, I'm just not good at writing. For me, this is a recollection about how a group of seemingly ordinary women did extraordinary acts of kindness for other people without expectation.

Today's generation needs to know the power of group energy. It's okay to use group energy on a large scale like staging protests but, little acts of kindness among friends can produce the same energy. You will be surprised at the things we accomplished as a group.

No one seemed to have the time to write; all the other Fairy Comaras were either busy with their grandchildren, volunteering for some church event, going to doctor appointments, to the senior center or, just plain computer illiterate. So, Antoinette decided to call the other Fairy Comaras and suggested that I do it; they all ganged up on me on the Zoom. After all, I didn't have grandchildren running all over the house so, I became the one to do it. My only hope is that I've done a good job in re-telling stories of the Fairy Comaras.

When we all got together to suggest which stories to write about, we were up to 40 stories and I held up my hand and said again, "A basta!" too much. I told them I'm not writing another War and Peace so we narrowed it down to about seven or eight stories that we all felt should be included; stories that involved us as a group.

So, Fairy Comaras, don't judge me if I repeat myself or get my dates or names wrong; I'm as old as you are and you're not the one writing it. Maybe we'll have an editing session if I haven't moved by then. Antoinette Fresca, this is my best shot, hope you're happy.

I'm the only Fairy Comara that's still living in the old neighborhood, Park Slope, Brooklyn, NY. I finally threw in the towel this year and decided to put my home up for sale. I had a nice young couple, both professionals, living in the downstairs apartment. They just gave me their 30-day notice; they found an apartment in Manhattan. I guess I'll leave the apartment empty after they leave; they say you can sell a two-family home faster if there are no tenants. However, I am concerned that now I'm in this big house all alone. Regrettably, it's time to leave Park Slope and hang up my wings and wand for posterity.

I always thought I'd leave Brooklyn in a pine box, feet first but, when the Fairy Comaras gradually started moving away some 15-16 years ago, the magic of our neighborhood started to disappear. Up until 2015, I'd still get a come over call to drop by from one of them or one pops in with an "I can only stay 5 minutes" which always lasts an hour. But, as the years passed, the visits are less frequent. And, I don't blame them; I'm having problems traveling myself. All of the Fairy Comaras, except me, moved away to be nearer to their children, grandchildren and relatives in Long Island, New Jersey, Connecticut, Pennsylvania and some even moved south to North Carolina and Florida to those gated 55 and over senior communities. Most of us are in our early or late 70's now; our parents are loving memories and our children have families of their own. Officially, the Fairy Comaras Thursday Evening Meeting Group ended in 2010. After 10-15 years of migrations of longtime neighbors moving out and new neighbors moving in, Park Slope took on a different nuance. The magic was gone.

My traveling days to visit them in Long Island, New Jersey, Connecticut, Pennsylvania and Florida are no longer possible because of my "Arthuritis" as our mothers used to call it. In the house I'm presently living in, the steps have become a real hindrance for me; going up to bed has a strategic plan all of its own and God forbid I forget to bring up something from downstairs, I just say fuck it, I'm not going down again. I have to be very careful and alert and even then, sometimes I lose my balance. I'm getting forgetful; I always leave my medic alert somewhere around the house instead of around my neck where it belongs. It's an accident waiting to happen. I told Antoinette I'm not looking at any houses with stairs in Brewster, NY. She's been trying to lure me there for about a year now.

The reason the Fairy Comaras don't visit me often is because they only travel by car; actually, their children drive them everywhere. Some of us never learned to drive and the trains require too much walking for us. I mean, who needed a car in Brooklyn unless you were visiting relatives from far away; if we went shopping, we'd take the train or the bus. I see them mostly at weddings and funerals now, but, we have Face Time on our cell phones and, for those of us who know how to use it, we meet on the Zoom. We don't get a big crowd on the Zoom even though our children help us; we never remember how to log on, me included. One of the Fairy Comaras, Theresa Guarino, passed away four years ago. She was 74 years old. She is the only Fairy Comara we lost so far. As youths, we used to think if someone was in their 70's and died they were old! Now we say the dead were taken so young. Rest in Peace, Theresa!

She was a nurse and our medical Fairy Comara at the Thursday evening meetings. She'd help all our mothers in recommending the right doctors or she'd diagnose some of their ailments herself. She helped a great many people both inside and outside of the hospital. Some of her elderly patients' children would give her a gift for the way she treated their parents even though she'd always say, "I'm just doing my job". She dated some of the guys in the neighborhood but, in the end, she married a doctor and became Theresa Christiansen; I think he was American of Swedish descent, I'm not sure, could be Danish or Norwegian, all I know he was Scandinavian. But we always called her Theresa Guarino. Our parents couldn't remember your first name let alone remembering your new married name so we always said Theresa Guarino and, then they knew who we were talking about. She helped me and my mother get early morning cardiologist appointments so I could take her there, bring her home and then go straight to work. We didn't have family leave back then; you had to use your vacation or sick days if you had to take the day off. Some of us would volunteer to take a Fairy Comara's mother to a doctor appointment if we couldn't take the time off.

God bless her, on her days off, Theresa would check in on our grandparents to make sure they were okay or bring them a certain lotion or medication from the pharmacy. She'd even bring her blood pressure monitor with her. And, if she saw something that was cause for concern, she'd call to tell us to keep an eye out for this or that or they needed to cut down on the salt. She diagnosed my mother's heart condition before she even went to the doctor.

The day before she died, a few of the Fairy Comaras, myself included, were with her. Her daughter sent us all a lovely group text message thanking us for the visits and the cheer we brought to Theresa up until her last day on earth. Theresa lived in a condo in Maplewood, New Jersey a couple of blocks away from one of her daughters. She wasn't happy living there but, when she lost her husband six years ago, she decided to sell the house. She was retired by then; there was nobody that she knew on her block and she didn't drive anymore. Too many crazies on the road in Brooklyn!

We laughed and we reminisced about who said what and who did this at the Thursday evening meetings. We remembered the time Signorine was admitted for pneumonia. Correct me if I'm wrong ladies but, Signorine got pneumonia when she was about 85, right? By the time she was admitted into the hospital she already had it about three or four days, she was already living in my downstairs apartment. I swear she never showed it or looked sick. Maybe, because I was coming home from work in the winter and it was dark in the hallway, it was so long ago, I can't remember the circumstances but, I didn't realize she was so sick. She always put on a good face when I came home from work; during the week, except for Thursday evenings, she'd stayed in her apartment and watched TV.

It was on a Wednesday morning; she called up to me from the hallway. It took three times for me to hear her because her voice was so low and hoarse. In those days you never thought to call on the phone if you lived in the same house, you yelled in the hallway. Signorine told me that she needed to go to the hospital, her face was as white as snow. I called 911 and she was immediately put in ICU. At that point, I called Theresa in the hospital and Black Marie Giordano, for support, because I knew Black Marie was home on Wednesdays. Theresa updated us on her condition during the day and she got her the best pulmonologist to take her case. Honestly, we thought this was it and we were going to lose Signorine. One night when we visited her in the ICU, she was mumbling like she was talking to someone but, Theresa and I didn't think she was talking to us. Her eyes were closed but under her eyelids we could see a lot of movement. She even was smiling. That was the night we called one of the priests from St. Agatha's, I forget which priest, to give the last rites. Just as he was about the do the prayers, she lifts up her right hand slightly and says, "non ancora" (in English, "not yet"). And from that point on she started to get better; after two weeks, she was discharged. I stayed with her the night she came home and we watched TV; when one of the commercials came on, I told her about how me and Theresa thought she was mumbling to someone and smiling. Signorine told me she had the happiest conversation with her mother in heaven. She thought she was going to join her but her mother told her non ancora, not yet. She said she was so happy to see her mother! I told her we heard her mumbling for maybe about five minutes but, she said it felt like a long conversation to her. Her mother died in Sicily many years ago and, at the time, she couldn't afford the air fare for her and her son. She carried that conversation with her mother in her heart until the day she died. I'm sure Signorine was there when it was Theresa's time to go. Her daughter said she died with a smile on her face. I hope by the time I go, there'll be a good many Fairy Comaras to greet me. Not that I wish them ill! God forbid!

But I digress… Our generation were brought up to value physical contact with friends instead of electronic; maybe we talked on the phone but, mostly we were a tight knit group who did everything together. Unlike today, where you lose touch with so many people in your life; we never stopped being friends. You hear nowadays about people who are friends 10 years and everyone thinks that's such a long time. We've been friends for over 65 years! And, even though we don't go out together anymore, we still get together online. The problem is there's no hugging and kissing on the Zoom or Face time, which I miss. Somehow Face Time always shows my turkey neck no matter how I adjust my cell phone! Everybody says I look tired on Face Time but, that's because I don't put my make-up on every day like I used to; whom am I getting all dolled up for? My phone?

Another thing, "The Zoom" as we call it, also shows our many wrinkles but it doesn't show the love behind them. When we look at someone's face, when they're right next to you, you also look into their eyes. On the Zoom, we seem rather one-dimensional. When you're physically with a person, their eyes tell you so much more instead of looking at two sockets on a screen. The Zoom wrinkles don't show the depth of the laugh wrinkles, the many fun dinner wrinkles, the partying and, yes, sad wrinkles. Wrinkles form the landscape of our lives. Our wrinkles showed our support for one another, through thick and thin; they provide a map of the struggles and joys in our lives. I'm not a big fan of Botox because it's like looking at a blank map; it wipes away all the detours you took in life, right or wrong. However, it's your choice to get it or not. I don't wish to get Botox. For us, the Fairy Comaras, every wrinkle tells a story of a person or family we either helped in some way, shape or form. However, our deepest wrinkles are our laughing ones; they show how much we laughed, laughing until our cheeks hurt. I'll be telling you a few stories about those wrinkles in the pages that follow.

To be honest, the reason I stayed in my house so long was because of the memories. But now, the memories are not enough for me to stay because the neighborhood can no longer give me any more memories. Everybody moved. I loved the house because of the people I grew up with, not the house. And then I thought to myself, "I really can bring those memories with me anywhere. I'm writing a few of them right now. The house was just situated in the right spot at the right time. And now those people left so I won't be so heartbroken when the time comes to leave.

We had such personalities in our neighborhood when we were young. There was Anna Monteleone who every day would tell anyone who would listen that her husband was sending her to an early grave. If he put out the garbage cans in the wrong place instead of the curb, we'd hear how she told him a million times where to put them and he doesn't listen. No matter if you were a stranger, she'd tell you everything he does that's going to kill her. Her husband was a quiet man, though, never said a word. Summer evenings, he would sit outside his house with his transistor radio listening to a baseball game; sometimes he fell asleep. And then, around 10:00, Anna would come out and yell at him for falling asleep. Then we'd hear her say, "Jesus Christ, help me, this man is going to send me to an early grave. Get inside, I'll take the chair in; you know you have to go to work tomorrow!"

Then, there was Nosey Rose; our mothers called her that behind her back but, we were never allowed to say it outside. Rose wanted to know everyone's business but her business was closed like a steel trap. My mother always used to tell me when Nosey Rose asked me a question about my family to say I Don't Know; she'll either think you're stupid or she'll take the hint. We had Bill the singing mailman; everyone knew when the mail came. Thank God he had a good voice. There was Al Pugliese who sat on his stoop all day with the crooked cigars and thought he was the mayor of our block. He complained about everything, the kids were too loud, they were all a bunch of bums, why do they have to play stick ball on the block, look at the way they dress nowadays. If he smiled, his face would crack. But, every holiday, Al and his wife would visit the neighbors' homes and give us kids a dollar. He even complained when the neighbors gave him a 70th Birthday party; he loved every minute of it even though he said it was a waste of money! Then there was Loud Lina; you could hear her five blocks away; she just had a loud voice like Ethel Merman. When we were teenagers, we'd bust her chops when she spoke to us, we'd say, "What Lina?" and then she would speak even louder. Eventually she caught on and would say, "Don't be fresh, I'll tell your mothers!"

We did have one unfortunate lady on Carroll St, I only remember her first name, Aurelia. According to my mother, she had a mental breakdown when she lost her five-year-old son to a brain tumor. She never really recovered from the grief. And then, one day, nobody really knows what happened, her husband was gone. And I think that really put her over the edge. One summer evening, she came down my block with only her underwear and heels, she had makeup on and her hair was perfectly in place. Poveretta! That poor thing, asking people if they saw her husband. I remember my mother and Carmela Fresca were sitting outside when they saw her and my mother quickly ran inside to get her a robe. My mother immediately took her inside the house and gave her a cup of coffee. The assholes on the block thought it was a big joke but, I saw the worry on my mother's face and she just told me that she was a sick woman. I don't know what happened but, after that, Aurelia didn't live on Carroll St. and all the women were hush, hush about it.

We had Ben Fanucci who every time you met him, he had a joke to tell you; some were clean and some were saucy. That's how he started a conversation with you. The only time he wouldn't tell you a joke is when he was an usher doing the collections at St. Agatha Sunday Mass but, he was always smiling as he passed around the collection basket. He smoked one cigarette after another and if he laughed, he'd cough so much, you'd expect a lung to come out any moment. We always knew when Ben was outside by that long cough. Ben didn't like Al Pugliese so, just to bust his balls, he literally gave Spalding balls to the boys on our block so they could play stick ball. He even got them a football to play on the street.

I remember snow days when we got about 18 inches of snow and didn't have school. There were at least 10 different snowmen (excuse me, snow-persons) on any block in the neighborhood. My mother used to save the buttons on clothes she threw out and one year, she came out with big black buttons with rhinestones on them; that year, I had the best snow lady on the block. I haven't seen a snow-person on my street in well over 10 years. All our parents bought their shovels and rock salt from Marty's Hardware Store on 5th Ave. What Amazon! We could get anything we needed within a 5-mile radius. Everybody shopped local. Sure, we went to A&S, Mays Department Store or Baker's for clothes and shoes but our everyday purchases were made in the neighborhood. Al Pugliese would try to con us with some ploy to shovel the block so he wouldn't have to do it but, we never listened. Everyone shoveled their own property except Frankie Boy; he did his parents and Old Sam. Old Sam would look for him on the block and even though we were in the middle of playing, Old Sam would call him to shoveled his property. When Old Sam died, Frankie Boy was still living in Staten Island and he drove to New Jersey for his wake. His son, Frank, the real Frankie Boy, recognized him, "you were the boy who always used to shovel our property". Frankie Boy, AKA now Tony Fresca told me he wanted to say, "and you're the son who did nothing for him" but, he didn't.

Frankie Boy, I'll never be able to call him Tony, sent me a Christmas card about 10 years ago with a letter; by then, he was retired and moved from Staten Island to North Carolina. He had a lot going on medically but, he proudly talked about his sons and his two grandchildren. I must have forgotten that Antoinette told me he got divorced because he referred to his wife, Claudia, as his ex-wife. I was stunned. When I called Antoinette and asked her, she told me she didn't say anything because, at first, they were only separated so she felt they might get back together. She told me she still keeps in touch with her ex-sister-in-law; she liked Claudia. She'd known her for over 30 years. She just told me they grew apart. Many years later, Claudia re-married but Frankie Boy never did, although he had girlfriends in the past. I didn't want to ask too many questions because Antoinette was and is very protective of her brothers.

The final reason why I'm going to put my house for sale is because Antoinette Fresca and her husband moved last year. They moved to the town of Brewster, NY, to live with her stepdaughter who is a teacher, electrician son-in-law and two grandsons, Stuart and Mark. Antoinette and her husband used to live next door to me in a large brownstone and, finally, it got to the point that they realized the house was too big to take care of at their age. As we all know, a house is like a child that constantly needs maintenance; the money was just floating out the window for two retirees on a fixed income. Besides, it was getting too much for her stepdaughter and son-in-law to pack up the kids and drive down to Brooklyn for the holidays or for Antoinette and her husband to drive back and forth to Brewster. They were too old to do the long back and forth drive even if they stayed weekends. Antoinette was tired of missing the boys' soccer games and recitals.

Her two married brothers, Frankie Boy and Emil, lived in Staten Island for many years but when their kids moved out and they retired, the brothers packed up and moved to a retirement community in North Carolina. Of course, they asked Antoinette and her husband to come, too, but she was a New York girl, through and through, and her husband wanted to be near his daughter. So, last year, they sold their house, pooled together their money with her stepdaughter and son-in-law and found a McMansion mother-daughter home on five acres of pristine land in Brewster, NY. It worked out with daycare because Grandma Antoinette, she didn't like Nonna, wanted nothing more than to smother her grandsons with everything they're not supposed to have…. hey, that's what grandparents are for, not negotiable! And, her husband enjoyed being outdoors and, it didn't hurt that the golf course was two miles away. When she moved, that was my cue to finally leave the neighborhood. I was the last Mohican.

Antoinette tells me there's a rich Italian-American community up in Brewster but she could be bullshitting me because she's been attached to my hip ever since she moved into my downstairs apartment back in November 1999. She emails me all the Brewster condo listings every day and what all the amenities are for each community, detail for detail. When she Face Times me, she has that excitement on her face that she's had all her life looking out for people! That is what Antoinette is all about; once Antoinette enters your world, you have a friend for life. She's a soul healer in every sense of the word. She definitely earned the Fairy Comara Tiara. If Antoinette goes before me, she'll be preparing my cloud in heaven or sending me an air conditioner if I go to hell. She'll definitely be part of the greeting party.

I keep on telling her I'm not moving just to bust her chops but, I'll probably move to Brewster. I'm a New York girl, too! And I consider Antoinette to be my "baby" sister from another mother.

Antoinette Fresca was Frankie Boy's younger sister; I was good friends with him back then. Antoinette was the baby in the family, the "peanut, we called her. I'd say hello to Antoinette when she was playing, we'd buy her an ice cream from the Mr. Softee truck or in the summer, we taught her how to do Double Dutch jump rope. When we came home from the clubs, we taught her the Hustle. But that was the extent to how well I knew her.

The Frescas lived in a brownstone on the corner of Union St. and 4th Avenue a hop, skip and a jump from the train station. My parents' home, also a brownstone, was further up and across the street, nearer to Agnello's Bakery on 5th Avenue. When we came home after we "disco'd the night away" with Frankie Boy, our first stop before going home was the Fresca house. They were the go-to home to hang out, her mother Carmela or Mrs. Fresca, as we called her back then, was always up watching TV or cooking something for Sunday dinner. Her husband, John, was in bed most days by 9 PM because he worked long hours at his business. Only on Friday evenings, he stayed up past 9 PM; the Frescas played cards with my parents, Joe Jr. and Laura Santangelo, sometimes my Grandpa Joe and the Schrables. They'd take turns at each person's house but they mostly played at the Frescas.

Little Antoinette used to listen by her bedroom window in anticipation of our arrival home; it provided the ideal excuse for her to stay up on a Saturday night and listen to our stories and laugh and laugh! My God, I laughed so hard back then, my cheeks would hurt. Carmela would call our parents and let them know we were here and they would be okay with it as long as they knew we were on the block. Sometimes, Carmela would tell them we came home at 11:00 PM instead of 1:00 AM so we wouldn't be reprimanded but, she didn't like to lie. Once we did arrive, she would cook us an early breakfast before we all went home or serve some coffee if she smelled alcohol on our breath. We used to buy mints for that but then our parents caught on. We taught Mrs. Fresca and Antoinette to do the Hustle. Even though the music was blasting, John Fresca slept through it! Antoinette liked one of us to comb her hair while we were talking; then her eyes would close and Frankie Boy would carry her to bed. When Carmela was in her 70's, sick with congestive heart disease and in the hospital, she confided in me that her and John wanted Anthony "Frankie Boy" to marry me. She said I would have made a good daughter-in-law. She also asked me to take good care of Antoinette which I thought was strange because she had two brothers. I said yes, I would, thinking this was going to be a no-brainer since her daughter knew everyone. She died about a month later.

Antoinette was closer in age to her other brother Emil; he always shared his Halloween candy with her or had a way of saying something to stop her from crying. They still talk to each other at least once or twice a week even though he lives in North Carolina. His children and grandchildren moved down there a few years ago so it's one big happy family and he loves the weather. Emil was quiet and more sensitive than Frankie Boy; he wasn't as boisterous. Emil never judged people; he may not agree with their thinking but, he respected them and he's been like that all his life. Frankie Boy was more outgoing, more like his mother, Emil was more his father. John Fresca was happy with just the simple things in life; he loved working and more importantly, he loved his family.

After Emil graduated high school, he went to Manhattan Community College and worked part-time with Irish Marie's father at the nearby public school.

Irish Marie's father, Hector, was the Janitorial Supervisor. After about a year, he quit college because he liked being an assistant janitor more than working in an office. Hector taught him everything but, with a stern hand. He told Emil, "You do a good job once, you never have to do it again" and even though Emil had to scratch his head thinking "well, of course!" after a while he realized how important those words were throughout his life, not just his job at the school.

Frankie Boy went straight to Brooklyn College, majored in Business and got his first job on Wall Street. His outgoing personality got him far in the securities industry and he did very well for himself. However, his job kept him away from his family too much which is probably why he got divorced but, who knows! Emil, on the other hand, didn't make as much money as Frankie Boy but, he was content and family came first. When Frankie Boy's neighbors in Staten Island needed work done in their homes, he recommended his brother Emil to make some extra money. And he did a good job the first time, like Irish Marie's father told him, and got plenty of side business. Emil worked as hard as his father and, like his father, his family was everything. He did all the work on his parents' house. John Fresca would show everyone in the neighborhood "look what my son Emil did in the kitchen" or " look at the beautiful job he did in the bathroom". Unfortunately for Frankie Boy, when you work in the stock exchange who sees what you've done so it was hard for John to boast about him; all he told the neighbors is that he's making a lot of money. When Emil retired with a good pension and sold his own house in Staten Island, it made sense to go down to North Carolina with Frankie Boy and buy a townhouse in the same gated community. I still keep in touch with Frankie Boy but, he's living in another world now and all he can say to me is, "thank God I don't have to shovel snow anymore!" And then, he'd reminisce about the things we did and tell me how much he missed those days.

Back in the 70's some of the Fairy Comaras went to work after high school, some to college. Then the weddings appeared followed by the christenings but, no matter what, us girls always stuck together.

Once everyone started working, we'd try to go out for dinner on a Friday or Saturday night. But once the kids started coming, it was hard to get us all together on weekends. So, we decided to meet every Thursday evening to shake the dust off from a week's worth of stress with some wine, food and conversation. At first, we took turns going to each other's house so that no one person had to prepare something all the time. Thursday evenings were a chance to get away from the husbands and kids for a couple of hours. After my mother passed away, we decided to get together at my house on Thursday evenings because I was the only one who didn't have a husband or kids. Everybody brought something; food they made, wine or cake. Also, other neighbors and friends were interested in coming so it was good to have it in one place. I don't know how it happened but the crowd coming to the meetings increased every month and the rest is history; and that's how the Fairy Comaras Thursday Evening meetings started. In just a year, we had people from all over Brooklyn come to us for a helping hand, to get a reading from me or Signorine or just to be with people from the old neighborhood.

I understand that with the COVID 19 pandemic, the social gatherings stopped but, to be truthful, there wasn't much physical interaction before the pandemic either. Maybe people would gather at a bar but how much of a conversation can you have at a noisy bar? And now, they're all glued to Facebook or Tik Tok or Instagram watching strangers or posting photos of their meals! This virtual world may be efficient but not effective. But, don't get me started on socializing in today's world, I'll get myself too aggravated to go on any further which defeats the purpose of this story.

Back in the late 80's and early 90's, we didn't have the internet ingrained into our daily lives; the Fairy Comaras Thursday evening meetings were the Humanet…we were twitter, Tik Tok and YouTube with a human heart and a kick ass attitude rolled into one. On Thursday evening, we could forget our problems for a couple of hours, or maybe get information on how to solve a problem. You got the latest news on who died, who got married, who got divorced and who moved. When we encountered a serious problem, we had to take the bull by the horns and help a friend in need outside of Thursday nights.

Like the time the Fairy Comaras had to call Captain Doyle to talk to Sylvia Cusimano's teenage son, George, because he was cursing and using his hands against his mother. One Thursday evening, she was hiding a bruise on her left cheekbone with make-up. Just so you know, Sylvia usually didn't wear a lot of make-up. I can't remember Sylvia ever having a husband although she did but they divorced when George was three or four years old. After a couple of years, George's father was no longer present in his life and his mother had to be both father and mother to him as best as she could while working full-time.

Little Marie Greco called Captain Doyle and he had a man-to-man talk with George and got him enrolled in PAL; after that, he was like an uncle to him. He straightened out. We had to step in for a lot of ladies in similar positions. George became a Physical Therapist; he works nearby at the 2nd Street Rehab Center. Sylvia was one of our regulars on Thursday evenings and, one-night, Black Marie got it into her head that, since George was graduating high school and going to a college in Massachusetts, maybe Sylvia might need some gentlemanly companionship. Shortly after that, she visited her Uncle Jimmy, Big Jimmy to us, and happened to mention Sylvia. Uncle Jimmy had just the right guy for her, "Marie, you know Danny, good guy, he works for me. Well, he lost his mother about three years ago and his father, Danny Sr., lives like a miserabla. He never goes out; he sits on the couch watches TV all day; he's

63 but he acts like he's 93. I mean, Danny and his wife can only provide so much support. Danny Jr. works long hours for me and he has his own family to take care of; he's stressed out about it and I can't have that happening to my crew." Uncle Jimmy said, "Marie, how about we arrange a date between Sylvia and Danny Sr.? I'll work it out with my Danny, you take care of Sylvia, ok?" Believe it or not, Sylvia didn't put up a fuss when Black Marie suggested it; she actually told her she was thinking about dating now that her son will be away at college. She just didn't know how to go about it; she hadn't dated in decades because of George. She felt it wasn't right to bring another man into her home. Anyway, she said she'd give it a try. Black Marie told her all about Danny Sr. Uncle Jimmy called Marie and told her Danny got his father to go; he had to pull teeth to get him to say yes but, he agreed. Danny brought his father to Men's Warehouse and got him a new suit and a nice pair of shoes for the date. Uncle Jimmy paid for a reservation for two at Joe Allen's in Manhattan, complete with limo service for this Saturday.

You know the saying; you have to kiss a lot of toads before you get a prince? Well, Sylvia only had to kiss one. She and Danny Sr. had a great time! They exchanged their life stories. Danny Sr. loved Sylvia's sense of humor; she used to crack us up at the Thursday meetings. And so, there was a second date and a third date and so on and so on. Danny Jr. and his wife loved her and George was happy that his mom found someone and he liked Danny, too! After George graduated college, Sylvia and Danny Sr. finally agreed to live together; they never married; it would decrease their social security. They bought a condo on Shore Rd near the Verrazano. Beautiful, I've been there a few times. Sylvia still lives there but, Danny passed away maybe five or six years ago.

Anyway, by 1999, the internet entered our everyday life at work and at home; people started sending emails instead of talking on the phone and then the cell phones and texting followed. Theresa Guarino was the first of the Fairy Comaras to have a home computer. By then, the Fairy Comaras' children were teenagers or college bound and, at the same time, they were taking care of their parents. Schedules started to fill up with football and baseball games, ballet classes; in addition, there were doctor appointments for their parents. We still got together one or two Thursdays a month until about 2005. That's when the gatherings started to dwindle in size. Who died and who moved were the main reasons; who wanted to stay home and play internet games, was another reason.

It was about then that the neighborhood began to change in personality; people would move in and out like a revolving door and pretty much kept to themselves. An apartment became a temporary domicile; a bed to come home to after work. Once the neighborhood changed, our gatherings petered off. Who knew these strangers to even invite them to a meeting? By 2010, it became difficult for many of the Fairy Comaras and guests to travel from wherever they lived whether it be Long Island, Staten Island or elsewhere and so, sadly, we had to close the doors on the Thursday evening meetings.

The Fairy Comaras' children weren't into our gatherings; they had their own generational mode of communicating. Our meetings were regarded as some old Italian custom from a bygone age. Why go to a Fairy Comara for help when you had Mr. Google to go to for expert advice on thousands of .com web sites who promise, for three easy payments, that they can put your life together in the privacy of your own home? Don't get me wrong, I think all the Fairy Comaras are thankful for technology; we couldn't talk and see each other otherwise. But nothing will ever replace the touch of a warm hand or a heartfelt hug just when you need it. When we used to have our Thursday night gatherings, there was an energy in the air. If we were a web site today, our address would be COMEOVER@Thursdayevenings.house.

Signorine was always at our Thursday gatherings. She was our resident tea leaf reader; she'd tell your fortune in Italian and broken English, and then she'd talk about her life back in Italy. She'd tell you for the millionth time that she shouldn't have married and come to the United States even though she kissed the American flag every time she came near one. Occasionally, we'd have a guest speaker come over like Captain Doyle and talk about how to secure your home from robbery or Theresa Guarino would get one of the doctors to talk about preventing heart disease. Theresa gave up asking doctors to speak because people were using Thursday as a doctor visit and the poor doctor would wind up being there for three hours or more talking to our mothers. After that, she gave the medical lectures. Little Marie Greco was our authority on elder care and she gave advice and how to take care of our parents or grandparents. Black Marie was a paralegal and spoke about wills, Living Trusts and current NY State divorce laws. I, Diane Santangelo, offered psychic readings and gave one or two lectures.

There's nothing in technology to replace those magical yet, ordinary day moments, in our lives. Call me an optimist but I continue to hope that one day, the pendulum will swing the other way and they'll be more Fairy Comaras Meetings sprouting up in the world. I don't care what day it is!

Now, our children patronize us, for sure; they don't have a clue about all the people whose lives changed because of us. "Noi siamo i vecchi pensatori" meaning, we're the old thinkers, the old farts, in other words. One good thing about getting old, we can get away with murder in front of our children, no filters and thank you, God, for that! They look at us with affection but roll their eyes, like we have no inkling of how the world works today. And the more they do it, the more we embarrass them in front of their friends. If we say something that's true but not said in public we're just ignored or they say "oh Mom, you don't mean that" with the fake nervous laugh. Fuck that, we say it anyway, and we mean it. When they get older, they'll realize we were right and their children will make fun of them, talk about instant karma. That's why the Fairy Comaras wanted me to write this book.

It's funny but as I get older, I say fuck a lot like it's a verb or an adjective. For me, fuck adds color to the conversation although some people cringe when I say it. Who cares! Every fucking author has their own style. Antoinette asked me to write this history and I'll put whatever fucking thing I want. In truth, I just wanted to get my quotas of fucks in this paragraph. It will annoy the hell out of her, Sister Antoinette of the Blessed Word that she is!

With the COVID-19 pandemic almost over, the idea of mingling and getting together actually supporting one another in the same location is getting back to normal again; but we still have far to go. No man is an island and we're starting to get agoraphobic with this technology. As I said, maybe the pendulum will swing and new groups of Fairy Comaras will be formed with a new way of channeling the healing, loving energy. Even with the dot.com websites, depression is at an all-time high. Maybe, in the future, there will be "tellacomara" gatherings in an actual room or a home instead of on a screen. I'm hoping that a new generation of neighbors and families will understand the importance of mingling, sharing the stress and supporting one another instead of exchanging mobile numbers so you can text or call. What the hell is texting all about anyway? That's not conversation, it's words without emotion.

A chain is as strong as its weakest link, a neighborhood is as good as its most difficult neighbors and a family is as strong as the last problem solved together. There are so many troubled people in the world that maybe a meal, a glass of wine and good conversation could just be the catalyst to getting them back on track. Who knows, stranger things have happened!

I've had people over back then who told us, if not for the Thursday night meetings, their lives might have taken a different direction. They'd come in with a frown and leave with a smile. Let's make it easier to love one another instead of pointing out their differences. Take that first step and you'll feel the energy of contentment. Someone's political beliefs are always 41 on my top 40 list of why I like someone. You are not defined by your politics but, by the people you interact with on a day-to-day basis.

If you're the kind of person who constantly says, "Why does everyone come to me with their problems?" then you're probably a Fairy Comara. If you find that you have to do everything yourself or you can never rest for five minutes without someone calling you with a problem then, you're probably a Fairy Comara. If you made many mistakes in the past but are good at advising, then you are a Fairy Comara. When we had the gatherings, we discovered there were many Fairy Comaras in the room; they just didn't know it.

The truth is, a Fairy Comara can't stop giving. If they stop, they'll be miserable. If we stopped giving, everyone would think we were acting strange or you're sick or something. If you feel like everyone goes to you for advice, be happy. It's your life purpose and be proud that you've been doing very well so far. Why else would they keep coming to you? Sometimes people don't listen to your advice at that given moment but, eventually the light bulb goes on and they remember that you gave it. Giving without expectation is the very essence of being a Fairy Comara. God doesn't send idiots to earth to do his work. Remember that!

The last Fairy Comara that moved out of the neighborhood, Antoinette Fresca, once lived in the one-bedroom apartment on the ground floor of my house; my house was a two-family that originally belonged to my parents. When both my parents died, as the only child, I became the owner. My father died first; he was a quiet man, rarely raised his voice except when I talked back to him but then he forgot about it. My mother died five years later; she was the animated one, at weddings she would always be on the dance floor, not with my father, he didn't like to dance, but with all the ladies and occasionally she'd borrow one of the husbands.

I think my parents loved each other. Other than hearing them fight over who went into the room and didn't shut off the light or who left the milk on the table, they pretty much got along. And they both wanted me to get a good education; I went to Brooklyn College and got a Business Administration degree and later started working for the Chase Manhattan Bank, now called just Chase, as a mortgage manager. Irish Marie also worked for a short time at Chase Manhattan but at another branch. I liked my job; I got to make many families happy by giving them mortgages or helping small businesses get a financial jump start. But, outside of work, the Thursday evening Fairy Comaras meetings were what I enjoyed the most. All the Fairy Comaras said the same thing.

When my parents bought their home, my maternal Grandma, Concetta, lived with us but she died when I was maybe 3 or 4. They originally thought to rent the downstairs apartment to help out with the mortgage but I think when I was about five years old my father's parents, Joe and Filomena "Philly" Santangelo, moved into the downstairs apartment. Grandpa Joe did all the repairs and painting; my father did not inherit his father's talent for home repairs; he worked long hours while going to school at night. When they died many years later, my parents rented it out to newlyweds. They eventually moved out later on to buy their own home. I was working at the bank back then and I got their mortgage approved. There was a professional couple who moved in but they didn't stay long. After my mother passed away, I offered the apartment to Signorine; I heard that her landlord was giving her a hassle.

So, I offered the apartment to Signorine. At that time, she was on welfare and her greedy landlord was always looking for ways to get her out of her rent controlled two-bedroom apartment so he could triple the rent. She no longer needed that big of an apartment anyway; between cleaning it and climbing two flights of stairs it was getting too much for her. We even got the landlord to pay for the U-Haul truck to move her things and she got back her security of $5.00, that's right, $5.00 that was her security back then, before WWII, over 60 years ago, when she moved in, can you imagine? She didn't have much furniture so when we did move her, it fit comfortably in the one bedroom. She kept her son's night table but, she gave the bed and the dresser to Sylvia Cusimano for her son, George. Since She and my Grandma Philly were such good friends, she was comfortable moving to an apartment she spent so much time in; good memories.

They were bosom buddies; they went everywhere together until my grandmother, Filomena "Philly" passed away. Signorine cried like a baby at the wake; she told people my grandmother was like a sister to her. When Grandma Philly was nearing her end, she stayed all day with my her and took care of her. By then, my Grandpa Joe was dead about 10 years. After the funeral, she baked my grandmother's lasagna for us. She begged my grandmother for that recipe and finally, Grandma gave it to her. Signorine would serve it at the Thursday evening meetings at Christmas time. Every once in a while, she'd make a tray so we could eat together and she told me stories about how my grandma helped her.

According to Signorine, my grandmother saved her life. My Grandma Filomena, Philly, as she was called, never talked about how she helped Signorine. All I remember as a child is that the two of them were attached at the hip. If Grandma was on 5th Ave shopping, then Signorine was not far behind. She acted as a translator for Signorine if they were talking to someone who didn't speak Italian. Philly helped her raise her son, Girolamo, through the ladies in the neighborhood. Maybe not by blood, but they were like sisters. If anyone asked where Philly was, Grandpa Joe would say she's with her sister from another mother.

Just so you know, Signorine, was not a weak woman. She was a survivor. Hands down, she was the Queen of the Fairy Comaras in our group, even before there was a group. She couldn't speak English that well, even after living in this country for over 60 years, but the people she helped and the people in return who helped her would be a book unto itself. Her magic was her amazing intuition about people, some would say psychic gift, but most of all she had a healing nature about her. She had that one touch or short embrace that made you feel loved; I can't tell you how many women left our meeting a little happier or their burden made lighter by Signorine. She was known at the meetings as the tea leaf reader; she read everyone who came to the house on Thursday evening, never charged, but we all tipped her just the same. She started in this country with little and she left the same way but, she told me the day before she died that we, the Fairy Comaras, and the Thursday evening meetings made her last years the happiest.

Hers was a sad story of betrayal by her husband who left her a single mother with a son in a foreign country. By the time she came to live with me, she was on welfare for about 15 years; by then she was an American citizen, don't ask me how she passed the test. She had the papers to prove it! Back then, if you were on welfare the city made your life a misery, checking on you constantly, maybe you were allowed a phone. When she came to this country, her life could have taken a very desperate turn if not for a fortuitous meeting with my Grandma Philly in church one morning.

As I mentioned, when my parents bought their home they gave the apartment downstairs to my grandparents, Grandma "Philly" Filomena and my Grandpa Joe. Let me tell you there is nothing better than to have grandparents living in the same house! My grandparents were still working when they moved in but then Grandpa Joe had to go on disability because of his back. Grandma worked in a small factory two blocks away sewing collars on dresses. So, when Grandpa Joe picked me up from school, he'd take me to the candy store or he'd take me to get ice cream. My mother would come home from work and scold Grandpa Joe because I was too full to eat dinner but, she could never get angry at Grandpa Joe for more than a minute. He used to tell the same jokes to me and I would always pretend I didn't know the punch line. When he had to go on disability, he became a daily fixture on the block. He would walk around for most of the day and stop in all the stores and converse with the owners or go to Uncle Jimmy's club to play cards with the guys. He was tough as nails and strong; before his back went out, he worked on the docks.

According to him, he came to this country at 14 years old, alone, with $1 in his pocket and two shirts and the pants he had on. His parents could not afford to feed him because of the famine in his town; they had three other mouths to feed. He lived with a cousin and got a job on the docks. He married my grandmother when he was 19 and my grandmother 17 and they struggled together. My grandmother worked in a sewing factory, Di Paolo's, a couple of blocks from where they had an apartment. When my father was born, Mr. Di Paolo was kind enough to keep her working part-time until my father was old enough to go to school. Back then, six-year-old kids were like 21-year-olds. My father would come home, do his homework and then do some chores around the house until my grandmother came home from work to start dinner. My father would tell me he sometimes had to wash his own shirts on the scrub board they kept in the kitchen and hang them on the clothesline. Grandpa worked a lot of overtime back then and they were finally able to rent a bigger apartment. When my father was all grown and married, Grandpa Joe gave him the down payment on his home and later on, they moved into the apartment on the ground floor.

Anyway, back to Signorine. Signorine's marriage was arranged between her parents and the groom's parents. The groom's family lived near Coney Island; the parents knew each other when they lived in Trapani, Sicily. They arranged the marriage without Signorine or her husband even knowing it. Her mother and father had two other children to feed and she was 16 and it was time for her to marry. She came to America with the money she got from selling the only jewelry she owned, gold earrings. The money was used as her dowry to the groom's parents. She came to this country with her mother's wedding gown and the clothes on her back. Her parents couldn't afford anything else with two other mouths to feed. They felt she'd have a better life in America.

She met her in-laws at the docks in New York harbor, her groom was not even there to greet her. He wasn't there because he didn't want to get married to someone off the boat. Ironically, he was born in Sicily but came to Brooklyn as a child. When his parents introduced her, he said two words to her and flew out the door to be with his friends. A week later they got married in church, no reception, no honeymoon and the next day, she was washing clothes and making dinner for a husband who gave her dirty looks and hardly spoke to her because she didn't speak English; he only spoke Italian to her when he needed something.

Her mother-in-law despised her because she wanted her son to marry one of the Italian-American girls in Coney Island but, her husband had the last word and they needed the money to fix the roof of their house. This was a marriage made in hell. Signorine was nothing more than a roof to them. Her husband was used to dating American girls. He was numb to her touch, he looked upon her as a slave. She'd fed him, ironed his clothes to go out at night and once in a blue moon they had sex. After three years, they had a son, Girolamo, who her husband rarely noticed, only when he was crying and that was because he was annoying. He would make any excuse to go out with his friends to "play cards" but she didn't have to be an American to figure out he was fooling around. Signorine told my Grandma Philly that one of his girlfriends knocked on her door to scream at her in English which she didn't understand, until her mother-in-law came down and talked to the woman. She never found out what the woman was screaming about because her mother-in-law never told her, she only remembers her mother-in-law slamming the door on the woman. All she knew was that evening there was a lot of yelling upstairs between her husband and his father. His parents were starting to realize that their son was not a good husband and a bad father as well. There were a lot of arguments, all in English, so she didn't know what they were arguing about. Her husband would come downstairs in a worse mood than before and take it out on her in Italian and many times he got physical.

His parents were always on his back and, with good reason. He kept on losing job after job. When he did work, he gambled his pay before his paycheck got to the house. One day, her husband told her that they're moving away from his parents; he found a nice 2-bedroom apartment in South Brooklyn (now Park Slope). He said he found a new job nearby and they could be a family without his parents' interference. Signorine thought her life had finally changed for the better and he was ready to settle down. Never happened. Two years after moving out and having lost another job, he left her. He got up in the morning and "went to work" and never came back. He left her $10 on the table for what she thought was for groceries and then adios, you're on your own. His parents wanted nothing to do with her; they had the nerve to tell her he left her because she wasn't a good wife so they didn't have to repay the dowry to her parents. They claimed they didn't know where he was; they wanted Girolamo to stay with them until she found a job but, she would never give up her son.

So, here she was in a country she barely knew, spoke no English, had no job, a baby son, with $10 and not a penny more; the rent alone was $5 and not a friend or anybody to go to for help. She couldn't go back to Sicily to her parents because it would bring shame and disgrace to her family. Besides, she didn't have the money to go back.

One day, in desperation, she decided to go to church; who else but God could help her at this point? She went to church early that morning with Girolamo in tow. Signorine was desperately praying in Italian to the Blessed Mother. That morning, it turned out, my Grandma Philly was also in church; and the Blessed Mother answered her prayers. Grandma Philly went to church every morning to say the rosary before going to work. She worked for Di Paolo's Clothing Company two blocks away; my father wasn't born yet. She was a piece worker; she put the collars on the blouses and dresses and by that time Mr. Di Paolo came to rely on her like a factory manager to organize the work. She didn't get paid for it but, Mr. Di Paolo was a good boss and a kind man; he used to come over to our house for a drink during the holidays.

So anyway, my grandmother heard her crying with her baby son in church. She stopped praying the rosary and got up from her pew and walked up two pews and sat next to her. My grandmother always carried a handkerchief in her purse; when she lived with me, she switched over to Kleenex. They came in handy to wipe away my tears when I fell down and scraped a knee. Since my grandmother spoke Italian, one thing led to another, Signorine told her story and my grandmother told her to dry her eyes because she was bringing her somewhere. Grandma Philly always lit a candle before she left church and she told Signorine she was lighting it for her today.

She took Signorine and Girolamo to the factory to meet Mr. Di Paolo. Mr. Di Paolo spoke Italian but he was from Rome so he had a different accent but, he understood my grandmother's Sicilian. My grandmother told him Signorine's husband recently died of cancer and she needed a job. She lied about Signorine's husband because she didn't want him to think Signorine was a putana, a loose woman. In those days, women were the fault for the breakup of any marriage, whether it was or it wasn't their fault. And from that point on, Signorine wore black for the rest of her working life. Long story short, Signorine was hired, not as a piece worker but as a regular worker making enough at least, to pay the rent and buy milk and bread. Signorine eventually took over my grandmother's piece worker job on collars after Grandma Philly quit to take care of Grandpa Joe.

Grandma Philly was a Fairy Comara but she didn't know it. She was the inspiration for me in creating the Thursday evening meetings; paying it forward helping people in the neighborhood. Like a true Fairy Comara, she rounded up all her friends and each one of them helped Signorine. She told her friends that her husband passed away, too, because, back then, there was less shame and disgrace if your husband dropped dead than if he left you. The ladies that were housewives took care of Girolamo after school.

Signorine was able to stay in her apartment and she never had to starve because someone in the factory always brought her leftovers, or she and Girolamo were invited at least once a week to all the neighborhood's family get togethers; Mr. Di Paolo even gave her his son's crib that turned into a bed when his son grew out of it. All the hand me down clothes, some not even worn, were given to her for Girolamo and every Christmas and his birthday, the ladies gave him gifts of clothes or toys. I'm not sure but, I think my Grandma Philly gave the money or the school took him in on a scholarship but, Girolamo went to St. Agatha's instead of public school. I remember my father having a conversation with his mother one night and he took out $20 and told her it was for the Girolamo Fund.

Grandma Philly kept her spare change in Chock Full of Nuts coffee cans. No kidding! She had about 10 cans in the pantry next to the soup cans. If I went to the store for her, she would tell me to go to one of the cans and take out a quarter. Grandpa Joe would call her a cheap skate for only giving me a quarter and then she'd relent and tell me to take another quarter. I think she used that money for Girolamo's education.

This was also the start of Signorine's tea leaf readings for the ladies in the neighborhood. She learned to read tea leaves from her grandmother but, she said she thought her grandmother was more of a psychic than telling fortunes from the leaves. She'd look at the leaves one time and then spout out that person's future. Signorine did pretty much the same thing but, back then, it was more acceptable to get a tea reading than go to a fortune teller. Only the gypsies did that back then and we all kept our distance because the Catholic Church didn't allow divination. Well, at least that form of fortune telling.

And, every 4th of July, she put a little American flag out her window with thanks to the country that gave her a start in life even though she missed Sicily. She went back to Trapani, Sicily, with her son to see her family, compliments of Big Jimmy and the Italian American Veterans Club but, it was only once.

When Mr. Di Paolo retired and closed the factory many years later, she had to go on welfare, which she never liked to mention. She had practically nothing in savings and then she got the "Arthuritis" in her hands. She couldn't get a job with her English, anyway.

By that time, Girolamo was about to graduate high school; he had a job after school helping our butcher, George the German, sweep up the cuttings, clean the butcher block and fix the displays. In those days and, even when I was a kid growing up, you didn't buy meat in a package; you had to go to a butcher and have the meat cut right in front of you. George the German would tell you his problems and the ladies would tell him theirs; it was a social as well as a commercial transaction. I remember coming into the store and seeing the big provolone balls hung from the ceiling; George always gave me and my mother a slice of cheese. To this day, the smell of provolone brings such memories. Grandpa Joe would go to the store just to talk to George the German and, maybe he came home with a pound of sausage if he wanted that specially for dinner. Grandpa Joe told me that when WWII broke out, the neighborhood didn't hold the fact that George was German against him. He was born in this country. My grandmother was glad to get Grandpa Joe out of the house; if she was on the phone, he would loudly say, "who is it?" and my grandmother would make a motion to shut up or he would notice dust on some piece of furniture and point it out to her. Grandpa Joe played cards at the Italian American Veterans Club with Black Marie's Uncle Jimmy or Big Jimmy, as he was called. Just so you know, we never saw another Jimmy or a Little Jimmy in the club. He was a big man but not obese. It's a mystery. Even Black Marie didn't know why.

But, back to Signorine. World War II broke out, Girolamo enlisted; Signorine wasn't too happy about it but, he was all grown up. He was stationed in Europe. Girolamo never came back. I wasn't even born then but, my grandma told me that Signorine just sat in the kitchen and wouldn't eat for weeks. The grief paralyzed her. She just stared at the wall all day. After that, she made sure that Signorine was never alone; she was invited to every party, every BBQ, every Sunday dinner at my house for the rest of her life. And my grandma's Comaras, Philly's Comaras, invited her to their house, too! She always had somewhere to go almost every day of the week. And every year on his birthday, Signorine would buy a cake and put a photo of Girolamo, in uniform, on the table. Philly's Comaras came over to help her remember him. Many nights, after Grandpa Joe died, Signorine would sleep over in Grandma Philly's apartment. When Grandma Philly died, my parents continued to invite her to dinner and every party. And, after my mother died, we, the Fairy Comaras, took over the task of taking care of her. She was never alone for too long a time until the day she died and, even when she died, she was not alone. She passed away on the recliner with 40 people sitting in the room! And that's the story of Signorine.

Frankie Boy was the first son born to John and Carmela Fresca. His real name was Anthony but, just to bust his chops, we all called him Frankie Boy except when we were around his parents. But I think they knew we called him Frankie Boy. Old Sam who lived on our block gave him that name back in the early 60's when we were kids. He wore big pants to hide a hernia he had for God knows how long. After he had the hernia operation, he lost a lot of weight but, he refused to buy new clothes so he always wore suspenders over his tee shirt in the summer to keep his pants up. The only time we ever saw him wear clothes that fit was when his son, Frank, got married and he had to wear a tuxedo. Sam owned the fruit and vegetable store in the middle of my block and he also sold milk and bread. Very handy store to have when a snowstorm hits or you forgot to buy vegetables in the supermarket for dinner that day. Anthony was always outside; he could never stay in the house no matter what time of the year it was. And guess who Sam would bellow out to shovel the snow on his sidewalk and entrance to the store? Anthony Fresca. For some reason, he could never remember Anthony's name and called him by his son's name although, we never saw his son help him. Old Sam always needed help carrying the metal garbage cans out on collection days so if he saw Anthony outside playing stickball or football in the street, he'd call him in a big bellowing voice... Frankie Boy, vieni qua! He'd give him a quarter which even for our day was cheap and some fruit or a zucchini to bring home to his mother.

Old Sam's son, Franco or Frank, married and moved to Bumfuck, NJ near his wife's family. I don't remember where he lived in New Jersey. I don't think anyone on our block ever knew Old Sam when he was Young Sam; his wife never left the house except to shop and his son, the real Frankie Boy, never hung out with us. Frankie Boy shoveled snow and put the garbage out whenever Old Sam called him because back then it was a command from our parents to obey our elders. We were taught to say NO first if they offered money, then we could take the money if they insisted. So, Frankie Boy took the quarter. The first time Frankie Boy got a quarter from Old Sam, he told his mother. She told him to donate it to the church on Sunday. After that, he never told her. There was a candy store on the corner that could burn a hole in our pockets; you could buy a lot of candy for 25 cents back then. Old Sam's son, Franco, was an only child and his parents made sure he had the best they could afford. We used to call him Frank; back in the 50's and 60's, the more American you sounded, the better, no vowels at the end of your name. It's the reason my parents named me Diane, instead of what they really wanted, Isabella. I don't know how I would be as an Isabella but Diane suits me just fine.

Franco went to St. Agatha's but, he stayed within his own clique. He was an A student; it wasn't in his best interest to hang out with us, the B and C grade crowd. Many years later my mother told me the reason why Franco didn't play with us; it was because Old Sam's wife, Paola, was born in Milan. She stuck her nose up to all the Napolitano and Siciliano families on the block; she wouldn't even allow her son to play with us kids. When the boys were playing stickball, he was learning to play the piano. Other than school and visits to relatives, he never went outside. He would just sit in his backyard. As soon as Franco was old enough to travel on the subway, he vamoosed to Bensonhurst to be with his Xaverian High School friends. The only time we saw him was when he was walking down to the train station. No one from the neighborhood was invited to his wedding. When Old Sam died, Franco closed the store and sold it to a couple of yuppies who converted it into a small restaurant. He put his mother in a nursing home in New Jersey because his wife and his mother didn't get along. And that was the last we heard of Old Sam's Franco. I saw him about five years ago at a wake and he seemed like a nice guy but I had to come up to him because he didn't remember who I was…. we had nothing to talk about because we had no memories.

The Frescas had another son, Emil, very soft spoken and nearest in age to Antoinette so they were always close. Emil had his other friends but he couldn't hang out with us because he was still much younger than Frankie Boy. Frankie Boy was lively and sociable like his mother; Emil was more like his father, quiet but forceful at the same time. When Emil was about 10, he got pneumonia and had to go to the hospital. From that point on, Carmela would always double bundle him up during the winter; we all wore a sweater under our coat, Emil wore two sweaters and a heavy coat, a scarf, boots and gloves. He was always dressed for a snowstorm even if it was 50 degrees outside. After he turned 14, he dressed himself for winter but snuck out of the house like a thief in the night before his mother saw him. When he retired, he and his wife moved down to North Carolina and he never had to worry about wearing coats, anymore.

When we were our late teens, Frankie Boy was our wild and crazy friend and, he had a car! He used to crack us up with his remarks about other people. Especially when we went with him to the clubs. The Fairy Comaras loved hanging out with him or going to the disco together. He always acted so macho coming into the disco with us girls like we were his harem but, he was and still is a great guy. Always bought us the first round of drinks. Of course, now, he prefers to be called Tony. Tony Fresca used to be VP- Sales for some big shot securities firm; I can't remember the name at this moment. He's retired 12 years now. When he got married to Claudia Paterno, his mother-in-law called him Tony because her son was also named Anthony so he got second prize on the Anthony name list. Of course, his mother and father, God rest their souls, called him Anthony because he was first on the Anthony list in the Fresca home.

Antoinette was the miracle girl that Carmela Fresca prayed for; she prayed every day and made offerings to St. Anthony to have a girl after two sons. Anthony was named after John's father and then Emil, who we just called Emil, no nickname, named after Carmela's father. After three years and nine months of many candle offerings in the church under the statue of St. Anthony and enough candles in the bedroom that John complained that he needed a fan to cool off, she got her daughter, Antoinette. Of course, she had to be named Antoinette; after all the hot flashes she gave to St. Tony No Baloney, he was the saint that delivered! Because of St. Tony, poor Antoinette had to be in every June 13th St. Anthony children's procession wearing a brown robe with the rosary beads hanging down from her waist sash; it was only until she stood out in the parade at 14, that Father Ignatius delegated something different for Antoinette to do like making the annual St. Anthony bread with her mother or frying up the zeppolas at the feast. Antoinette and the other fellow brown robed children would march in the parade all over the neighborhood so people could attach a dollar to the large St. Anthony statue held up by six men. The kids at school would make fun of her but her mother would tell her the old "sticks and stones may break my bones but words will never harm me" line. It still hurt her; we had bullies in our day, too! Emil used to beat the shit out of those bullies when Antoinette came home crying. That was OUR way of dealing with bullies.

Antoinette was a "guarded" child; she was never allowed to leave her mother's sight. She couldn't play at the other little girls' homes because they lived in apartment buildings where Carmela suspected there were strange men lurking behind the cellar door waiting to kidnap children. Her friends either came to her house or played inside the gate outside her home. Because she went everywhere with her mother, she was able to do a lot of good for the church and neighborhood. Carmela had a good heart and she helped everyone. They visited every neighbor's mother or father in the hospital. Antoinette was even a hospital volunteer; they used to call them candy strippers, I don't know if they even have that program anymore. Antoinette helped a lot of the neighbors fill out city or government forms that they couldn't understand. Over time, she made lots of friends and accumulated a lot of favors. This came in handy at our Thursday evening meetings when someone needed a connection for some family issue. The two of them volunteered for all the St. Agatha clothing drives and fundraising events. They knew all the priests, nuns and brothers at St. Agatha's; this was not good for us kids when we did something wrong at school but, thank God, the nuns and brothers were frightening enough. Antoinette sold chocolates and Christmas cards for the church and went to Mass every Sunday rain or shine. She went through 12 years of Catholic school, graduated with good grades and did one year of secretarial school before going out into the working world.

When Antoinette was born, their apartment was too small for two kids let alone three. John was starting to make good money then and so, her parents bought a fixer-upper brownstone in Park Slope, Brooklyn. Back in the 50's and 60's you could buy a brownstone in Brooklyn for $20,000 - $25,000; $25,000 wasn't cheap but, not so astronomically expensive like they are today. Also, people weren't making salaries like they do today, even plumbers, believe it or not! Now, you can't even look at a brownstone for under two million.

My parents lived in an apartment too, and then bought the brownstone next to Esther and Murray Schrable so that originally my Grandma Concetta and then later on my Grandma Philly and Grandpa Joe could live with us. That's the way it was, your parents came with to live with you. Sometimes, that wasn't possible and your grandparents lived in an apartment even though you owned a house but, they were always nearby and you saw them practically every day.

Back to Antoinette's family. John Fresca started out as a plumber's apprentice after the war, working for Viola Bros. He was a quick learner and a hard worker. Mr. Viola took him under his wing and taught him everything because his son, Bruno, wanted no part of the plumbing business; John was like a second son to him. John saved his money, got married and lived in a tiny apartment on 3rd Street for many years. In 1960, with three kids and a wife, he took the plunge and decided to start his own business, Fresca Plumbing. Carmela did the bookkeeping in their kitchen and his cousin, Pietro "Pete" Fresca worked under him as a plumber's assistant even though he didn't know what he wanted to do at the time. Sometimes a career just drops into your lap. Pete took over the business after John died; when he retired, he sold it to a large franchise.

John did very well; he had that sort of personality and he was reliable; he had a good work ethic and he charged reasonable rates for our middle-class neighborhood. He used to tell us kids, if you do a good job, you never have to worry about putting too much money into advertising; word of mouth is better than ads. It almost sounded like what Irish Marie's father told Emil. After living with a wife and two kids, in a two-bedroom apartment on 3rd Steet for 8 years, they bought a house to accommodate the whole family. John's mother and father left Calabria and came to live with them in the downstairs apartment.

And then, they had Antoinette. Back then, Italian-American homes had to be big enough to accommodate the many, many relatives who's visited them from Italy, too. Brownstones were good for having enough room to accommodate these visits and the parents who lived with them.

The Frescas always had a crowd on weekends; Fridays they played cards with the Schrables and Little Marie Greco's parents and sometimes mine. Saturday nights the Frescas were usually home or going to a wedding but, Sundays were definitely at the Fresca's. Many of their relatives came to visit from their town in Calabria; some stayed indefinitely until they could get a job in New York and become an American citizen. They knew that, in this country, hard work really did pay off and they embraced the American Dream. And, of course, they invited Signorine over so she could talk with people from the old country.

And despite their initial struggle in America, Carmela and John made sure their children got the best education so they wouldn't have to go through as much of a struggle as they did. When she lived in Sicily, Carmela told her children she lost both her parents to illness when she was in her teens; her eldest sister, Carla, took care of her until she married. Carla and her husband remained in Sicily because her husband worked for the government and he didn't want to lose his penzione. The sisters had an uncle in New York and Carmela decided to move to America. Many years later, Antoinette found out her mother's parents did not die of sickness but were murdered as part of a vendetta. Aunt Carla's daughter, Stefania, told Antoinette the story when she visited Brooklyn with her husband.

According to Stefania, after their parents were murdered, Carla and Carmela had to leave their town in the middle of the night and escaped to Palermo; they slept on the streets of Palermo until Carla found a job at a restaurant. She married a waiter who was waiting for his application for a government job to go through and, it did. Carmela lived with them for a little while but, once Carla got pregnant, it was time for Carmela to go to America.

I guess the vendetta part was a bad memory Carmela never wanted to pass on to her children. Back in those days, our parents didn't talk about their past except if it was a good memory; there were no ancestry companies back then and, to be honest, we kids never thought about our parents' past. We were more interested in the here and now. When we became adults, our parents began repeating themselves and would re-tell the same happy memories to us. That's all we knew.

However, as a result of her own past, Carmela kept a close eye on her sons to make sure they kept out of trouble or hung out with the wrong crowd like the gangs back in the 60's and 70's. The gang members used to sit all day on the stoops of other people with no education and most likely, no job in the future. We thought they were cool back then, smoking cigarettes, boozing, hanging out with the neighborhood sluts but, after we all went to work, we saw that we were saved by our parents. Frankie Boy and Emil had to tell their mother whenever they left the block and Carmela, like all our mothers, had a network of spy mothers who would tell each other where they children were at any given time. Today, we have cameras on every street who tape our movements, we didn't need cameras then, we had mothers who were all over the place and they had the telephone. People didn't have any reservations about telling other parents what their children were doing; they actually thanked them! Nowadays, if you tell a parent what their child is doing wrong, you might get an argument about it or told to mind your own business. Today's parents have to be afraid to reprimand a child lest they get sued.

It was not unusual for our mothers to call other mothers to tell them if we did something wrong! And God forbid we dared go off our block without permission! Children were only allowed to go to another street or avenue nearby to pick up some grocery item for our mothers. In the Fall or Winter, the mothers would each look from a window to make sure we were alright. And you knew you were being watched; all you had to do was look up and see one them looking at you through a curtain or even waving hello!

Ok, back to the Frescas. It wasn't discussed back then but Carmela had a miscarriage before Antoinette was born; it was a boy. But, as they say, God works in mysterious ways; three years and some months later she gave birth to the girl she prayed for; if the boy had lived, Carmela would have stopped trying after three sons and we would have lost a wonderful Fairy Comara!

So, needless to say, Antoinette grew up being VERY guarded not only by her mother but by her two brothers, her father when he came home from work and her grandparents who always sat outside in the little area. Every brownstone had a gate. These were finely designed wrought iron gates about 4 ft high sometimes with spikes on the top to deter any burglar coming into the house who didn't know enough to open the unlocked gate door and found it impossible to jump over a 4-foot gate with spikes. Everybody in the neighborhood had one; it was the middle-class thing to do back then. When we were kids, we thought they looked like crap and we could never hold on to them when we were trying to break a fall while roller skating. Some of my fondest memories were of roller skating with my friends, up and down the block, sometimes for most of the day.

Anyway, Antoinette's world was within those gates. She had friends, at least, the friends who could play with her inside her gate. She never went to other friends' houses except with her mother. In the summertime, Carmela would loosen the leash and let her go on the rides that came on our block or let her go 10 feet away to get a Mr. Softee but only if she was sitting outside.

During the summer, there were always at least two groups of five or six mothers sitting outside on summer evenings. They sat on beach chairs and had a Tupperware quart filled with homemade lemonade or iced tea when we got thirsty. When it was really hot, they would tie a cool wet handkerchief around their necks and refresh it every so often. Not everyone had air conditioners and, besides, it was a way to talk to one another about their lives instead of complaining about the heat. Some mother was always out if we got hurt or bruised our knee playing. It was a good "Humanet" as I like to call it; we had the beach chair groups at different spots on every block; "location trackers" on every street. No need for an app back then to know where your kids were at any given time!

And, this is another reason why I'm deciding to sell my house; I no longer hear the sound of children playing outside. It's such a wonderful sound to hear the voices of children laughing, playing stick ball or in winter having snowball fights, sledding or making "snow-persons". There are children on my block, I see them going into cars with their parents but, they're never out playing. Now they go to designated play dates or they're chained to a tablet for one reason or another. Every once in a while, the Latino neighbors next door will send up one of their kids to bring some specialty dinner to me. Yum! Their children are very polite but, I barely have time to ask them how they're doing in school before they're headed out the door. I can't blame them; I was the same way as a child. I wanted to leave so I could still play before the sun set. When I came home from work, I would talk to all the children and neighbors outside. I complained about the noise sometimes, stupid me.

But I digress… Antoinette was a protected child and she missed out on a lot of young adult experiences, too, like going to bars, dances, going to the beach in Coney Island as a mixed gender group. She went to the beach with her brothers and their friends but it was very rare. Every entertainment imaginable had a mother, father, grandparents, aunts and cousins. She didn't have the joy of sleepovers putting makeup on each other, the dances, the first not permitted cigarette or the bar hopping drunk times like us degenerates. She did go to her senior high school prom, with her cousin, in the limousine owned by Big Jimmy's cousin, Al, who owned a fleet of them. And, when she went to secretarial school she was allowed to go to dinner with her friends from school during the week. Weekends were mostly spent at home except when she went on her secret afternoon dates with Manny. I'll get to that story in a minute. Of course, her parents had young men in mind for Antoinette but, she never liked them and, sometimes her mother would even say that this or that guy was not for her! When she and Manny split up, she took up with a married guy so she still spent weekends with her parents.

And, that was just fine for her married brothers; they never had to worry about their parents being alone; she was the first responder if something happened.

As the Italian-American unmarried daughter living at home, it was understood that she would take care of her parents. Even if they were married, Italian daughters usually took care of their parents. Her brothers were married and living in Staten Island. They had jobs and families to take care of and usually couldn't get off from work. Antoinette took care of all their bills and her boss let her take time off to take them to the doctors when a medical issue arose. If repairs needed to be done, she'd call Emil and he'd drop over on the weekends to take care of it.

It may seem like an injustice but it worked out in the end for Antoinette. By living in the neighborhood so long, she got to know many people; she helped them and, on occasion, they were able to repay the favor. The extensive human network of people she helped allowed her to call upon them when the need arose; and, as a Fairy Comara, it was all about connections.

Like the time her mother had a stroke and went into the hospital; she couldn't be with her all day. By the time she came home from work, all the doctors had gone home. She went to Anthony "Cheech" Curcio and asked him if his son, Dr. John Curcio, by that time a famous cardiologist, could take a look at her mother and give his evaluation. Everyone in the hospital's Cardiac Ward was amazed that such a famous doctor from Manhattan would be visiting the hospital for one patient. Anthony Cheech never forgot how Antoinette and her mother took care of his wife and son when she had her hysterectomy. They did the cooking, the washing, took care of little John Cheech and Anthony never had to worry. And Anthony's wife, Ursula, never was alone; there was a whole stream of women coming in to visit, leaving some dinners or help her wash herself. Carmela and Antoinette made sure they told the neighborhood ladies about the situation. There were no secrets back then; you helped because you knew one day you may need that help, too.

Antoinette's asset was she had a giving heart and through that giving she was able to ask favors of them; not for her but for other people. No one said no to Antoinette! Frankie Boy told us one time his sister got punished because one of her friends only had one outfit for her Barbie and she gave her two outfits with heels and purses from her big Barbie closet. She had a little girl's dream closet of Barbie clothes, the car, everything. Her mother thought the friend stole them and then Antoinette confessed that she gave it to her. Her parents were furious because as immigrants they worked hard for their money but, now, as an older adult, I think those were the beginnings of Antoinette's goodness, her generous giving of self and who she is today. She knew everybody in the neighborhood and they all had a story to tell of one thing or another that Antoinette or Antoinette and her mother did for somebody. Antoinette had her tumbles along the way and she wasn't always good; she got into some risky situations before and after I met her again. And, that's why she's a Fairy

Comara.

Fairy Comaras don't always do the right thing; when they do the wrong thing, it's usually to themselves. God knows the Fairy Comaras had a full plate with their own troubles but they made the time to help others out. For the most part, we led normal ordinary lives but, what distinguished us was our ability to go the extra yard to make someone's life a little better. We didn't move mountains; we just cut them off at the top so that the troubled person could see the other side better. And many crossed that mountain to the other side because of one of us. A Fairy Comara helps everybody else before they take care of themselves. Many times, no one knew that we even helped them and, we never cared. Today, you get a medal if you help an old lady cross the street; you get the medal because you actually looked up from your phone and noticed.

In truth, there was/is a Comara in every family, some focused their assistance on only their families and some spread out a wider net. We cast out a wider net on Thursday evenings. If you think about it, every family has a mother, an aunt, a grandmother or a godmother who we can talk to or will cover for us when we're in trouble. They are the "go to" people we always run to for help. Back in our day, we had some male Comaras, like Big Jimmy in the club when we ran into some neighborhood problems or Captain Doyle when he had to put someone's son straight or if we teenagers were caught drinking and the cops stopped us. He'd give us the lecture and tell the cop not to report it to our parents, but we only got one "Get Out of Jail Free" card for that; the next time, he handed your ass on a silver platter to your parents.

A Fairy Comara accepts that they enjoy giving more than receiving; they're usually not good receivers. I know I have a problem with receiving; probably the other Fairy Comaras will agree, too.

But, as far as giving? …. boy, if you got a group of us together for a common goal, we were a force to be reckoned with! And God forbid you should be stupid enough to do harm to one of us or our family, then we accelerated your karmic payback. The Thursday Evening Meetings were an opportunity to get us all together and get to know other Fairy Comaras who came to the meetings from other neighborhoods.

Facebook has become a quasi-Fairy Comara to everyone; they post photos of their dinners like we were sitting next to them. Post the dinner at the restaurant and then pay for a delivery to our house and then we'll all be happy to view your dinner! You didn't need to snap a photo of what you ate to your friends because, we ate together. Another thing on Facebook, are the bleeding hearts who post one line and never tell you what's wrong. What is that all about? If you can't talk about it, why post it? However, I do like the fact that you find out who had a baby or who died.

Unlike Facebook, we helped you solve your problems then and there, no Face

Time shit and we didn't pray for you, we preyed on the problem. Through the Humanet, we were able to connect you to a solution, one way or another. Some ladies had problems that they didn't want to talk about but they came out through psychic readings with me. Things would come out that they didn't even tell their own family about; if they were abused, or their son or daughter was in trouble or even if they got into some hot water situations themselves; it would come out in the reading.

Back then, Domestic Violence hotlines were not really in gear or hardly used; it had to be settled by the Fairy Comaras. Even now, there are still victims out there who are ashamed or fearful of calling. Problems were first settled within the family and if you didn't have a family or they weren't sympathetic, then you went to the Fairy Comaras and we took over.

As children and as adults, we were taught to respect our elderly neighbors; we went to the store for them or helped them in other ways like Frankie Boy shoveling snow for Old Sam or taking Signorine to doctor appointments. As children we were taught to have a deep respect for our elders even though they always picked the wrong time to ask us to go to the store, or when they told you the same story fifteen times. You just stood there and listened. And when you grew to be an adult, you realized why you were told to listen because there would come a time when you would beg God to hear them speak one more time. We made sure they had plenty of food and lots of company. One Thursday a month, Antoinette used to pick up and bring some of the homebound senior women to the Thursday evening meetings, the ones who had no daughters living nearby. God bless Antoinette; it didn't matter if they were in wheelchairs, walkers or canes; she and another Fairy Comara would patiently and cheerfully fold up the wheelchairs and the walkers and drive them to my house. We'd always sent them home with whatever food we had left over. I remember how many of them walked out with Cool Whip tubs of leftovers! For many of them, it would be tomorrow's dinner.

Fairy Comara "Little" Marie Greco's first job was working at our local police precinct; she worked for Captain Doyle as his secretary. Later on, when she got married and had her first child, she moved to Massapequa and worked part-time as a Senior Services coordinator for Francone Senior Center. She was always good in making sure the seniors had good services like part-time care and housekeeping if they needed it. When Irish Marie started her own cleaning company, Little Marie used to send the cleaning jobs to her. She knew Irish Marie was a perfectionist; she made surprise visits to check on her staff making sure their house was thoroughly cleaned. She sometimes would come to clean someone's house even though they couldn't afford to pay for it.

In addition, Little Marie set up a special fund at Francone for poorer seniors from donations and raffles. She always presented a professional image; she was short but she had a big heart of gold. She had a way of making seniors feel special, not by patronizing them but by talking to them as adults and they so appreciated not being treated as a non-entity. She managed to get all these nurses and doctors in the area to speak to the seniors. She even had Frank Sinatra and Elvis impersonators perform at the center! And she made sure there was music playing in the community room. This she did in addition to bingo, arranging self-defense classes, latest social security changes, crocheting circles, card games and $1 Movies on Tuesdays; she got Blockbuster to comp the rental. And this was part-time; can you imagine what she could have done if she was full-time? She made it a point to get to know all the nursing homes and funeral directors, the priests or rabbis, the Caregiver agency managers and the insurance brokers and lawyers. They spoke or provided information on anything she thought seniors should know so they wouldn't get scammed. She always made time to listen to their problems. She also had a keen eye to zoom in when she sensed some form of abuse going on inside their homes. Francone Senior Center's director asked her to go full-time but, at the time, the kids were still young and she was caring for her parents too; it was just too much time out of the house.

As I mentioned earlier, Theresa Guarino, another Fairy Comara, worked as a nurse in our neighborhood hospital so she knew all the doctors and helped us to get appointments for our parents. She'd visit our grandparents and parents to check on them, explain medications, sometimes she even brought her blood pressure monitor. We'll discuss Theresa a little later. I'm going to repeat myself throughout this story because I'm old so, be patient.

Black Marie Giordano, nee Santorini, worked as a paralegal so she made sure we or our parents weren't getting the shaft on any outside business dealings. By the way, Black Marie was not black, she was a Sicilian with a swarthy complexion; as I stated, we had so many Maries in the neighborhood we had to differentiate one from the other. Black Marie always had a smile on her face; she had the patience of a saint. When legal stuff had to be explained to their senior citizen clients, the lawyers at her firm would send her to the conference room to do that because she would explain it over and over without losing her cool.

I, Diane Santangelo, worked in the same bank for over 40 years; I started out as a teller and worked my way up to mortgages in Park Slope and Bay Ridge, Brooklyn. I dealt mostly with people my age back then who were seeking mortgages or starting a small business. I also dealt with all the seniors and their many questions. I dealt with the seniors who had more money than God and complained about the cost of a container of milk or those who lived from one Social Security check to another each month. I knew almost everyone in the neighborhood; sometimes, I had to make house calls if one of our customers was homebound. I always brought them a complimentary pen and a plastic sleeve to keep their bank book. One time, one of my customer's daughters called me up and begged me to talk to her mother about stashing large amounts of money around the house, sometimes between the box spring and the mattress. They still had the Depression fresh in their memory even after 50 plus years ago when the banks had no FDIC requirements; they never trusted the banks since then. I convinced her to keep $100 in the house for an emergency and if she needed money from her account, I would bring it to her personally so she wouldn't be afraid of getting robbed. Her daughter and I canvassed the house and found $6,000 that she even forgot she had squirreled away in every nook and cranny.

Back then, you didn't have to Press 1 for an account balance, Press 2 to pay a bill, Press 29 if you wish to speak with a representative. You called the bank and a living breathing person spoke to you on the phone. I used to bring the bank's complimentary pens to the Thursday meetings because the old ladies loved pens! Antoinette used to go to the Hallmark store on 5th Ave and buy the little notepads with the flowers on it and give it to them, her own money. They acted like we were giving away gold! Just remember, a good hug beats a Thumbs Up on Facebook any day. By 2010, we were becoming the seniors. Sadly, we couldn't find any Fairy Comaras to replace us.

Our grandparents wasted nothing! I remember my Grandma Philly used to use the inside of an envelope she would receive and re-use them as grocery lists, she also used the front cover of last year's Christmas cards for gift tags. When paper towels first came out, our grandparents re-used them if they were used to wipe up a water spill. But they still used kitchen towels for the dishes. Now, no one hardly uses kitchen towels because they have germs; and they're sicker today than before. God gave most of us an excellent immune system; we need germs to keep that immune system working.

As a senior, I have one family right now that cares for seniors. I have Latino neighbors, on the other side of me, young married couple, the Beltranos, they have two children, the boy is 12 and the girl is 10. Very respectful, they always tell their kids to ring my bell and ask if I need anything in the store. They're renting the second floor in the brownstone that Rose Di Fillipo, Little Marie Greco's mother, owned. There's a single guy who rents the downstairs apartment but, he's always out. I've never seen the landlord. Mr. Beltrano told me he mails the rent to a management company. When it snows, Mr. Beltrano gets his shovel out at 5 in the morning because he has to get to work by 7:00 AM. He does his sidewalk and does my sidewalk as well. The Latinos, like the Italians, have a great respect for their elders. When I do need something in the store and the son delivers it, I try to shove a few dollars in his pocket but, he won't take a dime from me. Now, on those rare occasions when I make Lasagna, I'll call them and they send up one of their children to pick it up. Up until she moved, Antoinette babysat for the Beltranos when they went to a wedding or had to take care of some business together. Their kids ran to her house because they knew they're going to be treated to everything imaginable that Antoinette could do to entertain or feed them. They even came home with toys sometimes! Antoinette!!!

I remember when we got the Fairy Comaras together to help Esther Schrable when she had hip replacement surgery but, I'm getting ahead of myself. In the 90's, hip replacement surgery wasn't like it is today; today they send you home in one day. But I'm getting ahead of myself; I do that a lot lately. I'll get back to Esther later on in the story.

Cordless phones in the house were a big technological boom for us; no more stretching the cord to its max just to have a private conversation that couldn't last long. Now, all we do is talk on the phone, outside as well as inside, and we have a free hand to do other things more engaging like, for instance, bullshitting about nothing all day long and then saying we don't have enough time in the day to do the important stuff.

In the 2000's, the neighborhood slowly started to change; progress is good, don't get me wrong but, it just wasn't as friendly. Whenever I met the new neighbors on the block, they'd say hello but they kept mostly to themselves. A couple of years later, they were moving out to someplace else and someone else moved in for another two years.

My parents' house, my home now, was a few doors down from Agnello's Bakery. Every morning we took in the smell of cakes and cookies being baked. Agnello's closed about six years ago and opened a bakery in Staten Island where most of the Italian migrated. Next to my parents were Esther and Murray Schrable. The Schrables were the only Jewish family on the block; it made sense for them to live there because it was around the corner from their store, Murray's Department Store on 5th Ave. between President and Carroll Sts.

At one time, Antoinette secretly dated the Schrable's son, Manny, for almost two years; they really cared for each other. I think they both were around 16 when they started. They had to go on Saturday afternoon dates on the sly because Antoinette's parents would never let her date unless it was at home, under family supervision; dating unchaperoned at 16? That was never going to happen in the Fresca house. On Saturdays, she would tell them she was going shopping to A&S on DeKalb Ave. to buy something. After the movie or lunch, Antoinette would have to go in A&S and pick up anything so her parents wouldn't be suspicious. If she said she was going for shoes, she'd come home with pantyhose and say she didn't like the styles or they didn't fit right. Manny on the other hand just said he was going out with his friends. Parents didn't question boys as much as girls back then; I think parents still do it, although they claim they treat each child with the same caution. Antoinette's and Manny's parents were good friends. They had dinners together, went to the movies together and every Friday night, they played cards along with my Grandpa Joe Santangelo. I know, I repeat myself.

For a couple of years, Antoinette and Manny got away with it; with the parents, that is, but, some of us knew something was up, except Frankie Boy and Emil. We thought that Emil would have known because he was good friends with Manny. Even my mother knew because Antoinette used to meet Manny in front of our house and she could hear their conversations when the windows were open. My Mom knew how to keep a secret and they looked so in love; she didn't even tell me until the bomb dropped.

The bomb was when Antoinette and Manny decided to tell their parents. Antoinette told her parents at her family's Sunday afternoon dinner with her newlywed cousins present. Big mistake! Signorine was invited that Sunday, too. John Fresca was not a man prone to outbursts, some would say he was a quiet man, but he was a decisive man. He told Antoinette her mother would go over and talk to the Schrables about it. Not a single word more. Well, of course, Antoinette felt like all her fears were unfounded and immediately called Manny to tell him the good news.

After that, the next thing we knew was Antoinette was enrolled in secretarial school after high school and Manny Schrable was shipped off to Florida State University; the relationship between Antoinette and Manny was no more. Manny eventually married but Antoinette never did and although she was a looker in her heyday, no guy was Mr. Right after Manny. That story to be continued….

I think all us Fairy Comaras would agree that, after Signorine died, Antoinette Fresca became the Queen of the Fairy Comaras because a lot in this book is really about her. Until last year, she was the only Fairy Comara still living in the neighborhood. After the Thursday evening meetings started to fizzle out, I'd talk or visit her at least twice a week. The other times, she was still busy volunteering at the hospital or baking cakes for St. Agatha's Church Bake Sale. St. Agatha's was forced to close about 6 years ago because of poor attendance. No one gets involved with the church anymore, not even me I'm ashamed to say.

As I mentioned before, I really didn't know Antoinette because she was 10 years younger than me and, as I said, the only reason I know her is because I was friends with Frankie Boy. She was a cute kid, always had something blue on her; we called it Blessed Mother Blue because it was a light blue like the statue in church. We used to teach her how to do the Hustle when we dropped by after going to the disco, we even taught her mother Carmela! Antoinette still talks about those nights. Up until my Arthritis kicked in, we would occasionally dance when we heard Barry White on the radio.

But, as I said before, she had a restricted childhood and adolescence. Carmela was very protective of her, at least we thought so then; by today's standard she would be called a tiger mom. Carmela brought her with her when she went to have a cup of coffee in someone's house or to the church every Sunday. She was mostly around adults and she could only play with her friends if they played on her stoop. All I know is she had the largest collection of Barbie and Ken dolls with two Barbie cases of clothes. I think she still has those Barbies!

I'm giving you training on how to listen to the same story over and over again; someday it will come in handy when talking with your parents or grandparents.

Because she was the only girl in the family, Antoinette quickly got indoctrinated in helping others because her mother was involved in the church's activities, the food and clothing drives, she learned how to crochet hats with the sequins to sell at the church fairs, she went with her mother to the Methodist hospital to distribute the chocolate lollipops her mother made for the pediatric patients, and most of all she got to hear all her mother's friends' problems. In other words, she was an adult before she was a child and that helped her to be compassionate at an early age. When she grew up, she was a candy stripper at Methodist Hospital on Monday nights and Wednesdays she would call out the bingo numbers at St. Agatha's. You can always tell which section of the hospital she was working in by the never-ending decorations she brought for every holiday, even the Jewish holidays…she had the hearts for Valentine's Day, the green shamrocks for St. Patty's Day, tulips for the Spring, flowers for summer, Halloween, Thanksgiving, Hanukkah, Christmas and even Kwanzaa. The wards would fight over who got Antoinette. When she got older and couldn't get around as much, she became an Amazon Queen; she orders all her decorations through Amazon and sends them to the hospital. Up until last year, she made plenty of chocolate lollipops for the pediatric ward at Christmas.

In light of this, do I need to tell you how her parents' house was decorated? In Christmases past, the Frescas decorated every inch of their home, inside and out. Their home was a must see if you happened to be in the neighborhood and we even had people who heard about their house come from Bensonhurst driving by to look at the decorations. The lights, the moving figures, the music. They even put out a basket of real candy canes at night for the passersby. Frankie Boy used to be Santa at Big Jimmy's club and give out turkeys to the parents and toys for the kids. And after her parents died, she continued decorating the house for Christmas, even though she was the only one living there. She'd start right after Halloween and be finished by the day after Thanksgiving. But it wasn't too long before her brothers convinced her to sell the house and move to Staten Island. She sold the house, didn't move to Staten Island.

Back then in the 70's and 80's, college wasn't a must for a girl, at least in our neighborhood. So, when Antoinette graduated from Blessed Mother High

School, her parents sent her to a secretarial school and then, she immediately got a job on Wall St, through Frankie Boy, working for his company but in a different department. Back then, it really WAS who you knew. I think it's still the same but, now with these Human Resource outsourcing companies they tell me it's much harder. I'm still not too sure of that but, I digress. And, because Antoinette went to Catholic School, she was hired immediately because you received an excellent education in Catholic schools; they knew we worked hard; the nuns would never have accepted anything otherwise!

She worked for a Senior Manager, Fred Manza, who headed up the Marketing Dept.; Frankie Boy knew Fred only as a work friend but he met with Fred about hiring Antoinette. She worked for Fred for a little over 22 years until his promotion. Frankie Boy worked in Sales. Five years later, he moved to another job with a promotion, AVP, and a higher salary. By that time, Antoinette knew all his co-workers and she continued baking cookies for them even after he left.

After so many years working for him, Antoinette knew Fred Manza's family on a first name basis. She smothered his two children with gifts when they visited the office; she talked to his wife, Susan, almost every day. She loved working there and everyone in the company knew her. This was to be Antoinette's first and only full-time job.

Italian men like to hire Italian women because they know they'll be nurtured just like their mothers nurtured them; it's in our genes to take care of their needs. We're talking years ago not now. For the first five years, everything went pretty smoothly between Antoinette and Fred Manza. Every morning, Fred would have his bagel with cream cheese and coffee on his desk, courtesy of Antoinette, the mail would be opened and placed on his desk but only the mail that was important. She arranged all his meetings, travel, lunch reservations, and filtered all his calls. In addition, She bought all his wife's Christmas, Anniversary and birthday gifts; His wife caught on and she'd call Antoinette and thank HER for the beautiful gift her husband bought her. She even coordinated birthday parties for his kids. She went to all of his family events even after what happened after five years working for him.

According to Antoinette and, by the way, I only found this out through a reading I gave her back in 2000, is that Fred started getting a little too friendly with Antoinette. First, behind closed doors, he would tell her about the family problems at home then, it went to complaining about the wife and then he was depressed. A script as old as time but what did Antoinette know? With the cloistered life she led? All she did was go back and forth to work and spend weekends with family. And, I'm not saying this couldn't happen to even an experienced woman but, Antoinette was a blank sheet in the dating department. Well, long story short, eventually it got intimate.

What everyone didn't know or maybe secretly knew in the office was that every Wednesday they spent a good long lunch hour at the Marriott Hotel. She told me that, although Fred swore he loved his wife, she didn't understand his depression like Antoinette. And this affair went on for many, many years until Antoinette found out that Fred found somebody else who also understood his depression. This story is to be continued. It gets better.

Fairy Comara Irish Marie is not Irish, she's Puerto Rican, Maria Estella Rodriguez. We called her Irish Marie because she married a firefighter named Brian Fitzpatrick, Jr. Her parents left Puerto Rico for New York with their son, Hector Jr. back in the mid-50s. They stayed with relatives in Canarsie, Brooklyn until Marie's father, Hector, got a job, through a family connection, as a junior janitor at the public school on Garfield St. Hector, Teresa and their baby son, Hector Jr., moved to a two-bedroom apartment on President St. and 6th Ave in South Brooklyn, now called the fancy shmancy name of Park Slope. Hector was a stern man, never smiled but, his family came first. Marie's mother, Teresa, our mothers called her Terry, was the nurturer but pretended to be strict with her kids. Between the mother and father, I don't know who was stricter; I think her father delegated the mother to administer the punishment.

They moved into two-bedroom apartment with one child and two children followed. Three kids, son Hector, daughter Carmen and then Maria, Irish Marie; how they did it no one knows but they did it. And you never saw a cleaner home than Irish Marie's parents' apartment; that's where Irish Marie picked up her cleaning skills. They rented in a two-family limestone home on 6th Ave and President St.; the landlady lived alone in the downstairs one-bedroom apartment. When the landlady got too old to live there, her son sold the house to Marie's father and they brought Teresa's mother from Puerto Rico to live in the downstairs apartment.

Back then in the 60's and 70's, South Brooklyn was somewhat of an integrated borough, mostly European Jews, Italians, Irish, German, Polish, Cubans and Puerto Ricans. We had one black family up the block, their last name was Davis; what a nice family. They lived in a house near the corner; Mother was named Ida but, I've forgotten the father's name. They had two children, a girl, Cassie and a boy, Jesse. Later on, Cassie married and her husband and their two sons lived there for a while so she and her husband could save enough money to buy a house. I remember playing Double Dutch with Cassie; she definitely was the Double Dutch queen. If you could outdo her, you probably were from another neighborhood; we girls couldn't, so that never happened. We complimented her but, in our heads, we wished she'd trip on the ropes! She was the reigning queen. Years later at one of our block parties, when she was a mother of two boys, we dared her to do the Double Dutch again; she still beat us. When both her parents died, she sold the house because her husband took a job in Maryland. I wonder if she's on Facebook? Maybe we can connect again.

Our neighborhood was a mix of everything but more Italian, the common thread was that our parents or grandparents were immigrants; they all came here to escape poverty, bad governments or religious persecution in their homeland. Not everyone lived in a house; many of them lived in apartments. We had families who lived in apartments for 20-30 years with no intention of moving; not like the revolving door of tenants you see today. This was your home. Some families like mine saved enough to put a deposit and get a mortgage. And, if you can believe it, brownstones were considered low to middle income homes; you could get them cheap because you had to do a lot of fixing with old houses.

When my grandparents, Joe and Filomena "Philly" married, they also brought my Grandpa Joe's mother, Concetta, to Brooklyn from Italy because she was a widow. Grandma Concetta was old when she gave birth to my grandfather; my mother thinks she might have been 40-45 but she wasn't sure. They lived in an apartment in Park Slope for about five years; both my grandparents were working at the time and my Great Grandma Concetta took care of my father when he was a baby. Then, one day, according to what my mother told me, they heard about a two-family brownstone on President St. that was going into foreclosure because the owner died with no family. It was a real fixer upper but, little by little they got the house in working order. My grandparents lived on the first and second floor and Great Grandma Concetta lived on the ground floor apartment, she loved it and she ate dinner with my grandparents every night. She passed away by the time my father was in his late 20's. When Grandpa Joe and Grandma Philly were older, they sold the house and moved in with us. My father and mother were already married and I was maybe three or four when Grandma Concetta died so they took the downstairs apartment until my father could buy his own home.

To be honest I have a vague recollection of my Great Grandma Concetta. She had heart problems when she came to this country and she always had to take those nitroglycerin pills every day. I do remember her singing to me in Italian and she was always kissing me.

My father's parents Filomena "Philly" and Joe Santangelo, came to this country when they were young. They met at a Knights of Columbus Dance. Grandpa Joe worked on the docks in Bush Terminal and sometimes in Manhattan near the Hudson River. Grandma Philly worked in a sewing factory as a piece worker in Di Paolo's Clothing Co. in Brooklyn. By the time Grandpa Joe came to live with us, he was on disability for a bad back from working as a longshoreman so he was unable to maintain a whole house so they sold it and moved in with us. Grandma Philly continued to work at Di Paolo's.

On the holidays, Grandma Philly made the best cookies and pastries. Even though my mother knew how to make all of Grandma's cookies, they never tasted the same. And she made a mean lasagna and brasciole, too! My father would never say it to my mother's face but, he liked the way his mother cooked. Grandma Philly used to sell her trays of Stroffla "honey balls" to Agnello's Bakery during the Christmas holidays because even Mr. Agnello didn't make them as good as her! Now, it's a miracle if you find an Italian bakery in Brooklyn; we still have Savarese Bakery but, the line stretches around the corner almost every week just for Italian bread. I can't stand for hours with my Arthritis!

In an Italian home, the dining room was where everything happened; you discussed family matters or related news about one of the relatives and there were passionate discussions about the price of everything. What you never, ever heard was any discussion about the three tabu subjects: Sex, Politics and Religion. I wish that rule was still active today!

When I invited friends, who weren't Italian, to my home for dinner, they would always ask me why the people around the table were fighting? I'd tell them, they're not fighting, what makes you think that? Shouting was a part of my life and everybody on the block's life; we are a dramatic kind of people. And our laughing was loud around that table as well. On Sundays, there were always additional family members or friends invited for dinner. They were mostly related to my father's family because my mother had no family in New York. The kitchen was breakfast and lunch and doing your homework but dinner was in the dining room. It was a big thing to have a formal dining room back then and every family had a table that always had a clear plastic cover on top of their most expensive tablecloth. If the table just had an expensive tablecloth, then we kids knew that we had to eat in the kitchen because the other table was used only on holidays, for show. Sunday dinner lasted for hours and it was like we had a conveyor belt of food circulating around the table; food was taken away and replenished. I remember the large gallon of Gallo red wine on the table and 7-Up or Ginger Ale soda. And then there was coffee or espresso with desserts that all the aunts and cousins brought fresh from the bakery.

Living Rooms were for TV, listening to music and playing games. Now, they have TVs everywhere, in the kitchen, in the dining room and, I swear I saw one in someone's bathroom. Personally, I would feel uncomfortable taking a shit while someone was talking to me even if they're on the TV. And how long do you plan on sitting in that bathroom? Take the hint to get off the seat when the hemorrhoids commercial comes on!

When they bought their own homes, our parents had to do all the plastering, painting, putting up new kitchen cabinets, laying down the linoleum floors, wallpapering; they didn't have extra money to spend on labor so they had to learn how to do it themselves. Occasionally, if one of the neighbors knew how to do something, they did it and then our parents would do something for them. It always worked out. When he was a teenager, my father worked in a hardware shop putting down linoleum floors and tiles and he shared that talent with our neighbors. If you needed electrical work done then you called Little Marie Greco's father, Dominick Di Fillipo, an electrician and he'd do it at a discount or if you needed a plumber, you called John Fresca, and he would fix your plumbing. Mike Martorano did all the kitchen countertops on my block when Formica counters were the big thing, he did a good job on my mother's countertops. He would work at the houses of the well-to-do and imitate their style in his own home. He liked marble, too, and his bathrooms were always the coolest part of the house in the summer.

Years later, Little Marie's brother Jimmy went into medical school and wound up becoming an orthopedic surgeon. He started a practice in Manhattan and eventually married a nice girl from Russia who's a pediatrician. Dr. Jimmy Di Fillipo operated on my father when he needed knee surgery; he took good care of him. His office didn't accept my father's health insurance so, Jimmy waived the surgery bill. I think Dr. Jimmy is retired now or he moved his practice somewhere else; Little Marie would know for sure. I could really use him now because my left knee is giving me problems. Maybe they have a good surgeon in Brewster; I'll have to ask Antoinette. Anyway, no one charged one another, except for the cost of the materials or a slight charge. It worked out pretty good back then; we weren't exactly poor but who had that kind of money to outsource the renovations?

Funny thing about those times was if you had a doctor or a nurse in the family, the neighbors would take them aside at parties and talk about what part of their body was bothering them to get free medical advice. They never actually went to the doctor after getting the advice but, at least they could say they talked to a doctor or a nurse and this is what they told them. Nobody went to doctors like today, there was no preventive medicine back then; you went to the doctor when you were sick, even though a doctor's visit was way cheaper than it is now.

Antoinette's father, John, could never sit still at home; there was always a home improvement job going on with his two sons working by his side, not really what they wanted to be doing on a Sunday but, later in life it saved them a chunk of money when they bought their own homes. And, as far back as I could remember, there was always a revolving door of family doing repairs in their house and a lot of food cooked for whoever was doing the job. You wouldn't recognize Carmela unless you saw her coming out of her kitchen and usually Antoinette was right behind her. Their house always smelled so good! And on Sundays the smell of the sauce cooking, oh my God! Food was life to our parents; it was the reward for working hard in America, where you didn't have to wonder where your next meal was going to come from.

All the neighbors helped each other because they knew, at some point, they would need help for something else. They all wanted the American Dream and realized that we had to do it together in order to afford it and raise a family; I guess we were the village Hillary Clinton talks about, the village that looked out for each other. There was a sense of permanence and closeness. Our neighbors lived in the neighborhood 20, 30 years or more, whether it was in a home or an apartment. If one of the men lost their job, that family was fed with the leftovers of everyone on the block until he got a job. Of course, we didn't knock on the door and say, "hello, I heard your husband's out of work, here's a leftover." We'd do it subtlety, like sometimes our parents would make us' kids deliver it and tell that mother, that their mother, said to bring it to them. And, then, they had no choice but to take it because they couldn't refuse a child and we were off in a second to get back to playing. Hand-me-down clothes were not regarded as poor but functional common sense because kids grow out of clothes fast and why not pass it on to someone else? In the early 2000s, when the Yuppies came in, there was a store that sold used clothing, I believe it was called a Consignment Store. They still have them today but I'm thinking it's a store for worn designer brand clothing. I don't even know who some of my neighbors are to give them some of my stuff. No sooner do I make an acquaintance with someone on my block, they're moving. It's hard to make a strong connection when everyone moves in three or four years.

For many of us, our parents or our grandparents came to this country on ships speaking little or no English. They had very little money, they were sponsored by a relative and lived with them for a short time until they found a job. They learned how to speak English from reading the newspapers and listening to their co-workers. And when they came to live here, they wanted a new life where they could believe what they wanted to, work hard, have something to show for it, and give their children a better life than they had in the old country.

You didn't have to tell our parents to recycle, they recycled everything. Paper bags to cover our school books, milk bottles were glass and the milkman picked up the empty ones and re-used, diapers were washed and used again, the only plastic stuff we used were the plastic cups at parties and later on the Cool Whip containers. Our parents saved everything. Grandpa Joe told me when he was a kid and his shoes were worn out on the bottom, he had to fill his shoes with cardboard to cover the holes; he only had one pair of shoes. Throughout his life, Grandpa Joe had two pairs of shoes; one pair for weddings and other occasions and his everyday pair. He thought he was so fortunate just to own two pairs of shoes! My father tried to introduce him to sneakers but, he said no.

This was our grandparents' home now and they were here to stay and they brought that culture of cooperation and friendship with them from Italy. The neighborhood became the village from back home.

Irish Marie's mother couldn't speak a word of English when she came to Brooklyn from Puerto Rico; we had parents from Italy, Germany, Ireland, Poland, Latvia, Russia; I think we even had one couple from Finland who lived in the neighborhood not speaking English. They all helped each other with translation or they enlisted us kids to translate for them. And their translating skills were a sight to see and hear…. all of them screaming in their own language and then at the end you'd hear "understand?" They'd say "shuga bol", wonda bread or washa machina. They'd all say it in their accent and of course, as kids, we would be hysterical laughing behind their backs. If our parents sent you out to get regular bread, that meant Italian bread. Wonder Bread was for peanut butter and jelly "sangwich" and toast. God bless them, they kept our neighborhood tight and tried to understand and help one another. Signorine would say a whole sentence in Italian, which no one other than the other Italian women would understand and at the end of it say to everyone "capisce?" We'd all nod yes anyway. And while they were drinking "cawfee", Signorine would point to the "shuga bol". They learned "yeah" much sooner than "yes" so they became thoroughly indoctrinated with all the key words with a Brooklyn accent.

Except the curse words which we NEVER taught them; they eventually found out from one of the neighbors; our mothers belonged to the "we'll find out somehow" parents' group. They also shared our report cards from school just in case we told them that c's and d's meant we were doing well…that worked for about 5 minutes no matter what language you spoke. We had so many Maries in the neighborhood, we had to put something in front of their name so we would know which Marie we were talking about! We started to call Maria Rodriguez, Irish Marie when she married Brian Fitzpatrick. I don't remember what we called her before we called her Irish Marie; I know we never called her Spanish Marie although that would make sense but I think we just called her Maria. You had to see the look on people's faces when we would point out Irish Marie to people at the Thursday meetings. She definitely had the tanned Caribbean look no doubt about it. Back then we didn't get our panties in a knot over "perceived" racial differences. Yes, they were surprised but, it was a joke to see the look on people's faces. Can you imagine the look on peoples' faces when we first introduced Marie Giordano as Black Marie? We called her Black Marie because she had a gorgeous dark Sicilian complexion. No one took it the wrong way or as a racial slur. We did however have one Fairy Comara many years ago who actually was African-American, but her name wasn't Marie, it was Janette. Janette was a Fairy Comara before the Thursday meetings. She owned a fabric store on 5th Ave and she sold curtains, too. Our parents bought most of their curtains there. Grandma Philly bought her fabrics there but made her own curtains with her Singer sewing machine, the sewing machine with the peddle! She was always chatting with Janette. She was more of a Fairy Comara in my grandmother's group than our group but, she helped a lot of people in her family get jobs and she was generous to her customers in giving them discounts on curtains they liked but couldn't quite afford.

So, back to Irish Marie for a moment. Irish Marie held a secret and she held it for a long time before we all caught wind that something was wrong and it became apparent that we had to do a Fairy Comara Intervention. To be continued.

We had Fairy Comara Little Marie Greco, nee Di Fillipo, in our group. She was 4'11" always wore heels even her slippers had heels. I'll talk more about her later. Then there was Black Marie Giordano, nee Santorini, who wasn't black, she was Sicilian. Her father and mother, Paolo and Livia, owned the pizzeria and restaurant up the block on 5th Ave and she worked there evenings while going to college at New York University. She was one of the Fairy Comara disco regulars who would go out with us. Black Marie was always the one who could think of a good excuse when we stayed out late or in trouble, she was good at thinking of something at the spur of the moment. In the beginning she used to tell her parents she was sleeping over one of our houses so she could stay out late instead of being home by 11:00 PM. That scheme worked for a couple of months until they found out and then she thought of something else; she went to her uncle, Big Jimmy at the club. Black Marie's uncle, Big Jimmy, "managed" the Italian American Veterans Club which did contain veterans, many of them fought in WW2 and the Korean War but, it was a little more than that; everyone knew they were mobbed up. But, the neighborhood was safe and there was never any trouble on the streets. Uncle Big Jimmy solved the disco problem for us; he called in a favor with a limousine company on Bay Parkway and every time Black Marie went to the disco with us, we went by and came home in a limousine. Discos didn't start to get populated until 10:00 PM; all the parents were content with the limo arrangement and we got to stay out late.

Black Marie was married two times; the first one should never have happened. She met a guy at NYU, Preston Scott McManus, Jr., who was a likable guy but his family were WASPS and she didn't get along with the mother because she treated her in a condescending way. They got married while attending college; her father was against it because he thought she was too young but, he paid for a big wedding. Scott's family stuck out like a sore thumb and pretty much never left the reception table to converse with anyone and, to be truthful, Black Marie's family sort of stayed away from their table, too. When she would invite her in-laws to dinner they'd always ask if dinner was pizza as a jab to what her father did for a living. Ironically, when her mother-in-law had bypass surgery, none of his family offered to take care of her and Black Marie took time off from college and stayed with her for two weeks. But still, it wasn't enough. When Scott was offered a paid summer internship at Arthur Anderson on the West Coast, he accepted. Black Marie had one year to go before she graduated college so she stayed in New York. At first, he called Black Marie every day then a few weeks later he'd call two or three times a week and then once a week. When he came home, according to Black Marie, he was not the same Scott and long story short, Scott's parents managed to get the church to issue a quickie annulment. She later found out that her ex-husband married his childhood sweetheart and they moved to San Diego.

Black Marie went home to her parents and for a while, we all had to take her out so she wouldn't be so depressed. She was married, then un-married, no children and now, she was single again. Luckily, she still had her job as a paralegal at Bernstein & York to keep her mind off her life. She vowed that she would never get married again.

On Tuesday and Thursday mornings, Black Marie would take the garbage out for her parents before she left for work. One Tuesday morning, the sanitation truck came early and as Black Marie was hurrying to bring the garbage cans to the curb, this big guy comes over and offers to do it for her. He was the one who dumped the garbage in the back of the truck while the other guy drove. The next week, on a Thursday, the truck comes early again and once again this guy offers to bring the cans to the truck for Black Marie. He would only say good morning to her and she did the same. This went on for a month until he finally had the guts to ask Marie if she wanted to go on a date; she didn't even know his name although he knew she was a Santorini because the name was on the garbage can. His name was Sal Giordano. He got up the courage to ask her out; she never saw him coming. Timid but sociable, he soon blended in with our crowd. His family lived in Bensonhurst but, Antoinette Fresca's mother, Carmela, knew Sal's mother, Mary, because she was friends with Carmela's cousin, Concetta, and she got to know Mary at Concetta's son's christening party and other occasions.

Well, once again, the rest is history. After about two years, they got engaged. This time, Black Marie was cautious and waited. Black Marie got married, again, to Sal, church wedding because of the annulment and God Bless her father Paolo, he paid for another wedding reception. She was a Daddy's girl although he denied it. This one, he had no problem paying for; he liked Sal. This second time around wedding felt like the first time, for everyone, and the in-laws got along just fine. Black Marie would always pick up Sal's mother and, of course, her mother Livia and bring them to the Thursday meetings. They both spoke Italian and they were good company for Signorine.

When they came home from their honeymoon, Black Marie and Sal lived with her parents to save up for a home. Sal took the exam for the Supervisor position at the Sanitation Dept, got it and then the first child came. Black Marie worked as a paralegal for a law firm, Bernstein & York in lower Manhattan. When her son, Sal Jr., was born, she couldn't work the long hours needed at a law firm and wanted to resign but one of the partners, Joe Bernstein, who valued her work, offered her a part-time position at the firm so, she worked there for a couple of years until baby #2 came, a daughter, Annette, named after her maternal grandmother, and then it was too much. She had no choice but to quit. Her mother was still working with her father at the pizzeria; they needed her help on Saturday nights. After Annette was born, they started looking at homes and found a nice small one family home in the Gravesend section of Brooklyn.

Although Black Marie was no longer a paralegal, she was our legal Fairy Comara. On Thursdays, people would bring any legal documents for her to explain or she would tell them they needed a lawyer for this or that problem that required it. If she couldn't help them, she would call up her old firm, Bernstein & York, and Joe Bernstein would give them a discount. She helped Esther Schrable many years later when she needed some legal advice.

Black Marie had a stroke about five years ago. By then she and Sal had moved out of the Gravesend section of Brooklyn; Sal was already retired from the Sanitation Dept. and their children were married. They bought a home in Shirley, Long Island, to be near their daughter Annette, her husband and three grandchildren. She still has a little problem speaking when we go on the Zoom but, she's still the same Black Marie. I used to take the train out to Shirley to see her but, these legs of mine are getting slower and slower and all the steps in the subway and the Long Island Railroad are too much for me. Antoinette tells me she is going to organize a Fairy Comara Reunion at her house. Another alluring tactic by Antoinette to get me to move to Brewster.

As I mentioned earlier, occasionally we'd have a lecturer at the Thursday meetings as an educational segment in additional to all the neighborhood gossip.

Lecture: Thursday, September 9, 1994   Black Marie Giordano, Bornstein & York

Taking An Active Role in House Finances

Always worry when your husband says don't worry about it!

"Before I start talking, I want to say that I am married to a wonderful man for over 12 years. He's been a good husband, a good father, he treats his parents and my parents with the utmost respect and kindness. But there are times when a problem comes our way and he tells me not to worry about it and nine times out of 10, I should have worried about it. The only time you should not worry about it is when you're the one taking care of it, trust me.

Right away, you could see all the other women nodding their heads in the affirmative. Black Marie's lecture was about how to monitor the finances, without seeming to, if your husband's responsibility is to take care of the family finances. How to ask why don't I have to worry about it? In a way that is not intimidating or condescending.

"First of all, as a married couple, both of you should have access to checkbooks, bank account statements, mortgage and home owners' insurance, car insurance, etc. And, by the way, all these items should be locked in a fire and water proof case in case there's a fire or water problem in your house. Buy one, they usually sell them in a hardware store. You can get them at Marty's Hardware on 5th Ave. Say Black Marie sent you; he'll give you 10% off.

You should always know what's going on with marital assets on a continuous basis, even though, maybe, you don't understand parts of it, I'm just saying. Even if it's not your responsibility, take an interest. It's not like throwing out the garbage is his responsibility or you handling your children's homework; this is something that can affect your whole family so you have to take on at least the job of monitoring it on a monthly or quarterly basis.

You should have at least two months' rent or two months mortgage in your savings account. A certain percentage of income has to be put in the savings even if it means tightening your belt on other expenses. If you see that this is not so in your joint account then, you have to sit down with your husband and discuss what monthly expenses can be cut. But not in a way that it looks like you're telling him what to do.

Now we come to the part about HOW you discuss this with him. When you ask your girlfriends about something you may not totally understand or need some advice, you just ask them right out, correct? But, when you're speaking to your husband about the family finances you don't say, "Explain what's going on with this account!". They interpret what you said as "why are you questioning what I am doing?" Your girlfriend won't mind that statement but, he's not understanding why you are asking him; there must be a reason so he feels like it's an interrogation instead of a question.

So, what you should do is have the bills, the checkbook and whatever paperwork spread out on the table and when he comes in tell him, Thank God you're here I don't understand why these two figures don't match or why there is a withdrawal for this or for that." And if he says don't worry about it then, you ask him why you shouldn't worry about it. If he can explain it then it's ok but if he keeps on insisting don't worry about it, then you worry about it because he's hiding something. Of course, there may be nothing wrong with the finances but it always pays to monitor it for his benefit and maybe for yours; you could be the spender for all you know. And, then you have to tell him not to worry about it because you'll fix it.

You could see a lot of the women were afraid to confront their husbands even if both were working. Then Marie pulled out the proverbial Ace card and told them that at the law office where she worked there were a lot of women clients who had no clue what their husbands did with the money and then found out they are suddenly penniless. She also said this happens to parents who entrust their finances to an adult child, as an Executor, who may abuse the funds. If you have more than one child, make both Executors or have an outside party, possibly a lawyer, administer the funds as a trust to pay your monthly expenses. She gave the ladies time to absorb all of this and a few of them asked questions.

Because Black Marie was the lecturer, she brought some dessert favorites from her parents' pizzeria/restaurant. Signorine was on a roll telling fortunes and she made good tips that night which, being Signorine, she donated part of it for next Thursday's dessert.

When Black Marie couldn't go to the clubs with us, there was no limo service. Sometimes we'd all pile into Frankie Boy's car and go to the disco. On the way home, he'd invite us to eat at his house at 1:00 AM because the Frescas were always ready for company, something could always be heated up for us and Carmela was always up at all hours cooking and feeding us, what a nice woman. She could never sleep more than four hours, her brain was trained to wake up at 6:00 AM. God rest her soul, she loved to laugh. She'd listen to all our stories and we'd teach her to do the Hustle and she would practice with Frankie Boy during the week and strut her stuff at weddings. If by any chance one of our parents called and we were supposed to be in her house instead of out at 1:00 AM, she'd cover up for us. She'd tell them they were watching TV in the Livingroom and she'd send them home as soon as the movie was over. She only did that with one of our parents, I forget who it was, but otherwise once Carmela told them we were at her house, nobody questioned. Little Antoinette Fresca, I think she was about 9 or 10 then, would come down in her pajamas just to sit around and hear us talk. Carmela would tell her to go to bed, we protested and then she let her stay up. We taught her the Hustle, too, and she would practice with Carmela during the week. Those nights stand out as one of my most heartwarming memories; I think the other Fairy Comaras would agree as well. Frankie Boy still talks about those memories to this day.

With all the chatter and music, her husband John Fresca slept like a baby, God bless him. A bomb could go off next to him he'd just turn around and go back to sleep. He was a hardworking man and once he went into business for himself his days were 12-14 hours long. Carmela used to say only three times did he ever wake up during the night and that was when she told him they had to go to the hospital to give birth to her three children. Sundays were John's Day, the only day he had off; the relatives came over and they had the big Sunday meal around this enormous dining room table and that was without the extensions! Then, he would go outside with the men and smoke his cigar with his espresso with anisette and talk about whatever men talked about. This is what made him content. Quiet man but forceful; you didn't tangle with him. Although, when Carmela said no, it was NO, especially with anything having to do with the kids, that was her domain. She would always tell one of her sons or Antoinette, "Your father and I discussed this or that and we decided…." her children knew that no such discussion happened. Maybe, she may have mentioned it to John but he knew his input didn't matter. When they would ask him if mom talked about it with him, he would say to them, "yes, we decided" or "don't ask any more questions, your mother knows what she's talking about!" or "this is a good game (baseball or football) on TV, I'll talk to you after it's over" and that never, ever happened.

Then there is another Fairy Comara named Marie; we just call her Marie from Long Island, her maiden name was Marie Dominici and when she lived on our block, we used to call her Mary D, but then she married a lawyer, Polish guy, and we could never pronounce her last name so, when we were talking about her, we just said Marie from Long Island. After she moved to Long Island, she still drove down to Brooklyn twice a month to look in on her parents and then when her mother died in 1995, her father sold the house and she took him to live with her in Long Island.

When her parents were alive, she used to bring home four gallons of Brooklyn water because she claimed Long Island water changed the taste of her sauce and the macaroni. Her parents lived two doors down from Antoinette and, after she sold the house, she used to drop by the Frescas at least once a month to pick up her water and hear the latest gossip. When Antoinette sold her parents' house, she'd come to the Thursday meetings once a month to get her water from me. You'd think we gave her gold. She did that until about 2007 and then she really didn't feel safe driving long distances anymore, especially at night. Occasionally, she'd sleep over at my house on a Thursday night so she wouldn't have to drive at night but after 2007, she couldn't do it.

Marie from Long Island had a part-time job as a wedding planner. She was the planner for Emil's wedding and Black Marie's second marriage. She knew all the party vendors in Brooklyn and Long Island. If you had a specific theme to your wedding, she did a beautiful job of decorating the table centerpieces. She loved that job. Marie from Long Island had this way of speaking to people that calmed them. If Marie was at our meeting and someone was crying, Marie from Long Island would come over and you'd hear these whispers and, all of a sudden, that person started to smile and then a giggle and then she'd move on to the next casualty in the room. She taught Bennie Fiore everything about the catering business. When Bennie went into business for himself, Bennie's Party Palace, he asked Marie to be his regional manager for Long Island. Little Marie Greco used Bennie's Party Palace for all her family's parties; sometimes they catered to the Francone Senior Center for special events at a tremendous discount. When Marie from Long Island's daughter got married, she pulled out all the plugs and it was the best wedding I'd been to! I got to bring home the centerpiece! Marie from Long Island took in Chinese students into her home while they were attending college, no charge for rent. She taught them English, American life, how to cook Italian food and how to host the best parties. Now that they are married, they bring their families to her home and she goes to their home.

Then there was Fairy Comara Marie De Napoli and when we discussed her, we called her by her full name. Marie DiNapoli got married in the 70's, left her husband after one year, moved back with her parents and we never had to worry about calling her by her married name, Kunz. To this day, we still don't know if she ever got divorced because she never re-married and that was fine by her. Maybe, I'm wrong....I think she rented an apartment in Bensonhurst for about a year, maybe 18 months, after she left her husband but, after her father was diagnosed with congestive heart failure, Marie Di Napoli moved in with them and was hired as a third-grade teacher at St. Agatha's School on 3th Ave. During the summer, Marie DiNapoli and her mother crocheted baby blankets and sweaters to sell at the St. Agatha's Christmas Craft Fair. If you wanted to sweat profusely during the summer, you went to Marie Di Napoli's stoop and watch them both crocheting sweaters and blankets. All that wool over their laps, you broke a sweat just talking to them for 15 minutes.

Most of the kids in our neighborhood went to St. Agatha's so the mothers were always talking to Marie Di Napoli just to know how their kids were doing in school. Marie Di Napoli kept up on the latest church gossip so that was always a treat to hear. Marie's parents were from Calabria; she spoke Italian at home and English everywhere else. She was one of the translators for Signorine when she had to do anything on the outside or when Signorine was reading someone's tea leaves. In addition to being a teacher and a translator for Signorine, Marie Di Napoli was a foster care mother to two girls; their mother was addicted to heroin and couldn't care for them. What was to be a temporary arrangement turned permanent when their mother unfortunately died. Marie Di Napoli raised them until they were adults. Of course, the girls went to St. Agatha's! She became a grandmother about 15 years ago; one grandchild from one girl and two from the other. Marie moved to Far Rockaway, in 2009, to be near them all. She learned the Zoom at the Far Rockaway library so she's now our tech person when we have problems with the Zoom.

I, Diane Santangelo, gave psychic readings two Thursdays a month; the other two weeks were for our Fairy Comara lectures. We either invited speakers from outside or we had one of the Fairy Comaras speak about everyday life lessons. Our meetings even went beyond the neighborhood clan, we had ladies come from all over Brooklyn even as far as the Bronx. The Thursday evening meeting memories go down as one of the best life experiences of my life and the other Fairy Comaras as well! We talk about them all the time when we get on the Zoom. We had such good times and some dramatic times where our courage was tested! In fact, it was on the Zoom that they asked me to write all this down for posterity, so here it is. I must have told you this before, but I digress.

Signorine was our official greeter even though she spoke very little English. In addition to her "job" as official greeter, she arranged the coffee and cake table and she read the tea leaves for the girls waiting for a reading with me. She would go around the room and ask in Italian if they wanted one or just sit down to chat and then lead into a tea leaf session. It only took a minute or two so why not? I will say this, most of her readings were on spot. Little Marie Greco or Rosalie "Ro" Mancini translated for Signorine. In 5 minutes, she'd make you feel so much better for that short amount of time spent at my house. She had a special kind of compassion to feel for the people whose tea leaves she read and the intuition to zero in what bothered them. Sometimes even Little Marie was amazed at what came out of Signorine's mouth. When the ones who were waiting for me were called in, Signorine would come in first and either roll her eyes or groan before she brought them in and that was my signal to prepare for a biggie problem and get the Kleenex out. Her face was so expressive and animated. Sometimes, I'd think to myself what a lively young woman she must have been before all that tragedy happened in her life. Sometimes, I even wonder how she handled it.

Anyway, by the end of the night, we'd all tip her a couple of dollars for her readings and she'd save part of it for the next Thursday delicious meal or dessert. She kept a purse near her bedside and when I came down to visit her during the week, I would slip $20 in her purse; she never knew the difference. Or maybe she did? We would always offer her money for the desserts on Thursday night and she'd tell us not to worry because she had enough. Towards the end of her life, she was a little off on her predictions; we didn't give a shit, we slipped her a few dollars anyway. But I have to say her remedies for back pain and colds always worked. I wrote all of them down and still use them today. The other day, I caught a cold and I made her infamous mustard plaster wrapped in gauze and put it on my chest for an hour and lo and behold, I'm feeling better today!

We all loved Signorine, little thing that she was; she was shorter than Little Marie Greco! But I had a special promise to keep. As she got older, Grandma Philly would always say to me, "if I go before Signorine, please take care of her or I'll be crying in heaven". My grandmother and Signorine were best friends and she always made sure Signorine was taken care of, one way or another, by her or through other people in the neighborhood. When my grandmother died, Signorine cried like a baby. I kept my promise and Grandma Philly never had a reason to cry in heaven, may she rest in peace. She must be so happy to have her "baby sister" with her now. Anything Signorine needed there was always a Fairy Comaras who came to help, buy something for her or drive her to the doctors. And, of course, she lived with me so I took care of her at night.

Reminds me of the time Signorine, when she was in her 80's and lost weight. She was wearing a down winter coat two sizes larger than she was. You couldn't even see her face in that coat with a big down hood with fake fur trimming, it was just two hands and two feet sticking out of her body. And, when we told her the coat was too big, she kept on saying that they didn't make coats as good as they used to or, some other excuse other than saying she couldn't afford it. So, Ro Mancini went shopping at A&S Department Store when there was a big sale and bought a coat for Signorine. She took all the tags off and brought it to one of the meetings. She asked Signorine if she could use a winter coat because her daughter Donna bought it a year ago and now, she didn't like it because it was last year's fashion, or maybe that her daughter was pregnant and it was too tight, I really don't remember. Signorine took it because she thought it was used; her pride wouldn't allow someone to just buy it for her. And, every time she saw Ro Mancini, she would say how she couldn't believe her daughter didn't want to keep this coat. Signorine had to work for something to earn it. She wouldn't accept money unless it was for her tea leaf readings which, as I said, always were right.

Ok, back to Irish Marie...In addition to working at the bank, Irish Marie used to clean houses on the weekend for a few of the families along Prospect Park so her three children could attend St. Agatha's. She was working full-time at Chase Manhattan Bank back then, same as me, but in a different branch. She was so good at cleaning houses people were referring her to other people and she started to build up a good number of clients by the time her kids started high school. When her paternal grandmother passed away, she left her three grandchildren a small inheritance. Brian told her she should start her own cleaning business and that's what she did! Fitzpatrick Housekeeping, Inc. on 4th Ave and Carroll St. On weekends, I would pass by to see if she was in the office just to bullshit. Yes, I saw her at least two Thursdays a month but, you can't talk personal with 40 people in a room.

She was a drill sergeant at work; sometimes she'd do surprise visits to clients to make sure it was squeaky clean. When she told you, you could eat off the floor, she meant it! Back in the 70's and 80's, our neighbors cleaned their own houses, God forbid! However, the people who lived along Prospect Park were different, they were mostly doctors, lawyers, dentists, busy professionals who were an economic notch above cleaning their own homes. And God bless them. The only one in our neighborhood who hired Irish Marie in our neighborhood was Esther Schrable and that was when she and her husband, Murray opened their clothing store on 5th Ave. Irish Marie started cleaning her home when she was in 8th grade. Esther loved, loved, loved Irish Marie! Not because of her cleaning skills; Esther just enjoyed talking to her!

All our mothers went to Murray's Dept. Store to buy stockings, bras, girdles, ties for their husbands, knee socks for school, gloves, scarfs, you name it, they had it, Murray's was our Amazon back then. They always stocked "I need it by tomorrow" clothing; things you needed that day. Murray even sold men's suits. When Irish Marie was in 8th grade, she would clean their house twice a week after school. She would go to Murray's, pick up the keys and start cleaning before Esther came home at 6:00PM. Esther would only let Irish Marie clean her house because she knew Marie since she was a child playing with her son, Manny. Anyway, on the days she would clean their house, she would wait for Esther to come home and Esther would go over her homework with her. It was Esther who helped Irish Marie get good grades because Marie's parents were just getting their own grip on English. Even when she was not cleaning their house, Irish Marie would stop over at the store and if Esther wasn't busy, she'd help her with history or arithmetic.

Esther had a soft spot for Irish Marie; she knew Irish Marie worked hard at school and she was going to be something later in life. Esther provided the acceptance Marie so badly needed as a Puerto Rican in the late 60's and 70's. We had gangs back then, the Italians against the Spanish AKA Latinos; that was the way it was, all the gang members were pieces of shit and they never amounted to anything; they soon dissolved away from the neighborhood either through being arrested or having Uncle Jimmy at the Club pay for their moving expenses. They'd either moved away by foot or in a box, they decided to leave upright. Big Jimmy had to take care of it because it was hurting the local businesses and his weekly card games at the club. In addition, Captain Doyle had squad cars going back and forth of the avenues watching for gang fighting but also watching the club.

Irish Marie became such a good student that the nuns at St. Agatha's got her a scholarship to go to Blessed Mother Catholic High School which back then was a school where only a 90 average student could be considered, very prestigious and very expensive. That scholarship was anonymously donated to St. Agatha's specifically for Irish Marie. What we found out much, much later was that Esther went to St. Agatha's and spoke to the principal and suggested that maybe something could be worked out financially for Marie to attend Blessed Mother Catholic High School. Back then, the idea of a Jewish woman speaking to a nun was a rarity indeed! Probably still is! But Esther crossed the line and a scholarship was created by an anonymous donation to St. Agatha's. Irish Marie loved talking with Esther because she provided opportunities Marie never thought existed, she opened up a whole new world to Marie. After graduation, Marie wound up working for Chase Manhattan Bank, same as me; first as a teller, promoted to Sr. Teller and then promoted again to Mortgage Representative; the only woman and the only Latino in that position. Her father, Hector, would brag about her to the teachers where he worked. He was proud of all his children; Hector Jr. became a lawyer and Carmen was a teacher. But, Irish Marie looked like his late mother so she was special.

Esther had a good heart. When Irish Marie and her husband, Brian Fitzpatrick were just married and were bleeding money to fix up their fixer upper home, she would give Marie "special" jobs to earn a few extra bucks like cleaning out her closets and putting new liners on the kitchen cabinet shelves. At times, she would make up chores, especially near the Christmas holidays when Santa was expected to grant the Fitzpatrick children's wishes. But that ended in 1999, when Esther's daughter-in-law Phyllis hired someone else supposedly cheaper. Nevertheless, Irish Marie would always stop by Esther's to drop off something she baked, like her infamous arroz con pollo and platanos fritos; the food the doctor told Esther to avoid. She'd sit and chat with Esther and talk about the business, Brian and the kids.

Of course, that was before Irish Marie found out that Esther's aid, Gladys, the aid told Phyllis everything; who visited and what went on in her mother-in-law's house. The woman hardly ever cleaned Esther's house and she was slow as molasses to go to the store. After that, Gladys had an excuse for why it was not a good time to visit Esther. She gave excuses to many of the Fairy Comaras who rang her bell. Esther was cut off from the outside world. Phyllis convinced Esther to tell Irish Marie not to bring any Puerto Rican delicacies, because of the salt or any Christmas specialties because of the fat. Of course, Puerto Rican women don't know the meaning of the word NO; She got the treats to Esther by giving them to Esther's next-door neighbor, me, and I brought them over after Gladys left and took whatever was left over and put it in my refrigerator for her the next day. Sometimes Esther told me to give the leftovers to Signorine when she lived with me.

When my father passed away, it was me, my mother and later on, Signorine in the house. During the summer, I'd help my mother down the steps to our backyard so she could talk to Esther and Murray, when he was alive, rest in peace. She was older than Esther and had a harder time getting around. I'd take her to visit cousins and friends who moved away from the neighborhood or we'd go to the movies on 9th Street. She loved the movies; sometimes we'd stop by the Purity Diner for coffee. The steps were starting to be hard to climb, she fell once on the steps leading to the garden and became fearful of going out alone. When I barbecued in the backyard; we'd invite Esther and Murray to come over. Of course, Signorine was invited to everything we did! When my father and Murray passed away within five years of each other, my mother and Esther became even closer as friends. They still played cards on Friday nights with some of the other couples but, it wasn't the same without their husbands.

After Grandma Philly passed away, my mother and father rented the apartment to newlyweds, very nice couple, stayed with us a good six or seven years before she became pregnant with her second child. My parents never raised their rent in all the years they lived there. They bought a home in the Coney Island area; I got them their mortgage. Even after they had their first child, my mother and father would call them the newlyweds. We threw them a small housewarming shower before they moved out. At first, I was thinking about using the apartment for myself for a little privacy but, by then, my father passed away and my mother's heart condition started to worsen. I couldn't leave her upstairs by herself. We rented the apartment to a professional couple who were friendly but never home. I still get a Christmas card from "the newlyweds", in the form of a photo card with the newlyweds and their three grown children! And they always write a little something in the back thanking me and my family for the support we gave them when they started out in life.

The professionals moved out after five years; they found an apartment in Manhattan. By then, my mother's condition had worsened and she was pretty much confined to the house. So, now I had an empty apartment and I knew nothing about being a landlord. My mother was in no condition to show the apartment to potential tenants and I worked full-time.

It just so happened; Signorine was having landlord problems. Black Marie's mom, Livia Santorini told my mother that Signorine's apartment was rent-controlled. She told her Signorine's landlord saw what the other landlords were getting in rents from the yuppies looking for a short commute to the city. He couldn't outright kick her out but, little by little, he made her life very difficult. Things would break and it would take a long time to fix, he told her she couldn't store her grocery cart behind the cellar door, her TV was too loud; we all knew she was losing her hearing. Not sure why Signorine didn't get hearing aids; either she didn't have enough money or didn't want to admit she needed them. Signorine lived two flights up and that was beginning to be a problem. At the time, she was on Medicaid for her health and welfare, food stamps to pay her rent and food. Any extra money, she got from reading the tea leaves for all the Italian women in the neighborhood. When I came home from work, my mother told me the whole story. We both agreed it made sense to invite her to come live with us. Good decision. After my mother passed away; I felt comforted having Signorine in the house.

Signorine used to roam the neighborhood to socialize; she was never one to sit in front of the TV all day, only at night. She'd ring the neighbors' bell in the mornings after the kids went to school and the husbands went to work. If you were home, there was no doubt that even if you didn't want a reading that day, you let Signorine in and when she left, there was always a little something in her grocery cart to bring home. Sometimes the neighbors passed on a tea leaf reading and she'd just sit and chat over coffee and cake. Grandma Philly, rest in peace, always got her tea leaves read by Signorine, even if she had it done three times that week. If I was with her when Signorine visited, I'd mention that she already got her tea leaves read. Grandma Philly would shush me and tell me it doesn't matter because every day is a new day. After the reading, she would give her a couple of dollars and take something out of the Frigidaire that she cooked and wrap it up for her.

There was always a full refrigerator in Grandma's Philly's Frigidaire, it was amazing what she could whip up from nothing. If she bought chicken, she'd make chicken cutlets and use the bones and the dark meat to make soup; you never saw many bones in my grandma's garbage. If she bought chopped meat, she'd make a meatloaf but also meatballs for the Sunday sauce…there was always something leftover. She used to grow pumpkins in our backyard for us to carve at Halloween; Grandma had jars of pumpkin soup in the winter and she saved all the pumpkin flowers to fry, they were so delicious!

Grandma Philly was also psychic but she never applied her talent, she kept it between me and her, even Signorine didn't know. She was the one I got the gift from, I'm almost sure. And when it was just me and her, my grandmother tested me to see if I was psychic and once, she saw that I was, she taught me everything I know with two tablespoons of love and compassion. Signorine spoke to me in Italian and Grandma translated. I loved to sit at the table and listen to their chats over coffee; it was all in Italian, I understood not one word of it but, they spoke so passionately together. Sometimes there would be tears and sometimes I'd laugh with them even though I didn't know what I was laughing at!

When Grandma Philly passed away, I was working at the bank and still living with my parents. I was thinking of taking the downstairs apartment just so I could be close to her in spirit. But my parents decided to rent it to a newlywed couple who happened to see the FOR RENT sign on the window. By the time my father passed away, it was just me and my mother; the newlyweds had already moved out and we had a professional couple living there for about five years. When they moved out, I offered the apartment to Signorine for way less rent than she was paying for her two-bedroom apartment so she could use the extra money for her prescriptions. By then, many of my friends were married and moved away and some of the parents passed away. Signorine was a comfort to me because she was the last person from Grandma Philly's Comaras still living in the neighborhood. We still had Little Marie Greco's parents next door, Carmela and Antoinette Fresca, Esther Schrable and the Santorini's restaurant, though.

Marie Greco nee Di Fillipo AKA Little Marie was born into a short family; she married a tall man, Frank Greco from Canarsie and they lived happily ever after. Marie's parents were, well, little. Her mother, Rose, was 4"10, her father, Dominic "Dom", barely made it to 5 feet and her older sister, Camille, about the same. Marie Greco was 4'11, her brother, Anthony, was a whopping 5'4! Somebody in the past generation must have been average height for that to happen! You went into Marie's parents' house and you thought you were in a beautiful doll house; the kitchen cabinets were so low you could reach anything at eye level if you were taller than 5"4". For them it was a stretch. Her father and mother were so much fun; listening to them talk about the price of everything going up. If her mother offered you something to eat, she'd tell you how much it went up in price. Dom was a bricklayer and Marie's mother, Rose, a homemaker, we used to call them housewives but, I think homemaker is a better description. Rose liked the color pink and it showed in almost every room. If you came into their house and you were over 5'4", they would remark how tall you were! Rose didn't like heels; she wore a one-inch heel shoe if she went to a wedding. Little Marie wore them all the time until she moved to Pennsylvania to live near her son. She told us, "Who's going to know how short I am when I'm driving?" We told her as long as her feet touch the pedals, wear the flats.

Marie "Little Marie" Di Fillipo met Frank Greco when she was going to school at night for her associate degree in Human Resources at Kingsborough Community College. Frank was going for his accounting degree; he later went to Brooklyn College for his Bachelor's. He noticed her eating a pepper and egg sandwich on Italian bread in the college cafeteria; he was eating leftover lasagna from the Sunday meal and it was love at first sight! They exchanged lunches to see how the other's parents made it and they had their first date that weekend.

They had a big abbudanza wedding at Miceli Terrace in Brooklyn and a cake that looked like the Verrazano Bridge with her and Frank at the top and all the bridesmaids and ushers on the side! Had to be over 200 people, short and tall. Both Frank and Marie came from large families; and half the 78th Precinct was at their wedding because Marie's Brother Anthony AKA Tony the Detective worked there and the precinct knew Little Marie because she worked for Captain Doyle. Her mother always made the precinct struffli and stuffed shells at Christmas.   What a wedding! We got on the dance floor, danced the Hustle to the songs of Marie's cousin Vinny and his band, the Disco Infernos. Because we taught Carmela Fresca how to do the Hustle, she wowed the crowd with her moves. John never had a clue that she danced so well because he was always in bed by 9:00 PM. And then, Anna Cantare, cousin to Marie's father, the renowned celebrity at every Italian wedding in Brooklyn and Long Island, sang all the old Italian songs that brought back memories for our parents with tears in their eyes. We danced the Tarantella with our parents, even Signorine! We all had too much to drink but who cared, then there was the Venetian hour for pastries, coffee, Anisette and espresso. And, on your way out, they gave you bagels and the Sunday Daily News. What a wedding!

After she graduated Kingsborough Community College, Little Marie Greco didn't get a job in Human Resources; instead, she took an NYPD administrative job at the 78th Precinct about half a mile from her parent's house. She was hired to be secretary to Captain John V. Doyle. The job practically fell into her lap through her brother, Anthony "Tony the Detective". At the time, she wasn't getting any HR job offers and this job was 15 minutes walking time from home. Captain Doyle eventually put her in charge of the personnel files and she was able to do some HR with the police officers by recommending services for them and their families. She even visited their wives in the hospital when a baby was born. Little Marie helped every officer in the precinct at one time or another. She even started an after-work meditation class for them to relieve the stress. After she was married, her husband Frank used to give advice, free of charge, on money management and figure out if they could get a mortgage. He also did some of the police officers' taxes.

Little Marie loved, loved, loved her job! She loved the hustle and bustle of the precinct and who better than an Italian woman to do everything for a man! Captain Doyle loved her; he called her his work wife. She either made or bought his lunch, arranged all his appointments, filtered all his calls, wrote all his letters, made his coffee, picked out his wife's birthday and Christmas gifts and his two boys' gifts as well. Just like Antoinette, notice a pattern? She did all his research, helped all the cops with forms, girlfriend/boyfriend problems and coordinated all Captain Doyle's interdepartmental and outside meetings. She loved every minute of it! She was also entrusted with retrieving criminal records for the Captain and, sometimes, she'd find a folder on someone in the neighborhood that had a criminal record that we didn't know about; she never told us.

The joke at the precinct was that even though the offices were half glass, half wall, you still couldn't see Little Marie if she was standing. And don't think Captain Doyle didn't give Frank Greco the pre-wedding talk about how to treat his work wife.

After a couple of years, the newlyweds moved out of Little Marie's parents' home; they saved enough money to put a down payment on a house in Massapequa, Long Island. Even though she moved away, Little Marie continued to work for Captain Doyle for two years until her son Frank Jr. was born. Marie found a part-time HR job in Massapequa, Francone Senior Center. She was so good with the staff and the seniors, they offered her a full-time job but, she had a child to take care of when they first moved and then Joseph came along. When Frank got his CPA, he worked a couple of years for an accounting firm in Manhattan but, decided in the early 90's to start his own business in Massapequa. He always did the drive from Massapequa to pick up Marie's parents for the holidays. As the years went by, it became apparent that Marie's parents could no longer take care of their big, little home in Brooklyn. After Joseph was born, Little Marie asked her parents to come live with them. It would also help her to continue working part-time. So, Frank and Marie moved to a bigger home to accommodate her little parents. They found a mother daughter home in Massapequa. She sold her parents' home through her friend, Elizabeth McCarthy of McCarthy Realty. Maybe I'll use her, if she's still in business, when I decide to sell my house. Once the house was sold; the parents moved in but her mother and father didn't quite adjust to living in "the country" as we called it then. The Di Fillipo's were sad to leave the old neighborhood but, loved taking care of their grandsons while Marie worked part-time. Despite the distance, Marie and her mother, Rose, still came once or twice a month to the Thursday evening meetings; Rose looked forward to it! A few years later, Little Marie's father's health had taken a turn for the worse first with the heart and then with the lungs. After taking care of him and her grandsons on the days Marie worked, Rose was ready for a night out. Marie knew her mother was lost in Massapequa; she missed her walks to the store, the conversations along the way and the coffee visits. Rose Di Fillipo and Signorine would huddle in the corner on those Thursdays and talk about old times and she'd talk to the other old timers like Rose Mancini and Black Marie's mother, Livia, and compare ailments, trips to the doctor, and what the grandchildren were doing. Rose always brought something she cooked at home and we'd all rush to the table to snag a piece before all the cafones took it.

Many years later, when Rose Di Fillipo's health was failing and she wasn't able to get around, all she could mumble about was her times at the Thursday meetings. We all thought Marie Greco's father would pass away before her mother but it turned out to be the other way around. She had a stroke in bed one morning; they did everything they could at the hospital but, she didn't make it. After that, the father ambled around like a lost soul for about 18 months before he passed away; he was lost without her. They were married 49 years and she meant the world to him. He lost his parents at a very young age and she represented the only family he really ever had.

Little Marie never rented her parents' apartment until many years later when Captain Doyle's son got married. She rented it to the newlyweds for practically nothing so they could save for a house of their own. She also got to see Captain Doyle and his wife often which made her happy. Little Marie's TALL sons, thank God they took after Frank, went to college, got married, had children of their own but didn't remain in Massapequa; Frank Jr. moved to Pennsylvania with his wife and two kids because of a job re-location and the other son, Joseph, moved to Scarsdale to be nearer to his wife's family and the Metro North Railroad going into the city. Little Marie and Frank were still working back then and they drove to Pennsylvania and Scarsdale a few times a year; her sons tried their best to drop over but, they were so busy with one thing or another.

One winter morning in 2005, after Frank Greco finished shoveling snow on the driveway, he came into the house, made himself a cup of coffee and sat down to have some breakfast and read the newspaper before heading out to work. Little Marie headed to work before him and when she came home, she found Frank sitting in the kitchen same way she left him in the morning. He had a heart attack and died. After that, Little Marie worked full-time at Francone until she retired in 2011. She sold her house and moved to Pennsylvania to be near her son, Frank Jr. He found her a nice home 5 minutes away and had the kitchen remodeled so that she could reach everything; she's been there ever since. I talk to her almost every day either on the phone or the Zoom and she still is able to drive locally but not long distances and never when it's icy. Both her grandchildren are grown up and in college now and her son and daughter-in-law check on her every day. She misses Brooklyn but she misses the old Brooklyn, not now. She came to see me with her son about two Christmases ago; she said she thought Frank had taken a wrong turn to Manhattan with all the high-rise buildings; all the stores she grew up with were out of business.

But, let me talk about Signorine, Part Two.

Signorine died peacefully on a Thursday night on October 14, 1999, age 92, probably midway through the evening, during Ann Caracciolo's description of her trip to Lourdes complete with projector and slides. She even held up a small bottle of the healing waters where Our Blessed Mother appeared and she passed it around so that we could feel the spirit. She tried to bring back a few bottles for her mother and sister but they only allowed one bottle per person. We had the projector set up to show the photos on the white wall of the living room. No one knew when Signorine passed away because the lights were off, the wine was flowing, who was viewing the slides, who was whispering and some of us were probably napping, too. Ann had about 70 photos to show us which is good if we were actually in Lourdes with her but, we were all thinking maybe 15 photos were enough; we looked at all 70 slides anyway. Ann

Caracciolo worked as a dental technician for our neighborhood dentist so many of us brought our children there and that's how we got to know her. Every time Ann talked to you, she talked to your teeth, not your eyes, which always worried us because she might see a cavity and tell us to make an appointment. I only had one reading scheduled for that night so we had no choice but to look at all 70 of Ann's photos. By the end, it was getting late and everybody was ready to call it a night. We sacrificed a whole weeks' worth of gossip for Our Lady of Lourdes.

It wasn't unusual that Signorine fell asleep on the recliner after she set up the coffee and cake table; that was her "job" for the Thursday Evening meetings the last years of her life. I didn't realize that she had passed away until I tried to wake her up. She had a whole bunch of dollar bills in her lap. Nobody noticed.

In her heyday, she baked all the cakes and cookies and made the espresso and coffee; sometimes she made eggplant or chicken parmigiana, or lasagna if it was near the Christmas holidays. When she hit her late 80's and couldn't stand for long periods of time, we told her to take it easy and bought cake from Agnello's Bakery and Stella Doro Breakfast treats; Antoinette Fresca made the coffee and that was good enough. Also, a few of the ladies always cooked something and brought it to the meeting; we always had leftovers. If she had a little energy on Thursdays, she might do a tea reading but because she never remembered to bring her reading glasses, she would look at the person rather than the tea leaves and use her intuition to tell them everything about their life up to that moment and then future stuff. And, she was always right! While she was sleeping, we'd drop her a five or ten-dollar bill in her lap and when she woke up, she thanked the Blessed Mother. It was nice to have her downstairs in my house; when Grandma Philly passed away and then my father and mother years later, Signorine represented the OLD order of the Fairy Comaras; Signorine was one of the last ones still living in the neighborhood or even still living for that matter! Having her in the house was a real comfort to me and the other Fairy Comaras, too! I'm repeating myself; I know.

Every Thursday night, we'd hear the same story from Signorine, in broken English, about how bad she felt that she could no longer help us. And every Thursday night, we told her, now it's time to help her. And how she loved those Thursday nights! It was the only time she had the opportunity to help lots of people at one time and we all regarded her as the Queen of the Fairy Comaras; everybody who went to the meetings knew Signorine.

I worked at the bank back then, sometimes long hours during the week, it was hard for me to look after her so, I asked the other Fairy Comaras to check on her if they had the time or were in the neighborhood. I ordered her groceries from the supermarket on the corner and little John Curcio, John "Cheech" Curcio's son, delivered it on those big delivery wagons. He never got a tip from Signorine because she said he was doing his job but, I always stopped by the store and gave him a big tip. We used to call his father, John Cheech, don't ask me why, he had that name since we were kids. Little John Cheech was a hard-working boy, God bless him, he later graduated, went to med school and became a cardiologist. When I brought Signorine to him to check her heart, the first thing she said to him was "you no deliva the food no mo?" He told her," For you I'll deliver the food, Signorine!". When it became apparent that she could not care for herself, Little Marie Greco made sure she sent a nice young lady, Amanda Finch, from Francone Senior Center in Brooklyn. By then, Francone had a Brooklyn branch. Amanda attended college three days a week, the other days she took Signorine to the doctors, prepared her lunch and straightened up a bit. Irish Marie cleaned the apartment once a week. Amanda was going to Kingsborough Community College to be a certified day care worker. Did Signorine complain about her? You bet! But, when Little Marie asked her if she wanted another caregiver, she said no, she's a good girl. And so, we listened to the complaints with one ear and it went out the other. She just couldn't get used to being unable to take care of herself.

Amanda came to the wake; she said that Signorine always knew when she had problems at home. Signorine told me her mother liked to drink and her father couldn't take it anymore; he left his wife when Amanda was a teenager. Amanda told us that she didn't know how she knew it but Signorine knew that, as a child, she liked to have her hair brushed. When Amanda had a bad day at school or with her mother, Signorine would say "veni qua" and brushed her hair. It helped her forget all the problems she was having at home. Amanda went on to work at a day care center; when a child was out of sorts, she told us she brushed the kids' hair to calm them down. "She even taught me how to make brasciole!", she said. I was jealous; Signorine never taught me how to make brasciole! Amanda knew what happened to Signorine son. Signorine loved taking care of Amanda; it made up for the child she lost many years ago.

Her wake was packed all three days filled with all the "children" that she helped in one way or another. We were told stories about her that we didn't even know; she certainly got around in the Angel Dept. Amanda told us that her mother has cirrhosis of the liver and she asked Little Marie if she could recommend someone to take care of her during the day. She knew that Little Marie would only send the best caregiver for her mom. She told us Signorine helped her to forgive her mother. "One afternoon, we were watching TV and out of the blue she tells me that I should try to understand that my mom had a hard life and she thinks about the past too much. I told Signorine that my mother never talks about her mother and father or even her other family. One time when she was drunk, she threw her drink at my little brother because he asked if he had a grandmother so we never asked again. Now that my mom is ill but sober, she's kinder to me and my brother. And, recently I asked her about her childhood and she did, indeed, have a hard life. Her father beat my mother and my grandmother; he was an alcoholic, too. My grandmother left him; they got divorced. Two years later, her mother re-married. My mother told me her stepfather raped her when she was 15, and when she told her mother, her mother kicked her out. She went to live with a cousin in Queens, graduated high school and started working in Manhattan; that's how she met my father. They worked for the same company. She said she drank to drown out her memory of being raped. My father knew what happened to her but her drinking and rages were getting out of control. He wanted her to go to a psychiatrist but she refused so he left."

Once a week, Irish Marie had one of her staff clean Signorine's apartment. Amanda did little clean ups but not thorough cleaning. When Signorine needed her windows cleaned, Irish Marie did it herself for fear one of her staff didn't know "the technique". There was a technique with window washing in our neighborhood whether you lived on the ground floor or the fourth floor. You had to position yourself on the windowsill with half your ass sticking in, half out; it was an acquired sense of balance our mothers taught us. They used to clean them with vinegar and water and use newspapers to avoid the streaks. Irish Marie's mother used to worry the neighbors every time she cleaned the windows. Not to be impolite but, she had a big backside and everyone thought she had her full backside completely out the window but it was only half. She did it that way into her 50's and then Irish Marie did them. Her father used to say, "Who left the window open? Oh, it's closed. Those windows are so clean, it looks like they're opened!" Irish Marie was the apple of his eye.

On warm summer nights, Signorine would sit outside and she and Esther Schrable would talk for hours...yes, for hours, and they would be enjoying themselves even though Esther didn't understand Italian. Hand motions always did the trick. And on those warm nights, all the ladies would sit outside, sometimes the men but, usually the men were in the back yard listening to the baseball game. Each mother would bring out their beach chair, some cake or ice tea, sometimes a few of them would bring a thermos of coffee with paper cups. As I'm re-telling this story I'm thinking it might be nice to sit outside, on a beach chair, with Antoinette in Brewster.

As kids, we were so glad that our mothers were sitting outside because that meant we could stay out longer! And, they were outside when the Mr. Softee truck came or the kiddie ride truck came up our block. There was no haggling if we could go or not, they just gave us the money just to get us out of their hair so they could talk in their little semi-circle of beach chairs.

Every night, I'd come downstairs to check on Signorine or bring her clean laundry, we'd talk, she only in Italian and broken English and me, in broken

Italian and hand motions, or we'd watch TV together, she loved the Golden Girls and Bonanza! I don't know what it is with Italians loving westerns but they do and Bonanza was on every Italian's TV set in the neighborhood. Sometimes the TV would be on and I'd find her sleeping on the sofa. I'd turn off the TV, tuck her in right there with a blanket, and she would mumble something with an air kiss and a grazie at the end. I think she liked the sofa better than the bed because it was near the bathroom. She kept a photo of her son, Girolamo, in his army uniform, on the end table along with her rosary beads. She prayed the rosary at least once a day, just like Grandma Philly. Towards the end of her life, she talked about death but with a sense of joy. She'd be with her mother, her son, Girolamo and Grandma Philly. When I used to say she'd outlive us all, she would wave her hand in disbelief.

The night before she died, I put her nightgown on, put her slippers next to the sofa and just before I put a blanket on her she put her two index fingers together and told me that Antoinette was going to live here. She pointed her fingers to the floor. I thought she must be sleepy so, I just yessed her and covered her up. At that time, Antoinette was still living in her parents' home; I thought she must be thinking maybe it was tomorrow, Thursday, and Antoinette was coming over to help her get the food table ready. Yeah, that was it. No, it wasn't.

On Thursday evening, October 14, we had the usual meeting and nobody knew Signorine was dead until I went to wake her up. Antoinette was with me, thank God, or I would have lost it. We called the cops and then we called Torregrosso Funeral Home. A group of us chipped in for the wake, the limos and the burial. The funeral director asked us if we had clothes for her to wear; we brought her best black long sleeve dress, the one she wore at weddings. He asked us why black? And, we told him that no one would recognize her if she was dressed in any other color.

We gave her the best finale possible; we reserved the big room at Torregrosso because it was going to be a packed crowd. I had such a headache for three days with all the flowers. After the burial, we invited everybody to join us for lunch at Monte's on Third Avenue to recall all the laughs and memories we had with Signorine. I told everyone Signorine's life story because only a few of us knew what she went through. She had touched so many people in her life and, yet, very few people knew anything about her. She's in heaven now with my Grandma Philly and all her friends chatting like the old days.

Once she moved in, Antoinette took over the cooking and baking; we all knew we were in for a treat because she was a good cook! From that point on, we had delicious meals every Thursday; a big tray of antipasto, eggplant parmigiana, chicken marsala, cream puffs, jelly donuts, she made everything and loved every minute of it. She'd go around the room asking people if they were happy with the meal or she'd make little doggie bags for them to bring home. I had dinner for the rest of the week on her leftovers. The guests usually brought wine or cake. And did that wine flow!

But, I'm getting ahead of myself. Ok, where was I? oh, let me refresh your memory.

Signorine lived with me in the downstairs apartment for a little over 11 years before she passed away at 92; prior to that she lived in a two-bedroom apartment on Degraw St. She lived in that apartment for almost 70 years raising one son, Girolamo. When she first came to New York, she lived in a one-bedroom apartment downstairs from her husband's family in Bensonhurst. According to her, her marriage was arranged by her parents when she was 15 but she didn't actually get married until she was 17. Her husband turned out to be a real desgraziada; after two failed jobs, and one more about to end, he started drinking and staying out all night. With the drinking came the beatings which his family closed their eyes to and, when he moved her and their son to Degraw St, she thought he turned the corner on getting his life together. Not long after they moved in, he said he was going to work and left her $10 and never came back. This story was corroborated by my Grandma Philly; she and my grandfather were living in their house on Degraw St. with their son, my father Joe Jr.

The neighborhood back then was very close, they all spoke Italian mainly. According to Grandma Philly, she tried to find her husband and then about a year maybe two years later, she received a letter from him saying that he was living in Philadelphia. He managed to get an annulment and the paperwork was included in the letter. It was from some church in Philly that was heavily mobbed up. The search stopped and she and little Girolamo never heard from him again. There was no welfare assistance program back then and Signorine had no money. At the time, my grandmother was working as a piece worker sewing collars to dresses in a factory around the corner and she put in a good word for Signorine to get a job.

Back then, a village DID raise a child and little Girolamo was looked after by all the other kids' mothers. The neighborhood took care of all his clothing needs with the hand me downs from their children when they outgrew them. As the years passed, little Girolamo grew up with the rest of the kids, graduated high school and then decided to join the army when World War II broke out. Grandma told me Girolamo was the apple of Signorine's eye and she was so proud that he was fighting for a country that had given her so much.

He also did not come home but not for the same reason as his father; he lost his life, ironically, in a battle 10 miles from Trapani, Sicily where she was born. When the factory closed 12-13 years later, Signorine had to go on welfare and earned extra money by reading the tea leaves for all the women in the neighborhood. When I was a child, it was called the "visit" when Signorine came because no one wanted to rat her out to the church or police about the tea leaves; they were afraid the kids who went to Catholic school might let it slip. My Grandma Philly used to read the cards for people, too, without charging so I knew about such things and thought nothing of it. Back then, fortune telling was considered Devil worship. She was a great card reader but, she always had Signorine do her fortune. She'd send Signorine home with a leftover meal and a few dollars. Even if they didn't believe in those things, the neighbors called her to come for the "visit" because we all knew her story. She was much too proud to take a hand out. Italians always made too much food; she always walked out of their houses with a meal and a few dollars, too.

When her husband left her, she wore black because supposedly her husband had died of cancer. I only remember her in black but, Grandma Philly told me there was a time, before her husband left when she wore colored dresses and did her hair up nice. She never dated anyone because of her son; she didn't want him brought up seeing strange men in the house. After Girolamo died, she had a true reason to wear black for the rest of her life.

Depression and grief were different back then, no one went to therapists in those days. Besides, you didn't have the time to sit alone and cry in our neighborhood because there was always someone visiting, some house you were invited to and, of course, there was family nearby. When he was alive, Signorine and Girolamo were invited to every holiday my family celebrated in addition to her "visits". My grandmother worked with her and after Mr. Di Paolo's shop closed, she became a fixture in my grandmother's home. Grandpa Joe was glad his wife had the company because back then, he was working long hours on the docks.

During the summer, my grandmother sat outside with her beach chair, crocheting and there was always an extra chair for Signorine. Grandma Philly made sure she was never alone, ever. When she moved in, she felt my grandmother's spirit immediately and that comforted her.

When I started the Thursday meetings, Signorine was the official greeter and feeder. She'd be cooking up a storm in my house even before I came home from work. I got her a set of keys so she could start early. When I came home from work, she would greet me with a smile and a plate of food. I was so spoiled! I miss that smile. I knew her better than the other Fairy Comaras but we all loved her equally.

Grandma Philly passed away when I was in my late 20's. Five years after my Grandpa Joe passed away. In the 70s no one knew much about breast cancer; it wasn't even discussed in the home. It was only when my mother went down to dress her for some wedding that she saw two lumps, one near the breast and one below her armpit. By the time she was diagnosed, it had spread to both breasts and the lungs. She kept it a secret all that while. She was too frail by then for chemo. Signorine was there with her 7 days a week for four months before God took her to heaven. After that, the neighbors had to go to Signorine's apartment because she was so depressed, she couldn't even get up in the morning. In the beginning she couldn't bear to go inside our house for dinner but, after a while with time, she finally came over.

And when Signorine brought eggplant parmigiana to my parents, I had the fork ready! And, boy, could she cook! I loved her escarole, "scarole" with Italian bread. I remember brisk Fall Saturdays going to the store for my mother; I had to pass by Signorine's house. If she was looking out the window with her little pillow she used to lean on, she'd ask me, in broken English, "you eata?" and even if I ate a seven-course meal 15 minutes before, I would say I didn't. she'd feed me scarole on Italian bread with some milk; my mouth is watering as I'm typing. She would call my mother and tell her I was here so she wouldn't worry.

I couldn't speak a word of Italian and she understood very little English but, I look back on those days as so wondrous for what was never spoken. The smell of Clorox in the kitchen and the scrub board she kept on the side sink to wash her clothes with Octogon soap. My mother had Octogon soap in her kitchen but it was used to punish me for saying curse words! I still curse now but, back then you remembered the taste of the soap and were very careful. I still have Signorine's scrub board but, I don't use it.

And, when she came to live with me, I got to hear all her stories in broken English and spent more unforgettable moments with her as an adult! I felt like a kid again going down to my Grandma Philly. Even if she was crippled and hunched over with Arthuritis, with her signature black dress and stockings, she made 'scarole for me. It was usually when I came home from a long day at work, probably a shitty one, too. And that 'scarole sandwich, made with warm Italian bread, wiped the day away. In Spring, she planted tomatoes, peas, basil and took care of the fig tree that Grandpa Joe planted. In the summer I would pull out the BBQ and cook some chicken, hamburgers and Signorine's favorite, frankfurters. We'd call Esther to come over; she brought the wine. There was one BBQ when I think Signorine had more than one glass of wine and she put on the radio and tried to do one of the dances she saw on TV; I guess wine is a temporary cure for Arthritis.

Signorine's gift was that even though you didn't understand Italian, you walked away somehow understanding; you felt a little better than you felt 10 minutes ago. Anybody needed help, Signorine was there, if someone was having a baby, she was there to feed the husband and kids while they were in the hospital. If someone died, she went to the wake, funeral mass and picked up the pieces of your grief for years afterward. She never forgot the people who pulled her up during the bad times. And, she was always dressed for the occasion! I remember when Mrs. Russo lost her husband when he was in his late 50's. Signorine came to her house two, three times a week and cooked for her and her children for months. They watched TV together and then, later on, Signorine invited her to our Thursday evening meetings. From then on, Mrs. Russo had us to fall back on. Signorine made sure Mrs. Russo was never alone; she died 10 years later if I recall.

For some reason Signorine thought we all understood Italian even though many of us never spoke a word of Italian in our house; we may have had an Italian surname but, we grew up in the 50's and 60's where being an American to immigrants was a big thing, and so they wanted to do everything American, be everything American. Plus, they wanted us to learn English to interpret for them. We kept our culture in our homes. Back then, having a vowel at the end of your name was not viewed well by 60's Americans. I did not have to speak Italian in my home because both my parents spoke and read English fluently although when they didn't want me to hear something, they reverted back to Italian so I wouldn't understand. My father worked for many years as a Bookkeeper for the Brooklyn Casket Co. and then he went to Manhattan Community College at night for his CPA and got an accountant job in Manhattan, my mother got a job in the neighborhood public school cafeteria and she learned a lot of English from the kids as well as her co-workers. But, most of my friends were in charge of teaching our parents English or being able to translate official letters. Except for me, the other Fairy Comaras spoke Italian at home. If she would tell me a joke in Italian, I wouldn't understand a word until she laughed and, then we laughed together. I didn't know what the fuck she was saying but, I laughed anyway because I loved her!

I don't remember when we started the Thursday evening meetings, I think it was when most of us were in our mid- to-late 40's; Antoinette was much younger. By then, some of us, like me, lost our parents or had one parent still alive. The other Fairy Comaras got married, settled in with some babies, ran around like chickens without a head between work and family and then, when their kids were teens, they only were blessed with being mental wrecks but not so physically exhausted; just in need of a night away from all of the chaos. Thursday evenings were our Girls Night Out before there was an official Girls Night Out. We didn't need a restaurant or a bar; we had peace of mind in being with people we knew and from time to time, new people. And the wine was flowing!

When you combined Signorine's cooking, the flowing of wine and conversation, the lectures and my readings, those evenings were priceless. If you came in with problems, you could sort them out or get some advice because there was always someone who went through it or knew someone who could help you with it. It was more than lip service or a "group hug", it was group energy! When someone said I'll pray for you, that meant they were going to church, lighting a candle and then, actually praying for you.

The Fairy Comaras did it the other way around; we worked on your problem and then prayed that we got it right! Those people we helped, in turn, helped others, and brought other friends who needed help. In our heyday, we had as many as 50 people in my house. For some who came on Thursday just to chill, Girls Night Out became Girls Night Off; they'd put their problems on the shelf and left laughing with a merry heart. No matter what, problems or no problems, they walked out feeling better than when they came in!

Many of them brought their specialty appetizers, wine, and sometimes they cooked meals especially for Thursday! Even Esther Schrable, who never went to our meetings, would send over something she baked. We used to send her all the Italian leftovers we couldn't fit in our refrigerator because she loved Italian food; ours was always better than the way she made it. That may have been the reason she moved into an Italian neighborhood when you think about it.

Every Thursday, 5 to 7 of the Fairy Comaras came to my house to help with the guests. Each Fairy Comara had a talent to help someone and cooked something; who was going to bring trays of lasagna, eggplant or Chicken parmigiana, or they'd bring pastries from Agnello's Bakery. During Christmas, Esther Schrable would send over the best homemade Babka. When we told the group that it was Esther's Babka, everyone would dash over to the table. The only one who was given Esther's recipe many, many years later was Antoinette Fresca and she has that under lock and key.

Little Marie Greco usually brought her mother, Rose Di Fillipo, and the other Rose, Rose "Ro" Mancini as translators for Signorine.

Thursday evening was an opportunity to get the Fairy Comaras together to recharge their wands. Loud Lina would come with her daughter and her daughter asked us once if we could make her mother less loud but, that was out of our hands. We knew Loud Lina was coming when she closed the front door of her house. If she came for a reading from me, I would tell her, "Lina, write down your questions so everyone in the neighborhood doesn't hear them".

The network of support we had back then was better than Angie's List. All the people we got to know either through our parents or just walk-ins. Someone in that room could recommend a person, a service, a lawyer and more to someone with a problem. If you needed something fixed, we'd find or recommend someone who could do a good job and didn't charge a lot; if it was a problem that was more complex, maybe a domestic problem, then we'd take over and get to the bottom of it. The Fairy Comaras had an invisible wing on their right side and a pitchfork on the left. We were the ones God sent down so we could redeem ourselves from our less than stellar youth or maybe even a past life. We were the Oomphas of God, his trouble shooters for the times we lived in; you had a problem, we'd find a way to fix it for good!

For the record, Fairy Comaras are not angels; we still have to earn that.... we have a past and sometimes it's because of that past, that we may be in a position to correct the path of others. We became Fairy Comaras not because we viewed life from a cloud up above; we were not above reproach. In fact, we could teach you a thing or two about how to make bad decisions because we made plenty in our day. It's because we fell short, that we tried to lighten the fall for others, maybe even save them from falling at all. Our halos are gray, not white.

And, although I'm writing about our neighborhood experiences as Fairy Comaras, there were Fairy Comaras all over Brooklyn and the other boroughs. There was always an aunt, or a grandmother or a group of ladies you could go to; they were the people you could confide in without judgment. We were the Fairy Comaras for our neighborhood and the Brooklyn area. My Fairy Comara was either my Grandma Philly or Signorine. They're both gone now but, I still remember the things they taught me and the selflessness of their efforts to help others.

Thursday evenings, I gave readings or occasionally, I'd give a short lecture or someone in the neighborhood would speak. They'd come and speak about things we could do better like Fairy Comara Little Marie Greco, who worked for Francone Senior Center; her lectures were usually about how to lift our aged parents if they fell and when not to lift them, where to get hand grips for the shower, what questions to ask if we think they may be going into "demenza", dementia. She also spoke about using an aid (caregiver), we used that title back then and, what to expect and not to expect from an aid.

Usually when the time came for us to hire an aid for our grandparents, we called Little Marie because the staff there were trustworthy and caring. Back then, there weren't many grandparents who lived alone; most lived with their children and if they didn't, they probably lived nearby. There was always a network of support, even financial, in the home. They had Medicare but we paid for everything else. And, if we couldn't afford it, Little Marie would arrange a payment plan to suit our out-of-pocket expenses. She always managed to get a lot of financial support from the city through special grants so the aid's salary kept our family's cost down. In other words, we went to Little Marie for ways to keep our grandparents at home, not in a home. It was an unwritten rule that everybody in the house, including the grandchildren, took care of grandma and grandpa. Little Marie's lectures from time to time helped make life easier. And, she always kept her word; if she said she'd look into it, she did. In addition to Little Marie, Captain Doyle, her old boss, would come to the Thursday meetings once or twice a year and speak about crime prevention, protecting your house and the many services the New York Police Dept does for the community like providing the baseball uniforms for St. Agatha's Little

League baseball team or the Fresh Air Fund to get neighborhood kids out of the city and enjoy some country air.

In addition to readings, I did the Man 101 lectures on relationship training once or twice a year. Always drew a large crowd since, most of the people I gave readings to needed some boyfriend or husband advice. Signorine was in charge of making everyone comfortable while they waited. She hugged the ladies who came out of my readings crying or offered them food if they came out with a smile on their face. Sometimes she gave them a tea leaf reading just to make them feel better. She used a porcelain tea cup and saucer, the old ones with the gold trim and the dainty handle; and each person swirled the cup, asked a question and emptied the contents into the saucer. Nine times out of 10, bingo! The question was answered.

Signorine knew how to take the edge off of bad news with the tea leaves. She predicted that Rose "Ro" Mancini's daughter, Donna, would have a baby within a year. Ro's daughter had been trying for over five years and they were at their wits end. It was starting to put a strain on the marriage and her daughter was plagued with the thought of never having a family. One year later, her daughter gave birth to an eight-pound girl. When her granddaughter was born, Ro Mancini lit a candle in church and gave Signorine a dozen long stemmed roses. After that, Rosalie's daughter burped out two more babies, another daughter and a son.

Once the word got out about Ro's daughter, we got flooded with young women attending the Thursday evening meetings just to get a reading from Signorine. They only wanted to "consult" with Signorine, nobody else. Of course, with this new breed of women who didn't speak Italian or very little, Rose Mancini or Rose Di Fillipo did the translation. I remember Signorine got a lot of tips while she slept on the recliner; she finally treated herself to a comfortable pair of shoes. God forbid she should have one of us buy her shoes!

Around the Christmas holidays, Gina Leone asked Signorine if her boyfriend would pop the question and propose; Signorine said yes but not now. Gina was less than happy but full of hope. Later on, when everyone had left, Signorine told Antoinette that yes, Gina would get married but not to her boyfriend. As God is my witness, after the holidays, her boyfriend broke up with her because he wasn't ready to settle down. That was true because he met a girl at work and he didn't feel right betraying Gina which was noble of him, I must say. We found out later on that he went on his first date with this girl right after he broke up with her. At that point, Gina was crushed because Signorine had told her she would get married and look what happened!

Two months later, out of nowhere, a friend of hers invited her to her engagement party and Gina meets this wonderful guy, a teacher, Brendan Walsh, who lived in nearby Sunset Park and, just like that they got married the end of December during Christmas break, beautiful wedding! They had the reception at some catering hall on 18th Avenue, I forget the name, an abbundanza amount of food, live DJ, the works. I think they have two or three grown children now; I know the first one was a boy but, at my age, I lose track of who had sons and daughters and how many. The names and faces fly right over my head. To this day, Gina Walsh lights a candle in church once a year for Signorine. And even after she moved to Staten Island, she'd drive down for a Thursday meeting every now and then; sometimes she'd bring her mother, Sofia, along, too, so she could reminisce about the good old days.

So, anyway, when Signorine died, everyone chipped in to give her the grandest funeral at Torregrossa's; we reserved the big room. She went out first class. She received so many flowers that we had to put some in the main lobby and some we sent to St. Agatha's for the chapel. In those days, you waked a person for two or three days, then the funeral mass and then the burial followed by a lunch. Now, you're waked one day and you go right in the ground. Someone told me recently that they attended a Zoom wake, creepy! The room was packed for three days straight. Antoinette Fresca donated a Chasable to St. Agatha's Church. A Chasuble is the robe worn by priests when they say Mass. Gina Walsh, nee Leone, Ro Mancini, Black Marie and Irish Marie paid for the limousines. Uncle "Big" Jimmy paid for the wake. Me and Little Marie Greco paid for the funeral cards, funeral Mass and burial. All the bookies in the neighborhood who came to Signorine for the winning daily number and won, chipped in for the luncheon at Monte's for 50 people. Signorine lived her whole life just getting by but, in the end, she went out like a queen.

Antoinette Fresca was at the wake all three nights and we all thought, Madonna! Signorine must have really helped her! She was always at the Thursday meetings with her mother; after her father died, she brought her mother everywhere so she wouldn't be alone. And we all knew Carmela, she was Frankie Boy's mother but, she was our friend as well. Those nights after we came home from the disco! She never judged what she heard around that table when we had a little too much to drink and loose lips; she never told our parents. We always wondered how a woman whose life was so Catholic could be so open-minded. But, then again, we thought to ourselves, we weren't her kids so what did she care! Certainly, she kept Antoinette under lock and key when she grew up!

Anyway, speaking of Carmela Fresca, I found out later on that Carmela and Signorine shared a secret. That secret was revealed in a reading I gave Carmela one night. Carmela asked me to give her a reading about something to do with her sister Carla's illness, but, I couldn't help feeling that Carmela carried a heavier weight around her shoulders, a heavy weight of guilt.

When I began the reading, I told her, her sister Carla was ill and I pointed to my heart and she said yes. I asked Carmela, "Is there a way she could come here for treatment?" Carmela said that Carla was stubborn and refused her offer to come to New York. "I even offered to pay the air fare and doctor bills but, she said no." I comforted her and told her she did the best she could for her sister. Carla was five years older than Carmela; she was mother and sister to her at the same time. Just then, I had this image of tremendous guilt. After I dried her eyes, I couldn't hold it in so I just said to her, "Carmela, you carry such a heavy weight of guilt and sadness about you, why?"

She broke down and howled out such a cry, the people outside went into a hush, you could hear a pin drop. Antoinette knocked on the door after a while, "Ma, are you alright?" I just answered, "We're fine." I asked Antoinette to bring her some wine and I gave her another tissue. Everyone knew never to ask me about another's reading, I wasn't a priest but, what happened during those readings stayed in the little room off the side of the Living Room. Carmela, between tears, asked me if Signorine told me anything and I said, "nothing like what you're about to tell me". I knew it wasn't about Carla.

When she finally composed herself, she said, "It happened after Anthony started school; Emil was maybe 3. You know I had a miscarriage after Emil, right? John was working long hours back then, trying to start a business. He wouldn't be home until 8 or 9 o'clock at night; he would eat, watch a little TV and go to bed. Our love life was, how do I say it, few and far apart. I felt very unloved and alone. The ladies were fine for coffee or shopping in the afternoon but, I was depressed and just couldn't shake it. Regardless, I always had a smile on my face for my sons and John."

"One morning, it was my turn to arrange the flowers in church for a funeral mass at 10:00 AM and, of course, whenever I was in church, I always lit a candle to St. Anthony to give me a daughter. There was a man, lighting a candle alongside me. He had that sad face and after a few minutes, I asked him if the candle was for his mother or father, he looked about 35, 36 years old so that's the first thing you think of but, he told me it was for his daughter, Ellen, who would have been 6 years old today. She died last year from a brain tumor. No parent should go through the death of a child. After Emil was born, I had one miscarriage and I went into a deep depression. You were too young then to know but, your mother and some of the women on the block knew it. They took turns taking Anthony to school and my mother-in-law, God rest her soul, took over the household and watched Emil, until I could get back on my feet. In our time, we didn't talk about going to psychiatrist and, maybe we should have, because it would have helped instead of keeping all the loss and emotions in your mind all day long. My Antoinette talks to me about things that I would never have told my mother and we have a better relationship. My parents died when me and my sister Carla were teenagers. When John and I married I knew nothing about sex and my sister Carla lived in Italy. All she told me was, be a good wife and a good mother. But I only fulfilled one part and I carry my sin with me to this day."

After I refilled her glass of wine and she took a big gulp, she said, "Well, anyway, this man and I continued the conversation after we came out of church. He told me how she was his only child and how much he loved her; he took the morning off from work today to go to church and light a candle. He and another fella owned a car dealership in Coney Island. After his daughter died, his wife took a turn for the worse, she fell into a deep depression; the house was a mess, sometimes he'd come home and she was still in her pajamas, no dinner, she was a vegetable. A psychiatrist was recommended to him by their family doctor. The doctor got his colleague to lower the payments for her visits because they had spent all their savings on his daughter's treatments. Still, she never was herself again.

After that, he and his wife had nothing to talk about and she refused to let him touch her. She left for a short visit to her mother in Yonkers; a short visit that so far lasted six months. We talked on the church steps for something like 15 minutes more. For some reason, we were both uplifted by the conversation. We just connected and time stood still. Well, to cut to the chase, I saw him again at Sunday mass; John was home painting our kitchen. Sundays were really his only day to do anything around the house and God forbid we should have someone else do it! I had Anthony and Emil with me so I was trying to pretend I didn't see him because I didn't want the boys to see me talking to him. He didn't approach me but, when the boys went over to talk to Sandy Russo's children, I said hello. He asked me if we could meet for coffee at the Purity Diner sometime and, and…. I don't know what came over me, I said yes. Long story short, we started meeting for coffee every Wednesday, John's parents were living with us and they looked after the boys after school. I told them I was going to St. Agatha's to go over the St. Anthony Feast details with the ladies. I didn't know what excuse I was going to use after the feast was over but, I was just living for Wednesdays and didn't think that far ahead. To this day, I live with the guilt that I lied to John's parents! When they both passed away, I cried harder than John did because of how I deceived them. They were so good to me, treated me like a daughter."

"Anyway, one day this man suggested we drive over to see his car dealership in Coney Island, it was nice to drive around Brooklyn with someone who was interested in what I had to say and I could tell he really listened to me. I saw the car dealership and then, one thing led to another and he invited me to his house. He was the second man I went to bed with and I felt so alive during our lovemaking; I hadn't been loved like that in a long time; the sex was fantastic. Is that right for me to say? Till today, I remember it fondly but, always with remorse because I deceived my husband, his parents and my sons. I was intimate with him three times after that. The last time we went to his house, as I was leaving his house to go into the car, who do I see but Signorine! Of all people! Her doctor had a practice across the street from this man's house. You always get caught no matter how hard you try, Diane, eventually it catches up to you. My shame could not be mistaken as me and Signorine locked eyes.

After that, I didn't see him anymore; he must have felt the same guilt because he didn't argue with me. About a month after that, I finally had enough courage to go out and mingle with everybody and went to Signorine to confess. She asked to come in and she read my tea leaves. She told me I was pregnant and my heart raced.... oh my God! She told me to think fast. I did. John and I were intimate that night and eight months later, Antoinette was born. Everybody thought she was born premature and thank God she weighed six pounds, not like Anthony and Emil who were over eight pounds. And, thank you, Jesus, as you can see, she's all me, even the nose. I never told this gentleman that I was pregnant with his child. When Antoinette was born, I felt that I had given birth to the daughter that he lost."

I was numb....in my head I was saying "what the fuck? What the fuck! what the fuck did I just hear?" I had to control my facial expressions not to show the shock on my face! Carmela? Can't be! Carmela who is the Blessed Virgin incarnate of the neighborhood, who'd give you the shirt off her back? But, at that point, I realized that Carmela was a Fairy Comara. For all our goodness, there was always a little gray tint to our wings.

My response came after a pregnant pause, "Carmela, you prayed for a daughter and you got one! You got what you were praying for and the Devil doesn't like happy endings so this must be God's love. You have done so much for the neighborhood, the church, your family and your friends, do you really think you're condemned for this? I'm inclined to say that as odd as it may sound, God gave you both the gift that you had been praying for and he gave you and this man the comfort you so badly needed. You and John have been the best parents to Antoinette and your husband loved her, God rest his soul."

Carmela said, "My guilt is that I never told John" I said, "you probably told him now! He's probably saying how much he misses you and Antoinette!" I asked her if the man was still living there but she said she didn't think so; she didn't dare visit him at the dealership. I told her if she wanted to clear her conscience, she should at least tell the biological father; he had a right to know. After our reading, she did do that and was told by a young man at the dealership that he retired and moved to Naples, Florida with his second wife. He had a daughter and a son now but he didn't know where his children were living. The guy was the son of the man's partner and he took over the dealership when his father died some years ago. Knowing that this man had started a new life made Carmela feel whole again and she never again walked around like she was carrying a cross. And all through the reading, if you can call it that, more like a confession, she never said the man's name and I never asked. When Carmela died, I thought about telling Antoinette but decided it wasn't a good idea. I never mentioned it to Signorine and Signorine never said a word either.

This one goes to the grave no matter how close me and Antoinette are today. Sorry, folks, I'm not into negative drama. If it's not broke, don't fix it. I knew nothing good would come from this revelation back then and nothing will now. Now, if Antoinette does an ancestry trace, let the company tell her although, Antoinette isn't really into those things. As a matter of fact, only your eyes will read this part as I intend to delete it when I hand the books to the Fairy Comaras. I know I digressed with this story instead of the Antoinette funeral home conversation but, I felt I had to put this in.

So, anyway, Antoinette was at Signorine's wake all three days. And we were all wondering what could Signorine have done for Antoinette to warrant this kind of friendship? When I say WE, I'm excluding Little Marie Greco who knew why; I'm talking about the other Fairy Comaras. On the third day, Little Marie Greco pulls me over to the side and tells me that Antoinette is in the lobby and she wants to talk to me. Marie said she was going to go with me, too. Now, I'm really wondering what it could be that Marie has to go with me? So, I hesitantly said OK. We walk into the lobby and there's Antoinette near the water cooler sipping water from the little cone shaped cups they give you, probably on her fourth cup because she looked nervous. She had this fake grin when she saw me. The one from ear to ear like she saw Mel Gibson coming her way. I looked at Marie with a side glance like I'm being ambushed and she tells me it's alright which I didn't believe because she didn't have her truth face on, she had her I'm really sorry I put you in this position face. And, I know this from past experience with Marie. You have to understand, Marie Greco, Frankie Boy, Irish Marie, Black Marie, Marie from Long Island, we all played on the same block as kids, most of us went to St. Agatha's. We did everything together; went to the disco together and celebrated holidays together. We even went shopping together to A&S Department Store except Frankie Boy. And, we all had a different look that told all of us what was going on. A&S had the best Christmas display back then, outside and inside. They had a big Christmas tree in the main lobby near the elevators and decorations throughout the store! We did everything together and even after we married, we were still surgically attached at the hip!

Anyway, we all knew when something was up by our facial expressions, when we had a secret to tell, when we had a problem, who was a pain in the ass, etc. All of us had a certain facial expression that was distinctive, even Frankie Boy. We all had a different face to tell us what the other was thinking. We had IT, Italian Telepathy. One look, even a cough told us some shit was coming down the pike and our glances, sideways looks and even our hand motions told the whole story.

So, Little Marie Greco's face, even though I had to look down to see it, told me that she was in a sticky position and that she was going to shift it to me. Like I needed this right now with the wake! I was already dreading the idea of having to clean out Signorine's possessions and then pass an empty apartment every day until I rented it.

We did the how are you, kiss and a hug; Antoinette told me how sorry she was for me because I was so close to her and, I was, and thanked her. Then she starts telling me her brothers were asking about me and said to say they're sorry about not coming to the wake because blah, blah, blah the kids, work, not enough time in the day and then she hurriedly slips it in and tells me that she's selling her parents' house. She and her brothers discussed it, which didn't sound entirely true because when Antoinette told me this, she put her head down slightly and since I'm psychic I already knew what was coming down the pike. I felt she was reluctant to do the asking. She proceeds to tell me about the discussion her brothers had with her, word for word, and then ended it with the decision to sell the house. I didn't think she was for it in the beginning. Do you ever get these people who use 50 words when 20 will do? That's how she was talking…. a mile a minute. And I'm not one for long conversations so, I had to cut her off after we heard the long story about how the neighborhood was changing and these young professionals, we called them Yuppies, were moving into Park Slope and paying top dollar for brownstones. She told me the sale of the house would be split three ways since there was no mortgage. Her brothers told her she would be able to put a little away for retirement being that she was single and had to support herself. I looked at Antoinette straight in the eye and said, "Antoinette, so you want to know if you could move into Signorine's apartment?" and she said, "how do you know that?" and I said, "how many Thursday night meetings have you been to Antoinette?"

I can't tell you how many times people came to me for a psychic reading and say, how did you know? Who did you think you are talking to? Your manicurist? Always mystified me but, maybe they came in with doubt but, not to brag, they never came out in doubt even if they weren't told what they wanted to hear.

So, anyway, Antoinette finally came out with the ask, "is all right then for me to rent the apartment? Diane, I'm sort of pressed for time because we close on the house the end of this month and I've looked for an apartment in Staten Island and they're too small and I don't know anyone and it's too far to travel on the train to work. Of course, I would pay rent and I can do Signorine's job on Thursday evenings; you know I love to cook." And she was rambling on so much and in such an agitated state that I had to stop her. And I held up my hand and said Abasta! which means enough! I then asked her a question, "you know who I live next to, you really want to move next to Esther Schrable?"

Everybody in the neighborhood knew about Antoinette and Manny Schrable. They were friends as children and dated. Manny was friends with Emil Fresca because they were almost the same age; he was a fixture in the Fresca home since forever.

As I mentioned before and probably before that, Murray and Esther Schrable owned Murray's Department Store on 5th Ave between President and Carroll Streets; small store but they had everything from men's suits, dresses, bras, stockings, girdles, you name it, they had it.

My mother bought me my first training bra there which was sort of like the non-Jewish Bat Mitzvah for us Catholic girls. All the women in our neighborhood bought their girdles from Schrable's. You went to A&S Dept. store to shop but you went to Schrable's to get something you either needed right away or you needed a girdle. Esther Schrable was the girdle expert. She could just look at you and know what size girdle you needed; personalized service and you always wound up buying a pair of stockings for the girdle and Esther could tell you the quality of each of the styles. And, in addition, the Schrables lived next to my parents, so they were our merchants and our neighbors at the same time. I miss stores where you bought and exchanged conversation; it provided a contented shopping experience which I didn't appreciate at the time but, miss terribly today.

As I also mentioned before, Camella and John Fresca, Murray, Esther and Little Marie Greco's parents played cards every Friday night at Esther's house. If someone couldn't make it, Esther would call my parents from the backyard to come down to fill in. If Esther and Murray couldn't make it, then everybody went over the Fresca's house. The card games went on for over 10-15 years; in the summer there'd be a barbeque and everybody brought something for Murray to cook. You could hear them talking and laughing when they played outside and the laughing got louder when the wine and other alcoholic beverages came out. All was well until the Big Thing happened. Forgive me, if I repeat myself sometimes, think of it as last week's soap opera when you heard "previously on Days of Our Lives"; it's kind of a recap.

Not even her parents had a clue. But at 16, little, good Antoinette and Manny Schrable were going on dates. And this went on for two years! Their Saturday dates were usually going to the movies. Antoinette would tell her parents she was going shopping with her friends. She'd have one of her friends ring the bell to go and then the friend would disappear at the corner of the train station until Antoinette would call when she came back home. Sometimes their date was lunch, sometimes they'd just walked around for hours. For Antoinette, Manny was Mr. Right, the guy she would marry.

First of all, Antoinette's parents would never let her date at 16, her dating would begin as supervised dates in their home when God knows how old she would be; they were Old World. And she couldn't take a chance and tell her brothers because they might tell her parents. Emil knew Manny was dating someone but he didn't know who until the Big Thing happened. Emil might have suspected Manny was up to something, probably with a girl outside of the neighborhood but, he didn't have a clue it was his sister.

Back then, it was almost a rarity for a Jewish person to marry a Gentile; Jerry Lewis did it and Stiller and Meara but, it was not done so much in everyday life. According to what I was told, these "dates" went on for about two years and something had to be done. Manny and Antoinette were running out of excuses in order to be together. And so, when Manny pressured Antoinette to tell her parents that they were a couple, Antoinette agreed. Manny would tell his parents and she would do the same. It seemed like the right time; Manny was a graduating from high school that year and he would be off to college in Florida. They decided that Antoinette would also tell her parents that she would move to Florida, get a job near to the college and then, after Manny graduated, they'd get married.

What was she thinking? What guts she must have had to even think that she could move out of her house just like that? We live in different times; now, young people tend to get a job and move out on their own. Parents even help them move and help with the rent. In our time, you left your parents' house one of three ways: you got married, enlisted into the army or.... feet first horizontally out the door. A young single lady getting an apartment was viewed suspiciously. Our mothers would ask us "What can you do in an apartment that you can't do here?" What was Antoinette thinking? Sheltered all her life by overprotective parents; did she actually think they were going to tell her, OK Antoinette, Good Luck darling! Go with our blessing? But she was naïve; she definitely was in love with Manny, he was the one for her. Now, that I look back on those days, they were soulmates. And, as much as they tried to hide that light of love they had for each other, it had to come out.

Anyway, the Big Thing was told to me by my mother who heard it from Signorine. It happened at the Fresca's Sunday afternoon dinner; they usually ate around 2:00 PM. I don't know why she choose dinnertime, on a Sunday, to make an announcement like that; in hindsight, maybe she felt she needed the support, who knows. There was her mother, Carmela, John, Frankie Boy, his friend Eddie from Flatbush, Emil, cousin Frederico "Rico" and his wife, Joann, who just got married a month ago and, of course, Signorine. Rico and Joann went to Italy for their honeymoon and couldn't wait to show their photos. Back then, Europe wasn't a vacation destination or a honeymoon spot our parents could afford; most of them didn't even go on a honeymoon. We drove to the country or to the beach on vacation, maybe, if our parents saved the money, we went to Disney World. You did not vacation in Italy unless you had family there. And, if you did go, you lived with your relatives for 2 or 3 weeks, no hotel, that would be an insult! Maybe you got to go outside of the town to do a little sightseeing. Those trips were like family reunions not a vacation.

Now, couples spend their honeymoon in places all over the world; sometimes they combine the wedding with the honeymoon and then every guest has to fly and book a hotel room to attend the wedding. I'm not saying there's anything wrong with that, it just wasn't done unless you had money. Showing photos of their trip to Italy was a big thing for Rico and Joann. It wasn't the Big Thing, though; the photos were supposed to be the big thing that Sunday, but they weren't. Joann's father was a funeral director; he had the money to pay for the wedding and the honeymoon of his only daughter. Rico and his wife lived in the apartment above her parents' home on Ocean Parkway so they could save for a home.

Funny how things turn out. Rico had been studying for the police officer's exam at the time while working as a temp in Manhattan. Occasionally, his father-in-law asked him to help out at the funeral parlor when they were a man short. Well, this went on for some time and Rico was a quick learner. Joann's brother wanted to be a doctor and had no intention of going into the business. He wanted to take care of the living, not the dead. Anyway, Rico left his job, stop studying for the police officer's exam and started working for his father-in-law. He went to school, took the exams and got his funeral director's license or whatever they call it. His father-in-law made him a partner and they opened another funeral home in Queens; they did very well. Of course, Joann wasn't too happy about it; she saw how her mother had to go to weddings alone because her father had a Saturday funeral but, later on, Rico hired two managers when he branched out to three funeral parlors and then, Joann didn't have to go alone to weddings so much.

So, anyway, looking at their honeymoon photos on that particular Sunday was supposed to be the big thing. Nobody asked for the photos after Antoinette's announcement.

So, after the antipasto, brasciole, meatballs and spaghetti, everyone was full, and there was lively conversation across the table. Anthony "Frankie Boy" was telling everyone about his job, John Fresca asked Joann about her family and how they were and Signorine put her two cents in and was telling them about her rotten landlord. It was when everybody was ready for espresso with anisette and cake that Antoinette chose to make her announcement; coincidentally, that was when the photos were supposed to come out. I know all this because whenever an Italian tells a story they have to include what meal was served. Food was the prologue for any story. For drama, it mattered that Carmela made brasciole because you didn't make brasciole every Sunday, only when you had company. It was the drama building up to the story. If it was just pasta and meatballs, that wouldn't be dramatic enough because every Italian in the neighborhood was having the same thing. According to my mother, Signorine's meal description went on for about 15 minutes before she got to the Big Thing. In addition, Signorine had to tell us about Rico and his wife, where they went for their honeymoon and also how fast they rushed to get out the door after Antoinette announced the Big Thing.

Signorine was the town crier in our neighborhood and she told a story with such passion. Conversations back then were not measured by how many characters you had left on a screen; it was storytelling with so many stories in between; some had nothing to do with the original story! It was told with such gusto you didn't care how long it took to hear it! And, you wouldn't dare interrupt or talk over the storyteller because it was impolite and listening was valued. Nowadays, you speak two words and you're interrupted, who listens anymore. Just so you know, anatomically speaking, you can't talk and listen at the same time. You're either doing one or the other and it's probably talking. Listen and Silent have the same letters.

Maybe you could call Signorine's stories gossip but, I knew my mother and many of the other mothers and fathers. When they received bad news, the intention was that maybe they could do something about it. Like when Marie Fusco's dog passed away. She had a small dog, a mutt, named Champion, a pain in the ass barking all the time but, she loved that dog! She treated him like a baby. Her husband told us he thought she loved the dog more than him. Champion was old when he crossed the rainbow bridge. When my mother heard this from Signorine, she told me she was going to go over to Marie's for coffee because she needed the company.

Or when we heard that Sal Balzano's wife, Marie, yes, another Marie, had a miscarriage; all our mothers brought food so she wouldn't have to think about making lunch and dinner for Sal and her son John. Marie Balzano used to come to the Thursday meetings after her three sons were teenagers, yes, three sons. She gave up trying for a girl after son #3. We cared about each other when we heard bad news and we celebrated like crazy when we heard good news. My mother was a good listener, she could tell me exactly what was told to her with the same passion as Signorine, only in English.

So now comes the Big Thing. Everybody is full, relaxed, contented...who's burping and then saying excusa except for Frankie Boy who made everyone laugh when he burped. Everyone laughed except Antoinette; she was so nervous she didn't even touch her cannoli. Her father was the first to notice, "Antoinette whatsa matta, you don't feel good?" Because not eating a cannoli was a noticeable thing to us. And, God forbid, you only ate half! That really caught our attention. She stuttered a little bit but then she said, "I have something to share with you all". Of course, when Signorine told the story, Antoinette said, "hey evybod, Ima gonna say somting" we didn't use the word "share" in that way. This is pre-Facebook. And then, Antoinette said "I want to tell you all some good news". So, Frankie Boy says, "Hey, Antoinette, you got a job?" and then everybody was so glad and they were asking what kind of job it was? where? Nobody would talk about how much she would make until the family was alone. Italians don't talk about money even if extended family like cousins are at the table. The family would wait until everyone went home and then they'd ask Antoinette.

Well, anyway, with all the family asking questions and telling her how happy they were for her, she couldn't control the table. Finally, after she shouted "I didn't get a job!", they all looked at her with a staring glaze; what the hell was she going to tell them? And then, stuttering yet again, she said, "I even have better news, Manny asked me to go steady (old term, AKA dating exclusively) and I said yes! He'll go to college in Florida and I'll go down and get a job down there. After he graduates, we'll get married." You could hear a pin drop after that news.

According to Signorine, she never saw a calmer face on John Fresca that day. A calm face but, the eyes gave it away. His eyes didn't blink and then when they did, he said "This is Manny you're talking about, Esther's son?" Antoinette's face went from elated to serious because she didn't know what was going to come out of her father's mouth next. Carmela had her head down pretending to eat her Sfogliatelle. The cousins were just curious because they didn't know Manny. And then, he said "Manny is a nice boy, he comes from a good home. I always liked him" but, nothing else. Frankie Boy and Emil, looked at her wide-eyed in shock and said, "that's nice, Antoinette!" because they knew that this was not going to be the end of it; there would be more discussion after Rico, Joann, Eddie and Signorine left. They both experienced their father's calm many times, it never ended well.

But Emil had to let the cat out of the bag by blurting out "Now I know where he's been going on Saturdays" and that was the nail in the coffin. Antoinette dropped her glass of water all over the table; she wanted to pinch Emil but he was too far away. It was time to keep quiet. And, even after everybody had left, nothing was said. John turned on the TV, watched his shows and promptly went to bed at 9:00 PM.

Carmela, on the other hand, asked Antoinette to help her straighten up the kitchen and put the dishes away. She asked her, "How long have you two been dating?" and Antoinette replied, "we haven't been dating, he asked me for a date" at which point Carmela says, "well, who was the girl Emil said he was seeing on Saturdays?" By the way, the kitchen story I'm telling you, was not from Signorine. She had long gone home. This is what Antoinette herself told me after she came to live with me. Anyway, Antoinette didn't know what to say except, "I don't know". At which point the expression on her face told Carmela she was lying.

Italian-American mothers should work for the FBI, nothing gets past them. I had the same thing going on with my mother! The shady guys I dated on the side that I thought she knew nothing about; it came out at a later time during an argument that would blind-side me. Cut me off right at the knees. Our mothers were secret seeking missiles on two legs. They'd zoom in at the right time and catch you off guard. God, I miss those arguments now. And, I miss the wise advice and the unconditional love that came with it. All of us who were parents, grandparents now, try to do it but, we don't have "the look" like they had, hard to explain in words but it was a certain look that told us they weren't buying our bullshit. When we were young, we had to go to confession for lying; we'd look at the other kids in church to see who lied the most and prayed the longest; if you had to pray the rosary, you had some big-time sins!

Well, long story short, with the back and forth, Antoinette told her mother confidentially, yeah right, that they had been meeting Saturday afternoons for two years. Her mother told her that it was good she finally told the truth but, she should be ashamed of herself for lying to her and her father for so long. Antoinette watched a little TV, got her uniform ready for school and went to bed. At the time, she worked part-time after school as a cashier for our pharmacist, Joseph Turco, on 4th Ave and President St. Joe Turco was the nicest guy in the world; he became a pharmacist after WWII with a GI loan to go to school. His father was a bricklayer back then and he used to put a few dollars away through the years for his son to get an education but, since he didn't need the money, he wound up giving it to his son to buy his own pharmacy. Because he had no daughters, Joe always treated Antoinette like a daughter and he always gave her a few dollars more than she should have gotten on payday. Every once in a while, Carmela would make Joe Turco's favorite dinner, lasagna, and Antoinette would bring it to him. Antoinette was also in charge of doing the Turco Pharmacy Christmas storefront display; she did a good job! She created a different holiday theme every year! Joe told me he thought Antoinette bought some decorations out of her own money. He couldn't be sure because he didn't remember what he had in his Christmas decoration box but he did remember that he hadn't seen some of the decorations on display. She even decorated around the store when it wasn't busy. She did such a good job that Esther Schrable asked her to do their storefront for Christmas even though they were Jewish.

Signorine only put up a Nativity set at Christmas; she had a small plastic one she bought from John's Bargain Store. On one of her secret Saturday dates with Manny, Antoinette, as usual, went to A&S to buy something to bring home. She saw this beautiful 12-piece Nativity set from Italy with the manger, animals, the three kings and of course, the holy family with the creche of wood and hay, on sale for $29.00 which was steep for those days and more so for a 17-year-old but, she bought it with the last $30 she had in her wallet. Lucky that she had a token to get on the train! No metro cards then, folks. Metro cards may seem the efficient way to travel on the subways but, it's not the most environmental; at least you could recycle the tokens over and over again. The plastic gets trashed. And using your debit card to take the subway? Talk about taking your privacy away.

When she came home, she told her mother she was giving it to Signorine; she walked over to her apartment and gave it to her that day. Antoinette said that was the first time she saw Signorine cry and she hugged her so tight she couldn't breathe. She had to use her saved money hidden in the panty drawer of her dresser for lunch and train fare for school that week. Her mother knew where she hid it and during the week when she did laundry, she slipped the $30 back into Antoinette's pouch; probably Antoinette didn't even know it, because she never counted how much was in it. After Signorine passed away, I gave it back to Antoinette; she puts it up every Christmas. We never knew it but, underneath the manger, Signorine wrote in Italian "given to me by an angel, Antonietta". But, once again, I digress.

Ok, back to the Big Thing, so the next day, Monday, Antoinette got up and went to school and while she was out of the house, Carmela and John went to Murray's Department Store to have a talk with Esther and Murray. After that, there were no more Friday night card games with the Frescas. Manny Schrable was packed off to Florida State University. Antoinette was told the Schrables were against Manny dating Antoinette because of the religion thing and that Manny didn't need to be distracted from his studies. Manny didn't answer any of Antoinette's calls she made from the phone booth; her heart was completely broken. She was angry at the Schrables; from then on, she refused to talk to them other than a cordial hello. She enrolled in a secretarial school and after a year, she went to work for Fred Manza. The Frescas still shopped at Murray's Dept. Store but, it was never the same. After college, Manny went to a Dentistry school in Maryland. Right after that, he married Phyllis Bornstein, started his own dental practice in Manhattan and lived in Queens in an apartment next to Phyllis' parents. They had one daughter, Allyssa, and a little after she was born, they moved to Great Neck.

However, Antoinette never got over it. All we knew in the neighborhood was that Manny went to college in Florida and Antoinette went to secretarial school for one year after high school. Some of us didn't even know that they were dating. All Frankie Boy told us was that they had been dating a little while but then they broke up. Frankie Boy actually knew the whole story but he didn't go into it, it was a family matter; he found out through his mother who told him not to say anything because of their friendship with the Schrables.

No matter how many dates Antoinette went on, she never could find Mr. Right. When her father had a stroke at 67, he sold the business to his cousin Pietro "Pete. She resolved that she couldn't get married using the excuse that she had to take care of him and her mother. But that didn't stop Antoinette from having another kind of "date"; one that worked out just fine with no excessive commitment. Not a soul in our neighborhood knew about it; not even the Fairy Comaras! It came out in a reading I gave her many years after.

After secretarial school, Frankie Boy got her a full-time job on Wall Street working for a Senior Manager at his securities firm, Fred Manza. She and Fred got along perfectly. When it comes to high maintenance, Italian men are #1 and who better than Antoinette to maintain him. She did everything for Fred, his, calendar, letters, flight arrangements, planned the department's holiday party, got him his morning coffee and bagels, ordered his lunch when he was in the office and made reservations for lunch when he went out with clients. She even picked the gifts he gave to his wife for her birthday, wedding anniversary and Christmas. Fred's wife, Sue, knew she picked them out and always bought the best gifts for Antoinette, of course, from Fred. And, Antoinette did one more thing for Fred.

Every Wednesday they went for a long lunch at the Marriott Hotel. Everyone in her department sort of knew about Antoinette and Fred but they looked the other way. They looked the other way because Antoinette was Antoinette and who could dislike her! She was the kindest person to work with and she helped everyone there with their own work! They only questioned why such a pretty girl with values like that didn't find a husband. Unbelievable that this could go on for almost 20 years but, yes, it did go on for that long. Once a year, they'd travel together to an annual two-day conference in Poughkeepsie to meet upstate New York clients but, other than that it was Wednesday afternoons. When she came to live with me, I didn't have a clue until one of our Thursday evening meetings. This story to be continued because it gets even better.

So, let's get back to the story about Signorine's wake and Antoinette asking to live in the apartment downstairs, As I said I was a little taken aback. "Antoinette, you know who I live next to, right? Esther Schrable. And, I know that you haven't talked to her for over 20 years ever since you and Manny broke up. You'll see her every day; she sits in her backyard sometimes. It's been seven months since she had her hip replacement surgery; she's in a wheelchair. How's living next door going to work for you?" She said, "Of course I know that she lives next to you, but I want to stay in the neighborhood. It's convenient to go to work and please, don't make me move to Staten Island because my brothers want me to move there but if I say you offered me the apartment, I can give the excuse that you were lonely and you needed someone to keep you company." I said, "Keep me company? What am I? 90 years old? I work five days a week and host the Thursday evening meetings, I have a pretty good social life on weekends. Why would you say I'm lonely?" She said, "No, that's what I would tell my brothers." So then Little Marie Greco chimed in, "Diane, now that Signorine is gone, may her soul rest in peace, Antoinette can take care of the guests like Signorine did and you know Antoinette is a good cook; it certainly beats cake and Stella Doro cookies every Thursday. You don't have the time to cook. Look, she wants to remain in the neighborhood, she knows nothing about Staten Island and her sisters-in-laws are home with the kids, what is she going to do over there? And what a long commute she'll have from Timbuktu to Wall Street, she'll be traveling all day!"

So, I said, "Antoinette, you know this is a one-bedroom apartment. Where are you going to put all your stuff from your home?" Antoinette said she promised to give most of the furniture to her cousin Edouardo, "Eddie", for his new home in Bay Shore and Bennie Fiore is getting the Dining Room set. Her sisters-in-law had their own modern furniture layout and it wouldn't match. All I'm saving is the kitchen and Living Room set and my bedroom furniture. I said, "then, I have no problem with you renting the apartment. But I warn you not to stir up any trouble with Esther. She just had hip surgery and the surgery didn't go as well as expected so she's in a wheelchair. To be honest, she looks like she's in a fog half the time anyway." She said, "well, like the priest tells us, you have to forgive and forget like Christ. I have no problem being cordial." (Yeah, right!)

Antoinette and her brothers got their one-third share of the money from the sale of the house; Frankie Boy gave her a little more than a third because she was unmarried. God bless, he really didn't need the money. Frankie Boy always had a big heart; that's why he was always shoveling everybody's property. Antoinette also gave her sisters-in-laws one piece of jewelry from her mother's collection out of the goodness of her heart. However, she'd never part with the gold cross and chain her father gave to her mother; the gold cross with the diamond in the middle. Her mother loved that cross! Carmela wore it only on special occasions like weddings and Christmas. She gave Frankie Boy her father's watch which he still wears today and to Emil, her father's cross and gold chain and his tie clip.

So, back to Antoinette moving in; after hearing the WHOLE story from Antoinette, I told her she could move in and I warned her again about Esther. I told her I didn't need those negative vibes in the house, it inhibited my readings. Two weeks after we buried Signorine, she moved in and she moved in with more than she said she had but, she managed to find a place for it, even her Barbies, including the Barbie and Ken car. She never gave them away; can you believe it? Probably some of you still have them, too! She asked Tony Slice if he would put up wooden shelves for the Barbies and he picked out a nice one, no charge. Tony Slice told me, "When my mother was in the hospital for her bypass, Antoinette was a volunteer on her floor. She visited my mother every day, it was the highlight of my mother's day when she came over because she would bring her cookies and something to read; she gave my mother a get-well card signed by all the people in the neighborhood. She'd sit with my mother and let her know what was going on with this one and that one and my mother started to get the color back in her cheeks again. When me or my sister would come to visit at night, it was Antoinette did this and Antoinette told me this and Antoinette brought Father Giudice from St. Agatha's to pray with her yesterday and now I'm feeling better!" He's never even think to charge her for the shelves, it would be mala faccia, not good.

In fact, he even put a new carpet in the bedroom for her, no charge, only the cost of the carpet. I also think he had a crush on her when they were kids but, Antoinette's eyes were only for Manny. Tony Slice got married to a nice girl he met at work, we all went to the wedding but, she didn't seem like she could be one of us; she lived in the Bronx. After that, the only time we saw Tony Slice was when he had a job in the neighborhood, a wedding, or at a funeral.

By the way, his name wasn't Tony Slice, it was Anthony Fiore but we all called him that because he was always trying to lose weight and when we'd ask him if he wanted a piece of cake, he'd say "just a small slice" or "just a slice" if it was pizza. It did no good because he was always chunky. He'd go home, his mother would put the conveyor belt to his mouth and he'd eat like there was no tomorrow. There was no such thing as just a slice in the Fiore home which is why his mother had to have the bypass surgery. He's doing fine; I get a Christmas family photo card from him every year. I think he lives in White Plains now.

Antoinette moved into my downstairs apartment on October 30th when the Autumn chill and leaves swirling weather arrived. In the beginning, Antoinette's interaction with Esther was almost next to nothing except when the warmer weather came; Esther's aid, Gladys, would wheel Esther into the backyard for some fresh air. Upon moving in, Antoinette volunteered to close up my yard and cover the fig tree my Grandpa Joe planted; Signorine loved and cared for that fig tree! There were so many things to do in the apartment, she barely had time to put up her Halloween decorations and make Trick or Treat bags for the neighborhood kids.

Let me tell you that our Thursday evening meeting crowd got bigger when everyone heard that Antoinette was cooking! Good Bye Stella Doro breakfast treats! She made pigs in the blanket, stuffed shells, eggplant parmigiana, Thomas' English muffin pizzas, I love them! She even made little calzones one night. Add to that, that she served cake and Italian cookies from Agnello's Bakery and made espresso for those who didn't want coffee or tea, can you imagine? Our guests purposely would not eat their own dinner on Thursday nights because of Antoinette's "snacks".

And, she was able to connect with all our friends and listen to their stories which to be honest, I hadn't the patience for, even to this day. I'd ask for the Reader's Digest version from Antoinette. She'd look at all the photos of babies, children, grandchildren and weddings each lady took out of their purses, all 200 of them on any given Thursday! She also listened to their heartache stories as well. It was the heartache stories that made her a Fairy Comara; the many people she helped in the past that made life manageable for them.

Like when Mrs. Maresca's daughter, Rosemarie, needed back surgery. The doctor told her if she didn't get the surgery, she would be in a wheelchair by the time she was 25. Mrs. Maresca couldn't afford the cost of the surgery, $5,000, on her salary as a school cafeteria lady. Mrs. Maresca's "husband" never appeared, at least no one had ever seen him, so it was understood that there was never a Mr. Maresca; that might have been her maiden name, who knows. No one talked about it and that's the way it was in those days. We had a few such single mothers in the neighborhood, it was none of our business. And even if it was our business, who wouldn't want to help a sick child?

Antoinette started a Maresca money drive and made the rounds around the neighborhood for donations for Rosemarie's surgery, without Mrs. Maresca knowing it. I think now they have Go Fund Me online. She raised $ 3,500 between making her rounds and sneaking around Mrs. Maresca on Thursday evenings. When Black Marie told her uncle, Big Jimmy about it, the club made up the difference of $1,500. At the next Thursday evening meeting, Antoinette told the crowd coming in about Nancy Maresca, her daughter Rosemarie's surgery and there was going to be a raffle tonight so she could win. "No charge, just put Nancy Maresca's name on these tiny slips of paper in the hat. Only one per person" I hope Antoinette was joking about the one per person rule! So, everybody put Nancy's name in the hat and near the end of the meeting, Antoinette announced the winner of the raffle. She pulled a piece of paper out the hat and said, "Nancy Maresca!" Nancy was so excited to win anything, she was happy already. And then Antoinette opened up the envelope containing the secret prize, she told her it was $5,000".

The floodgates opened and Nancy just sat there and cried. She thanked the Blessed Mother first, again we get no credit, and then all of us for having the raffle. In her mind, only the Blessed Mother could have made this wonderful miracle happen. Antoinette told Nancy the raffle was $1; she wanted to buy five tickets but, she told her only one per person because she wanted to give everyone a chance to win. She believed it. Maybe later on, Nancy figured it out but, she never let on. Her daughter, Rosemarie, got the surgery and became a nurse. She later helped Antoinette in another situation involving her cousin

Eddie when he had to have emergency surgery but, I'm getting ahead of myself.

And then there was the time that Black Marie broke her arm and couldn't help her father cook for the Christmas holiday crowd at the restaurant. Antoinette stood in for her and helped with the Friday and Saturday night dinner crowd, no charge. Black Marie told me her father wanted Antoinette to come work for him she cooked so well. When Carmela got sick and couldn't shop on her own, Black Marie's father would see Antoinette walking home from work and he'd give her a platter of some hot food, for her and her mother, just so she wouldn't have to cook. When Antoinette moved in with me, Black Marie's father sent over a tray of cold cuts for one of the Thursday meetings, no charge.

One Thursday evening, Antoinette was talking to Little Marie Greco's mother, Rose DiFillipo, 4'11", another one who always wore a little heel. She asked Antoinette, "Have you seen Jim the Drunk lately? He looks like he's been in a fight". Everybody on the block knew Jim the Drunk; he was the neighborhood drunk and we took care of him. Why? Because he was a veteran. We didn't know anything about PSTD back then, if a guy came back a little off kilter, we used to say he was shell-shocked. Jim probably never went to the VA because back then, they would just see an alcoholic not the mental part; PSTD was not considered a mental disorder. He smelled like shit and occasionally one of our mothers would bring him some clothes and take him to the baths on 4th Ave. He never harmed a soul except himself.

Rose told her that one of the teenage gangs in the neighborhood were strutting around the other day with nothing to do; when they saw Jim huddled in an empty storefront, drunk as a skunk, they decided to rough him up a little. This was no harmless gang and everyone in the neighborhood was afraid to interfere for fear of them taking revenge on their families. When Rose Di Fillipo approached Antoinette about Jim the Drunk, she had to find out more. Rose told her that she heard from Joe Turco who owned the pharmacy on the corner of 4th Ave, that the boys were kicking Jim while he was sleeping one off in the front door of an empty storefront across the street. He didn't see anything more because a customer came to get his prescription. When the customer left, Joe looked across the street and there were no boys and no Jim. And then, later on, Jim's walking on 4th Ave all banged up, he could barely stand and he wasn't drunk. Joe helped him inside and cleaned and bandaged up his wounds; he bought him a coffee from the diner across the street and slipped him a few dollars. That's all Rose knew.

Captain Doyle had officers watching 4th Ave because that's where these gangs mostly hung out but, unless they had an eye witness to their crimes, they couldn't arrest them. And, nobody would come forth because they remembered what the gang did to Old Sam. Old Sam witnessed one of the gang members stealing a 6-pack of beer from Dilbert's Supermarket and he told the police what happened. One of the gang members must have been within an earshot of Sam telling the cops in the patrol car.

Old Sam used to leave the empty wooden crates outside at night in front of the store so he could set up the fruits and vegetables faster in the morning. A few days later, at midnight, they set fire to Old Sam's store by setting fire to the crates. Sam, his wife and his son were saved by Jim the Drunk who happened to be stumbling through our block. At first, we all thought he was drunk when he was yelling "fire!" but then, we looked out the window and saw the blaze. The front door was on fire so Jim pulled the awning down and Sam, his wife and son slid down the awning with Jim catching them, one by one. The Fire Department came and contained the fire and no one was hurt. Old Sam didn't go down to the precinct to make a report. From then on, he became blind to anything that was going on in the neighborhood. But he always gave Jim some bananas or apples, maybe a dollar or two, whenever he passed by.

Back to the story, so when Antoinette heard about Jim the Drunk getting beat up, she went to St. Agatha's rectory and told Father Giudice about it. Father Giudice was close to Jim; both of them were veterans. Sometimes, he would let him sleep inside the church if it was too cold outside or give him some warm clothing from the donated clothes the church collected. When he was sober, Jim actually went to church to pray and one time he asked Father Giudice to contact his sister in New Jersey. He gave him her phone number; Jim said he tried to call about 15 years ago but, she hung up. Jim hadn't spoken to his sister since then.

According to Antoinette, Father Giudice told her that Jim told him the reason she hung up. He had what we would now call a meltdown, on Thanksgiving, at his sister's home in New Jersey. His brother-in-law threw him out and forbid him in their home. He was also starting to drink heavily. His sister tried to get him help but he refused it and after that, she wanted nothing to do with him. Somehow, Jim landed in Brooklyn; after that, he had no contact with her. Antoinette asked Father Giudice to call his sister; maybe time heals all wounds. Father Giudice did call his sister and she cried because she thought Jim could never forgive her for abandoning him. She told Father Giudice if he wanted to come home, it was okay because her son left for college and she wound up getting a divorce from her unfaithful husband last year. He could come stay with her, she had a guest room. She would take care of him and get him the help that he needed; the VA Hospital was two blocks away from where she lived. When Antoinette heard all of this, she decided to take matters into her own hands. She asked Father Giudice to come with her down to the club to talk with Big Jimmy about Jim the Drunk.

Big Jimmy knew Jim the Drunk because he used to run some "errands" for him. He collected the football sheets and money from people in the neighborhood;

he never took a dollar from those football sheets. Big Jimmy would slip him $50 a week to do this and other errands. This was the height of the football sheet season and he was looking for Jim the Drunk to make the collection. Antoinette told him that the gang on 4th Avenue beat Jim up because they thought he had the money from the football sheets and Jim was afraid to come into the neighborhood. Jim wasn't afraid to come into the neighborhood, he always was so drunk; he had no fear when he was drunk. Antoinette didn't know if the gang beat him up because they thought he had the football sheet money but, she stretched the truth as much as the truth could be stretched. You have to respect the urgency of this matter. Big Jimmy told Antoinette and Father Giudice that he would take care of it.

According to Captain Doyle, who told Little Marie, who told Antoinette, the strangest thing happened at the precinct. Two days later, Frank Forni from Big Jimmy's club comes in with three of the gang members all with bruises on their faces barely standing up and Frank said he witnessed them trying to rob a woman's purse on 5th Ave. No one questioned why it would take three boys to rob one woman; the gang members admitted their guilt because they wouldn't live long if they didn't confess. Frank said he was a witness. Whoever was left of the gang disbanded out of fear because they knew Frank Forni didn't fool around. Unlikely witness that Frank was, Captain Doyle took the report anyway and the boys were locked up. Big Jimmy got his football sheets and errands done and Jim the Drunk could go back to being, well, Jim the Drunk. For taking care of Jim, Father Giudice got a nice donation from Big Jimmy's club to buy uniforms for St. Agatha's new football team, and he announced their donation at the weekly bingo game. But that wasn't enough for Antoinette.

Now that, that problem was solved, she started to work on getting Jim in contact with his sister. But first, she was going to contact her herself. The first phone call with Jim's sister, her name was Bridget, was emotional and Antoinette told me his sister was crying and full of guilt for listening to her husband. Blood should always be thicker than water and now she felt that Jim would never forgive her. Antoinette asked her if her offer to bring Jim home was still on the table and she said YES! Antoinette realized that she couldn't do this all at once so she waited for the day after Thanksgiving. The week before she sent a money order to his sister so she could buy him a decent set of clothes to keep at her house. She also wanted to give Bridget money for train tickets to come to Brooklyn but, Bridget said it wasn't necessary. Bridget drove but was afraid to drive into the city. Next, she invited Jim the Drunk and Father Giudice for dinner and cocktails the Friday after Thanksgiving. The mention of cocktails was enough to persuade Jim to come over. And now the stage was set.

Friday after Thanksgiving, Father Giudice took Jim to the baths and then to the barber shop to get a haircut and a shave. He pulled out a nice shirt and pants, even a tie from the clothing drive and gave it to Jim. They arrived at Antoinette's apartment, bottle of wine in Jim's hand from the both of them. And, after the initial drinks had been imbibed, she announced that dinner was ready. When all three of them were seated, Antoinette blurts out, "Oh, I forgot to tell you, I invited one more guest to dinner." Jim by that point was so distracted by the smell of the food, he already started eating like there was no tomorrow. We're not sure if he actually heard her. Antoinette went into the kitchen and she comes out with his sister, Bridget. Antoinette and Father Giudice were tense; which way was this going to go? Please God, no meltdown!

It turned out to be a pretty good idea on Antoinette's part, thank God! The minute Jim noticed Bridget, he put down his fork, got up from his chair and asked his sister to forgive him. Bridget said, "Forgive you? please forgive me!" and from that point on, you needed a wet vac to dry up all the tears. Antoinette cried and Father Giudice got misty and then they hugged them and they all sat down to eat. Do you know, for the rest of the evening, Jim didn't touch a drop of alcohol! He still drank the next day but, not as much; he had to collect the football sheets for Big Jimmy so he had to be sober for at least part the day. Bridget asked him to come live with her and he said yes, he would like that but, what about her husband? So, yada, yada, yada Bridget told him about the divorce and the nephew in college which made Jim proud of his nephew. She would look after him from now on and get him the care he needs at the VA.

Through the tears he said yes because he came to the realization that he needed help and that's the first step to recovery. So, on Saturday, Antoinette and Black Marie went down to the club to talk with Big Jimmy. By the way, there was never another guy named Jimmy in the club so we don't know why they called him Big Jimmy. There was more than one Frank in the club; Frank Forni and Frankie Giancarlo but no Jimmys. Maybe, it was the obvious, that he was overweight but, most of the guys at the club were overweight, too, so we'll never know. She told him all about the dinner, the sister in New Jersey, and his sister wanting him to come back home.

Big Jimmy made a deal with Antoinette; let Jimmy finish the football season until the Super Bowl and then he could go with his blessing. He told her by next football season he should be able to find another guy to do the sheets and he had other people to run his errands already. He just gave Jim the Drunk the job to earn a few bucks. When he left us, after the Super Bowl, his clothes and shoes were paid for by a donation from the Thursday Evening Meeting Club, a duffel bag donated by Agnello's Bakery filled with underwear and socks, and car service supplied by Big Jimmy and off he went to New Jersey to live with his sister. Before he left, he thanked and hugged Antoinette and Father Giudice and most of all, he thanked God for giving him his life back.

Antoinette kept in contact with Bridget for a couple of years and they exchanged Christmas cards. Jim joined the AA meetings near his sister's, he got some meds from the VA but didn't like the way it made him feel. He really didn't need them because he got a job at Home Depot through AA and, most of all, he had his family back. Many years later, Bridget and Jim paid a visit to me and Antoinette. This was later, after Big Jimmy passed away; I think it was only me and Antoinette still living in the neighborhood. He wasn't well, we could tell, but he was happy to see us. His sister said he had cirrhosis and some heart problems going on, but he was under a doctor's care at the VA. In an emotional moment that I'll never forget, Jim stood up from the table as we were having coffee and Entenmann's Cheese Danish, I remember it down to the cake!

Anyway, Jim stood up, took a crumpled piece of paper out of his pants pocket and read it out loud. "Antoinette, I am here today to thank you for pulling me out of the gutter. You saved my life. Why you picked me out of everyone in this neighborhood, God is the only one who knows. You saw something in me that I didn't see for many years. I have given up drinking because of you, you re-united me with my dear sister, Bridget, who spoils me rotten. I'm now able to enjoy football games with my nephew; he even taught me how to drive a motorcycle!" For which Bridget interjected, "I wasn't for it" and we all looked at Jim with the BE CAREFUL look. Jim continued, "I wish I could thank Big Jimmy for giving me all those breaks" he looks up to heaven, "Jimmy, there were times when I took a dollar or two for liquor and, I think you knew it, but felt sorry for me. And thanks to all the guys I knew during the war that didn't make it for saving my life; please put in a good word about me with the Big Guy until we meet again." Jim was never a crier but he got misty and we all had tears in our eyes.

About two or three years after Jim's departure, Father Giudice became Bishop Giudice and was transferred to a different parish. Just as I was about to clear the table with Antoinette, the bell rings. And who was at the front door but, Bishop Giudice. Antoinette knew he was coming but said nothing. Jim leaped up from the table and hugged him so hard the bishop jokingly told him was going to crack his ribs. He blessed Jim before he and Bridget went home and gave him the same rosary he used when he was praying for him those many years ago. Later, Bridget told us that Jim rehearsed what he was going to say to us for two days.

As I said, Bridget sent Antoinette a Christmas card every year with a short note telling her what they were up to, family stuff. The last Christmas card she received was from Jim about 2-3 years ago. He wrote that Bridget passed away during the summer; she suffered a stroke in May and then another more fatal one two months later. He told Antoinette that he was going to sell the house and move in with his nephew's family after the holidays and he would send her his new address. He never sent his new address so we never heard from Jim after that; my psychic intuition is Jim probably died shortly after to join his sister. We all thought he would go first. I'm glad our vets are getting the needed care for PSTD; they deserve everything for their service to this country.

Once a month, sometimes twice, we'd have a lecture. Sometimes I would give a lecture or Little Marie Greco would give a lecture on senior care or one of the other ladies would speak about something of interest to us all. Even Signorine gave a lecture, of course translated by Rose Di Fillipo, on how to tell the difference between a well-made garment and a cheap one even though the cheap garment may cost a lot. FYI, it's all in the stitching! Now, everything is made cheap as far as I'm concerned; I wish I could buy something that says Made in the USA for a change. I have a sweater I bought over 30 years ago, USA made, button only came off once and no holes. We make good stuff.

Anyway, my lectures were based on psychic readings I gave where I saw a pattern or repetition of a similar problem; sometimes the lectures were on how to avoid relationship pitfalls or they were about financial tips because I worked at a bank.

We also had outside people come to speak like Captain Doyle on preventing burglaries and self-defense. We had Joe Turco's son, a lawyer, come in and talk about making a will, Frank Ciccone from Ciccone Insurance talked about securing inexpensive life insurance and the current funeral costs which many of us didn't realize cost so much. We even had one of the Torregrosso brothers talk about a lay-away plan for your funeral from wake to burial. It was good for us because who had time to read pamphlets with everything going on and the guys who came to speak knew that we always had a large crowd.

My lectures, on the other hand, were not so professional; they were based on whatever subject or what issue came up repeatedly in the last six or seven months and needed to be addressed. I was labeled "the unpopular psychic"; you were either very pleased or you hated my readings because of what I had to say which you knew to be true. People came away with a smile or a frown. So rather than specifically dealing with a problem on a person-to-person basis, I'd give a lecture in the form of an allegory or dramatic statement such as:

Thursday Evening, May 18, 1989 Lecturer: Diane Santangelo, The Unpopular Psychic

A Man is the Purse to an Already Accessorized Outfit

I told all the ladies to take out their purses and put it on their lap. By then, everyone had eaten so, they were all ready for the lecture and talked out with each other. You could always tell who was single in the room because they usually had a small purse; the Chanel mock-ups with the chain shoulder strap or with just a big zippered wallet. The married women on the other hand, had the big hobo bags or the bags that looked like mini briefcases. Their bags had to be big because they held things for work and home and maybe a sandwich for work. So, anyway, I told them to give a good look inside their bags, maybe take a few things out if you couldn't see the inside too well. And then I began...

"I would probably say most of you purchased that bag based on a set of criteria: first, the look of it, if it was a leather bag, which I see most of you have, the leather has to have a certain feel to it. Is the leather stiff or is it stiff in the beginning and will becomes comfortable as time goes by? Second, you looked inside this purse to see if it could fit everything you carried; a wallet, keys, your work lanyard, your small purse for your tokens (no Metro Cards then), your make-up, and depending on how much you have to do during the day, a list of the things you have to get done. Third, you looked for how many pockets it has; do some of the pockets have zippers to keep your keys from falling out or important papers you don't want to lose or maybe change if you had to take the bus? Fourth, can this purse match with most of my outfits or is it a one-time deal purse?"

"A purse without pockets may look good but, you'll never find anything inside it. You'll have to rummage through, maybe feel around for the shape of the thing you're looking for; it's a mess and you'll tire of that purse and put it in the closet. Only LaBorsa or Boosta' bags have no pockets because the couple are just starting out. Later on, the pockets will come".

For those who don't know or have never been to an Italian wedding, the La Borsa "boosta" bag is a white satin bag the bride carries for guests to either drop our cards filled with money, when the bride and groom visit each table or we bring it to the bride and groom at their table as we are leaving. We all did it and I think we still do it now; Italians didn't bring a gift, gift back then. Now, when one of the Fairy Comaras' grandchildren gets married, they tell me to go online for their wedding registry; I'm not having any of that, let them take my money and go buy it themselves.

"All you ladies, take a good look inside your purse." Rose Di Fillipo asked if the partition inside the purse counted as a pocket? I told her only if it has a zipper. Gina Leone, she wasn't married then, asked me if we counted the outside pockets, I said, "of course! Those are the pockets we use for our outside life whether it be work, subway tokens, badge to get in the building, ladies room key. But, make sure the pocket is not bulging because that could be a problem; it means family and work are not getting equal attention. If you're at a job that has your pockets bulging inside and outside of the purse, it's time to leave. The shape of the purse will look shitty and you'll look like shit as well. Your job is taking up space inside the purse and you won't be able to fit your needs and the needs of your family into the inside pockets."

I said, "The title of this lecture is, A Man is the Purse to an Already Accessorized Outfit and, I can already see by the look on some of your faces what you're thinking, "Diane, my husband means more to me than a purse! What is this? Is this going to be a Women's Lib issue?" I said "No, this is going to be a lecture about picking the right guy and maintaining a good marriage. A few of you have spoken to me about your own relationships and I thought that this analogy would help you to make good relationship decisions and be content with who you are."

"First of all, your purse is an important part of your everyday life, it is no trivial thing. So don't give me that look like I'm pazza (crazy). Some of you may change your purse to go with your outfit but ultimately each purse must supply the support you need to carry on day-to-day. You are frantic if you can't find your purse at home or in the office. Your life would stand still if you couldn't find it, so don't tell me the importance of comparing a purse to a man is a trivial comparison. As your life progresses, that purse contains your whole life up until the present. If you lost or someone robbed your purse, you'd be a total basket case, it's like losing your identity. Your wallet alone contains all your identification, and the photos of your family, maybe your driver's license, doctor's numbers to call when you're out of the house or working, your purse contains train tokens for the week, important lists of things you have to get done, and all the things you'd have to do for your husband because he has only two or three pockets, am I right or wrong?"

"When you first meet a guy, the first thing you look at is how he looks, just like a purse. You look him over and you start to chat. Is he a tough leather purse or a soft one; you need to get a feel for what kind of a guy he is first. If it's tough leather, do you think it will soften? Does the purse have a sturdy handle, in other words, does he have a good job? That's important because the purse has to contain your stuff and his and you don't want it to snap off one day; you need a sturdy handle to hold all the stuff or else the purse is useless. It's even better if the purse has a sturdy handle and a sturdy shoulder strap; he may be in a low-level job but he's going to school or he's learning a trade. Is he family oriented? Does his family come from a long line of sturdy handles? Is the leather cheap? Does he like to go Dutch on dates? As we all know, cheap leather doesn't last long no matter how good it looks at the cashier. More importantly, is this a purse you can be comfortable with? Can you see yourself walking every day with this purse or is it that you picked this purse just for show but not for go? Looks fade but, personalities either get worse or they get better; if that purse was uncomfortable from the very beginning, the odds are it'll get worse. Purses for show become purses that go… once the LUST-er is over, you're stuck with a lousy purse that you can't imagine why you bought it to begin with."

"Ladies, look inside your purses! how many pockets does it have inside?

The one who had the most pockets was Black Marie's mother, Livia. Most of the ladies had three or four pockets. She had about 10 pockets inside; some of them were on the outside of her purse. It looked more like a duffel bag but, she needed every pocket because she had to carry a lot of stuff; her and her husband's medications, receipts from the restaurant (their business) and all the telephone numbers on little slips of paper for emergency calls. Black Marie told everyone that she bought her mother about seven or eight little black address books so she could organize all the family telephone numbers but, Livia said she didn't have the time. The house, the kids, medications and the restaurant (the Santorini's business) had to go in one purse. I lifted her purse, Madonna ! it weighed a ton. If that purse ever got stolen, I pity the guy who stole it, he'd get a hernia! Livia told me she bought this purse about 22 years ago, in Martin's Dept. Store, on sale. If this purse represents her husband, she'll keep it for another 22 years! She loved her old bag! You had to laugh.

Not to change the subject, but we always liked when Livia came to the meetings. She always brought delicious food from the restaurant. And, the chicken parmigiana was to die for! She made the sauce herself for every entrée at the restaurant, no Ragu! Their restaurant was always packed on Friday and Saturday nights. They worked their fingers to the bone from just a pizzeria to a full-fledged restaurant, God bless them.

"How many pockets are devoted to just your stuff?" Most of them said the zippered or deep pockets because it held their house and/or car keys, their eyeglasses, maybe a lipstick or a pack of cigarettes. Mary Fusco's daughter, Lisa, asked "what if the leather is tough and you go to the shoemaker and get it softened, does that count?" And I said to myself, there always has to be a smart ass. But I said out loud, "Lisa, you thinking of sending your husband to a masseuse, he might like that! Everybody laughed. "Lisa, just don't buy the purse to begin with!" Women have that urge to be fixers but, you can't fix something that thinks it doesn't have to be fixed. "If you picked a tough leather purse, you can bring it to the shoemaker every week, wear it every day, even stomp on it, it will still will be rough. Who keeps a purse like that for long? Maybe somebody who thinks she'll never find another purse to match her outfit? Maybe. Can you imagine that rough purse banging against you every single day; maybe you'll keep it for a year so you don't have that much buyer's remorse. But ultimately, you'll either trash it or give it away to the church."

"If you picked a purse with very little pockets, you can't add an additional pocket. So, you either stick with that purse (stay married) or you decide to donate it to the church poor box (and get divorced). In a way, I pity the next poor woman who gets that purse because she is going to wind up getting rid of it herself. It will be an uncomfortable purse no matter who owns it."

Barbara Ciccone, funny lady, asked me if her purse has a gold chain interwoven in her shoulder strap does that mean she's looking for a wealthy man? Back then, the popular purse was the Chanel style purses with the quilted leather design with a gold chain interwoven around a leather strap. No one could afford Chanel but, we improvised. I told her, "Those chains are gold plated so watch out." And then Signorine got up from the recliner to go to the bathroom and as she's leaving, she said something in Italian to Rose Di Fillipo. Rose translated, "what good is the money? There are no pockets on nightgowns." And we all had to think about it for a minute because we had never heard it explained that way.

When Signorine came back, she told Rose she put another pot of coffee on the stove because this was going to be a long lecture. Ou fa! She never was awake for the end anyway! Sometimes we left her on the recliner and just threw a blanket over her. When she woke up, she'd go down to her apartment or clean up the already cleaned kitchen with Clorox. I remember getting up on Friday mornings with the smell of Clorox in my nostrils until I got to work. In the 50's 60's all the women in our neighborhood used Clorox, we even had a man deliver it to our house; they didn't have the Clorox label, they used to call it "giavellotto" or Giavell water. The Giavell man would come every two weeks, collect the empty gallon and give you a new one. Our mothers used a lot of Giavell; everybody's house smelled the same. Anyway, I proceeded to talk about pockets.

"Every purse should have more than one or two pockets, meaning that the man you select to spend your life with should always be a source of love and support; love for you and love for his family. How do you know he'll be this way? By the number of pockets he already has in his life. I'm not saying he wears a purse; I'm just saying it figuratively. Does he have a pocket for his parents, his friends, his dog, his sisters and brothers. Are those pockets small? That's a factor. Small pockets don't hold much and are usually the first to tear in the purse. Or are they deep enough to hold many things. Does he have a zippered pocket of his own? Does it hold his keys, his work stuff or does it hold many secrets?

You know damn well that your purse holds your whole life in it. Figuratively speaking, the number and depth of the pockets in your purse carry the stability in your life. Even if you change purses, most of the time, you'll put the same stuff in another purse with the same number of pockets. The man in your life should have deep pockets; be able to be a loving and supportive partner. Can you depend on his pockets or do they rip or tear from use right away? A purse with one pocket is not going to make you content either. To run a household, take care of children maintenance details, fix stuff, pay bills, run errands; you're going to need more than one, two, three or more pockets! But remember, pockets wear out when you constantly put heavy items like your keys and change in the same spot. Make sure that you have pockets of your own to hold the things you have to do in life. Leave his pockets alone! For example, if you're going to school at night. Does he have pockets to take care of the kids while you're trying to improve yourself, perhaps, leading to a better paying job? Don't overload your pockets to make room for his stuff. He has his own things to do! If you're doing everything in the house and all your pockets are full to capacity this becomes a losing relationship."

"You can only pick out a good purse if your outfit is in order. In other words, you have to have your shit together in order to pick a good purse. Your outfit projects who you are and how well you are put together. If your outfit looks like it was put together running from a burning building, then, maybe it's time to take a good look at yourself. That outfit has to look good and most of all, feel good in order for you to select the right purse." Everyone groaned when I said child maintenance details because only a childless woman like me could coin a phrase like that... child maintenance, how sterile!

"A mother should have the title of CCMO, Chief Child Maintenance Officer attached to the end of their name. Everybody liked that title.

"So, while the purse itself may be perfect for your outfit, don't buy it unless you check how many pockets it has and how that pocket will conform to the wear and tear of your everyday lives. And, most of all, that purse should never hurt you; if you're carrying around a purse that always digs you in the side or causes your shoulders to hurt from carrying it, it's time to change purses no matter how good it matches your outfit."

And then I started to talk a little more about the outfit because the outfit is everything.

"I know some of you girls pick a black purse for everyday but, that doesn't mean you wear black; it's not primarily important what color your outfit is; your outfit has to fit and look good for you to start your day. It's your outward projection to the world. How that outfit makes you look and feel is fundamental to selecting your purse. Always select an outfit that compliments who you are and is comfortable; just because someone else's outfit looks good on her doesn't mean it's going to look good on you. Ill-fitting outfits never look or feel good on the wearer; you can hardly wait to get home and tear it off so you can be yourself. Whatever you choose, make sure you are always comfortable in that outfit. Doesn't matter if you wear traditional clothes or the latest fashion, if you're thin or plus size (in the 80s and 90s we said fat, not nice, but we did say it that way), you, the person, must project out. When you project your true self outward, you'll always carry the right purse because that purse is part of who you are. If you are a flamboyant personality then be flamboyant, it will be your calling card to a man that can appreciate you. Sometimes, a flamboyant purse can make you loosen up and start picking the right outfit for you! But it doesn't happen that often. Even if you have to go to work in a suit and heels every day, you can accentuate that outfit with a crazy brooch or some cutesy bracelets or earrings just to remind yourself of who you are when you're putting on lipstick in the Ladies restroom."

"A purse will find you and know what kind of outfit he wants to be walking with just because you gave him a sneak peek through the little flamboyant touches you add on. Once you know who YOU are, a good relationship will follow because you'll accept nothing less. Your outfit, if it's comfortable, will always be matched to the right purse with enough pockets. And by the way, if your purse looks a little disheveled, maybe there's a wayward string hanging out, maybe some of the zippered pockets are hard to open when you first buy it doesn't mean the purse is no good. I've seen many a good-looking purse start to break down after the first year and purses that seemed a little rough around the edges have lasted for years. It's all about the pockets! But, first and foremost, it's about the outfit. "

I thought this analogy of the purse would really do the trick but, it didn't. The following Thursday was readings night. They would all come in and show me how many pockets were in their purses but they're love lives were still shitty. Maybe it had to do with their outfit, did they think about that? Antoinette asked me a question which I thought odd, "What if you're always wearing the same outfit when looking for a purse?" At first, I thought she was asking because blue was her favorite color. I said, "Well, if you're a police officer, soldier, nurse then I can see wearing the same-colored outfit every day. You may like a certain color but, the comfort of the outfit is what it's all about." And then she said, "What if the purse is shared?" I wanted to ask her to elaborate on her question but, the ladies started to exit and the food had to be cleared so Antoinette was busy saying goodbye to everyone and I was folding up the chairs.

Even if you weren't getting a reading from me, you came for Antoinette's food and the conversation. You came for the conversation, to take a break from being the General in your household managing everything and everybody; you got to put your purse down and take a breather. You could be YOU at our meetings. And after a couple of glasses of wine, the real you came out and then, the laughs. How I miss the laughs, the hugs and everybody chatting at the same time with one another. If the President of the United States was making a surprise visit to your house on a Thursday evening, you'd drag him to our meetings rather than stay home. As each meeting ended, we'd hear "See you next Thursday!" As the neighbors started to move out, it would be "see you next month" then twice a year. The new neighbors weren't into Thursday meetings, they kept to themselves. Some of them did come to one or two meetings but, they didn't live in the neighborhood long. We never heard from them again. But I digress…

Back to the purse. I had a lot of women who came to me with purse problems. If they were married, we tried to find some pocket alternatives to their existing purse. If they were single, I just told them to get another purse. Some listened, some didn't, and then they came to me with married purse problems. For example, Mary Anzalone came to me for a reading with a purse problem when she was single. Her problem was that her purse belonged to another women, his wife. Mary's purse also had another girlfriend that, according to Mary, he only saw because he had a child with her. It would seem that this purse had a lot of pockets but the pockets were only for him and nobody else. I told her that she had to let the purse go because it didn't belong to her. It didn't match her outfit because it was a purse that was coordinated with another outfit. Supposedly, the other girlfriend was borrowing the purse so he could be a father to their child. Mary said he was not in love with this woman, he only wanted to see his child, which I thought was total bullshit.

I told Mary that she was meant to have her own purse; women generally do not share their purses with other women. So, we went over what she needed to do and I told her that the perfect purse was just around the corner if she put on the right outfit first before looking for a purse. I normally give a 30-minute reading but for her, she needed 15 minutes more because I had to explain the purse and the outfit over and over again. After all of this, as she's about to leave the room, she says to me "but do you think he likes me best?" and I showed her the door and told her to enjoy the food.

After the meeting ended and we started to clean up, I condensed the details of

Mary Anzalone's story to Antoinette and told her it was a secret and she got all flustered when I mentioned that the guy was married. Irish Marie came over to us and said, "By the way, I may have the perfect guy for you, Antoinette. Brian works with him, Mike Cardone." But, Antoinette, being ever faithful to her illicit arrangement with her boss told Irish Marie about Mary Anzalone. Some secret! It all turned out well in the end. It just so happened that Irish Marie found the right purse for Mary. Mike Cardone just ended a relationship that lasted a few years; he was just getting back on the saddle and was a little shy. Irish Marie knew Mary Anzalone since Mary was a kid so it was not unusual to invite her to dinner on a Friday night. Brian invited Mike, saying he was having a gathering; meanwhile, it was only the four of them.

Meanwhile, Mary Anzalone was still wondering if her purse liked her better, the purse that belonged to another woman also used by yet another woman, so she didn't take Mike and the dinner too seriously. She was still wondering if I could be wrong about her purse. However, Mike thought she was likeable and he asked her if she would like to go to dinner and a movie the following Saturday. She said yes thinking that he'll probably cancel during the week, she had dates cancel in the past. It turned out they had a lot in common; maybe she could have her own purse after all! So, long story short, they went on another date, thunderbolt still didn't hit yet although, her interest was piqued. And then, lo and behold, she realized that this could be the purse to match her outfit and a month later, she called the other purse to tell him to take a long walk on a short pier. Mike and Mary got married about 13 months later. So now she's Mary Cardone. And, she is very happy with her purse with the many pockets. I still get Christmas cards from her; her two daughters are all grown up now; I think one of them graduated college and is already working. Some of us went to the Cardone's 25th Anniversary Party five or six years ago; they both were fattened up and content. I asked Mary if she knew what happened to that other used purse but, she said she only heard that he got divorced and was on Wife #2 but, she had no contact with him for over 26 years. Thank you, Fairy Comara Irish Marie! Thank you, God, for Mike Cardone.

Occasionally, we'd have some not so traditional people come to the Thursday meetings like Sonny Bustamanno. During the day, he worked as a window dresser for Century 21 in Brooklyn but, at night he was Stephanie. Back then we used to call them transvestites but, I guess a better term would be what we use now, transgender. If one of us girls saw a purse or a coat we liked in Century 21, we'd tell Sonny and he'd get the 25% employee discount for us. Sonny worked two jobs so his mother could get the best treatment when she got breast cancer; they're making great strides today to eradicate this cancer but, back then chemo and radiation were the only treatments and many of us could not afford the expensive treatments or what we call now, the co-pay.

Sonny made sure she got the treatments and the home care through Little Marie Greco when he worked during the week. Unfortunately, it didn't work for Sonny's mother and she passed away at 59. Whether he was Sonny or Stephanie, you could not find a better human being with a kinder heart. And he loved to bake on the holidays, made the best zuppa di mussels for our Christmas Eve Meal of the Seven Fishes gatherings, too! After his mother died, he sort of went in the closet instead of coming out and finally came out as Stephanie but, only on the weekends and on Wednesday Night Bingo at St. Agatha's. If you didn't know him, you never knew he was Sonny. Looked gorgeous every time; to this day, if I'm going to a wedding, I'll call Sonny/Stephanie to put on my make up. All our mothers who went to Bingo knew it was Sonny but, back in those days it was "look the other way" on gay or lesbian people in the family and in the neighborhood. My mother's explanation for Sonny was that he was going through a phase; he'll meet the right girl someday. She never believed that Liberace was gay either; she used to say, "They always think that about men who love their mothers!" Sonny/Stephanie would give some of the bingo ladies a lift home in his car from St. Agatha's, even though the church was only three or four blocks away. When Little Marie Greco's mother passed away, he drove me, Antoinette and Irish Marie, all the way to Massapequa for the first evening of the wake and then after that to the Purity Diner for coffee and cake, his treat. He'd never accept money from us even when he was Stephanie. He/she is currently living in Dumbo with a man who accepts him for who he/she is and they come to visit me every so often or when I need him to put on my make up.

We went out to the disco with many gay friends who "didn't find the right girl"; best dancers in the world, I have to say, and they always knew what the latest dances were besides the Hustle. We had Joseph Paterno and Frankie "Dive" Costello, not to be confused with Frankie Boy Fresca, as our escorts into the disco. We called him Frankie Dive because everywhere we'd go, he'd say, "what kind of a dive is this?" They weren't dives but, he'd say it anyway. Imagine these two handsome men escorting six, seven of us dressed to the nines. All the guys inside must have been saying that Joseph and Frankie had a good life or, a big you-know-what. The both of them went to the clubs in Manhattan if they were looking to pick up someone. Back then, Manhattan was more cosmopolitan than the Brooklyn clubs; there were no gay bars in Brooklyn back then, at least, to the best of my knowledge. Even us girls would go to the gay bars; it was the only club where we could pour our hearts out to men and not have to worry if they were listening to us because they wanted sex. Gay men make the best friends.

Little Marie Greco spoke at many of our meetings. Many ladies who attended brought their mothers with them; they appreciated the information and available services she provided. However, sometimes she'd talk about her old job at the 78th Precinct.

Thursday Evening, July 20, 1995 Lecturer: Little Marie Greco, Coordinator, Caregiver Services, Francone Senior Center.

Lending Money to Men – You Can't Afford it!

"You know, when I worked for the Police Dept, I learned a lot about loaning money to family, friends and, especially, lending money to boyfriends. And how did I learn this working for the Police Department you may ask? Because of the many people who came to the precinct, desperate for justice, why? Because they were now in trouble because someone didn't make good on a promise to pay back the money they loaned them. Captain Doyle was especially sympathetic to the single mothers who came in looking for a way to get back that money; money they desperately needed to pay their rent and put food on the table. God bless him, the Captain sometimes took money out of his own pocket to, at least, give the mothers relief for one day. And we'd always hear the same story, "he told me he'd pay me back once he got his income tax refund" or, "it's a short-term loan, I'll pay back all of it in a month", or even worse, "baby, this loan is for us so we can start a life together." We heard this a lot. And, the Captain would always ask the magic question, "Did he sign anything like a promissory note or even sign his name stating that he owed you this money?" Almost 100% of the time the answer would be no. Why? For a number of reasons; he said he loved me, I never thought he'd do that to me. A lot of the time, they said it was a verbal agreement, he promised. Or, they told us "I couldn't ask him to do that, we're family." Or, better still they made them feel guilty by saying, "don't you trust me?"

If you are in a position where someone you love be it family, friend or lover comes to you for a loan, make them sign a promissory note. If Jesus Christ came down and asked you for a loan, make him sign a promissory note. At least, with Jesus Christ, you'd know you'd get the money back with a little extra because he tells the truth. He'd sign the promissory note. If that person intends on paying back the loan, they should have no problem signing a promissory note, no matter how they're related to you."

"In 1990, women earned 70 cents for every dollar a man earned doing the same job. Let me repeat that so it sinks in, in 1990, women earned 70 cents for every dollar a man earned doing the same job. And, despite that disparity in the gender income gap, it always seems like women are put in the position of money lenders. And why is that? Because they know we're better savers! We save as much of those 70 cents as we can while men are spending that extra 30 cents in the bar or on enhancements to their already colorful lifestyle. Whether we're married or single, we're saving for something that will improve our lives or our children. We're saving for a new car to get around and take the kids to the doctor or soccer games; or maybe saving for a much-needed family vacation. We save for our children so they can have the things other kids have, we save for their college fund, we save to take them to McDonald's once a week or to Coney Island in the summer. We save all the money our children receive on their birthdays or Christmas so they have something to start their adult life. We could even be saving for a home of our own or even for our own education. We are savers. Now, you will say that some women spend their money as fast as they make it but, they're the exception and obviously, they wouldn't be able to lend money to anyone!

Little Marie took a survey, "Raise your hands if you save all your kids' gift money in a separate account?" Every mother in the room raised their hands. Who is saving for a home? four hands went up; we had a handful of single mothers that night so, maybe two hands went up. Little Marie asked them if they ever lent money to a man who didn't pay them back? Almost every hand went up.

She asked the audience why did they think that happened? Black Marie Giordano started by saying that if you asked a man you loved, be it family, friend or boyfriend they would be insulted to have to sign a promissory note.

Little Marie told her "If someone is going to pay you back, they'd take no insult signing a promissory note. If I knew I was going to pay someone back after I received my income tax refund, I'd have no problem signing it because I know I'm going to do it. Lending to boyfriends is probably the worse lending decision a women can make. Boyfriends can be a lasting relationship that leads to a firmer commitment or they can be part of the parade of toads you have to kiss in order to get a prince. Either way, you have a 50-50 chance of getting it paid back in full.

But, if you have a signed promissory note for a loan of up to $5,000, you have a 100% chance of getting it back in small claims court. Over $5,000, you have to get a good lawyer to get the full amount of the loan repaid with a promissory note and you better have proof that you gave the money directly to him. You still have to get a lawyer but, at least you have adequate proof. Men consider loans made by women to be a gift. Afterall, they loved you and did you great favor by fixing that broken door or fixing your car and the occasional dinner out. And, if you're the one who break off with them, they doubly feel they don't have to repay the loan!

If a man borrows money from a man, he's more inclined to pay it back because he knows he'd get his ass kicked. Men don't give gifts of money to other men unless they have no expectation of getting it back like giving money to a friend for his wedding or another occasion. However, if he lends money to another man, he'd better pay up. I'm not saying that some men don't get scammed by other men, it's just that most of them will come after the guy, if he reneges on a promise. That fear is non-existent to a man asking for a loan from a woman because he knows he can get away with it. And, if you only have a verbal promise, it's pretty much his word against yours and the courts can't help you. That's how these women ended up in Captain Doyle's office. They had nothing to prove that it was not a gift and they wanted the police to arrest them. And he couldn't help them. But, with a signed promissory note, it's just like kicking his ass without flexing a muscle."

Black Marie's niece, Joanne, attended this meeting and she had a question, actually two questions: "Is it necessary to get a promissory note if you're planning a wedding? I'm engaged and we're in the process of looking at halls for the wedding reception. My fiancé just started working after graduating college so he doesn't really have anything saved yet. I've been working since I'm 18 and have a bit put away in the bank. Most halls require a deposit of 10% once the date and space has been reserved which could be about $2,000 dollars. I told my fiancé I would put down the deposit if he would agree to pay me half of the deposit, $1,000, in six months so that I could use the money to pay for the invitations and flowers. He said he would do that but, I know he has student loans, pays his own car insurance; he lives with his parents so he doesn't pay rent. Should I ask him to sign a promissory note? And if yes, how do I word it?

"Good questions, Joanne! To answer your first question, yes, you should ask him to sign a promissory note. Until you are married, your savings are yours and his is his and they are exclusive of one another. There is also the possibility that you could break off your engagement. How will you get that money back if you break up under bad circumstances? Then, it becomes your problem if you're out $1,000. What if you broke off the engagement, he could feel that it was your fault and you should pay out of spite? A promissory note is a contract that if your engagement is terminated, both of you will be responsible in meeting those vendor commitments. You may have lost $1,000 for your share of the deposit but, you shouldn't lose $2,000. With regard to your second question, a promissory note should be no more than a paragraph long stating that X agrees to pay back X in the amount of X and will re-pay that loan within a certain time frame, for example:

I, Your Name, agree to lend, His Name. the amount of $XXX, paid by check or cash (your choice although it's better to give a check to trace it) for the purpose of… state reason such as my half in guaranteeing a hall for our wedding or if it's a loan to someone else for a different reason. I, Name of Borrower, agree to pay lender, Your Name, the full sum borrowed of $XXX by DATE specific date or month? Six months? whatever.

Your name and the person who is borrowing the money should be below it printed and signed by both parties with a date.

Always keep a copy of the canceled check used in lending the money. In your case, Joanne, keep a copy of the canceled check you used to pay the hall or a bill of some sort. If possible and time permits, get the promissory note notarized. The bank usually has a notary on staff or Anthony Cheech is a notary and he'll do it for a couple of bucks. If a man or anyone knows they will pay you back, they'll have no problem signing that note, end of story."

Little Marie now directed everybody to the side table for coffee and cake. Joanne went up to me and asked me for a reading but it was getting late; I asked her to come to my house the next day but she had somewhere to go. She told me that she was unsure of getting married but the families got along and the pressure was on; she was getting cold feet. I told her to talk to her aunt (Black Marie) alone with nobody nearby and open up to her. Black Marie was not a bossy person, we all knew her since our teens and she never gave us that impression, she was never judgmental. Well, Joanne did just that. On the drive home, Joanne told her aunt exactly how she felt and that she knew that her family was for the marriage but she was unsure if she was making the right decision. Black Marie confessed that she never really liked him but she was only going along because she was in love with him. Black Marie told her to postpone the wedding; she would talk to her parents.

Joanne first asked her fiancé if they could postpone the wedding date and he gave a grunt and said OK but, he sounded sort of relieved, too. They broke off their engagement about seven months later and they both married different people. Two years later, Joanne married a guy about 4-5 years older than her and she didn't have to worry about the deposits or the other wedding things because he was a saver, too. His family had connections with one of the owners of a reception hall in Long Island and they didn't even have to leave a deposit so that worked out! Nobody worried about the money. It must be because they were really in love and there was no doubt in Joanne's mind about getting married. Black Marie wore this silver gown at the wedding that was so beautiful she wound up having it altered as a cocktail dress. She wore it to all the weddings until she gained 15 pounds as part of the aging process. She keeps it in the closet for when she goes on a diet. That hasn't happened so far. She told us she wants to be buried in it but, I've never seen the deceased waked in a spaghetti strapped silver cocktail dress but, knowing Black Marie, her niece Joanne will find a way.

Que sera, sera, whatever will be, will be…. the future's not ours to see, que sera, sera. Remember that song? If I recall, Doris Day sang that song but I remember it as my Grandma Philly's song. She used to sing that song to me when I was a child. It was usually at night to get me to go to sleep when my parents were out or when I was sick with a cold. One time, when I had the measles; she came into my room to comfort me and give my mother a rest. She sang that song and I forgot all about the dots on my face. To be honest, I was terrible as a sick child, always grumpy. And I was afraid of needles so it was a big ordeal to get me to the doctor's office. I thought it small compensation that the doctor only gave me a lollipop; I wanted a Barbie doll. Usually, my mother would take me afterwards to the candy store to pick what I wanted. But the real treat was spending the whole day with my mom because she worked, maybe it was not the same for her because I was a drama princess. I think I was needy because my parents worked and this was my way of stealing some time with my mother because she took time off from work to take care of me. I had her for the whole day or days when I was sick. When she couldn't take off from work, she asked grandma and grandpa to stay with me. Even then, God bless her, Grandma Philly had pains in her knees from the "Arthritis" but, she'd come up slowly with grandpa right behind her. She had other things wrong with her but, she never told us until it was too late.

By then, Grandma Philly was only working one or two days a week at Di Paolo's factory; China had cornered the market on inexpensive women's clothes and Mr. Di Paolo's orders were dwindling yearly. The big department stores no longer sent in orders. A couple of years later, he was forced to close the shop. Grandma Philly always said he was a good man and, a good boss to all the ladies in the factory. Mr. Di Paolo's mother worked in a factory in Italy under terrible work conditions; Mr. Di Paolo's father died fighting World War 1. She had a child to support and took any job she could get. By the time Mr. Di Paolo was getting ready to take his mother with him to New York, she died of lung cancer. The single mothers in Mr. Di Paolo's shop were the last to be laid off because he thought of his mother's struggle. When it was time to lay off everyone, he gave the women 2 weeks' pay as severance even though it was coming out of his own pocket. Grandpa Joe was home on disability because of his back but, eventually, he retired on a pension. He used to be a dock worker down at Bush Terminal but could no longer haul the freight off the ships. He worked 6 days a week for 30 years before he went on disability. One day, he woke up and couldn't lift himself off the bed. I remember my father taking him to the hospital. He was a proud man and was reluctant to have my father carry him to the car and drive him there. My father said he was once a strong man with bulging muscles and thick hard hands. My father's knees would shake every time he knew he'd did something wrong. But, as hard as those hands were, he had a soft heart. He always used to take Blind Pete, who begged on the corner, for a beer and a sandwich. It must have been hard for my father to see that strong man slouching when he walked because his back was so twisted.

When I was sick, Grandma would take care of me and Grandpa would sit in front of the TV until my mother came home. Yes, he'd pop his head in the room to see how I was feeling but, he didn't really know how to speak to me. He did a lot of hugging though, or he'd kiss me on my head. He'd ask me if I needed anything and if I did, he'd ask Grandma to bring it and then he'd plop his ass on the couch to watch TV again. Half an hour later, he'd be asleep. If Grandma went to shut off the TV or change the channel, he'd tell her he was still watching the show and she'd check on him 15 minutes later and he was asleep again. He liked to hear the TV, it made him sleepy.

Grandpa Joe died first from pneumonia. He went out one day to shovel the snow with his coat on but not buttoned because he said he sweated too much when it was buttoned. The next day, he started feeling achy and developed a cough and this continued for days because he was too stubborn to go to the doctor. He would tell Grandma that all he needed was a shot of whiskey. Long story short, the ambulance came and Grandpa was in Intensive Care with pneumonia. He didn't improve and died nine days later. Grandma was with him every day. She said she knew he was going to die because he said he dreamed he saw his mother. His mother held out her hand for him to grab it but she was too far away and he was unable to walk. He talked a lot about the old days and he told her something she hadn't heard in a long, long time. He told her he loved her. And that was it, the next morning we got the news that Grandpa died. I was about 11 or 12 years old then and it didn't wholly sink in that Grandpa was no more. It was only as an adult that I realized how much I missed him. Grandma died about 10 years later from breast cancer. She always had company downstairs and after Signorine got laid off from Di Paolo's, she was a daily fixture in her apartment. Grandma Philly never complained; after my mother found the lumps, she went into the hospital for a mastectomy but, it was too late. After she died, my parents rented the apartment to newlyweds and it was strange not to be able to go downstairs to visit Grandma.

I was still living with my parents when I was in my 30's. By then, I had many relationships that could have been the road to marriage but dissipated for one reason or another. In my 20's, I was dating a guy from work that really seemed to be solid but, he was Jewish and back then Catholic/Jewish marriages were not encouraged. So, begrudgingly, we agreed this was going nowhere and decided to date other people. My parents were somewhat relieved although, I think they would have supported my decision to marry him. I had him over for dinner many times; we dated for a year and I still hadn't met his parents so, that tells it all. He left the bank shortly thereafter and I never saw him again. I often wonder how his life turned out; I hope he is happy if he's still alive. He was a good man with a great sense of humor.

So, anyway, the newlyweds lived downstairs. Both my parents were retired by then; my mother retired from the school cafeteria but worked part-time at the Brooklyn Public Library for a couple of years. After the library job, she decided to retire full-time so that she and my father could do more things together. They went to Italy once and went on a cruise to the Bahamas with another couple. They stayed a week at a cousin's house in Pennsylvania to attend their son's wedding; after that, they didn't travel long distances any more. I didn't notice at first but, my father was having trouble breathing. I mentioned it to my mother and she said he went to the doctor and it was just a bad cold. It was two months later that I found out that he had lung cancer; my father told my mother not to tell me because he didn't want me fussing over him. All the chemo, all the radiation, unfortunately, didn't work; two years later he passed away at home. Everybody in the neighborhood came to the wake and to his funeral mass. The Schrables next door had a tree planted in Israel in his memory. My mother died 10 years, 9 months after we lost my father. She had heart problems for a long time; each year stymied her activities because she was tired most of the time. Before she passed, she was homebound; on weekends I would help her to the backyard to talk to Esther Schrable.

I knew the end was near because when I came home from work on a Friday night she cooked my favorite, meat loaf, for dinner. She cleaned the kitchen, did some laundry and didn't look a bit exhausted. I told her I was surprised to see her so lively tonight; she told me she woke up this morning like it was 20 years ago and decided to take advantage of the energy. We watched a little TV; I filled her in on what was going on at work and then she kissed me and said good night. She died in her sleep during the night; doctor said it was a heart attack. When I found her that Saturday morning, she had the most peaceful face like she was sleeping. I just told her to say hello to Dad and that I loved her.

I decided to keep the house. The house was paid for and my neighbors and friends were still living in the neighborhood, it made sense to stick around. By then, the newlyweds had moved out; they had one child and another one on the way. My parents never raised their rent in all that time. My father used to say, let them save for a down payment on a home. They were nice to my parents; the wife would drive my mother to the beauty parlor to get her weekly hairdos and nails done or drive my father to the hospital for his chemo treatments when I couldn't get the time off from work. They were always grateful to my parents because they treated them like family, not like tenants. I helped them get a mortgage from my bank. After that we had a professional couple renting the apartment. They moved out three years before my mother died. When they moved, I was lost. I had no experience or the time to interview prospective tenants. It was then that I heard about the shit Signorine was going through with her landlord and it seemed the right time to ask her if she wanted to move into the apartment. After my mother died, I decided to start the Thursday evening meetings.

It seemed like every time I came home from work there would always be four or five ladies in Signorine's apartment. Some came to get a tea leaf reading; some came to just get her thoughts on what to do; of course, one person was always there to translate. I didn't mind, Signorine was getting on in years and she couldn't have groups coming to her old apartment; she feared the landlord might complain about the noise or accuse her of operating a business in her apartment. He was looking for any reason to evict her. She always had to go to other people's houses; she didn't mind back then because they would invite her to lunch or dinner after the reading. It helped her to save money on groceries after Mr. Di Paolo closed the shop. She had no choice but to go on welfare in order to pay the rent. By the time we started our meetings, she was in her early 80s. She was having a hard time walking, especially in the winter; I thought it was about time people came to her.

So, originally, I started the Thursday evening meetings to get everyone together to get tea leaf readings from Signorine and if they wanted a reading from me, I was there, too! Little by little these meetings increased from five ladies to 10,15 20; we provided the dessert and coffee. Most of the time, people would bring something they cooked or maybe cake or a bottle of wine. Signorine was in charge of setting the table. I'd try to find any chair in the house to place in the Living Room, including four folding chairs in the closet. It got to be too much to put them all away in the different rooms at the end of the night. I asked Antoinette one Thursday if she knew of anyone we could rent folding chairs from or buy cheaply?

She picks up the phone and calls Bennie Fiore, Anthony Slice's brother, owner of Bennie's Party Palace, to ask about the chairs. Bennie told her that he had some old folding chairs in the back of the store that he no longer needed because he bought new folding chairs with cushions. The story about Bennie and Antoinette is that he had a crush on her, even though she was much older than him. He's married now but, still, he'd do anything for her.

According to Antoinette, when Bennie was in his teens he got into a little trouble with the law. Like any teenager, he was looking for a quick buck. A couple of guys in a truck happened to see him sitting on his stoop and they asked him if he'd like to make $35 moving furniture because they were a man short. He jumped into the truck. He thought he was moving furniture from one house to another. Actually, he was an innocent accomplice to a robbery. One of the suspicious neighbors called the cops and Bennie and the other two guys were arrested. His parents were beside themselves when he called them to come to the 78th Precinct to make bail. Bennie's mother called Carmela Fresca because they needed a translator. Antoinette was friends with Little Marie Greco who, at that time, was working at the precinct for Captain Doyle. Antoinette told her the whole story; they both knew Bennie and how he always wanted to be a wise guy. So, long story short, Captain Doyle decided not to press charges out of respect for Little Marie. But......but, he had to learn a lesson. So, he decided to give him community service. He had to help at St. Agatha's setting up the bingo hall in the auditorium on Wednesday nights. He had to set up the tables, mind you with two other people, set-up the folding chairs, make the coffee, slice the cake into slices for sale. And then, he had to clean it all up. Long hours and hard work.

At that time, Antoinette was the bingo caller when Father Giudice was called away for some priestly function, usually last rites, rest in peace. This she did for free as she always did for St. Agatha's. Her mother played bingo, too. After a few Wednesdays, Antoinette noticed that Bennie actually liked doing what he did on Wednesdays, setting up, serving people coffee and cake, talking to people, selling bingo markers. So, one Wednesday, Antoinette was talking to him while helping with the folding chairs; she told him he would be good at arranging parties. She told him her brother was having a Super Bowl party this Sunday and maybe he would like to cater and serve at that party and she would pay him. He did a wonderful job with the Super Bowl party; Frankie Boy and his friends were pleased. Word got around and soon he was catering other parties in the neighborhood. By the time he graduated from high school, he knew this was what he wanted to do. He started working as a waiter in reception halls, then started booking and managing weddings; he became a pro in the business. And 10 years later, he started his own business, Bennie's Party Palace, on 10th Street; he catered bridal showers, weddings, christenings, Christmas parties and even business meetings. The Fairy Comaras gave him plenty of business; he did all our bridal and baby showers. Antoinette was instrumental in getting him started doing corporate meetings at her job. By that time, he had a staff handling some of the smaller events. So, when Antoinette called him to ask if he had any folding chairs he could sell to us, he gave them to us, no charge. The next day, here comes Bennie in a truck and 50 folding chairs, with small engraved plaques saying Bennie's Party Palace with the phone number, and two rectangle folding tables.

Antoinette knew everybody and everybody owed her for some act of kindness she or her mother gave them. And she gave without expectation. Even after the Thursday evening meetings ended, the Fairy Comaras were always a phone call away to help out. We haven't lost our mojo yet.

After we started doing the lectures a few years later, we were drawing in maybe 30-40 people every Thursday. Bennie's mom came to the meetings, too, and she never forgot what Little Marie Greco and Antoinette did for her son. When Antoinette moved into the apartment and realized her parents' Dining Room set wasn't going to fit, she gave the set to Bennie's mom and years later, when Bennie's mom passed away, he gave it back to Antoinette and then she gave it away to someone else. And, still in mint condition, because Bennie's mother had a tablecloth and a plastic cover on that table. Trust me, when she gave it away, again, it was as brand new as the day she gave it to Bennie.

As much as I dislike table cloths, they keep tables stain and dent free. My mother always had a tablecloth with a clear plastic over it. I never saw the top of her dining room table until she passed away. One day, I decided to leave the table bare. When Signorine saw the table, she looked at me like I had three heads. She was always afraid to eat at that table. She'd spread paper towels where she ate and never drank anything while eating fearing she'd spill it. After a while, we just ate in the kitchen. When friends my age came over and saw the dining room table, they praised me for finally letting go of the table cloth, the older ones thought I was crazy and thought my mother must be turning over in her grave. Our parents were immigrants or first-generation Americans; they worked so hard to buy that furniture. It was a source of pride for them; it was expected to last a lifetime.

Today we change the furniture to suit the nuance of our current lives and most of the time, it's not good furniture, corrugated hardwood they say, lasts maybe five years and then you have to throw it out. Our living room couches were plastic, too! That was a biggie. In the summer, my father would have to put my baby blanket on the couch if he wore shorts otherwise his skin would rip off and become part of the couch. Anyway, enough about folding chairs and tablecloths.

As I said, in the beginning the gatherings were small but, as they grew in size the neighborhood realized that these gatherings contained women who either worked at jobs where they could help them or knew people to refer them to if they had a problem. We had close friendships with each other; it was me, Little Marie, Black Marie Giordano, Irish Marie, Antoinette, Theresa Guarino from 7th Ave, Marie from Long Island and of course, Signorine. By then, Little Marie Greco started working for Francone Senior Center in Massapequa but, she came two Thursdays a month even though it was a schlep and she always brought her mother. By then, her mother and father already sold their house and moved in with Little Marie. Her mother never assimilated into Massapequa; she had to depend on Little Marie to get around and she missed being able to shop by herself on 5th Ave. Her husband would drive her to the supermarket but, you know men, everything is rush, rush, rush. When Little Marie drove, she felt better but she wasn't used to depending on family to get around. She liked driving with her son-in-law, Frank, because he always had some stories to tell her about work or about what his parents were doing. He listened to her stories even though she knew he heard them before. He was a likeable guy and he took the time to visit them in the morning before he went to work.

Ok, more about Theresa Guarino. She lived on 5th St. and 7th Ave. She was a nurse at our nearby hospital. On the side, she sold handmade earrings, bracelets and necklaces. She came to the meetings to advise if anyone had any medical questions. She lectured about the warning signs for strokes, Diabetes, and helped direct them to the proper physicians. Because of her schedule, she couldn't attend every Thursday evening meeting; when she could attend, she'd put out a display of her jewelry. Her brother, Barry, real name Bartolomeo Guarino, was a firefighter and he worked with Irish Marie's husband. She later married a doctor, Swedish guy. She passed away four years ago in her sleep. She deserved to pass away in her sleep because she was a damn good nurse, a good friend and, helped a great many people with their medical needs. Theresa used to drop by after work or even on her day off to visit our mothers or fathers who were sick. She looked in on my mother and recommended a good cardiologist. She and Black Marie were responsible in getting Esther Schrable a good Physical Therapist to make house calls and help Esther regain her strength after her hip surgery.

Irish Marie was taking these yoga classes back then; she taught meditation and yoga classes at one or two of the Thursday meetings. She would teach the other more limber ladies how to relieve stress through yoga; our mothers never participated; how can you do yoga in a dress? For some reason they never wanted to wear pant suits, they felt strange in them. They usually talked with Signorine in the kitchen and had their coffee and cake ahead of time or they would sit in the back and critique the yoga classes. It wasn't until we started taking care of them that they wore pant suits either because they needed physical therapy or to keep their legs warm if they had Arthritis. They looked kind of cute in sweat pants, too! Summertime they would wear sandals; they always had peds on though. And, what a job convincing them not to wear a girdle!

My mother wore pant suits on the weekend but, not at work. When she got sick, I would call the car service to take us, with her wheelchair, to A&S Dept. store to shop for her pant suits. They had very good merchandise back then, it was worth it to pay a few pennies more for a few more years of use. She was never comfortable wearing pantsuits every day but she knew they kept her legs warm. Another good store across the street was Martin's; that was like the Saks Fifth Avenue of Brooklyn; expensive stuff but when they had sales you could get some really nice coats and outfits for weddings.

One time, we asked Irish Marie to give a lecture, not a yoga class. Irish Marie could be loud and boisterous but, in truth, it took a long time for her to believe in herself. She never wanted to stand up and speak; when she taught yoga, she was always sitting so no pressure there. We asked her to give her first lecture in 1997 after she started her own business. So, anyway, Irish Marie gave a lecture that people are still talking about and the analogy was perfect.

Thursday, June 12, 1997: Clean Your House, Solve Your Problems – Irish Marie, Owner, Fitzpatrick Housekeeping, Inc.

Irish Marie gave everyone her homemade lavender soap as a gift for coming. I think they call it SWAG now.

"You want to solve your problems…. clean your house. I bet you've been solving your problems this way for years and just didn't know it…. and…. each particular problem is addressed by what part of the house you take on to clean:

Floors…ahhhhhhh, the deeper issues in your life. You have to be very careful how you mop the floors; you could be pressing all your negative thoughts into the house. Try to avoid cleaning your floors when you're angry, you're creating negative energy and everyone who steps into your house will either feel uncomfortable or be in a bad mood. I've seen this happen many times. If you have your house cleaned, beware, they could be rubbing deep negativity into your floors. I have a woman in her 40's who works for me; she cleaned for three of my customers and they all said her work was impeccable, but every time she left their homes, either the kids would get sick or the parents would be sick. If they had guests overnight, the guests did not get a good night's sleep. How did I know this was happening? I would go to my customers' homes, every now and then, to make sure we're gaving them the best cleaning service and I would inspect the homes to make sure there were no corners cut in cleaning.

When I went to inspect one of the three homes this woman cleaned, I'm not going to say her name, I felt a bad vibration, a density to the house. In a casual conversation, the customer said that within the last three months her kids, her husband and herself were sick with colds almost every week. She wasn't blaming the woman who worked for me, we were just talking about our families. But I knew something was not right with the house the minute I walked in; I can't explain it, except maybe I felt claustrophobic. I asked permission to use her bathroom and in those two minutes I was in there, I felt a negative energy that gave me a headache. I felt like the walls were going to crash into me. I didn't say anything to the customer but, when I came back to the office, it just so happened that this woman was clocking out for the day.

I asked her to come into my office. I told her she's doing a great job, very efficient. And then I said, "how do you like cleaning so and so's house?" Are they nice people to work for? How do you feel when you clean their house?" I must have taken her by surprise because she just shrugged her shoulders and said they were very good customers, always friendly. And then I asked, how are you doing? And she said she was fine but there was a hesitation in her reply. "Do you like working here?" and she said yes, right away! In fact, she told me that she was going to ask me for more hours during the week. And, because I am who I am, I asked her if she needed money and, of course, she was too proud to accept a handout. She lived in an apartment all the way out in Canarsie with her elderly mother, her husband and her 10-year-old son. She told me last year, her son was getting fevers almost every week and he was always tired. The school asked if he was getting enough sleep because he often slept in class and was disciplined for it. Prior to that, he was an excellent student and got very high grades.

So, she took him to the doctor; bad news, Leukemia. He needed blood transfusions frequently and multiple doctor visits which was manageable because she was working part-time for me. Her husband was working and he had employer covered health insurance. The insurance covered a lot but there was a deductible and the co-pays were sometimes high, especially when her son was hospitalized; she admitted that financially, they had to cut corners.

Her mother earned a few dollars crocheting hats. Some had the sequins on them and some just had a crocheted flower in the front. I bought a few hats from her; my mother used to love them, especially the sequined ones, God rest her soul. St. Agatha's used to have a Christmas Craft and Jewelry sale. Little Marie Greco's mother, Rose, manned the corner booth selling scarves and hats. I bought about a dozen hats from her mother and asked her to display them; they sold like hotcakes."

Little Marie Greco said she bought two hats for her and her mother; she gave the sequined hat to her mother. She told us her mother still wears it. I told Irish Marie I bought a hat for Signorine. Signorine bought the matching-colored scarf. Black Marie wanted to know who made the scarves but nobody seemed to know. Some ladies thought they may have bought a hat but, couldn't remember. And then, Irish Marie had to get back to the story.

"Anyway, she told me that three months ago, her husband was laid off from his job. No job, the unemployment checks were not enough and most of all, no health insurance. Her son needed a blood transfusion last month and between the transfusion and the hospital stay, the bill came to over $10,000. They used their savings but, now she can't sleep thinking about the next doctor visit and the next transfusion. Her husband looked for jobs every day and he went on a few interviews but, no job. He was good at painting and he got an offer to paint one of the neighbors' bedrooms but, that was it. He was good with his hands but, that wasn't his job. He learned that all from his father.

I ended the meeting with me agreeing to give her more hours. I told her when she has a doctor appointment for her son to tell me in advance and I'd work her hours around it. But I knew, even with the extra hours, it wasn't going to be enough.

I had an idea to go to Big Jimmy in the club. By then, he was semi-retired; he only came to the club, once or twice a week, to play cards and shoot the shit with the boys. He had already passed the baton to Eddie San Marco; Big Jimmy is now in an advisory capacity. Anyway, I went down to the club and Big Jimmy was in the back eating Chinese food."

Big Jimmy always had the time, and sometimes the patience, to listen or to help the Fairy Comaras. When we were teenagers, we used to bust his chops all the time to get a free soda. He always had a wad of 10-dollar bills to spread around to us; he'd tell us to keep out of trouble but, he knew we weren't listening.

"So, anyway, I sat down with Big Jimmy; he asked if I wanted an eggroll or something but, I wasn't hungry. I told him the whole story. So, he said to me, "this guy wants a job like his office job? I know a few people I could call". he opened his desk drawer and pulled out a piece of paper. But a thought came to him. He told me, "I just heard Home Depot is hiring." With that he takes out a wad of business cards. I told him he's good at painting and he knows how to do odd-jobs like light plumbing and carpentry, too. "Let me call this guy right now 'cause he owes me a favor." He called up the guy and Big Jimmy asked him if there were any jobs in the painting department and the guy says yeah, they just lost a manager and now they only have two kids who barely know anything about paints. The back and forth went on, Big Jimmy asked him what it paid and the guy tells him to have the guy come in tomorrow. Big Jimmy told him he had to be covered by health insurance immediately; normally, you have to wait three months before you get employer health insurance. But he owed him a favor and something was worked out.

So, her husband got the manager job; she told me he loves it. They recently moved to a larger apartment nearer to Home Depot. And, most of all, when she cleans people houses, no more worries and no more sick houses. Her son, receives his transfusions, on time. Remember that customer I told you about who told me they were always sick? Sick no more. In fact, she gave a referral for this woman to clean another house so I didn't have to worry about how I was going to make up the extra hours.

When you clean your house angry or sick with worry, then your house will carry that vibration; you'll have a sick house. If, on the other hand, you're cleaning while on the phone discussing how a problem can be solved that's good; you're lessening the negativity because you're looking for a solution. Some of the best spiritual moments of enlightenment can be experienced while cleaning and talking on the phone. Years ago, you could only clean so far because of the telephone cord but now you can bring it anywhere. You want to wipe the slate clean or banish them altogether while you're mopping or vacuuming or whatever, you should be thinking of the steps you have to take steps to solve the problem...... start thinking of the problem before you mop the floor and then think of the solutions while you're doing it and then wring it out of your life. If you're on the phone, you can get feedback from outside instead of you thinking of a solution all by yourself.

You clean in steps; you should be thinking in steps with a positive result. If you're not on the phone, you should ask God for the solution while you're cleaning instead of thinking how you can solve it yourself. I used to think about my problems cleaning my kitchen and I never discussed it with anyone. My kitchen was the source of endless arguments with my husband almost every day. I rubbed my anger and frustration into every crevice of that kitchen. One day; it was a bad day emotionally for me, I asked God to help me. And who rings about 10 minutes later but, Diane Santangelo. She called about somebody who needed a house cleaned because their house was being sold and she must have tuned into me because I gave no indication I was in a bad state. Suddenly, the flood gates opened up and everything just poured out of me and I told her my problems. Long story short that problem was solved, the Fairy Comaras went to work and took care of it. I could have kicked myself for keeping it inside for so long. Bottom line, don't clean when you have unclean thoughts; call someone to get a solution.

Laundry...nothing really bad going on but, the folding part could potentially become a problem. Watch out how you fold your clothes....

neat, sloppy, folded carefully, only your clothes are folded and not his? Or, you're so controlled that you fold his nicely but neglect your own? There may be larger issues going on behind the scenes. Do you think you're the only one who can fold clothes right in your family and resent the fact that you're always the one who has to do it? Do you feel suffocated by the number of loads of laundry you have to do each week? Feel like you're becoming a mummy when folding sheets? Then, be a little less neat and take the extra 10 minutes to get outside. The best therapy is to hang clothes on a clothesline; they smell fresh and it opens you up to higher and more positive thoughts. It's relaxing actually. Our parents never had a problem with laundry, even the ones that worked. Sometimes, my mother would be hanging clothes and one of the neighbors would come out in the backyard to chat with her. I know most of you have a washer and dryer but, you have to be aware if you're folding your clothes with resentment; you'll be putting so much negative energy in your clothes and your family's clothes. That could be the reason you have a lot of arguments in your home; your family is walking around with unhappy clothes. Don't laugh! If you think about it, your hands are transferring whatever energy you are sending out into every fold.

Countertops …. As I said when I spoke about kitchens, you can be rubbing in negative thoughts and holding in unresolved issues that you think are unsolvable. Everything can be solved. Are you obsessed with keeping the countertops not just clean but, nothing on the surface? There could be denial problems or you hope your clean countertops will clear your mind. Never happens. You can't have a happy family and a clean kitchen at the same time. There has to be coffee cups or some remnant of the family breakfast or dinner around the kitchen. Cooking is messy and yes, there is a system to clean the kitchen after dinner but not so clean that it looks like no one lives there. You're spending too much time trying to give the appearance that everything is as it should be when it isn't. If you have a lot of stuff on top of your countertops but, your countertops are clean, then that's okay. My mother always liked all her spices to be on the countertops and she had utensils hanging on the walls behind them. Her kitchen would seem messy but it was clean and she loved cooking in her kitchen because she had all the things that made her happy easily visible.

Windows indicate a resolution to end or begin a new venture…" seeing" things in a new light…it's good to clean windows……windows are the "eyes" of your house, they see inside and out. Now, it's easier to clean windows so you should have no problem and yet, in some homes, windows are the most neglected area. You want to see things from a different light, not be confined by poor vision, clean your windows.

Cleaning the Medicine Cabinet…. another good move…. you're starting to move forward in your life; cleaning out remnant medications of old maladies that you no longer experience. Trash it! When you save medications that you no longer use, it's like you're fearful that you'll get it again. Expired meds you should trash as soon as possible, I wouldn't trust its potency.

I know everybody here has a clean bathroom so I'm not going to go into what to do with that; I'll only say one thing, if your bathroom has seven different types of shampoo and conditioner bottles all over the place and enough make-up to apply to 10 people, it may be time to make choices in your broader life. Pick the ones you use daily and only the make-up that you always wear and not the cast-offs. The bathroom is your inner sanctum for thinking about life.

Dusting: A desire for harmony in your life even though you know dust is all around you. If you have dust in places you rarely go, that's one thing. But, if it's dusty everywhere that means you're too pre-occupied with other things that cause disharmony in your life. Or it can mean you don't care because there are larger issues that need to be addressed and you'd rather cover them with "dust" so you don't have to face them.

Cleaning the Lamps…. knowing what can and cannot be done in the present to resolve the problem……keeping away from the hot spots in your life but, still projecting some semblance of order. Make sure you have the right lighting in your rooms or you're liable to mistake what you see both physically and spiritually; what you may be thinking you see in the way of any given problem, may not be it. Good lighting promotes clear vision.

Don't even get me started on closets and basements! …if you are afraid of opening your closet because everything will tumble out, you have too much of your past locked up behind closed doors. Cluttered basements produce negative vibes at the foundation level. There's stuff down there you never use, have a tag sale or donate it to charity."

Then we had a Q&A. Some of the ladies had specific questions about what products her company uses to clean houses and cleaning out problems in other parts of the house. Someone even asked how you clean out ghosts! And then she closed the lecture.

By the way, I received permission from Irish Marie to tell the story about why her own kitchen at one time was like a hurricane hit it. Kind of unusual for a lady who owns her own cleaning service, no? Even before our phone call, I was the first to notice something different about Irish Marie when I visited her.

She was quiet and Irish Marie was never quiet. When she came to the meetings, she talked with a few people but, not a lot; at least, not like she used to. She'd laugh but not with the same gusto. And then there was that time I called about a prospective customer and, after a few back-and-forth talks, she bawled her eyes out on the phone. Brian was starting to drink heavily. Coincidentally, it started when she started her own business but, she didn't think that could be the reason because he was the one who encouraged her to do it. Nevertheless, it started first with beer and then escalated to the harder stuff. He was getting shitfaced at every party and BBQ they had. Her kids were starting to notice and she would provide any excuse to calm their fears. This is what she told me on the phone. I told her not to worry, we'll think of something.

But then, the following Thursday evening, she asked me for a reading. Correct me if I'm wrong but, I think this was the Thursday evening when Jean Balzano brought her son Nicky, age 10, to play the violin for us. Nicky had just won First Prize in the Brooklyn Musical Championships and Jean was so proud. He played about 20-25 minutes and then Jean had to take him home for bedtime. The rest of the evening was devoted to readings. Signorine passed away the month before so Antoinette and Irish Marie set up the coffee and cake table.

After Nicky's recital, Irish Marie asked me for reading; I had a few people lined up before her so, she got herself some coffee and chatted with the ladies. I've given Irish Marie readings in the past like when she wanted to know if starting a business was the right thing to do or if her teenage daughter was going to be a pain in her ass for the rest of her life.

But this reading was different because Number 1, she had a lot of make-up on; she hardly ever put on make-up. But that night, trust me, she had enough foundation on to cover a wall. But all the foundation and make-up in the world couldn't cover up the bruise on her cheek. So, while Antoinette was in the kitchen, I asked her where did she get the bruise on her cheek. At first, she said something like …what bruise? And then she said she'd tell me later because people were starting to arrive. I thought nothing of it because Irish Marie was always a little clumsy; she'd hurt herself tripping on a pebble. A lot of times she'd get a black and blue on her arms from cleaning on the job. Esther Schrable told me Irish Marie took a fall as a result of trying to clean her top kitchen cabinet shelves so we were all used to seeing her with bruises on her arms but not the face. Number 2, at her reading, she cried even before she asked me a question so I told her let's just do a general reading. I usually ask the seeker if they have a specific question and then we go on to a general reading. Irish Marie said she didn't have a specific question but I knew she just was unable to say it. So, I just focused and then it came to me in full blown images.

How do you tell a woman that there's deception in her marriage but, you can't confirm it? The image popped up right in my head and I couldn't explain it. My non-psychic self is thinking that Brian, for all intent and purposes, is a good guy. He'd do anything for you. He put all my ceiling fans up in my house, no charge. He coordinates the annual block party on his street and he always has a smile on his face. Adores his children, never stops talking about them. So, why did I get this image of Brian and the word deception? And how do I say this to Irish Marie? Well, I said it anyway. And that's when the whole story came out.

She told me last week, they had a big argument over something Betty Cammamano told her. One morning, Betty Cammamano was taking the subway to work. Betty and Irish Marie were friends since high school and they stayed friends. They invited each other to their kid's birthday parties, communions, confirmation and a BBQ during the summer. Irish Marie pointed out that it was Betty who noticed that Brian was drinking a lot at their son's Confirmation party. She didn't make a big deal of it at the time. They had the Confirmation party in the backyard so he wasn't driving and quite frankly, she noticed it, too, despite the fact that she was moving all over the place to serve her guests. Irish Marie was and still is one of those people who can't sit down; she always has to be moving. Even when we went to the disco, she'd dance but, she was always looking around to see if there were any people she knew and bounced around all night until we'd went home. She was the first one sleeping in the car.

Well, anyway, one morning Betty got on the train to go to work in downtown Manhattan. The morning rush hour is always busy and by the time the train got to her stop, it was standing room only. Betty was scanning the train car to see if by some miracle there could be a seat but, as any subway rider knows, if there's a seat on a packed train, it's probably because some unfortunate homeless person is sitting in the seat next to that empty seat and before you're 10 feet from the seat you smell the aroma. It's not Chanel #5, I'll tell you that much. While she is scanning, she sees Brian on the train. So, she started to move closer to say hello. As she is trying to move forward, she sees Brian turn his head sideways to kiss the woman who was seated next to him and he had his arm around her. Betty at once knew it couldn't be Irish Marie; Irish Marie had dark hair, now it's grey but back then it was a dark brunette so it couldn't be Irish Marie. This woman was dark blonde with highlights. So, right away, Betty started to back track to her original position on the train. By that time, she had to get off at Fulton Street. When she got off, she turned around to look inside the train but she couldn't see anything because there was a whole slew of people getting off and on. As she was walking to work, she convinced herself that she probably was mistaken. It was the morning; she didn't have her bagel and coffee yet. It couldn't have been Brian; she knew the mind without coffee plays funny tricks on you. She worked all day and came home at night and forgot all about it."

So, Irish Marie continued, "Betty has only one child, a son, Paul, he's 11 years old and, occasionally on Friday evenings, she takes Paul to the Tiffany Diner for dinner and then to a movie. It's usually a monster or action movie but she doesn't care. Her husband usually stayed home to watch a ball game or some show but, Betty enjoyed these mother and son bonding nights. They go to the new multi-plex movie theatre in Bay Ridge that has three or four movies running at the same time. Well, anyway, last Friday, after they finished their dinner, Betty had to go to the bathroom. She always went to the bathroom in the diner because the bathrooms at the movies weren't always that clean and there was always a line. Besides, if you put it off, you know you'll have to go in the middle of the movie. You have to go way around the corner of the Tiffany Diner to get to the Ladies Room. As Betty was just about to sprint to the bathroom, she sees Brian, yet again, in a booth with the same woman. They were talking to each other but she was holding his hand across the table. Betty knew she would have to pass their booth to get to the Ladies Room so she turned around and went back to her booth. Now, there was no mistake. She and her son paid the check and got out of there like bats out of hell. They went to the movies and when Betty came home, guess who called her? I did. Betty's husband told her that I called about half hour after she left; nothing important, I just wanted to say hello which was true to a certain extent. Betty told me panic started to come over her and her husband looked at her strange but, the commercial was over so he went back to watching TV.

Well, Betty called me back the next day; she hoped I wasn't home so she could leave a voicemail but, I answered the phone. Betty was conflicted. She thought that maybe me and Brian were separated? She was wondering if she should ask or even if it was her business to even ask? Betty is my friend; how could she not tell me? Betty had a mountain size drama going on in her head. Finally, she just blurted it out. She told me about the diner."

I'm going to try to make a long conversation short because many of the Fairy Comaras know this story, especially Antoinette Fresca and her posse of Black Marie, Little Marie and Theresa Guarino, God rest her soul.

At first, Betty started out with the usual greetings like, "how are you?" Irish Marie's father I think was still alive then so she asked about him. Irish Marie told Betty that she actually called last night because Brian was working yesterday and she wanted to know if Betty wanted to go to dinner, just the two of them, like old times. Well, there was lengthy pause on Betty's side; in fact, Irish Marie thought they were cut off; she had to say "Hello? Hello?" Long story short, Betty spilled the beans. She made Irish Marie promise not to tell Brian who told her and, Irish Marie told me she didn't tell Brian who told her. It was Saturday and Brian would be home from the firehouse at 5:00 PM. She had a few hours to cry her eyes out; the kids were out with their friends. After the cry, she composed herself and made dinner. Well, Brian didn't come home at 5:00 PM; he came home drunk at 9:00 PM. Needless the say, everything came out and, of course, he denied it. Irish Marie admitted she hit Brian first but whether it was an accident or not, he threw a punch at her and she landed on the floor. The kids came out of the living room crying and screaming. Brian, seeing the look of horror on his kids' faces, dashed out of the house.

Thank God, Brian's father called and told her he was spending the night at their house. Brian's father liked Irish Marie and without questioning her he just told her two people are in a marriage for better or for worse; him and his wife were going on 49 years married and it wasn't always a picnic. Brian's father is a retired firefighter and he admitted sometimes the stress of being New York's Bravest can take a toll on a man. He told her he was going to talk to him tomorrow. Irish Marie decided to keep her mouth shut rather than tell his father about the affair or the physical fight; he already knew Brian was drinking when he came through the door. Brian stood over Saturday into Monday when he had to go back to work. He came home Tuesday to get some clothes when Irish Marie was at work. So, she called his parents and, after a little back and forth diplomatic questioning, they said he left Sunday afternoon. Irish Marie made up a story that he must have done an extra shift. He came home Wednesday but, she couldn't even look at him although he did try to talk to her.

So, here we are having a reading and she asks me what's the outcome? Are they getting divorced? Is he in love with this woman? So, I asked her, "Do you love him?" And, after her initial rant of "No, I don't love him anymore, how could he do this to me, he should drop dead, I always put him first how could he do this to me, I'm better off without him" and this went on for about 10 minutes and I was calm although, I told her to lower her voice because the other people could hear. So, I asked again, "do you love him?" she said, "you're going to think I'm crazy but, I do; we went through too much together. I'm so confused because he was there for me when I started the business, he helped me with the kids when I had the foot surgery to remove the bunion on my left foot, he cleaned, cooked and took care of the kids." I said, "What about when he had the side construction business going, before you started your own business, were you there for him?" Marie told me that, at the time, the kids were small and she was still working full-time at the bank and cleaning houses on the side. "He had his buddies at the firehouse and his father to help out. I was sad when that side business panned out; he just couldn't get the clientele needed to make a profit. And, the guys in the firehouse had families to take care of and no time to help him; some even had their own side business so, it just didn't work out." I said, "That must have been hard for him, Marie. His father had a side business for years when he was a firefighter and he quit when he got too old. I wonder how Brian felt that he failed." I asked, "Since you had the business, Marie, how many times did just the two of you go out to dinner or to a movie?" Marie said it was almost non-existent because of their different work schedules, the kids, the house and her cleaning business were just starting to make a profit. Something had to be done about this situation, but first we had to take care of the drinking.

I had another reading after Irish Marie and I told her I was sorry but, I had to end it. I told her not to worry; Black Marie and Antoinette are helping me with the clean-up tonight. Between the three of us, we'll come up with something. I told her to go home; she was too much of a mess to speak to us as a group; it was easier for us to discuss a game plan without her. It's better that she didn't know what we were up to, she might say something to Brian in an argument. Better she knew nothing for now. Mind you, the Fairy Comaras kept no secrets from each other; if we had something to say to one another, we said it. Not like today, where everyone speaks in riddles and mask their true feelings and then they go home and talk about each other. Friends should be solution-based not rumor-based.

After the meeting ended and everybody went home, Antoinette, Little Marie and Black Marie stayed to clean up. After Signorine died, we put some flowers on the recliner she sat on; no one sat on the recliner on Thursdays. Gloria Saccomano was at the meeting and I asked her to stay because her son, Vincent, worked at the same firehouse as Brian. Gloria may not have been a full-fledged Fairy Comara but, she could always be depended upon if we needed a favor. We asked Gloria to talk to her son and see what he could dig up about what's going on with Brian; maybe the guys in the firehouse noticed any changes in Brian's behavior. Did they notice he was drinking a lot, too? Anyone who's had to deal with an Italian mother knows you can never say no to them. She'd only have to ask Vincent and he did it. They have a honing system that knows immediately if you're lying to them. Vincent would tell her the truth about what he found out. If Italian mothers worked for the CIA, they'd get any secret out in an interrogation, no waterboarding needed. They just had a way of finding out. Once we found out what Gloria found out from her son then, Antoinette and Black Marie would start the ball rolling. Little Marie asked Black Marie for some legal advice and then she took her mother home.

Well, maybe a day or two later, Gloria dropped by my house; she had just dropped off some clothes at St. Agatha's for Father Giudice's used clothing drive. She had a load of information to tell me. It seems, Vincent had an argument with Brian a week before she spoke to him. He couldn't talk fast enough. He didn't even mind that Gloria was taking notes on the kitchen table. Gloria was a little forgetful; she had a million post-its all around her house. And now, I do the same thing, too, only I don't use post-its; I use the note pads that I get from all these charities asking me for money. Some, I contribute to, the rest I say "no, thank you". So, I have all these notes on my kitchen table, do this, do that, call so and so, buy toilet paper. Now I put dates on those notes because a few times I forget to throw out the toilet paper note and now, I have a dozen, 24 count rolls of toilet paper. Of course, it became very valuable during the pandemic. But I digress.

Anyway, Vincent told his mother that the guys at the firehouse knew something was up with Brian but, being men, they weren't going to talk about it. Men don't do that and anyway, in their mind this was a home problem. Vincent said usually the men get telephone calls from their wives or girlfriends when there was a problem but Brian was getting a call once a day. At first, they thought something was up at home and he was talking to Irish Marie. It soon became apparent that it was not Irish Marie because he was all laughing and giggling and talking low. Even the guys who had girlfriends didn't talk to them every day. And still, the guys didn't think it was any of their business; this was a family matter. But when Brian came in two times with alcohol on his breath and a little tipsy, then they had a problem. This impacted the safety of all the men in the firehouse.

The second time he came in with alcohol on his breath, you could smell it six feet away. And this was about a week ago. Frankie Valdaro, Antoinette's cousin, took him to the side and said something to him and then they sobered him up with lots of coffee. Thank God it was a slow day for them and the neighborhood. They had a grocery run, a fire inspection, possible gas leak and they put out a burning garbage can. However, Frankie Valdaro told Vincent that Brian had a Comara on the side which was kind of insulting to us girls but, we needed the information. Drunks have diarrhea of the mouth; they'll tell you everything. Her name was Stephanie but Brian didn't give him a last name and he said she lived in Flatbush (Brooklyn). Frankie Valdaro lives in Flatbush so he asked where and Brian told him that she lives two blocks away from the Kings Bar on East 45th St. He meets her there all the time.

At that point, we had enough information to go to Black Marie's uncle, Big Jimmy. So, Antoinette and Black Marie went down to the club. Irish Marie cleaned Big Jimmy's house for the last 10 years; his wife was too old to clean the house the way she wanted, she had the Arthritis, too. The first time Irish Marie cleaned the house, Big Jimmy's wife said she only wanted her to clean her house because she used the Giavell (Clorox). And, of course, she made friends with Irish Marie through the years. She always put a little extra in the envelope before Christmas and Big Jimmy would always send her a tray of pastries on Christmas Eve.

I remember they went on a Saturday because I was home. Anyway, Antoinette and Black Marie went to the club to speak with Big Jimmy, Uncle Jimmy to Black Marie. The minute you entered the club you were overwhelmed by the amount of cigarette and cigar smoke in the front room; nobody thought to open a window. A few of the guys there were playing cards or watching the races at Belmont. The club had two big rooms, the front room was where all the light business was conducted; it had a bar inside and if we were playing outside in the summer, Big Jimmy would call his sister, Livia, Black Marie's mother, and tell her to send us kids down to get some soda. My favorite was Manhattan Special, not Coca Cola. It's probably the reason why I drink 5-6 cups of coffee today! The back room was divided into two rooms: a small kitchen and Big Jimmy's office. Only serious stuff was discussed in Big Jimmy's office; it was bug proof. During the summer they used to play cards outside and have BBQs in the backyard. I went to a few of them, they cooked everything… chicken, hamburgers, sausage and peppers, everything. They bought all the chicken and meats from George the German so they were the best cuts. By this time, Big Jimmy was getting long in the tooth; he gained a few more pounds but until the day he died, he always wore a suit to the club. He was still in control but he was mostly a consultant; he delegated like a good leader should! He'd never stayed at home; his wife would have none of that plus he couldn't smoke a cigar in his house.

Anyway, the two Fairy Comaras went into his office. He was on the phone but he got off quickly. Black Marie did most of the talking. She told him the whole story about Irish Marie and Brian. When he heard that, he couldn't believe it. Irish Marie was like a daughter to him. "What do you want from me? I could get somebody to knock the shit out of him." Antoinette said, "no, no, that's not going to help in this situation although, I feel like we should kick his butt, too". To this day, Antoinette doesn't like to use curse words; I think one time we heard her say bastard. Black Marie said, "Uncle Jimmy, we want to know about this woman; we want to know what we're dealing with." She told him about "Stephanie" and the King's Bar. She described her to him per Betty Cammamano's description. Black Marie asked, "Uncle Jimmy, I want you to check her out and see what information you can get on her, that's all. We'll take over from there." Uncle Jimmy said, "I'm on it as we speak, I'll send one of the guys to the bar and see what we can find out about her. You say she lives two blocks from the Kings Bar? I'll make inquiries."

The meeting was over and after that, Big Jimmy asked us if we wanted some linguine with clam sauce in the kitchen. Black Marie called me when she got home and told me Step 1 was put in place. Step 2 was up to Antoinette.

Well, by this time, Irish Marie and Brian were not on speaking terms and, of course, the kids noticed it immediately. Irish Marie's father, Hector, came over that Sunday for dinner and noticed the difference immediately. It was an extremely quiet Sunday. He noticed the drinking, too. Irish Marie wouldn't ever tell her father about the other thing. She couldn't utter the words without crying her eyes out. It's better he didn't know because he liked Brian. Brian's father came over during the week when Brian was home and noticed the drinking, too; especially when you go to your son's house at 10:30 in the morning.

Antoinette's task, AKA Step 2, was to get the guys in the firehouse to do an intervention about the drinking. We thought there might be a problem getting them to do it but, we figured the best Fairy Comara to send was Antoinette. Practically everyone in the firehouse owed her a favor. For years, Carmela and Antoinette Fresca were the firehouse's top fans. In her heyday, Carmela helped a lot of the guys with babysitting their kids so they could go out to dinner with their wives or to a wedding. When Frankie Valdaro's infant son was colic, Carmela made her special fennel seed tea with honey and brought it over to them. When Gloria Saccomano had her gall bladder taken out, Carmela would bring dinners for her husband and Vincent the whole time she was in the hospital. Antoinette was a candy stripper at the hospital and she'd bring Gloria all the beauty magazines and some cookies. Some of the men Carmela helped have retired but their sons replaced them; they knew Antoinette because she baby sat for them or she was friends with their mothers. Once Carmela got too old and couldn't do it anymore, Antoinette became the babysitter; she does the hospital visits and dinners now. They'd do anything for her…. but, would they do an intervention?

First, she had to find out what evening Brian wasn't working that week so she called her cousin, Frankie Valdaro; he was married to her cousin Jeanette. Frankie told her Brian wasn't working Wednesday evening; she told him she was going to drop by the firehouse with her homemade cream puffs. When Frankie asked her why was it important that Brian was not there, she told him because she already made cream puffs for Irish Marie. Believe it or not, Antoinette told me he said OKAY. She told him to call her the minute the guys were in the firehouse and Step 2 was implemented. I love Antoinette's cream puffs; they're fluffy and she's not cheap with the cream.

She went to Key Food to get the ingredients and on her way home who should she see but Esther Schrable being wheeled to the car service that pulled up. They made contact and if looks could kill on Antoinette's side, Esther would have been laid out on the floor. Antoinette never got over the fact that Esther broke up her relationship with her son, Manny. But, that's another story for later; let's get back to Irish Marie.

God bless Big Uncle Jimmy, he always got the job done, God rest his soul. At his wake, they had to open two rooms in Torragrosso for people to pay their respects. They were taking flowers out each of the three days and giving them to the church; the place smelled like a funeral parlor but, of course, it was a funeral parlor, but you know what I mean. They had about 10 Mass card stands around the rooms completely filled. The priests at St. Agatha's received about 20 Chasubles; they were set for years! Somebody, we still don't know who it was, donated a solid gold Chalice. If Big Jimmy had a problem getting into heaven, all the Masses said for him gave him a pass. He was loved but he was feared.

About three days later, Uncle Jimmy called Black Marie at her mother's house and told her to come to the club after work; he had something for her. He didn't like explaining things on the phone but, Black Marie understood; then, she handed the phone to her mother so she could talk to her brother.

When she came into the club, Uncle Jimmy told her to come in the back to his office. He told her to pour a cup of espresso for herself and take some cookies; there was also stuffed shells and meatballs. She told him no because she'd be up half the night and she couldn't stay long. So, they're sitting in his office and Uncle Jimmy takes out an 8 by 11 envelope with a bunch of notes in it; he couldn't remember everything that Johnny T told him so he took notes. He told her that he sent Johnny T over to the Kings Bar and he canvassed the neighborhood. Johnny T knew the area well because he grew up there. After he got married, he moved to Manhasset, Long Island but, he still knew a lot of people from the old neighborhood so he asked around. Johnny and his friends used to hang out at the Kings Bar because the owner was an uncle of one of his friends and they could drink for free. It just so happened that the nephew owns it now. Johnny and his friend did the back and forth about the old days for a while and exchanged information about their families. After that, Johnny T. asked his friend if he knew a Stephanie who frequents this bar? All that was known at the time was that Brian was seeing a Stephanie with dark blond hair with highlights who hangs out in this bar a lot. That was all Johnny T. had to go by. Johnny's friend was a little nervous about saying anything but Johnny told him that he was just checking her out for a friend who's interested in dating her. And then the guy started laughing…so, here's what Uncle Jimmy told Black Marie.

"This guy told Johnny that if he wanted to know all about Stephanie, her last name is Wozniak, all he had to do was come to this bar any Thursday, Friday or Saturday night. She's a real putana, good looking but she's all about the money and the gifts. Lately, she's been coming to the bar with two different guys but, he heard there's another one who is single that she'd drop everything for because he's rich. He never comes to the bar. The two guys that she comes with, one is blond and that is probably Brian and the other one is a Sicilian type, darker, could be Greek. One time, when he was bringing wine to their table, Johnny's friend saw the blond guy give her an envelope with money in it. Probably the other guy is giving her money, too. He said she works for a dentist in the neighborhood. He goes to that dentist so he sees her there. She has an apartment in one of the two-family houses two blocks away.

Sometimes, Marie, a man goes astray, it happens. Don't tell your aunt but, there was one time and only one time I went astray; the kids were babies and your aunt had a handful taking care of them. But it was only for a short time. If as you say, (Irish) Marie wants to save the marriage, I have a plan. Just give me a week, maybe two, and I'll get the goods on this Wozniak woman and Brian will be back in her arms. Ok? You hungry? We have stuffed shells and meatballs in the kitchen"

They kissed, Uncle Jimmy asked her how she was, how were the kids and they said good bye. Then, she went to my house and told me everything; I called Antoinette to come upstairs. She told me Frankie Valdaro will call her this Wednesday evening and let her know when the guys were in the firehouse. Steps 1 and 2 were out of the starting gates!

Step 2: So, that Wednesday evening, Frankie Valdaro called Antoinette and told her to drop by; he was dreaming of those cream puffs all weekend. Antoinette also brought cream puffs for Jeanette and the kids and warned him that he better not keep them in the firehouse for himself which he swore he wouldn't do.

When she opened up the box of cream puffs the guys were like moths to flame so the first part of her job was done! She had them in a good mood right from the start. And then she did the usual thing, she asked about their families; she knew all of their families through one interaction or the other; she either babysat for them, went to their wedding, visited them in the hospital when they got hurt or had a new addition to the family. She was praying the alarm wouldn't go off and she could say what she had to say.

You have to understand, Antoinette was omnipresent, she knew everyone even people outside of the neighborhood; that was her nature. When my air conditioner failed to turn on, on one of the hottest days of the summer, I called Antoinette to see if she knew anyone. In two hours, a guy rings my bell, tells me Antoinette sent him to fix my air conditioner. Turns out it just needed freon. When I asked how much? He tells me no charge, he owed Antoinette a favor. But I digress.

Anyway, I can't remember exactly what Antoinette told me decades ago about the firehouse intervention but here's the condensed version:

First, she told them that she wasn't completely honest about why she brought the cream puffs; she had a very important favor to ask them. Of course, the guys said they'd do anything for Antoinette. And then, she started to explain. "I don't know if all of you are aware of it but Brian has a drinking problem, a serious one. If it continues, he could not only lose his job, he could lose his family. He needs an intervention. And before you even ask, he's not going to go to a therapist; you know you wouldn't either…. you're men, you can't help it, it's like asking you to ask for directions, not going to happen." There was a lot of hemming and hawing going on; they were hesitant to get involved. She didn't want to bring it up but she had to; she told them he was using his hands on his wife. Not only that, the kids were starting to be afraid when he came home. He was yelling at them all the time for the littlest of things. Something had to be done. Frankie Valdaro suggested taking him to a bar and having a long talk with him but, we knew that was not a good idea! Hello! Frankie! He has a drinking problem! The one thing we forbade her to mention was the girlfriend on the side. Step 2 was not to include Step 1.

Antoinette suggested a plan. A few of the guys who were home during the day, when Brian was also home, had to pay him a "surprise" visit. It had to be at a time when Irish Marie was working and the kids were in school. She already warned them that he was going to be on the defensive but, they should just barge in; she told them she was going to call Brian's father to be there because he noticed the drinking. Brian needed to hear it from family and it couldn't be his mother. This was good back-up in case he got violent; Dads can always put you in your place! So, five of the guys said they would go; no decent firefighter likes to hear one of their brothers is hitting his wife and their children are everything to them. They're not chatty unless they're talking about their family; then they're like a bunch of hens.

I just want to say one thing before I start talking about what happened with Steps 1 and 2. Antoinette was told what happened at the intervention but she did not get a long blow-by-blow story from them. Men have a problem with figurative narration; in other words, they're the Noun, Verb and Direct Object gender …no adverbs, no superlatives, hyperbole. The only men who speak figuratively are politicians and poets. Men speak in short sentences and their stories are paragraphs rather than pages. So, just saying, I'm telling what Antoinette heard from Frankie Valdaro.

Step 2, Intervention, was accomplished the following Tuesday. According to Frankie Valdaro, who told Antoinette, who told me, five brothers and Brian's father came to Brian's home at 10:00 AM. If they were hesitant about how they were going to approach this, they didn't have to think long because when they rang the bell, Brian greeted them with a beer in his hand. Brian said, "hey, guys, what's up? Come in!" Brian's father came in last and it was only when Brian saw him, he knew this was serious. He dumped the beer into the kitchen sink and went into the Livingroom. He was angry. Right away, he said, "Did Marie put you up to this? Because I don't have a problem." And his father shouted out, "No, it was me, I put them up to it, shout at me if you want but we're here because you're drinking too much and you're going down the drain like that beer can you just got rid of in the kitchen. What the fuck are you doing drinking at 10:00 in the morning? You think that's normal? You ever see me drinking in the morning? You know what your mother would do to me? You'd be visiting me in a cemetery." And then he and Brian had a back and forth about him not being the perfect father, either, and how many times his father had to pull his ass out of trouble. Frankie said that Betty's son, Vincent, finally interrupted and calmly pulled the conversation back to Brian.

"Listen, buddy, we're not here to pass judgment, we know the stress of juggling our job, family and for some of us juggling another job. It's a lot of pressure but, you can't give in to it. Drinking makes it go away for a night or in your case, a morning, but the problems are still there when you sober up. You're lucky you have a father who talks to you; my father just beat the shit out of me and told me to grow up. It worked but, I like your father's way better. I guess what we're trying to say is we all noticed the drinking. We saw Frankie pull you to the side that day and pump you with coffee because you came in drunk. Bottom line, we depend on each other going into a fire and right now, you're our weakest link. And what's more, you're letting your family down, too." Brian got on the defensive and started raising his voice and saying he was going to quit the Fire Dept., all bullshit beer talk. One of the guys made some coffee in the kitchen.

Frankie told Antoinette not to get mushy but, Brian was crying and some of the guys were crying, too. That was all he was going to say about the crying is that they cried. Antoinette asked who else besides Brian was crying but then Frankie was getting tense on the phone and just said one of them was Brian's father. He thought Barry Guarino, Theresa's brother was crying, too. Brian told them he felt like he was getting swallowed up by his family; Marie's business was doing very well, his side construction business, not so well. The kids were off in their own world with their friends, it wasn't Daddy! Daddy! Daddy! when he came home; the house felt empty. And while he loved Marie, he felt invisible. And then, he lied to the guys and his father and told them he rang up a gambling debt, $10,000. He had to take the money from the kids' college fund. Me, Antoinette and Black Marie knew that probably was bullshit; the only time Brian gambled was when the Lotto was over $50 million; he gave "Stephanie" the money. According to Johnny T, it was all a racket she had going on with married men, per explanation in Step 1.

Anyway, Brian told them he stopped but, he still had to replace the money in the kids' fund without Marie knowing and it was weighing on his mind. His father offered to replace half the money, provided he end the gambling; after all, it was his grandchildren but, Brian said no, it was his problem. What more guilt can a person have than when someone offers to help them with their lie, right? Talk about what a tangled web we weave.

One of the guys, Arty Maldonado, said his wife wants a new kitchen and he could use some help with that and Eddie Dugan said he needed a patio in his backyard; he just bought his first house. Some way, somehow, the guys told Brian they'd put the word out about his construction business to their families and friends and the $10,000 would go back into the kids' college fund. Brian swore on his son's Communion Missal, they couldn't find a Bible, that he'd stick to just a beer watching baseball. Frankie Valdaro was/is a very emotional guy and without him even saying it, we knew the guys had to get the Kleenex out for him. He retired many years ago, he and his wife bought a two-bedroom condo in New Jersey near the Goethals Bridge; I think they still live there. I'll have to ask Antoinette.

Anyway, Antoinette told me they ended the intervention about two hours later; after that, Brian asked them if they wanted to order lunch but, they said no although his father stayed behind; the guys thought maybe they had more to talk about as father and son. Frankie told her even though Brian swore he was off the bottle, the guys said they would watch him. The firehouse had a wedding and a christening to go to next month so they would keep a close eye on how many times he went to the bar. Step 2 was a lot easier than we thought!

The following Monday, Step 1, Uncle Jimmy calls Black Marie and said everything was taken care of and not a word more. That morning, Brian found a large brown envelope in his locker. It contained photos of Stephanie Wozniak with not one, not two but three other guys. Some were taken at the Kings Bar and some were of her and a guy coming out of her apartment. How that envelope got there, nobody knows. That night, we sent Uncle Jimmy 3 lbs. of Italian cookies from Agnello's Bakery.

At the Thursday evening meeting that week, Irish Marie had a big smile on her face. She never asked but she knew we waved our wands for her. She asked Antoinette if she was doing anything the first weekend in May because they needed a baby sitter. She and Brian were going to a Bed and Breakfast up in Mystic, CT. Brian never went to the King's Bar ever again. Antoinette's brother, Emil, sent him to a few side jobs in Brooklyn and word of mouth got him more side jobs. All was well.

By this time, Little Marie Greco already left the 78th Precinct and was working at Francone Senior Center in Massapequa; she was dying to do a lecture on Elder Abuse so we gave her the floor. Many of our guests were taking care of parents and their children at the same time; sometimes we had to farm out/outsource the care of our parent(s) to caregivers, we used to call them aids but now it's caregiver which I think is a better title. Did we feel guilty? You better believe it. But the American Dream of owning a home for our generation, took two incomes, not one anymore.

March 4, 1999 Lecturer: (Little) Marie Greco, Coordinator, Senior Services, Francone Senior Center

Recognizing the Signs of Elder Abuse

Marie started the lecture asking the audience who is currently taking care of a parent or parents at home? Five or six hands went up. She then asked how many have outside support caring for their parents? Two hands went up; one of them got their caregiver from Marie's place. How many have parents living alone and have to check on them at least once a week? Another 15 hands went up.

> "Well, by looking around the room, I know this lecture may not be directed to you but, it may be for someone you know, either a neighbor, your parents' friend or even someone in your extended family like an aunt or an uncle."

Little Marie borrowed a screen from her job and used her laptop for her PowerPoint presentation.

Slide 1: (Little Marie used a pointer for each slide, because she couldn't reach the top, and read it out loud.)

According to the National Council on Aging (NCOA) and the Centers for Disease Control (CDC) the five types of Elder Abuse are:

1. Physical Abuse – obvious signs of continued bruising or other marks that never go away.
2. Emotional – verbal or threatening remarks, harassment, living in a hostile environment, keeping them homebound and away from friends
3. Neglect – older adult is deprived of basic needs such as food, water, proper bedding, lack of hygiene, dirty clothes or medical neglect
4. Financial Abuse – stealing from the elderly, using their credit cards for outside non-patient purchases, using their home for illegal activities such as selling drugs or storage for stolen goods, illegal transfer of property.
5. Sexual Abuse – yes, it does happen!

Everyone in the audience let off a sound of disgust. They couldn't even imagine it!

> "For number 1, it's pretty easy to detect but, not always. Sometimes, the elderly hide their bruises because they don't want to get a family member arrested, or they're afraid of losing the support and having to go into a nursing home. So, they put up with the abuse. It may not even be a family member, it could be a caregiver; most caregivers are angels from heaven but, not all of them. Some caregivers shouldn't be

caregivers because they may not have the patience.

We had an elderly lady who would come to the Francone Center on Wednesdays to play bingo; she always wore a sweater inside which was okay because she claimed the center was too cold for her, didn't matter summer or winter. She'd complain about how hot the center was in the winter but she wouldn't take off the sweater. One summer day, she came in with not only a sweater but a scarf around her neck, not the woolen ones, the silk ones. If she had been dressed up, we wouldn't have thought a thing but, her clothes were worn out, the sweater was shabby and her shoe soles were old and dirty. So, one of our staff, Jean, was suspicious and she came over to her and admired her scarf. Jean told her the scarf was on all wrong and she would fix it; the old lady protested but Jean went ahead and fixed it anyway. Sure enough, there were hand marks on her neck and bruising as if she'd been choked."

"We are required by law to report these things and long story short, a social worker at the center was called to the community room. When she examined her, she discovered other bruises throughout her body, on the arms, hence the sweater and on her legs, she always wore pant suits. Nothing strange about wearing pant suits, most of the elderly wear them for comfort."

"It seems that her grandson was kicked out of his parents' home and came to live with her two years ago. Her children told her not to let him in but, she couldn't have her grandson living on the street. Besides, she could use the help. It turned out to be a nightmare arrangement; he was unemployed, on drugs and selling them from her basement. She would smell the smoke coming up from the basement and complain about it and then, he became angry and either threaten to hit her, curse at her or actually hit her. So, one Wednesday when she was at the center, we arranged to have the cops come to her house with a warrant and they discovered the drugs, arrested the grandson and we later discovered he was funneling money from her bank account. So, the grandson not only was guilty of physical abuse but numbers 2,3, and 4 on the slide."

"However, the biggest abuse is financial abuse either by children, extended family, a neighbor or a caregiver. Financial abuse can be done whether the perpetrator is in the house or out of the house. And that's what makes it the easiest form of abuse, especially if the elderly person is not able to administer his or her own money due to some disability or dementia. Emotional Abuse is another unseen-to-the-naked eye kind of thing because the outside world can't see it. Keeping them inside every day away from social interaction, constantly yelling at them, leaving them alone all the time. These are killers for the elderly. A lot of times their protests to go out lead to threats to put them in a nursing home because "they're too demanding" which to them is scarier than remaining alone at home. They lose their will to live and wait for death; they miss out having a full life in their golden years. And sadly, as hard as it is to believe, sexual abuse, number 5, does happen to our seniors. I see the look of horror in all of your eyes but, I have encountered it in my experience, it's disgusting, I know."

Slide 2: Check On Your Elderly Neighbors

1. Get acquainted with them if you see them outside. If they live next door, invite them to your home for lunch or dinner.
2. Offer to do shopping during inclement weather; snow and icy weather prevent them from even buying the basics like bread and milk.
3. If they allow you, visit them in their home. Is their home a mess because they can't do it or if they smell like it's been sometime since they've bathe themselves, find out if they have children; they may not be aware of the situation. Or call me and we can schedule a visit to decide whether they may need a caregiver to clean and cook for them. If they cannot pay for one, we have the resources to connect them to free services done by qualified volunteers.
4. If they protest or say they don't need anyone's help, just give them your phone number to call you just in case they do need help and let it go. Some seniors are just stubborn or they fear that you may be a con artist. Maybe they're ashamed to have others see that their house is a mess.

   "One of Francone Center's seniors, an elderly gentleman, confessed that he would never let his son or company in his house; if his son picked him up for the holidays, he would wait outside for him. His fear was that they'd see the mess and call his son and he'd put him in a home or he would take him to live with his family. He loved his three grandchildren, not so much the daughter-in-law. According to him the feeling was mutual. And he admitted he's no angel to get along with either. His wife took care of all the cleaning, cooking and paying the bills but, when she died a number of years ago, he was lost without her. They were married 51 years and for a long time he just let things go except for the bills. His wife was very organized and when she got sick, she made a list of the bills that had to be paid and what time of the month to pay them. But the cleaning and the cooking were way out of his zone so his house got cluttered and dirty. He told me, at this point, he doesn't have the energy to do the cleaning and wouldn't know where to even start. The washing machine he could maneuver because the detergent came with instructions; the dryer, however, was a problem. He didn't know how many wet clothes to put in the dryer; he thought maybe too much would break the drum. So, he put two garments at a time and boy did his electric bill skyrocket!"

"One day, with his permission, me and Irish Marie went to his house; I needed her assessment on what kind of a job this was going to be and the cost. She said the kitchen she could have someone come in and do it in a day; it was mainly a lot of boxes, dishes in the sink, clearing and cleaning of the countertops and probably cleaning out the refrigerator of all the expired food. The living room was the problem; newspapers stacked high, the carpet was dirty and worn. The couch and recliner had holes in it; he had a cat who used it as a scratching post; the cat died two years ago from old age. Dust everywhere and the curtains looked as though they've been hanging since his wife died. Both the kitchen and the living room definitely needed a paint job. The bathroom was a "ugh" moment…. definitely a Giavell (Clorox) job and the shower curtain smelled of mold. Irish Marie said she could try to clean the carpet but it was too worn and it was shredded in some areas. Brian could probably do the painting but, right now he was working on two big side jobs and probably wouldn't be able to do it for months. However, Brian's father had nothing to do and Irish Marie's father was a retired janitor, he painted all the time, maybe we could get the two of them to do it. Her mother-in-law was always looking for any excuse to get her husband out of the house, because all he did since he retired is look at the TV all day and wait for the mail to come. I volunteered to buy the paint and brushes."

"Irish Marie gave him a low-ball ridiculous price because he was on a fixed income. She came in on her day off and cleaned up the whole kitchen, including the refrigerator. After she cleaned out the refrigerator, she realized there was no food in there so she took him food shopping. Not only that, she cooked him a nice hot meal. He had a tear in his eye because the kitchen felt and looked like his wife was still alive. And he sure liked the company, Irish Marie could chew your ear off while she was cleaning, sorry Marie!   Antoinette and Diane were assigned with bathroom and curtain purchases; Diane went to A&S and bought a whole new bathroom set; shower curtain, bathroom rug, soap and toothbrush dish. She cleaned the bathroom; even cleaned out his medicine cabinet. Antoinette's mother, who passed away a year ago, rest in peace, saved all her curtains; she was always afraid that she might have a need to use them again. It never happened; she just bought more and more."

To be honest, all our parents had a thing with curtains, even me, I have to confess. My mother had curtains for all four seasons and one for the Christmas holidays. A window without curtains? Looks like a bordello! God Forbid!

"So, Antoinette looked in the closet and picked out a nice set of drapes and sheer panel curtains that would go with the Livingroom; they were pastel colors so they would go with whatever color the guys painted the Livingroom. Anyway, Brian's and Irish Marie's father picked up their brushes and headed to the old guy's house. I left them six gallons of paint: two eggshell finish gallons for the living room walls, one gallon gloss white for the windows and woodwork and one gallon white for the ceiling. The other two gallons were for the kitchen which was small. Came out beautiful. Brian's father did the walls and ceiling and Irish Marie's father did the windows and the woodwork. It took longer than we expected because they got friendly with the old man and before you know it, they were watching the baseball games in the afternoon or a western. It was all good, though; this elderly gent couldn't be happier having the guys around; he probably wished the job would take longer! They still visit him at least once a week and Irish Marie sends them off with tubs of leftovers. I went to Franklin Carpets in Massapequa; I buy all my carpets from them. I spoke with John the owner about this elderly man and the fact that he was on a fixed income but he needed new carpeting in his Living Room. John said he had some discontinued styles in the back and if she gave him the measurements of the room, he might be able to give him 50% off. I asked John what was he going to do if he couldn't sell them? Throw them in the trash? I got him to sell me the carpeting for 75% off. I got the measurements from Brian's father who knew about putting down carpets and about a week later the old carpet was replaced by powder blue carpeting. Antoinette put up all the curtains in the Livingroom and a little valance curtain for the window in the kitchen. We didn't know what to do about getting him new furniture, we could only spend so much. But his house looked great inside, no clutter, nothing.

Now, when his son picks him up, he asks him to come inside for a little while. He told us for Father's Day, his son bought him a new couch and recliner. He still comes to Francone once a week on Tuesdays. We show movies on Tuesdays for 50 cents; you get a movie, coffee and cake. One time he told me he wasn't going to attend movie day because "the guys", the painters, took him to the movies last week and he already saw it, can you imagine?"

Ro Mancini asked Little Marie if this guy needed more help; she was dying to get her husband out of the house. A few other women who had retired husbands told Marie what their husbands could do and what time you wanted them there!

Slide 3:

> If circumstances force your family to make the decision to place your mother or father in a nursing home, please contact me first. I know where the best run homes are in Brooklyn, Queens and Long Island and I can assist you in getting placement.

> "It's hard enough placing a parent in a nursing home and then finding out that they're being neglected or the place is not clean. And God forbid, they were being abused in some way. Adequate home caregiving is hard with both husband and wife working; you barely have time for yourselves. Dementia, Alzheimer's or if your parent is in wheelchair are serious challenges for both the parent and the adult children. These illnesses can be trying and demand huge amounts of time from a family. With Dementia and Alzheimer's, they eventually will have to be placed in a nursing home or require 24-hour care in yours or their home. Call me first before you do anything else."

That Thursday, Little Marie brought two dozen Thomas' English muffin pizzas, wine and soda because SHE was giving the lecture. So, we didn't have our usual cake and coffee. Even the women who already ate dinner ate the pizzas. There were no leftovers. I've tried to make the pizzas like her but, I've no patience these days to make my own sauce and that was the ingredient that made Little Marie's pizzas taste good!.

When it looked like Signorine couldn't take care of the apartment any more, Little Marie took care of it and sent Amanda Finch. Even though Little Marie worked in Massapequa, they had a "sister" office in Brooklyn; at least once a month, she went back and forth to Brooklyn to coordinate the senior events and services in both offices. It also gave her an excuse to see her parents; sometimes she'd sleep over just like when she was a kid. They still kept her bedroom with her little bed and her little desk and furniture. It looked like a dollhouse on steroids. Her mother liked the color pink; Little Marie never wore pink, I wonder why. Her parents' house had a pink bathroom and pink bedrooms; going to her parents' house was like going into the belly of a salmon.

Anyway, Amanda tidied up Signorine's apartment up until she died on that recliner. Signorine was a drill sergeant about cleaning; her apartment was always clean and she was healthy enough to complain about Amanda's cleaning skills.

Thank you, Comara Little Marie! And, thank you Comara/Nurse Theresa Guarino, rest in peace, for always getting the best doctors for Signorine. Thank you, Comara Antoinette, for making sure Signorine had cream puffs and bubbly conversation all the times you visited just to keep her company. Thank you,

Black Marie for getting us a no-cost wake at Torregrosso through Big Uncle Jimmy. Each of us did small things and when the whole group got together, it was a "Comaracle"; ah, the power of group energy!

Speaking of Signorine and Torrogrosso, let's get back to when Little Marie told me Antoinette wanted to speak with me in the lobby. Antoinette at that time had a buyer for her parents'/her home. Although she hated to admit it, the house was lonely and there were just too many memories. She'd walk in every evening from work and expect to see her mother in the kitchen asking her about her day and her father watching the news on TV. She missed the smell of dinner when she came through the door. Frankie Boy had been hounding her to sell the house a year ago but, she felt it was too soon to sell after her mother's death. She told him she had a lot of loose ends to take care of before she could sell. Her brothers weren't after the money; Frankie Boy certainly didn't need the money. In the end, it was Antoinette and Emil who benefited from the sale of the house; Frankie Boy was only interested in taking some mementos of his parents. To cut to the chase, the closing was October 30. Now, she needed someplace to live by November 1. And, she wasn't moving out of the neighborhood or near her brothers in Staten Island. She wasn't comfortable living in a neighborhood where you don't know anybody; to her, it was the same as living alone in a big house. Let's just say, at that time, it wasn't her time to move out of the neighborhood. Besides, having her brothers near her would be a cramp in her current lifestyle; they definitely would have disapproved. Frankie Boy would bust a gut if he knew who she was seeing on the side.

If you recall, when Antoinette asked me to rent Signorine's old apartment to her, I said I was surprised because I lived next door to Esther Schrable and I knew the story of why they no longer talked to each other. At least, at that time, I thought I knew the story of the big break up between her and Manny. I warned Antoinette that Esther just had hip surgery seven or eight months ago and she was in a wheelchair; she didn't need the aggravation. Esther had a caregiver, named Gladys, who stayed with her during the day. She used to wheel Esther into her backyard when the weather was good. However, we all thought it was strange that Manny didn't call Little Marie at Francone for a caregiver. He knew Little Marie since they were kids. When I asked Esther why, she told me her daughter-in-law, Phyllis, arranged everything.

Esther's daughter-in-law, Phyllis, could do no wrong. All I heard was Phyllis did this, Phyllis did that but, I could count on one hand when I ever saw her visit her mother-in-law. In fact, Manny paid a visit once a month to check on her. This was when he had the dental office in Manhattan. When he moved his practice to Long Island about two years later, Esther only saw him on holidays. As a matter of fact, it was about seven months ago that I started to see and hear strange things about Esther.

Last year, she fell in her house and had to have hip surgery. Once she was discharged, her daughter-in-law Phyllis, hired a caregiver, Gladys, to care for her. She was always in a wheelchair. If I saw Esther in the backyard, I'd come out and chat with her like we always did. The minute I started chatting, Gladys came out and told Esther it was time to go inside because it was chilly, or it was too hot, or it was going to rain, you name it, every time I'd start to talk to Esther, inside she would go. If one of the Fairy Comaras rang Esther's bell to say hello, Gladys gave the excuse that "it's not a good day for Esther" or "She's sleeping, poor thing. She had trouble sleeping last night." It seemed like she was blocking the world out of Esther's life. After a while, the only time I saw or talked to Esther was if I was doing something in the backyard in the summer; she looked loopy all the time or she fell asleep in the wheelchair. This was not the Esther we all knew and loved but, I chalked it up to old age or maybe this is what happens when you had hip surgery. I knew nothing about hip surgery at that time. What I did think was strange was every time she wasn't loopy and we'd start a conversation, Gladys would show up and say it's time for her nap. A nap? She's always napping outside! But Esther would always say that Phyllis told her the doctor said she needed lots of rest. And Phyllis knew what was best!

So, I knew Antoinette's apartment led out into my backyard and they were bound to encounter one another. Antoinette gave me the story "Oh, it was years ago! Esther's the one who doesn't speak to me. You know me, I talk to everyone." Now, I knew Esther Schrable, God rest her soul, she passed away about 12 years ago. She was a sweet woman, highly educated, kind to all of us as kids especially Irish Marie. She was not the type of person who bore grudges so, I took what Antoinette said with a grain of salt. Aside from whatever Frankie Boy or Antoinette told us, we never heard Esther talk about it to our mothers or us; she never mentioned Antoinette or said anything negative about her. And, after the hip surgery, I couldn't carry on a long conversation with her; her name never came up.

Just a short recap of an earlier story, probably for the third time. Esther, Murray and son, Manny Schrable were the only Jewish family on my block. They owned Murray's Dept Store on 5th Ave; all our mothers shopped there. It's true when they say the only difference between a Jew and an Italian is religion. The Murrays blended in perfectly with us; they came to all our birthday parties, Communions, Confirmations, weddings. We went to Manny's Bar Mitzvah and Wedding except for the Frescas, they didn't go to the wedding because of the Antoinette/Manny break up. But before the break up, almost every Friday night the Schrables played cards, always with the Frescas, sometimes my parents and sometimes Little Marie Greco's parents.

Anyway, we all knew Esther. Esther was pretty progressive for her time; an intelligent and very open-minded woman for the times we lived in; she came to America from Magdeburg, Germany during World War II. Her parents were killed in the Breitenau Concentration camp. Esther and her sister, Hannah, who were barely in their teens, escaped by being hidden by German neighbors, living from house to house. Somehow, they were given fake papers to leave Germany and sent to their aunt in London. Because London was going through its own problems, the aunt sent them to live with a Jewish family in the Midwood section of Brooklyn as part of a Jewish refugee initiative. The sisters always hoped they would re-unite with their parents after the war but, it never happened although, inquiries were made for years. They found out a few years later after the war ended that they died in the camp. Esther learned English, went to high school and worked part-time in the pizzeria on the corner. After high school, she went to Brooklyn College at night while working as a full-time Buyers' Assistant at A&S Dept Store. She learned a lot about the retail business at A&S; there were a few buyers who took her under their wing, mentored her. It came in mighty handy when she and Murray opened their own department store.

Although she would never say it, Esther was the backbone of the business; Murray knew it. She did all the inventory, the account books, met with the vendors and looked in the magazines for all the latest styles. Murray was the front man; he did all the schmoozing with the customers, Esther schmoozed, too, but Murray had a way of selling a garment. I think in 1960, she became a US citizen. I remember as a child going to her Citizenship Party in their backyard. I wonder if the other Fairy Comaras remember the candied apples she used to make on Halloween for our trick or treat bags? Remember when we could eat them with real teeth instead of the ones we take out at night? Although the Schrables did not celebrate Christmas, they always gave the kids on our block a little gift from the store like mittens or scarves. And our parents invited them over for Christmas or to watch the ball drop with the music of Guy Lombardo on New Year's Eve.

Esther met Murray at Brooklyn College; they were in the same business administration class. At the time, she was dating another guy she met at a dance but it wasn't serious. After class, Murray would always think of a reason to talk to Esther about something in class that he "claimed" he didn't understand; eventually he got enough nerve to ask her if she wanted to go for coffee. Esther claims she knew he was into her from the beginning but she played hard to get. She used to say, "Why buy the cow when you can get the milk for free?" Murray popped the question in one year and they married six months later, after graduation. She told me that one of her mentor Buyers in Bridal gave her a wedding dress free of charge because it was a sample and her size. Her sister Hannah was her Maid of Honor; she was the only family attending the wedding except for the people who raised her here in Brooklyn; they walked her down the aisle. She said she had a feeling that day that her parents were next to her and Murray, and that sort of gave her some comfort.

They got married and according to Esther, because her parents were deceased, her mother-in-law treated her like a daughter, not a daughter-in-law. They lived on Ocean Parkway with Murray's parents for about a year, both working, scrimping and saving every dollar for a down payment on a house, the house next to me. Two years after buying their house, their little miracle, Emanuel, Manny, came along. When Manny started going to First Grade, his father had an idea. Murray happened to walk by an empty store front on 5th Ave. He checked out how many people passed by and what stores were around the area and started thinking about opening his own business. They took a chance starting a business back then with limited savings but soon it made a profit. No one else sold women's undergarments in the area and once they started selling blouses, dresses and children's clothing, business really picked up.

Esther used to drop Manny off at school and then work in the store, then pick him up and he'd do his homework in the back. And, of course, she handled the business end, as well, while Murray worked the front with the customers. Those were long hours, especially during Christmas holidays or Communion time when the boys and girls had to get suits, dresses and veils. They worked all the Christian holidays. And, when one of us was having a rough time financially, they gave us credit so the kids looked their best; we always paid them back. My mother bought my Communion dress and veil at Murray's; I think all of our mothers did! I got my first training bra there.

And when Signorine would come in to buy her black stockings, they knew they had to bargain with her because Sicilians love to do the deal. Murray would tell her the price and then she'd say, "tu mucha, tu mucha." And she'd tell the story, over and over, that she worked in a factory, she knew what he paid for clothes wholesale. So, they'd drop the price 10 cents, just so she could feel like she got a bargain; after all, she was a good customer! They kept Signorine in black stockings for years! At Christmas time, they'd always put an extra pair in her shopping bag. When Murray had to have his gall bladder taken out, Carmela Fresca worked the front for two weeks refusing to be paid; Esther gave her one of the new dresses that came in from the vendor. Manny played baseball and football with the Fresca boys, especially Emil. John Fresca used to say that he should claim Manny as a dependent because he practically lived in their house. Of course, he was joking, he loved Manny. And Signorine cooked Esther a hot meal every night Murray was in the hospital so Esther wouldn't have to come home late from the hospital and cook dinner.

The store did very well for many years until the mid- 80's. By then, they not only had to compete with the big stores like A&S and Martin's, they also had to compete with the Kings Plaza Mall and then Caesar's Bay. In addition, their long-time customers were moving out and the new neighbors were shopping in Manhattan or at the malls. The kibosh on the store came when Murray died in 1989, he was 62. He had a short illness, pancreatic cancer; within a year he passed away. By then, their son was already married and living in Great Neck. I think that was the first time our parents and, likewise the Fairy Comaras, went to a Shiva in Esther's home. She always kept a beautiful home. Our parents had photos of themselves on their wedding day and their kids growing up; Esther had Monet, Renoir and Rembrandt reproductions. She was always into the arts and museums. She took Manny to Broadway plays which none of our parents did. She belonged to the Ethical Society in Brooklyn, took night classes at John Jay High School and, of course, coordinated the Sukkoth holiday tent at Temple Beth Elohim. She even read the New York Times and finished the crossword puzzle in a day. Our parents read the Daily News. Before she broke her hip, she used to call me to come down and get the New York Times Book Review; she knew how much I loved to read.

It was very fortunate that Irish Marie befriended Esther; she did a lot for Marie. As I mentioned, those two souls came together when Irish Marie, then Maria, used to clean her house to get extra credit from St. Agatha's. Maria cleaned Esther's windows and Esther opened windows to the outside world for her! She became Marie's mentor and helped her and the Fitzpatrick family through some rough times. Before she broke her hip, Irish Marie knocked on the door and told her, "It's time to change the curtains and clean out the refrigerator, I'll do it" or it's time to get the garden ready for summer." Irish Marie never charged her. And, in addition, she'd made sure the rest of the house was clean. When he was alive, she would make Murray his favorite, arroz con pollo, and drop it off on a Friday night. When Irish Marie's mother got very sick, the Schrables visited her in the hospital once or twice before she passed away. Esther used to embroider; she gave Irish Marie the most beautiful table cloth for her bridal shower. Everyone remarked about how beautiful it was; and the next thing they said to Marie was, "you better put a plastic cover on top of that tablecloth!"

When Murray passed away, Esther was like a yin without a yang. Even though she still celebrated the holidays with her son or with us, she was different, it's hard to explain. Thankfully, Esther was the saver in the family and she put away a nice bit of money for their retirement.

When Frankie Boy worked on Wall St., he advised Esther to put some of her money in interest-bearing CDs and some solid stocks; she did very well for herself. She even had a college fund for Manny. Frankie Boy invested some of Esther's, my money and a few of the Fairy Comaras in Microsoft stock back in the late 80's and we got a very good return on that stock. When he told me how much the stock was worth about 10 years ago, he said, "Now you don't have to shovel snow anymore!" Every time I talk to him, he always asks me how much snow did I get in Brooklyn this winter and after I'd tell him, he thanks God he doesn't have to shovel snow in North Carolina. Antoinette told me he's thinking about buying a summer house in Brewster; she probably sent him multiple house listings like me! If he decides to buy one in Brewster, that will definitely persuade me to move there. It would be nice to have him around! Maybe we can dance to the hustle again while we're still not using walkers!

Speaking of Frankie Boy, he was the one who told us that Antoinette and Manny broke up. When we asked him why? He just muttered that it was because of the Jewish/Catholic thing. Now, of course, these marriages happen all the time but, back then, it was rare; at least, in our neighborhood. People of different faiths were starting to marry but, not as much as today. Frankie Boy said his father told Antoinette that the Schrables wouldn't allow it unless Antoinette became a practicing Jew and there was a back and forth for about two minutes until Antoinette said she would convert and that's when her father lost it and started shouting at her, which he never did, and then nothing more was said. However, when Antoinette told me her story, the story changed a little. She told me, "Esther was the one who objected. She wanted Manny to marry a Jewish girl." She was an emotional mess that day and, every day since then. I think that's why Antoinette had an affair with a married man for so long; she couldn't deal with the heartbreak. Her confidence in having a long-term relationship was a little above zero.

After that, the Frescas and the Schrables continued to be friendly but not as friendly. The Friday night card games and the BBQs ended. Carmela would go into Murray's Dept. Store once in a while but she mostly shopped at A&S. When Manny and Phyllis got married, the Frescas were invited to the wedding but, didn't go. I think what also bothered Antoinette was that Esther could dismiss all the closeness and love she and her family had for the Schrables because of religion. In other words, it was all Esther's fault.

So, now we move fast forward to about 20 years later. Murray is dead, Manny and Phyllis have a daughter, Alyssa, about 18 years old, a good granddaughter. I've seen her visit Esther at least once a month. She just started at New York University. Esther sold Murray's Dept. Store after Murray died; she mostly stayed at home except for bingo at St. Agatha's, her committee activities at the synagogue and her annual cruise to the Bahamas with her foster family from Midwood and her sister Hannah's family from Yonkers.

Carmela and John Fresca passed away, Signorine died and Antoinette asked me to rent her Signorine's old apartment. Antoinette sells her parents' house, moves in with me. Esther had hip surgery seven months ago; she's still in a wheelchair, has a caregiver, Gladys, that was not hired through Little Marie

Greco's company, Francone Senior Center, and Esther and Antoinette are neighbors. And this is where our story begins.

Antoinette moved in right after she and her brothers closed on the house on October 30; just in time for the holidays. After Thanksgiving, my parents used to put Christmas lights and garland around the two-door opening of our front door; we had little lighted trees on each side of the doors. Our indoor Christmas tree was always positioned near one of the front windows. When they died, I just did the front window Christmas tree. I had the energy back then but I didn't have the motivation to do the front entrance; the front door was always me and my father's job. He took such care and loved doing it. Doing it solo just didn't do it for me.

Antoinette had all her holiday decorations put in storage on 9th Street; and I mean every holiday decoration: St. Patrick's Day, Easter, Halloween, Thanksgiving (she had paper mâché turkeys all around the house) and especially Christmas. When she moved in, I was dating a nice gentleman at the time and he invited me to his family's house, in Connecticut, Thanksgiving weekend. I thought it would be nice to get out of the city. After my parents died, Black Marie usually invited me and Signorine for Thanksgiving. She always had about 30 people at the house. Big Uncle Jimmy and his wife came every year, turkey supplied by Uncle Jimmy! When I told Black Marie I wasn't coming this Thanksgiving, she naturally was curious to know where I was going and I told her I had been "keeping company" with a guy I met at a friend from work's birthday party two months ago, "keeping company" was the phrase we used back then instead of dating. We knew dating but, our parents understood "keeping company" better. Black Marie wanted to know everything about him but, I didn't have time because I had a dentist appointment in a half an hour.

The Fairy Comaras were always ready for a wedding and after two months I wasn't ready to walk down the aisle. Knowing them, they would be planning my wedding before I got engaged! He was divorced with two daughters. He told me this year, his ex-wife had the girls on Thanksgiving and he was getting them Christmas; they alternated every year. So, at least I knew there wouldn't be any awkwardness with his daughters so soon into our relationship. I didn't even tell him about what I did at the Thursday Evening meetings. For now, I liked him and he liked me. We were getting along very well.

Anyway, the Wednesday before Thanksgiving, I took off for Connecticut. I gave Antoinette a number I could be reached in case of an emergency. She was going to Frankie Boy's house in Staten Island for Thanksgiving. I had a really good time in Connecticut; his parents had a great big old New England house, with the barn and the big backyard. And they were ever so gracious to me including his sisters and their families. Thank God, back then, people obeyed the golden rule at holiday dinners; no one talked about politics, sex or religion.

We would never even think about making that a topic of conversation; it was mostly family talk. Now, that's all you hear. How anyone can think by having an argument about which political party you belong to will change the other person's mind is beyond me. Luckily, these days, I don't hear much talk around the table about religion. No one discusses religion because it's not a big issue anymore, I guess. Besides, nowadays, you may have a few atheists around the table. I can just imagine our parents hearing that a person at dinner was an atheist! Ou Fa! To be honest, I could care less what religion you are or if you're an atheist; I know some atheists today that treat people better than Christians, Jews or Muslims combined. But I digress…

Sunday after Thanksgiving, my date gave me a lift home. He drove to his parents the Monday before Thanksgiving to have some quality time with them. Ironically, that was the last Thanksgiving he would spend with his father. Three months later, he told me his parents went to Aruba in January to escape the winter for a little while and his father had an aneurysm in their hotel room a couple of days after they arrived. He died in the hospital that night. His mother, God bless her, kept it all together in the days following his death; she made all the arrangement to have his father transported to the funeral home, her daughters helped her with the arrangements and the burial. After that, she never went on vacation again; she feared dying in a foreign place.

So, back to Sunday…I got home at around 6:00 PM; it just started to get dark out. We kissed and waved goodbye and, all of a sudden, my house just exploded with Christmas lights. Lights on the windows, lights on the staircase, an enormous Nativity with little string lights in front of Antoinette's apartment windows, a snow man and snow lady and a Santa that said Ho! Ho! Ho! Thank God it was winter or my mouth would have caught a lot of bugs. And then, a minute later a small crowd assembles to look and as I'm going up the stairs, one crowd walked away then another crowd came to look. When I put my suitcase down, I just sat in the chair for 30 seconds to take it all in and I hear Antoinette's footsteps coming up. Her first words…" Surprise! Welcome home! I saw you get out of the car and I wanted to turn them on right when you pulled up to the house! I got it all done on Friday and Saturday; Bennie helped with the decorations." I asked her if she put up all of her parents' decorations on my house and she said "I know, I'm sorry, I know it's not enough, I gave half to St. Agatha's. You think the house could use more?" I said, "No, I don't want to take away from the Christmas tree near the window that I usually put up". And she said, Oh, yeah, I forgot about the tree." And then while I'm was about to eat my soup, the phone rings and Little Marie Greco says, "Is this the Spata Residence" and then proceeds to go hysterical laughing on the phone. For those who don't know, people came from all over the tri-state area to see the Spata Residence Christmas Lights and Decoration Display in Dyker

Heights, Brooklyn. I think it's become a must-see tourist attraction site; they come from all over the country and even Europe! Can you believe it? So, that's why Little Marie peed her pants on the phone. Then Irish Marie called, another one who wet her pants along with her husband Brian, and then Black Marie, Theresa Guarino and a few other Fairy Comaras. And then whoever came to the Thursday night meetings, Antoinette used her camera to take photos of them in front of the house as a memento.

My relationship with this guy broke up, not because of the Christmas lights; he thought they were cool! Long story short, I don't think he was ready to cut the cord with his ex-wife. We broke off a couple of days before New Year's Eve. I wasn't into three-way drama relationships. And there was no drama when we broke up; he knew he wasn't ready. We remained "distant" friends.

For a couple of years, I had the Santangelo/Fresca Christmas Light Display and also the Valentine's Day display, St. Patty's Day, Easter, Memorial Day, July 4th and Halloween displays. She denied it, but Antoinette did add to the collection every year. I told her as long as I can get down the outside stairs and it's not blocking any entrances, it's okay. You HAD to say yes to Antoinette; she had enough exuberance for both of us. And, if you put up a fuss, she'd whine and wear you down anyway. I figured as long as I'm not the one doing it, go for it! Antoinette called her holiday displays one of her greatest achievements until she came into Esther's life again. This is a story to tell your grandchildren, Fairy Comaras!

I think it must have been a warm day in late March when Antoinette decided she was going to freshen up the backyard garden and plant some hyacinth, tulip and daffodil plants to get ready for Easter. We both felt sad when we had to take the gauze covering off of the fig tree; Signorine took such good care of Grandpa Joe's fig tree. In the Fall, she would get the burlap and cover the entire tree. When she died the year before, we forgot to gauze the fig tree in October but, we didn't kill it. Antoinette did it in November. That was Signorine's pride and joy. Antoinette wants me to dig up the tree when I sell the house so she can plant it in her backyard, I told her we'll see.

Well, Antoinette must have been so distracted with pruning the fig tree that she didn't hear or see Esther wheeled out to her backyard. Esther saw her, though. You know how sometimes you speak out at the same time you're thinking of something? It just comes out. Well, Esther says out of the blue, "She loved that fig tree!" and Antoinette froze while she was on her knees. Antoinette finished taking off a few dead branches and just stuffed it in the trash bag, picked herself up and said, "Yes, she did, God rest her soul" and walked into the house. But once she was inside, she realized how much older Esther got from just a year before her hip surgery. And she looked like a scumbari, sloppy; you never saw Esther looking disheveled. She always dressed up even to go to the supermarket. She told me Esther had these old blankets covering her legs, I mean bed blankets not throw blankets with a sweater clearly too big for her and then a shawl. She looked like a bag lady. Her hair wasn't even colored and she always had her hair and nails done at the beauty parlor every Wednesday, rain or shine. Seniors got a 10% discount on Wednesdays. I told her I noticed the change, too. Antoinette asked, "how long do you have to stay in a wheelchair after hip surgery?" I said, "To be honest, I don't know anyone else besides Esther who's had hip surgery so I don't know". I told her to ask Theresa Guarino, she should know, she's a nurse, they know everything.

And, Antoinette did ask Theresa Guarino; it was at the Thursday evening meeting. Theresa's work schedule didn't usually allow her to attend every Thursday evening meeting but, this one she made. So, they got to talking. Theresa couldn't remember how long ago it was that Esther had the surgery and so she asked me and I told her about 7 months ago. Theresa yells out "7 Months? she should be doing a jig around the house by now. She should be done with physical therapy by now." I told Theresa and Antoinette I never saw Esther go out of the house since she was discharged from the hospital. But then again, I worked; if she had Physical Therapy, it was probably during the day when I was out. Theresa said she would check out when Esther had Physical Therapy, "after her surgery, she probably got PT on 7th Ave and 2nd Street. They work with our hospital and the Hospital for Special Surgery in Manhattan. If she didn't get PT there, then I'll call up friends at Coney Island and Victory Memorial. Those are the only two places they would send her for therapy in Brooklyn." I told Theresa that two times I tried to visit Esther to chat with her but, her caregiver, Gladys, said either she was napping or she was not having a good day. Irish Marie happened to be standing next to me and she said she was told the same thing, too! And then Marie Greco's mother said she did visit but Esther looked so sleepy; Gladys said it was the medication.

Antoinette doesn't have big ears but if she did, they would have stood straight up and poked out of her hair. The little voice in her head told her something wasn't right. She had that faraway look on her face and we all saw it. So, after the meeting, as we were cleaning up, I said to Antoinette, "What are you going to do about Esther?" And she said, "what makes you think I'm going to do anything?" And, we both looked at each other and smiled because we knew SHE was going to do something. No matter that it was Esther, she was a Fairy Comara, and she was Antoinette.

Theresa called Antoinette Sunday afternoon on her break. She told Antoinette she couldn't find Esther going for physical therapy in Brooklyn. She found out from one of her nurse friends, Eileen, who worked at the Hospital for Special Surgery, that Esther had her surgery there and was hospitalized for about two weeks. She had PT while she was there but very minimal. She was discharged with a prescription to get PT at the 2nd St. office but she never appeared. The 2nd St. PT office knew nothing about it; she had never been there.

Theresa told Antoinette that Esther's doctor, Dr. Millburn, was one of the best Orthopedic surgeons at the Hospital for Special Surgery but, a month later, her daughter-in-law informed him that she was taking her mother-in-law to live with her in Great Neck; she would find her a doctor and physical therapist nearby. Theresa told her Dr. Millburn operated on Ann Caracciolo's mother's hips about the same time as Esther and she was walking and doing her everyday activities after two months; she could even climb stairs where she couldn't before the surgery. And, she was much older than Esther. She said she would try to dig a little deeper.

Antoinette knew the only way she was going to find out anything more, if there was anything to be found, was through Esther. But she'd had to find the right time when Esther was out in the backyard on the weekend. I remember Easter was April 23 and, the weekend before, Antoinette was out in the backyard putting up the Easter decorations; a few of the little ones on the block were invited for an Easter egg hunt. She also was starting her food shopping to make the traditional Fresca pizza rustica handed down from daughter to daughter. My mother made a good pizza rustica, too. I have the recipe somewhere; probably packed away in one of the black hole closets. Too much work. Antoinette also made Easter breads. She made three pizza rustica pies that year; one for me, God Bless her! One for Frankie Boy because she was going to his house for Easter and, one for Esther. Carmela always made a pizza rustica for Esther and Murray and, she thought that this would be the thing to break the ice. For years, we told Antoinette to let it go but, it wasn't the right time, I guess. Now was the right time. Who knows how much longer Esther will be around? She looked pretty sick.

Antoinette decided to bring Esther's pizza rustica on Good Friday evening; after all, Esther was Jewish, she could eat meat on Good Friday. She couldn't go Saturday because she was staying overnight at Frankie Boy's house to help her sister-in-law, Claudia, with the cooking and the baking. One of the Fairy Comaras who was unemployed at the time told Antoinette that they knew when Gladys came and went for the day. She came in 9:00 AM and left around 5 PM.

Antoinette made sure Gladys had left so she wouldn't get any excuses like me and Irish Marie. She had to ring the bell twice but finally Esther answered, "Who is it?" Antoinette says, "It's Antoinette!" and Esther says "Antoinette who?" I don't know if she was just busting Antoinette's chops but, after that, she told her to hold on because she had to shut off the alarm. Years ago, we sometimes forgot to lock the door to our homes, nobody got robbed. Now, with the neighborhood changing, even I gave in and installed an alarm. Different times. I just worry that if the EMS have to come into my house, how can I shut off the alarm if I'm lying on the floor. Anyway, after all the "hold ons" Esther was shouting out, she finally opened the door.

Well, you could have knocked Esther down with a feather if she wasn't already sitting in a wheelchair. I wish I could have seen that scene; Antoinette Fresca bearing gifts after all these years. She probably thought she was dying and bringing her last meal. Esther saw that it was pizza rustica through the Saran wrap and that alone was enough for her to say, "Why don't you come in?" And Antoinette did. At first, Antoinette gave some half-ass excuse like she made extra rustica. Trust me, you don't make extra rustica, it takes a long time and it's expensive, all those meats! But then, Esther asked her if she wanted some tea or coffee? The problem was Esther couldn't reach the top shelf from the wheelchair; Gladys told her she should only have one cup of coffee a day for her health. So, Antoinette got the coffee and made a pot with the Mister Coffee. She asked Esther where she kept the sandwich bags and Esther told her they were in one of the drawers under the sink. She put enough coffee for a pot in the bag and told Esther to hide it for tomorrow evening after Gladys left. When she worked in the store, Esther always had a pot of coffee on the little burner they had in the back. She loved coffee! Sometimes, she'd wouldn't have lunch; all she wanted was a cup of coffee and maybe a roll with butter from the luncheonette next door.

"Esther, I heard you had hip surgery about 7 months ago. How are you?" Esther responded that the surgery did not go as well as expected. "I go to a doctor in Great Neck where my son lives because my daughter-in-law Phyllis says he's a specialist. He's the best in Great Neck! I went a couple of months ago; he just renews my meds. There's nothing more they can do for me." And then she went on about how her daughter-in-law is an angel, "Phyllis, drives to Brooklyn, picks me up and brings me to a doctor in Great Neck and then brings me home. What daughter-in-law is going to do that?" So, Antoinette asked, "So I gather the physical therapy didn't work?" Esther told her that her daughter-in-law conferred with the doctor and he advised against physical therapy because she had brittle bones. She might fall and break the other hip.

Antoinette wasn't buying any of that but she said nothing. Esther went on about what a good daughter-in-law she had and how she checks with Gladys every day to see how she's doing. Antoinette asked her if she wanted a piece of pizza rustica now and Esther said, "I'll get the knife, you get the plates" Antoinette told her it was Good Friday so she couldn't have meat; she already had pizza for dinner. She asked her where the napkins were kept and she said they were in one of the bottom drawers; the drawer was filled with nothing but napkins you get in a diner or the luncheonette on 5th Avenue.

Antoinette asked to use the rest room; she knew it like the back of her hand from going in the house so many times. As she's walking from the kitchen to the Living Room and then passed the bedroom, she noticed the house was in shambles. Cups and paper plates on the side tables, bags of garbage near the recliner, the carpet looked stained but, she couldn't see that well because there were no lamps on around the house. Who was cleaning this house? The bathroom was so gross, Antoinette put toilet paper around the rim of the toilet seat just to sit down. Something was amiss; Esther always had a clean house, thanks to Irish Marie. Why didn't she call Irish Marie? She had the money, didn't make sense. What did Gladys do all day? A dozen questions were running through her mind.

Anyway, Esther asked about Frankie Boy and Emil; Antoinette talked about her nieces and nephews' achievements. The words felt like marbles coming out of her mouth but Antoinette asked, "How's Manny and the family?" Big one for Antoinette. Esther told her, "Manny's doing very well; he has his dental practice in Great Neck now. Less of a commute and he's part of a medical group to share the cost. He used to visit me once a month when he had his practice in Manhattan; he works morning, noon and night with this practice, now, I only see him on the holidays. He lives in a big house in Great Neck and my granddaughter, Alyssa, just started New York University. She comes to the house once a month after school but, she doesn't get along with my aid, Gladys; she thinks she should be doing more for me." Antoinette asked, "Did Little Marie Greco send this caregiver?" Esther said, "No, Phyllis, got her from an agency somewhere on Long Island. Phyllis said she came with outstanding references."

Antoinette mentioned that Irish Marie and Theresa Guarino tried to visit her a few times; Esther knew nothing about it. She said, "I was wondering what happened to my favorite girl, (Marie), but I thought with her new business and a family she was too busy. I was hoping to see Theresa, too, because I had some questions about my medications that she might know about, like the side effects. I'm always sleeping."   Well, Antoinette didn't want to ask too many questions, although she had many, trust me, and it was getting late. Antoinette asked her if she needed help to get into bed and Esther said she could manage; Gladys always puts her nightgown and robe on before she leaves. And as Antoinette was reaching for the door knob, Esther said, "Antoinette, I'm so glad you dropped in tonight. It meant so much." Antoinette's heart was racing and she was on the verge of tears. But all she could say was, "Ok, good night, remember to put the rustica in the refrigerator, I'll see you soon."

Antoinette came home and immediately called me to come down. Antoinette recounts a conversation like she has a tape recorder in the room; she remembers every detail. One of her job responsibilities at work was to take the minutes for every department meeting so she's had good practice. She told me everything Esther said and how the house looked. The minute I heard about the condition of the bathroom, I said something was wrong. Esther always kept an immaculate house. Also, Esther had a beautiful garden; her garden was the hangout for all the butterflies in the neighborhood. She did all the gardening until recently. Now it looks disgusting; weeds all over, I didn't even see a flower bloom last summer. I know it must be killing Esther to have to sit and look at her garden now.

I told Antoinette that I will take care of the garden, "I'll go on a Sunday when Gladys is off and I'll bring her out in the back to watch." Antoinette just nodded her head but she had that faraway look in her eyes. So, I said, "Well, what are you going to do about it?" And at first, Antoinette gives me this bullshit reason why she can't get involved, "I can't do anything; she has a son, daughter-in-law and a granddaughter. It's none of my business. I just wanted to make nice with Esther since I was living next door." Blah, Blah, Blah! It was getting late and I had clothes to fold, so I said good night and went upstairs. But I knew that her mind was racing 90 miles an hour. There was no way she was going to dismiss what she heard and saw at Esther's tonight. And there was no way she wasn't going to involve us.

What really got Antoinette moving was when she saw Esther in the backyard the next morning just before she went to Frankie Boy's house. Esther told her that she told Gladys about the visit. Gladys told her not to let anyone in after she left because she might forget to put the alarm back on. Then Gladys came out with half of her pizza rustica and told Antoinette this food was too rich for Esther and handed it back to her. Gladys told her she had a slice and it was delicious. God help the person who gives an Italian back food that they made especially for them!

The Monday after Easter, Antoinette called Little Marie Greco from work. Marie happened to be home; she took off Easter week because her children were off from school. Coincidentally, I was invited to Little Marie's house for Easter that year so I gave her the scoop on Antoinette and Esther. She told Little Marie the story with as much detail as she told me on Friday night. All she knew was the first name of the caregiver, Gladys. Marie and her sons took a drive to Francone, all the seniors there loved when the boys visited. Marie had so much cake and pastries left over from Easter, she brought some with her. She went into her office, called Antoinette back and looked on her computer; there was no one with a first name, Gladys, working for Francone in Long Island or Brooklyn. Antoinette told her the daughter-in-law hired her from some agency in the Great Neck area. Marie knew all the caregiver agencies on Long Island; she'd have to give them a call.

Theresa Guarino was one of the first of the Fairy Comaras to have a home computer. We considered her to be our tech go-to person when we bought computers many years later. Theresa had an email! She was on AOL which she explained was short for America On Line. Theresa was so into emails at the time; the minute she got home from work, she'd fire up the computer, which took a long time back then, and read all her emails and replied to them. She'd sit with her dinner and type away. I mention this because Antoinette sent Theresa an email from work. She typed up a short-condensed version of the Esther story. She wanted Theresa to come visit Esther one evening this week and explain her medications to her.

Well, Theresa, God rest her soul, called her that night and they arranged to go to Esther's on Wednesday evening, her day off. At first, Theresa suggested going by herself in the afternoon to see Esther but, Antoinette told her she probably wouldn't get in because Gladys always had an excuse for why they couldn't visit her. Theresa remembered she tried once and got an excuse from her, too. She told Theresa the best time to come was 6:00 PM. Gladys left at 5:00 PM every evening but just to be safe, it was better to go at 6. Antoinette told her she might come along just for company.

That evening, I asked Antoinette her what she was up to but, she said in a whisper she had to have a little more information before she could tell me. I don't know why she was whispering; it was only the two of us in the house but, never mind. So, they agreed to go that Wednesday at 6:00. Antoinette said she'd bring pizza pie and zeppolas; Esther loved zeppolas.

According to Antoinette, they rang Esther's bell, and again with the "who is it?" from Esther! Esther shut off the alarm and then she opened the door. Her first words to Antoinette were, "I must be dying, two visits in one week? Come in! Theresa I'm glad you came, too; I have some questions about my medications!" When they sat down, Antoinette put the pizza and zeppoles on the kitchen table; she also brought paper plates, cups and napkins and three cans of 7UP. As they were eating, Esther says, "You know I told my daughter-in-law, Phyllis, that you visited me, Antoinette. She was delighted that I had the company; but she said if you want to visit me just make sure Gladys is there to help."

Now, before we proceed, I have to tell you that whenever Antoinette gets her horns twisted, she gets a twitch in one eye, I think the right eye. Hasn't happened in a long time but, that night the twitch came back. Even Theresa noticed it and when Esther wasn't looking, she whispered, "what's wrong?"

Anyway, when they finished eating, Antoinette said she would clean up while Theresa explained the medications and side effects to Esther. Instead of putting all the paper plates, cups and napkins in Esther's garbage pail, Antoinette took out one of Esther's plastic shopping bags from the pantry and put the garbage inside. When Antoinette looked in the pantry, there were about 40 boxes of macaroni and cheese and about two cans of tuna fish. The only things she had in the refrigerator was a bottle of seltzer, small container of Half and Half, butter and some overripe bananas; the freezer was empty except for two ice trays. She couldn't believe that Esther lived so frugally; she had the money. Esther did her banking at my bank, Chase Manhattan. I used to see her often when she was well. Antoinette cleaned the table and put everything back exactly as it was; not neat, just like it was before.

By the time Antoinette walked in, Esther was sitting in the Living Room in her wheelchair and Theresa was in the recliner near her. Esther had a little table next to the recliner with all her meds, aspirin, TUMS and a plastic cup with water in an old Tropicana orange juice bottle. Theresa looked at the high blood pressure medication and explained what hypertension was and why she was taking it. In the past, Esther had a love affair with salt; she stopped using it but so many other foods contained salt in them, especially canned or fast foods. Theresa advised Esther to eat more prepared foods like chicken and fresh or frozen vegetables. Later, Antoinette asked me to check her account and see what her balance was; I wasn't allowed to divulge that information but, you'll forgive me later.

So, then Theresa picked up the other bottle; it was Lopressor, for the heart. "Esther, do you get chest pains?" Esther said no but she gets palpitations and she's always tired. Theresa told her this medication can cause drowsiness or dizziness when you first start taking it. "How long have you been on the Lopressor?" Esther said she's been taking it for about six or seven months, she couldn't remember. Theresa told her, "maybe when you first took Lopressor it caused a little dizziness but, after about a month, you should be used to it. It shouldn't make you that drowsy now." Esther said that maybe the Lopressor combined with her hip surgery medication, OxyContin, could be the reason. Theresa held her hand up and asked Esther, "Why are you on Oxycontin? It's been over 7 months since your hip surgery, you should be up and walking without any pain, you should be doing a jig right now." Esther told her that Phyllis spoke with Dr. Millburn. Esther said, "I have to stay in the chair at least a year before it heals; no physical therapy until then." Well, Theresa knew that was pure bullshit; the hospitals schedule post operative physical therapy immediately after discharge but, she said nothing to Esther. Antoinette and I knew nothing about hip surgery back then so we didn't question her being in a wheel chair; Theresa on the other hand, knew all about hip surgery. She took care of hip surgery patients at the hospital and, after surgery a day or two later, they were scheduling them for physical therapy in the hospital and PT at an outside location.

Theresa asked Esther, "So, you haven't had any kind of physical therapy since the operation?" Esther said that she had one or two days of light physical therapy in the hospital and they were originally going to send her to the PT place on 2nd St but, when she returned home, Phyllis told her that the doctor said that she'd have to wait a year because she had to heal. And that's why he prescribed the Oxycontin because she was in a great deal of pain and still is in pain seven months later. Theresa knew that the doctors wouldn't prescribe Oxycontin for seven months; they usually try to wean the patient off of it gradually. The last medication, however, was the biggest mystery. It was a bottle of Klonipin which Theresa knew was a tranquilizer. "This medication, Esther, is a tranquilizer. Why do you need this medication?" Esther said, "Sometimes I want to get out of the chair during the day; I can get into bed alright as long as I wheel the chair next to it but, I shouldn't try to do any standing during the day. So, I get agitated and depressed about how my life is now. Gladys told Phyllis about my depression and Phyllis told my son about it and he wrote up a prescription for Klonipin. Phyllis picks it up at her pharmacy in Great Neck because they're cheaper; she brings me the pills about once a month or she gives them to Gladys. Gladys lives in Floral Park so sometimes my daughter-in-law drives there and gives it to her." On this one, Theresa couldn't keep her mouth shut, "Esther, we all love Manny (as she glanced at Antoinette for a moment) but should he be the one to write this sort of prescription? I mean, he's a dentist not a doctor. These pills are strong; 1 mg, four times a day. That's very high! No wonder you're falling asleep all the time. And, the prescription is for Gladys Hickson, not you. Why is that? And you take this medication every day?"

Esther explained that the pharmacist might ask questions if Manny was prescribing for family so Manny put it in Gladys' name and she added, "besides, I didn't want everyone to know my business so Phyllis discussed this with me and we felt this was the right way." Theresa said, "You should see a psychiatrist or a psychologist and talk about this to him. I can recommend a very good psychiatrist; he's affiliated with our" ….and before she could finish, Esther shouted "NO!" and then she calmed herself down a little and said sorry. "Phyllis told me that if I see a psychiatrist, he'll only prescribed the same drug and if he sees no change, he might recommend a nursing home. I'm not depressed with the house; I want to stay right where I am. I've seen what those nursing homes look like; I'll be more depressed. The only way I'm leaving this house is feet first horizontally." Theresa and Antoinette could see Esther was getting agitated so they decided to drop it. It was getting late, anyway.

Mental illness was not discussed openly like it is today; and even today, it's hidden within the family. It hasn't changed that much. People talk about it and may know a little more about it now and many seek treatment but, it's still not as transparent. The only thing we found odd about Esther's prescription was that the prescription was not written by a psychiatrist. What was Manny thinking to give his mother these meds and in someone else's name?

However, before they left, Theresa sat down next to Esther, held her hand and said, "Esther, I have a favor to ask you. Do you trust me?" "Of course!" Esther said. Theresa continued, "Even though Antoinette is a pain in the ass, do you trust her?" Esther nodded and said, "I never thought she was a pain the ass." Theresa looked up at Antoinette with a smile and said, "that's nice, Esther, but she is a pain in the ass. Do us one favor, don't tell Gladys that we were here tonight. Don't say a thing to anyone just for now. Look, Antoinette took all the garbage from tonight and she's going to put it in her garbage can. Just promise us you won't say anything to Gladys or anyone just for now, ok?" Esther said, "sure, but why? I can have company." Theresa said, "Antoinette told me that Phyllis told Gladys to tell her that it would be better if we visited when Gladys was around; that's not possible because we all work. This is the only time we get to visit." So, Esther understood but, not fully, and said she promised she'd say nothing. Before we went, though, Antoinette made Esther another sandwich bag of coffee for tomorrow night. They helped Esther into bed, turned on the alarm and left.

Theresa said she had to go because she had laundry to do; she had the early shift tomorrow. She would contact the doctor who did Esther's hip surgery at the Hospital for Special Surgery; Theresa saw the hospital discharge papers with his name and phone number on the kitchen shelf. That was a start. She wanted to know why the surgeon was against physical therapy; she'd get one of the hospital doctors to call Dr. Millburn up and find out. The Klonipin was the bigger mystery. But, should we call Manny? Antoinette said she was not going to contact Manny; she was uncomfortable and both she and Theresa decided to hold off on contacting him until the other information was gathered. Antoinette said she would call Little Marie and give her Gladys' last name so she could search this Hickson woman further.

As I mentioned before, Antoinette asked me to look up Esther's account at the bank. She told me about all the macaroni and cheese boxes in her pantry and the empty refrigerator. I told her that Esther had the money to buy filet mignon; Murray had life insurance and Esther invested in that Microsoft stock through Frankie Boy, like us. When I looked up Esther's account, she only had a savings account with about $1,000 in it. Antoinette told me she was going to call up Frankie Boy and find out about Esther's stock portfolio.

And, after all of this was done, here's what the Fairy Comaras found out:

1. Once Little Marie Greco got Gladys' full name, she was able to find out who she worked for; Glady Hickson never worked as a caregiver. Nobody in the tri-state area had her down in their books. Maybe she was just a private caregiver? Or she had no experience and Phyllis hired her off the street or from a referral? Irish Marie said she'll ask

around with some of the housecleaning companies in Queens and Long Island. At that point in her life, Fitzpatrick Cleaning Services was doing pretty good; Irish Marie had clients beyond Brooklyn, she was sending people to Queens and Long Island. Irish Marie found out that Gladys worked for a cleaning company located in Hempstead; she cleaned two neighbors' houses on Manny Schrable's street in Great Neck. But last year she suddenly quit because of a bad back. She's was never a caregiver, she cleaned houses. Maybe Phyllis heard she quit at the same time as Esther's surgery and offered Gladys the job? Irish Marie already knew that the house was a mess. She told us she tried to visit Esther but this Gladys told her she was sleeping and then the second time she tried, she said Esther wasn't feeling up to company. Little Marie told Irish Marie that the Fairy Comaras were getting together after the next Thursday meeting to compare their notes on what they found out and Irish Marie said she'd come.

2. My job was to find out the status of Esther's checking and savings account. I was quite surprised to find out that currently Esther had no checking account and only $1,000 in savings. When I looked at her balance from seven months back, she had a checking account with $1,500 in it and a $77,000 savings account. I knew when Murray died, he had a $100,000 life insurance policy; whatever remained from the insurance, after funeral expenses, she put in the savings. When I looked now, $76,000 was withdrawn; I saw it was a wire transfer to Bernstein & York. Very strange. But then I remembered that she and Murray had a stock portfolio; Frankie Boy handled the Schrables' mutual fund account, including the Microsoft stocks. Even though the Frescas and the Schrables did not socialize, they still kept Frankie Boy as their broker. He took very good care of their retirement money. So, I asked Antoinette to call Frankie Boy and see what was up with those assets.

   Antoinette did call her brother the next day and she told him the whole story; I'm sure he was thrilled to hear a long story at work. He mentioned that Emil was still friends with Manny. They still went midnight fishing in Sheepshead Bay in the summer. He'd call Emil and see what he could learn. So, anyway, Frankie Boy told Antoinette that the only stock Esther has with his company was the Microsoft stock and Manny was the beneficiary if Esther died; it was a joint account set up originally for Esther and Murray. After Murray died, she switched it to her and Manny. Last summer, Manny with Esther's approval withdrew some money from the account in order to pay for her granddaughter Alyssa's college tuition. Manny handled all of that and he had the money wired directly to New York University. Manny only took out for the tuition and that was around July of last year. Of course, Frankie Boy had to add that Manny asked about her and to send his regards. He told Antoinette that the mutual fund account she had, approximately $600,000, was transferred to Bernstein & York.

3. So now we had to find out about Bernstein & York. It just so happened that Black Marie was there that Thursday evening and before everyone left, I asked her to stay a few minutes longer. Her children, Sal Jr. and Annette, were teenagers so she wasn't in a rush to go home if you know what I mean. Anyway, we asked Black Marie if she knew of a law firm called Bernstein & York. "I worked there; don't you remember? I worked there full-time before Sal was born and then part-time until Annette came along. Then it became too much for my parents, so I left. I still speak with Mr. Bernstein from time-to-time; he's always asks me if I want to come back. He keeps on saying he's going to retire but he was saying that when I worked there so I'll call him and see if I can get the inside scoop on Esther."

When you put combined energy on solving a problem, options present themselves like Black Marie and Bernstein & York. Black Marie wasn't even supposed to be part of our meeting; not that we wouldn't include her. When you work as a group, you'd be surprised how many options, answers and inspiration are culled from the universe to help you. Start a Fairy Comaras chapter near you; you never know.

Ok, back to #3. Black Marie contacted Joe Bernstein the next morning. They actually met for lunch the same day. Joe, at this point, didn't have many clients because of his advanced age so his calendar was clear. She told me he was so glad to see her and she showed him photos of her children and he showed her a wedding photo of his granddaughter. How time flies. While they were having dessert, Black Marie popped the question, "Joe, I have a favor to ask of you. It's not for me but for a very dear friend of mine who I feel is being taken advantage of financially. You may know her, Esther Schrable?" Joe immediately knew her; he mentioned that his firm got the account last year. "Sure, I remember the Schrable account; we set up a trust for her. One of our lawyers handled the account; I was included in the first meeting with Esther and her daughter-in-law. Why? You think there's something fishy going on?" Marie nodded yes. She said, "So, what you're saying is that Esther set up a trust and her daughter-in-law is the Executor?" "Correct", he said.

"Joe, we have reason to believe that Esther may not have agreed to the trust or she wasn't in a right state of mind. And we also believe that she is not getting the right monthly allowance for food, clothing and miscellaneous needs. Her food pantry is filled with nothing but boxes of macaroni and cheese, there's hardly anything in the refrigerator! Her clothes are worn, some with holes and her bed blanket is shredding. I need you to find out what money has been already spent on the trust and who's getting it; it's certainly not Esther. They have her on this cocktail of drugs that my friend, a nurse, says is not right. She's had hip surgery with no physical therapy for seven months" Joe interrupted, "I had both hips replaced; they had me in light physical therapy in the hospital and I went to PT two or three times a week for about six weeks. She should be walking around by now." Black Marie agreed with him. "So, you can see why we're concerned. Can you help us?" Joe said he'd make inquiries as soon as he got back to the office. He'd get back to her soon.

And true to his word, Joe Bernstein called Black Marie on the phone two days later. He told Marie he could not send any paperwork to her but he could read off the details on the phone.

"A living trust, in Esther's name for $676,000 was originally created six and a half months ago. In addition to the trust being created, a codicil was added to her will and her son and daughter-in-law are listed as beneficiaries of the remaining amount upon her death. However, Esther's daughter-in-law, Phyllis, was named the Executor of the trust and she currently manages the expenses for the house as well as Esther's living expenses. And this is where it gets murky. There doesn't seem to be anything unusual in expenses; Esther's house is paid off, she has the usual house expenses for heating, electricity, gas, phone, home insurance, prescriptions, doctor visits. Her grocery expenses are a little high; she shouldn't be eating only macaroni and cheese dinners because her monthly food bill is averaging $1,000 a month."

Joe continued, "According to one of the partners handling this account, Phyllis compiled bills for the last six months to substantiate these charges. However, by law, Phyllis as Executor of the trust is entitled to be compensated 5% of the estate's remaining balance upon her death. That provision was modified in June to read that Phyllis is to receive $10,000 per month as executor instead of being paid at the end. This was done at Esther's insistence because she has a granddaughter going to college and Esther is paying the tuition. The trust was signed by both Esther and Phyllis but, I was not there at the signing to verify the signatures. But my colleague said everything was on the up and up. There were also some credit card bills that were paid within the last six months and were paid in full each month. Some were pretty steep for purses and shoes. Didn't you say her clothes were worn?"

That was all Joe could tell her and Marie thanked him so much for getting this information so quickly. And again, Joe Bernstein asked her if she wanted to come back to work. She said she'd come back but, only if she worked for him, and he said he'd look into it but Marie knew his duties had been so drastically reduced there'd be no necessity. She felt good, though, that he asked.

4. I asked Theresa Guarino if she knew of any surgeons who Esther could visit in the evening to get a second opinion regarding her hip surgery status. Theresa said we could bring Esther to the hospital and one of the doctors there should be around to give us a second opinion. She said, "But before we can start any physical therapy, we have to first verify that

Esther is in any condition to walk again after being sedentary for seven months. We'd need to have a scan taken to see if her legs and hips are up to any physical therapy. If she can start PT, it could only be done after Gladys left so that might be a problem getting someone to come so late to Esther's house." Theresa said she would ask around to see if any of the physical therapists on 2nd St. would be able to come to Esther's and earn some extra money. Antoinette said she'd pay for it and on the days the therapist didn't come, she'd do the exercises with Esther at night. We had to figure a way for Esther to pretend she's taking the Klonipin, though, and that would mean we'd have to tell her some things about what was going on. Would Esther even believe us? When Murray was alive, I used to see Phyllis and Manny at the house. After he passed away, I only saw Manny occasionally when I was coming home from work; he'd stop by Esther's with some Chinese food and they'd share a meal. Until last year, he'd pick up Esther for the Jewish holidays and she'd stay overnight and then Manny would bring her home the next morning. I never heard Esther say a bad word about Phyllis; it was always Phyllis cares so much about me, she did this, she did that, and only recently, she said that Phyllis calls her every day. How do we convince her not tell Phyllis what was going on? We had a hard time not thinking the worst about Phyllis.

Times like this, I wished Signorine was still alive. She would know what to do. So, when we were hesitating about going into this hornet's nest, we took the Tarot cards out to see what we should do.

I shuffled the deck, then Irish Marie, then Black Marie and finally Antoinette shuffled and then said, "We ask these questions in the name of Jesus Christ!" To this day, Antoinette is the only one who has a plastic bottle of holy water at home and she sprinkled some water on the cards. She placed a funeral card with the Sacred Heart on the table. You would think she lived in the cardiology ward with her collection of Sacred Heart pictures! She has them everywhere in her apartment. If I had to look at them all day, I would want to rip my chest open and show Him my heart.

We asked the Tarot if, first: Is Esther in trouble? Second, are we doing the right thing and third, if yes, who should tell Esther? Antoinette certainly couldn't be the one to tell Esther for the obvious reason. She'd think Antoinette was still bitter over the break up even though she brought her pizza rustica Easter time.

So, we shuffled the cards and each of us pulled out a card, four cards and one more as the wild card, five cards.

First card was opened by me was the Hermit card; that was probably Esther because she's homebound. But the Hermit could mean self-discovery and clarity. So maybe Esther is going to be enlightened. Ok, ok, so here was Esther, the Hermit.

Second card, Antoinette pulled out. The Tower. I had to look that card up because I didn't know what it meant from memory. "The Tower signifies that what you thought were solid foundations are crashing around you. Destruction and chaos may follow but these events are happening FOR you not TO you."

Black Marie said, "So we are right! I felt it." Antoinette thought to herself that maybe the card was for her but, then she let it go.

Third Card, Black Marie. Eight of Wands. I had to look that one up, too. I may be psychic but I hardly ever used the Tarot back then. Now I use it to pull up a card to see what kind of day I'm going to have; it's hard to do the Tarot for yourself although, some people tell me they do it all the time. Anyway, Eight of Wands: I said, "You feel trapped by your thoughts and your situation. It may look like you have no choices but, those around you can provide the support you need to make certain choices."

OMG, that's the card we needed to see! That's it, we have to say something. Who was going to do it?

Fourth Card, Queen of Wands, Irish Marie pulled this card. This card represents a woman who is a social butterfly, leads an active life and has many connections. Confident and courageous, she is not afraid to speak up in the name of justice.

We all looked at Antoinette. "I thought you all said I shouldn't be the one to tell Esther? I can't tell Esther all by myself; I need a few people to come in with me. She's not going to believe only me." So, I said let's see what the wild card says.

Wild Card, Three of Pentacles

Collaborate together to create the environment for change. Collectively you have the wisdom and inspiration to get the job done. Black Marie and Theresa were chosen to go with Antoinette and tell Esther. Theresa would bring her to the hospital to have Esther examined by a doctor on Monday, her day off. She arranged to have one of the Orthopedic surgeons she was friendly with, Dr. Imperiale, examine Esther at 6:00 PM and do a CAT scan.

The next day, Friday, I volunteered to visit Esther and tell her what we were going to do. Esther and I always had a mutual respect for one another and after my parents passed away, we socialized every once in a while. We went to see Cats in 1995 and she came to a few of the Thursday meetings before her hip surgery. When she first came home from the surgery, I visited and brought her cannolis, her favorite, and flowers. She seemed so alert; a little uncomfortable from the operation but, other than that, she was looking forward to walking on the avenue without pain and maybe even traveling.

I went to Agnello's and got some cannolis and rang the bell. I didn't wait for Esther to say "who is it?" I just said, "It's Diane, next door" and after a minute Esther opened the door. Very important thing that Antoinette didn't mention was that Esther has to stand up to open the door. So, that was a good sign; I wonder how many other times she needed to stand up to retrieve stuff around the house? Anyway, I started up the Mr. Coffee, put the coffee cups and plates on the kitchen table and we sat down with our coffee and cannoli. I'm not one to mince words; I'm very direct and Esther knew I had something to say.

"Esther. I see you can stand but obviously not for long periods of time. Theresa wants to bring you to the hospital to get a second opinion on the surgery. Even though the surgeon told Phyllis that you have to wait a year, Theresa thinks it's suspicious that they didn't even try to give you physical therapy considering most patients get it immediately after they're discharged. They can take a CAT scan of your hips and legs and find out what's the problem. If there is no problem, Theresa wants to see if physical therapy will give you more mobility. What do you think? You want to go on Monday with Theresa?" Esther thought about it and then said, "I'll go, but first, I'd like Phyllis or Manny to be there if they can make it". How was I going to phrase this to exclude Phyllis and Manny?

"Esther, I just want you to know that Theresa and the doctor are doing this free of charge; if you had to go to get a second opinion, you would normally go to a doctor's office. This is being done because well, you know Theresa, she wants to make sure that all options have been taken. There can't be too many outside people in the hospital, it wouldn't look good for her. Besides, you know what Phyllis told Antoinette, right? We can only visit you during the day when Gladys is there." Esther remembered what Antoinette was told but, I didn't elaborate any further.

"You'll be in an out of there in minutes, you don't want Phyllis to drive all that way at night for only five or ten minutes, right? If the results are the same as you had seven months ago then, nothing's changed and no one has to know. If the results are hopeful then Phyllis will be told and she can take over. Theresa is acting on a hunch, no sense getting everyone in an uproar. Now, I want you to do nothing and most of all say nothing to Phyllis, not even Gladys or Manny. You'll have to trust me on this one; I've never steered you wrong so far. You can't even say I was here tonight. I don't want to argue with Phyllis about this, no drama. Theresa would be here tonight but she's working. She'll come and take you there on Monday around 6:00 PM, ok?"

So, Esther agreed. I cleaned up the cannoli crumbs off the table, washed and put the coffee cups away, kissed Esther and left with the garbage. I called Theresa and left a message on her home phone, "It's on for Monday at 6".

We almost got snagged that Monday; Gladys left at 5:45 instead of 5. When Theresa got to Esther's she had her nightgown on and she was kind of woozy; she was given Klonipin, probably in the afternoon. This is an accident waiting to happen if she's alone at night! Luckily, Theresa brought one of the male nurses, Kenny, to help her get Esther into and out of her car and put the wheelchair in the trunk. Dr. Imperiale was there waiting for them and he started examining Esther's legs and asked her if she could stand up; the Klonipin made her unsteady but she was able to do it with help from Kenny. The doctor said her leg muscles were good for someone who had no physical therapy for seven months but, he wanted to do the scan in case there were any obstacles or scar tissue near her hips. The scan results were clear; he said her surgery was a success and said if she was given PT seven months ago, she would be walking on her own by now. Theresa asked for a copy of the scan results. The doctor asked why she was on Klonipin and Theresa told him she was prescribed the medication for anxiety and depression. They both looked at each other and the doctor said, "If she had received her physical therapy seven months ago, she'd probably wouldn't be depressed now. She's on Lopressor which can make you somewhat lightheaded and add to that Klonipin?" Theresa added that she was on OxyContin too; she has to be weaned off it. He continued, "In my opinion, there's no reason why she couldn't start PT now, it would take much longer but, she should be back on her feet in six or seven weeks." That was enough for Theresa.

Well, in our minds, that confirmed that we had to take action on this; time to put our Fairy Comara energies to good use….and quickly. First, we had to tell Esther about the surgery, the results of the CAT scan, her Trust and the meds. We were just hoping she was lucid enough not to say anything to Gladys about tonight's visit to the hospital.

I remember the next day it was sunny and warm; I had a dentist appointment in the morning but, I took the whole day off from work. You never know how you're going to feel after root canal but, it turned out to be relatively painless. So, around 1:00 PM, I decided to sit outside in my garden and get some Vitamin D and, also to see what the hell else Antoinette planted in the garden. The fig tree looked great and Antoinette had a little plaque made to hang on one of the branches that said, "in memory of Signorine". I turned around and Esther was outside in her garden, which by the way was full of weeds. Esther never kept a garden like that; that garden was her pride and joy and she always had the best looking and healthiest hydrangeas! As soon as Esther was up and around, I'll go over and take care of it. I went over to say hello to Esther; Gladys was sitting next to her. It was mostly small talk until Esther's phone rang inside and Gladys got up to answer it. Once she was inside, I said, "Esther, we're coming over tonight to visit, don't tell Gladys, ok? We have the results from the doctor. You didn't say anything to Gladys, did you?" Esther said no. I whispered, "don't take the Klonipin this afternoon, put it in your mouth and spit it out, hide it somewhere, ok? When Gladys came back out, she told Esther that it was Phyllis on the phone. "She was just checking on how you were doing today." After about two minutes, she tells Esther that it's getting chilly outside and it's time to go inside. So, I gave Esther the look and she gave me the look, too.

At 7:00 PM, Me, Theresa, Black Marie, Little Marie, Irish Marie and Antoinette rang Esther's bell. Thankfully, Esther had already turned off the alarm so she opened the door right away. Esther was so happy to see Irish Marie, Black Marie and Little Marie; they hugged and kissed and Esther asked about their families. Antoinette went into the kitchen and started up the Mr. Coffee and when coffee was served, it was time for business. Although Theresa and Black Marie did most of the talking that night, we all went to show Esther that we cared for her and that what we were about to tell her was true.

Theresa started by saying that Dr. Imperiale thought there was a very good chance she'd walk again. Her hip healed very well. She showed Esther the scan results and explained everything to her. She told her the doctor said her leg muscles were still strong and, with some physical therapy she should be able to walk on 5th Ave and go shopping again. Esther told her, "I went to the best hospital for hip surgery and that doctor told me I could never walk again. The surgeon said he did the best he could." Theresa asked, "The surgeon told you that?" Esther said, "Well, no, not directly. When I was discharged, Phyllis and Manny met with the surgeon. Phyllis filled me in afterwards, I was still in a lot of discomfort and painkillers at the time." Theresa tried to skip the subject of possible deception and just said, "Why not prove the surgeon wrong and get some physical therapy and see how that goes? I can have a physical therapist come to your home, in the evenings, and do some strength exercises with you. Remember little George Cusimano, Sylvia's son? Well, he's a physical therapist now, he works on 2nd Street and, he said he'd come to your house two or three evenings after work to do the exercises. Antoinette will drop by on the other nights and do the exercises with you, too"

Black Marie and Sylvia Cusimano were good friends and George knew Esther since he was a kid; he was happy to do it. Black Marie offered to pay him but he waved his hand and said no, it was the least he could do to thank her for fixing his mother up with such a nice guy. I think Black Marie mentioned Esther's story to Sylvia and she passed it on to her son. Esther and Murray used to give Sylvia credit at the store during her lean years and she never forgot how they helped her back then. And, then Esther said, "I'm going to call Phyllis and tell her all about this and what you girls are doing for me!" And then, Black Marie gave her report to Esther.

"Esther, you're aware that you have a Trust set up by Bernstein and York, right?" Esther said, "yes, a Trust was set up to pay all the house bills, repairs, food, clothing whatever else came up. Phyllis told me that she took the savings and whatever was in the checking and set up the trust. My son works long hours and has to manage his own dental practice, he has no time to take care of this stuff so, after I had the hip surgery and because I wasn't able to do a lot of things on my own, Phyllis agreed to be the Executor. She's home and has the time to take care of all this for me. I'm blessed with a good daughter-in-law." Antoinette was so good, she didn't open her mouth or make a facial expression when she heard Esther say that; she behaved, I have to say.

Black Marie continued, "Esther there's a little more in the trust than your savings. Did you know that Phyllis transferred your mutual fund money into the Trust? You have around $600,000 in the trust right now. Frankie Boy told Antoinette that Bernstein & York made the transfer with Phyllis' authorization as Executor. I used to work for Joe Bernstein as a paralegal and he told me about it. Phyllis pays all your expenses but, did you know that she takes out $10,000 a month to be your Executor? And that your food, clothing and other expenses come to around a $1,000 a month? Antoinette had to get something out of your pantry the other day and all she saw were macaroni and cheese boxes and very little in the refrigerator, why are you scrimping on the food?" You can afford to have more than that with what you receive as a monthly allowance! Your hair is all gray; you used to have your hair colored every month and your hair set for the week! In fact, based on the budget for this trust, your personal allowance should be $2,000 a month even if you live to be 100. Irish Marie used to clean your house and she never charged you a lot, you know that; how come you stopped the cleaning? At the rate Phyllis is taking out in Executor fees, in about five years, you'll have nothing."

Little Marie chimed in to say, "you're currently paying Gladys $500 a week per the trust, why? She sits with you, makes macaroni and cheese, doesn't straighten up, does she bathe you? Esther said, "Gladys helps me in the shower and I sit on the bath bench twice a week, she dresses and undresses me and she makes sure I take my medications." Little Marie said, "that's a lot to pay for just a companion and a pill dispenser." Remember we're talking about 20 years ago; that was a lot back then. "I could get you someone to do that for a third of the price! She stays with you from what? 9:00 in the morning to 5:00 PM, what the hell does she do? None of the caregiver agencies have her on the books, who hired her?" Little Marie was starting to get agitated so we gave her the look.

This was quite a lot for Esther to absorb so we said nothing for a while. We honestly thought, at this point, that Esther was going to throw us all out of her house. Who the hell were we to get into her business? But she put her head down and we saw a tear drop down on her lap. Antoinette rushed into the kitchen to get her a glass of water but, her first words were, "I'll take another cup of coffee" and then she said, "My granddaughter Alyssa was here last week and she wanted to know about the macaroni and cheese and I told her it was because I didn't have as much money as she thought and Alyssa told me that I should have enough. Her mother told her she pays her tuition out of her Executor fees. She even offered to pay her own college tuition so I could have more to live on but I said no."

Antoinette then spoke up and said, "Esther, Alyssa's tuition is paid for from the dividends of the Microsoft stock. Frankie Boy told me Manny took it out last year when she started college. Her tuition doesn't come out of the trust. The only reason why the funds were not transferred to the trust is because Manny is solely handling that and the stock is doing very well; well enough to pay her tuition for the full year just in dividends."

And then I spoke up. I took Esther's hand and looked her right in the eye, "Esther, you know we all love you and we have nothing to gain by telling you this information. Believe me, we all did not go into this research with the intention of casting suspicion. In your heart, you know something's not right here; you worked in business most of your life. You managed a profitable business with Murray. So, you really can't blame us if we're a little suspicious after finding all this out, even if it involves Phyllis whom we know you love like a daughter. There could be another explanation for why these things were done. You're going to have to trust us for now and not say anything about the physical therapy or the Trust to Phyllis, Manny or even Gladys until we investigate this further. Do you trust us? You can't tell them that we were ever here. We're going to clean up after coffee like no one was here and next week George Cusimano will start giving you exercises. When Gladys gives you the

Klonipin, shove it in one of the cushions so that you're alert for the PT. You don't need a tranquilizer, you need PT. Can you promise us you will do this for us until we get to the bottom of this mess?"

Esther was clearly in a fog on hearing all of this and we didn't know if she really believed us. We had to take a chance that she did believe us and said nothing.

Black Marie said, "George will probably drop by tomorrow night to do an assessment and what portable equipment to bring for the first physical therapy session. When he rings your bell, he'll identify himself as Sylvia's son and say he's from 2nd St. That's how you'll know it is him and not some thug." And, we reminded her not to take the Klonipin from now on, throw the pills in the weeds in the back, no one will see it. Pretend to be sleepy until 5:00 PM! Irish Marie told Esther that she will drop by more often in the evenings and once this mess with the financials is cleared up, she'll come over and give the house a deep cleaning…. FREE! Thank God, she trusted us; Esther didn't say a thing to Phyllis and Gladys and allowed us to proceed.

After about six weeks of physical therapy in the good hands of George Cusimano and practicing with Antoinette the other nights, Esther was standing upright, not hunched over as before and, getting around with a walker and then walking with a cane. After listening to Esther for six weeks constantly asking, "Are you hungry? I'll make you some mac and cheese" George told her yes. But he told her to get it herself using her cane and she did it! And she reached up to the top shelf of the pantry and then walked over to the stove to make his mac and cheese. It was at that point that she cried while making the mac and cheese. It was hard for Esther having to sit all day in a wheelchair to fool Gladys and having to act sleepy for Gladys to believe that she took the Klonipin. It was also hard to accept all that we told her and the fact that she was starting to walk on her own.

One day, while she was pretending to be sleeping in the chair, the phone rang and Gladys answered. She was whispering because she thought she was sleeping but Esther clearly heard her tell the person on the other line, "when is the doctor coming over for the evaluation?" And then, "You want me to give her two pills a day? I'm worried." And then after a pause, she said, "Yes, yes, I will start today and I'll see you the following Thursday." Esther thought, that's a little over a week from now. What doctor? Evaluation? For what? So, after Gladys left, she called Antoinette and told her to come over; it was important.

Antoinette and Irish Marie came that evening and Esther told them what she heard. At this point, Esther didn't even use a walker to get around; she used a cane sometimes at night when she felt sleepy but, otherwise, she was walking; she was starting to walk a normal step for her age. So, here was Antoinette's plan, "next Wednesday night, me, Irish Marie and Diane are coming over. We're going to give you a shower, Diane is going to find a nice pantsuit in the closet and wash it because it's probably dusty and smells like camphor balls and I'll style your hair. Then on Thursday morning, I'll come down around 7:00 AM, put your clothes on and make sure your hair looks good. Irish Marie will tidy up as best as she can without causing suspicion. Absolutely no Klonipin and when the doctor visits, I want you to stand up and ask him if he'd like some coffee. It's going to blow everyone's mind. You understand? Gladys is going to be curious as to why you're wearing good clothes and just say something like I felt like wearing one of my pantsuits instead of the shmate I usually wear. It's going to be nice out, I'd like to go in the garden today and then change the subject. After the doctor leaves, Phyllis may stay, she'll obviously have some questions. All you should say is that you saw some exercises on the Richard Simmons' show for people in wheelchairs and you thought you'd give it a try. That may throw her off, for now. On the other hand, she may be extremely happy that you're finally getting back to normal. You'll know."

That Thursday morning, Gladys was indeed surprised to see Esther looking so well groomed. And Esther repeated everything Antoinette told her to say. And when the Klonipin was given to her, she put it in her mouth and then spit it out when Gladys turned around. And, after lunch, when Gladys gave her the Lopressor medication with a glass of water, Esther pretended not to notice that it was a Klonipin and spit it out. Good acting, I have to say. And the Academy Award for the Best Actress Pretending to Be High goes to Esther Schrable!!!

When the doctor came at 2:00 PM with Phyllis right behind him, Esther was ready. He examined her throat, her heartbeat, her eyes and ears, her blood pressure was a little high but, not worrisome. He asked Esther, "Are you able to get around this house in that wheelchair? What about bathing yourself, getting into bed? And Esther replied, "Oh yes, I can take care of myself very well." Phyllis interrupted, "Now Mom, it has to be hard getting around here at night and I worry one day you'll fall and be down on the floor with no one to hear you. Maybe, you, we, should consider 24-hour care?" Esther told the doctor, "Look at my daughter-in-law how she worries about me like a daughter. Phyllis, I'm alright." And then Esther said, "Doctor would you like a cup of coffee?" Without even waiting for an answer, Esther got up off the wheelchair and proceeded to walk from the Living Room to the kitchen and made the Mr. Coffee. Then, she walked back to sit back in the wheelchair. Boy, to be a fly on the wall on that day to see the shock on their faces! What a site that must have been. Just to see Phyllis' face would have been enough!

Phyllis said, "Mom this is such good news, I'm ecstatic! How did you manage to walk?" Esther said, "Determination and watching the exercises on Richard Simmons on TV; he has exercises for people in wheelchairs." Well, the doctor was busy and since Phyllis drove him there from Great Neck, she had to drive him back so there was no time for her to ask any more questions. When Esther told us what happened we thought how strange that Phyllis had a doctor from Great Neck make a house visit, which is rare in itself, but from Great Neck to Brooklyn?

On her way-out, Phyllis grabbed Gladys' arm and whispered, "how could you allow this to happen? I'll call you." Esther heard her and, it was at that very moment that Esther regrettably realized Phyllis was not the Phyllis she thought she was and, that made her sad; but it also made her more determined. Finally, she could walk around the house all day instead of at night! Her only hope was that Manny was not involved in this as well!

That night, Black Marie, Little Marie and Antoinette brought Esther a pizza for dinner and she told us the whole story. She told us that Gladys was quiet for the remainder of the day; she sat outside with her in the garden but, hardly said a word so Esther read the newspaper. Little Marie was worried about tomorrow morning when Gladys came back; what more could she do to Esther? Since Antoinette worked the nearest from home, Little Marie told Esther that if Gladys made her feel threatened, she was to call Antoinette at work right away and she would there in 20 minutes. Antoinette wrote down the number with no name on it and told Esther to keep it in her pocket. Esther walked to the bedroom closet and pulled out another pair of pants and a flowered blouse and told us she's wearing it tomorrow!

However, the next morning it wasn't Gladys who came through the door; it was Phyllis and, she came in all bubbly bearing flowers and bagels, too! I think for that fleeting moment, Esther might have thought that maybe we were wrong about her. But minutes later, she came back to reality when Phyllis told her over bagels and coffee that she had to let Gladys go. "Mom, now that you're walking and probably wanting to go out and about, I think it's best that we get a certified aid to take care of you; someone who has a little nursing experience and knows how to properly bathe you, cook a decent meal, help you dress and make sure you're safe during the night. Maybe 24-hour care? The sidewalks are not leveled, I'm afraid you'll take a tumble and break the other hip. You need someone to help you cross the street when you get your hair done, or shopping, stuff like that." Esther said she didn't think she needed 24-hour care, maybe someone to clean the house or tend to the gardening. And if she fell, she saw this thing on TV called Medical Alert that you put around your neck and you press the button and they send help right away. Phyllis asked her, "and how are they going to get into the house if it's locked with the alarm? What if you fall and you're unconscious for hours? Who's going to know?" and then she said, "Let me do some research into this and I'll get back to you." And then Esther said, "Well, I'll save you some time, call Marie Greco from Francone Senior Center in Massapequa; she would know how to go about getting someone." That took Phyllis off her guard for a moment because she said "Oh yeah, right. I don't know Marie Greco but, I'll call her and see what she says". Esther only had Little Marie's home number but she could leave a message in advance of Phyllis calling. Phyllis said, "don't worry, I'll call her." She wasn't expecting Phyllis to call.

Poor Gladys, she took the blame because of us but, we didn't feel that guilty because all this while she was doing what Phyllis was telling her even though she knew it was wrong.

Esther had Gladys's telephone number so she was elected to call her to find out what happened. Maybe we could get the dirt on what was going on; she was let go immediately, she had to be pissed off. We told Esther to call her tonight while the anger was fresh. Esther called around 7:00 PM and luckily,

Gladys was home. She didn't want to leave a message because she was afraid that Gladys might return her call the next day when Phyllis came in with her replacement. It sure wasn't going to be someone Little Marie recommended. Esther told Gladys she knew nothing about her being let go and how sorry she was that it had to happen, "I thought you took good care of me, I told that to Phyllis after she told me she let you go. You were always so sweet; but Phyllis thinks I need 24-hour care with someone trained in caring for me." Butter would have melted in Esther's mouth!

And then, with the vengeance of a harpy, Gladys said, "Esther, Phyllis is not looking out for you, it's the complete opposite. I know she's your daughter-in-law and you love her but, she is a two-face and, I'm telling you, you better watch your back. She doesn't want you to get 24-hour care at home; she wants to sell that house right from under you and ship you down to an assisted living community in Tampa, Florida. She already has the brochure. The doctor that came to examine you, he's a doctor but, he's also her boyfriend. But, he's not stupid enough to lose his license to put down the wrong information. She's been draining your trust by about $10,000 a month plus whatever she cut from your food allowance. She plans to leave your son, get his money from the divorce and by the time your son transfers the trust to him, it will be nothing. She's was ready to get the papers ready; she made me give you two Klonipin that day instead of one, I'm sorry. I knew the minute you got up and walked around that you didn't take them and I'm thankful of that; seeing you walk yesterday was just a miracle from God."

And, she told Esther other things Phyllis said about her; Esther told us she didn't want to get into it because it was too hurtful right now to talk about it.

Well, Fairy Comaras report to God so technically she's right; it was a miracle. Gladys added, "Whoever Phyllis sends will report directly to her and watch every move you make. And Esther then asked, "Is my son involved in this?". Gladys said she didn't think so; she didn't think he had a clue what was going on. Gladys said, "He came to see you last month and you looked disoriented in your wheelchair, so maybe he felt it confirmed what Phyllis had been saying to him all along. Esther, take care of yourself, watch your back."

After she got off the phone, Esther shook so much she couldn't stand without holding on to the wall. She just couldn't imagine that this was going on; she knew Phyllis liked wearing expensive things but, Esther felt that if her Manny wasn't complaining about the money, why should she? And to find out what Phyllis thought about her just shook her to the core. Had Phyllis felt this way all these years? She called me up as soon as she was composed and told me what Gladys said. Something had to be done and quickly.

Irish Marie was visiting me that night; after I got off the phone, she suggested we call her granddaughter, Alyssa, to have a talk with her since she seemed to be the only one who questioned her grandmother's condition before we did. Maybe if we show her everything we've learned so far, she could be the mole to see what her mother's next move will be but, would she do it? Afterall, it was her mother! We had to take the chance. So, I told Esther to call Alyssa; at that time some of us had one of those Nokia cellphones; all the youngsters had one, including Alyssa. She lived in the university's dorm with another girl. Esther had the number and she called her. Esther asked if she could stop by on Friday around 6-ish before she went home to Great Neck. Alyssa said yes, she would. Alyssa didn't have time to stay on the phone long because she was stepping out with a few of her friends. Friday would determine if Alyssa believed her Bubbe or tell her mother about us; it was a risk Esther/we had to take.

I was the most familiar with Alyssa because I lived next door. Manny would bring little Alyssa when he was picking up Esther and Murray for Passover or Rosh Hashanah to go to his house. She was a cutie and she loved her Bubbe and Zeyde! From the conversations I had with her recently, she seemed to be a smart young lady. She'd always asked me how Esther was doing. Now that she attended NYU, she'd pay a visit to her Bubbe at least once or twice a month. Of course, in the last seven months she must have thought her Bubbe was going downhill so, if her mother said anything about Esther's declining health, of course, she would believe it. One thing for certain, she may get angry at the Fairy Comaras for interfering but, she'd have to admit her Bubbe looked great. And so, we waited until Friday; the WE were me and Black Marie. Little Marie and Irish Marie couldn't make it, Theresa was working and Antoinette was uncomfortable being there and we understood. Antoinette remembered Alyssa as a child when Manny brought her over to visit Esther and Murray or if by chance, he visited Emil at her parents' house. Although she was always cordial and loved Alyssa, it was too emotional for Antoinette. She still loved Manny; she probably thought that Alyssa should be the child that they had.

A couple of days later, Black Marie received a plain 8x11 envelope with no sender address. Inside were copies of the expenditures on Esther's Trust for the last seven months and a recent request by Phyllis for an additional Executor percentage for administrative tasks towards the "pending sale" of Esther's house. Also included was new banking information and a wire transfer number Phyllis supplied for Executor fees for administering the sale of Esther's house; in other words, checks would no longer be mailed to the Great Neck house. Black Marie owed Joe Bernstein a lunch and a big hug and a kiss on the cheek!

A new caregiver, Virginia, came in the next morning; she was very nice and all that but, she was very reserved. She told Esther that she would be with her from 9 to 5 for the next two weeks and then 24 hours once she could get her home needs straightened out because she had a teenage daughter. Esther asked her what agency she worked for and she said she wasn't working for any agency at the moment. Her agency moved to Manhattan and she didn't want to travel to Manhattan so, she resigned. She was hired by her daughter-in-law who was friends with one of her former patient's niece. Esther asked Virginia," what happened to your patient?" She replied, "She unfortunately passed away last month from medical complications." Virginia told her that it was just by coincidence that she happened to be between jobs. "Between jobs? Does that mean if you find a job you'll be leaving?" Esther asked. Virginia abruptly corrected herself and said, "No! I meant it was lucky that I hadn't found a job yet or else I wouldn't be able to accept Phyllis' offer." Virginia went over Esther's medications and Esther informed her that she no longer needed to take Klonipin for depression. She was walking and getting around nicely; she planned on doing a little gardening now and going shopping. Virginia asked, "Did the doctor tell you to stop taking the Klonipin?" Esther said, "Well no, but I took that medication for depression and I no longer need it. My son prescribed it for me temporarily." She said, "Well, I'll have to check with your son or Phyllis about this and see if it should be discontinued before I stop giving it to you." When it was time to give Esther her meds, Virginia watched her swallow them with a glass of water. She couldn't hide the Klonipin under the cushion this time.

When Antoinette came to see her at night, Esther was a mess and she was very disoriented; she told her she couldn't hide the Klonipin. Antoinette took the bottle of Klonipin and looked at the size of the pills. Antoinette left Esther and went back to her apartment to look over her vitamin supplements; she said she'd be right back. She was a vitamin freak; she had about 10 vitamin bottles on her shelf. When she compared the Klonipin pills to her iron pills they were a perfect match so she took out the Klonipin pills and put in the same amount of iron pills. It might just work if Virginia didn't look carefully. Then she went back to Esther's and told her she could take the Klonipin tomorrow because they were iron pills; she put the bottle in the same position as it was on her meds tray. Antoinette hoped she understood; Virginia obviously gave her the two pills that Gladys was supposed to give her. She got Esther ready for bed and told me what happened. It was Wednesday; Esther had to be alert for Alyssa by Friday night. The following evening, we invited Esther to our Thursday meeting. She was good mastering the staircase going up but had a little trouble going down the stairs. She mostly lived in the basement apartment since the surgery. The upstairs hadn't been lived in since then. But we got Esther to the meeting safe and sound.

Esther was ecstatic meeting all the old crew from the neighborhood. Everybody was so happy to see her; Little Marie's mother knew about Esther through her daughter and said, "Welcome back to the land of the living!" Antoinette had it catered by Black Marie's father that night so we had all of Esther's favorite Italian food. She ate like there was no tomorrow. Sylvia Cusimano was there; she told her that her son was so happy that the physical therapy worked. Esther told her, "Your son saved my life and he was so patient with me!" We took her home at around 9:30 and got her ready for bed; we noticed that she had a message on her phone so Antoinette retrieved it. It was Phyllis; she called at 6:30. She wanted to know how the new aid was working out. Quickly, Antoinette handed the phone to Esther and told her to call Phyllis back. "Tell her you fell asleep in the Living Room and you didn't hear the phone ring. Phyllis will probably figure it was the meds." So, Esther called and Manny answered the phone. He was happy to hear from her; he asked if something was wrong. Esther said, "No, nothing's wrong. I'm calling Phyllis back, she called around

6:30 to find out how well the new aid was taking care of me." "Oh, you have a new aid? What happened to Gladys?" he asked. Esther told him that Phyllis felt she needed more professional care with longer hours. Well, that didn't surprise Manny because the last time he saw Esther was months ago; he spoke with her frequently but, he had the practice to run and he was spending long hours trying to make enough to keep up the lifestyle that they or rather Phyllis had. "Mom, Phyllis is at her Zumba class and then having dinner with her friends tonight. I'll tell her you called." Esther said, "Tell her I'll call her tomorrow and that everything is fine, I'm going to bed now." And after they said I love you and good night to each other; she hung up and gave the phone back to Antoinette. As we were leaving, I whispered to Antoinette, "Zumba my ass!".

Friday night came and Alyssa came around 6:15. The plan was that Esther would first reveal what was going on and then, me and Black Marie would pop in about a half hour later to back her up with the information. We rang the bell and Alyssa answered the door and uttered a hesitant hello. And then she said, "I'm not trying to be rude but this may not be the best time to visit my grandmother; we're having a family discussion." And then I said, "we're here because of that discussion; we have some things to show you. May we come in?" And then we heard Esther from inside tell her it was alright for us to come inside.

Black Marie and I laid everything out to Alyssa; Black Marie had the paperwork from the Trust and she circled certain items such as the household allowance and the Executor's fee. She told us that she knew her mother took $10,000 out each month; she said it was high because Bubbe wanted the money to go towards my tuition. We both said NO! and we showed her the Microsoft stocks and how her father was paying her tuition from the dividends earned from the stock. I said, "Alyssa, look in your grandmother's pantry. There's nothing but macaroni and cheese for her to eat. The refrigerator is empty except for some Half and Half and a package of frankfurters. Take a look if you don't believe us. She should be eating Filet Mignon. Your grandmother should be getting an allowance of $1,500 a month to pay for food, someone to clean the house, get her hair done if she wants and shopping. Look at her, her hair is gray, her nails haven't been done in seven months. And, look at this house, it's dirty; when have you ever seen your Bubbe's house in this condition? She hasn't been out of this house in months. Look at the monthly credit card expenses. Where did that money go? There's a line item for caregiving so the allowance is not paying for that, where is this money going? Why wasn't your grandmother given physical therapy after her operation? Your mother told Esther that the surgery wasn't successful and she couldn't get PT. How is it that we brought her to the hospital, took x-rays and discovered the surgery went well?"

I showed her the x-rays from the hospital to prove it. I told her she should have gotten PT immediately after the surgery. Your grandmother is walking because we arranged for physical therapy these past six weeks and look at her! She's her old self again!" Esther got up from the wheelchair to show her how well she was walking. I said, "and how long has it been since you've seen your grandmother this alert? Seven months, right?" I realized I was raising my voice and decided to stop.

Black Marie chimed in but gently, "And why is your father, a dentist, prescribing Klonipin, a tranquilizer, for his mother? The prescription isn't even under her name, it's under Gladys' name. We don't think it was your father who prescribed it, we can't be sure but we think your mother might have taken a sheet from his prescription pad. We know your father a long time and he wouldn't prescribe Klonipin under a different name or even in your Bubbe's name, he would be breaking the law. He'd have a psychiatrist examine her and prescribe her meds. Right now, legally, he's at risk of losing his license and jail time. Why is the Klonipin medication under her old caregiver's name, Gladys Hickson? And recently, your mother tried to prove that your grandmother was not capable of living in her own house. She came to the house with some doctor from Great Neck to confirm that she was unfit. She wanted Gladys to give her two Klonipin that day, instead of one, so she would be in a wheelchair and disoriented. Your grandmother heard it herself. It didn't work because we told your grandmother to pretend to take the Klonipin; she was able to walk around with a cane when the doctor examined her. She surprised them all! The next thing we knew, your mother fired Gladys a couple of days ago and now we got this new woman, Virginia, who watches your grandmother swallow the Klonipin pills and is going to make sure she's back in the wheelchair." Black Marie had her serious but concerned look; we all knew that look and her voice was slow and monotone.

Was Alyssa confused? Sure, she was! But Marie had to lay all the cards on the table for her. Alyssa just said, "I don't know what to say, it's incredible. My mother always speaks so lovingly about Bubbe. Why would she do this?"

And then, I had to open my mouth, I couldn't hold it in, "We can't verify it but, after Gladys was fired, she told Bubbe that your mother was having an affair with the doctor who came over to examine her on Thursday. After the show she put on with the walking, there was no way he could say she was unfit to take care of herself. She was coherent, dressed nicely and she was walking! Gladys was a witness to all this. So, she fired Gladys and now she's hired this woman and plans to sell the house and put your grandmother in a nursing home or some old age community in Florida. Then, she'll put the money from the sale of this house into the Trust that she's taking money out of, plus an additional percentage for handling the sale when it's sold."

Alyssa asked if she could bring the bottle to her mother to get an explanation and we told her no, we replaced all the pills with iron pills. I told her we have the meds at my house; I didn't mention Antoinette did it. I said, "We're still trying to decide where this is all going; we need to get all our ducks in a row on this before we can be absolutely certain. However, we do have one favor to ask of you. Would you bring your father next week so we could talk with him? We told Alyssa she is not to say anything to her father, especially her mother, until we explained everything to him like we did with her. She wasn't for it but, she reluctantly agreed.

We really didn't know if Alyssa believed us; after all, it was her mother we were talking about and I definitely crossed the line with the information on the boyfriend. And then, Esther walked over to Alyssa, looked in her eyes and said, "Alyssa, you know I loved your mother like my own daughter but the facts speak for themselves. I don't know about this so-called affair Gladys was talking about but, the money, the meds, the doctor, it's all true. If not for these ladies, I'd be waiting for death. I'm afraid to say it but, sometimes in the best of families, money can be their ruination. Trust the ladies and I'll see you next week with your father, ok? All of this will be straightened out next week but, please, for Bubbe, say nothing for now, ok? Look at you, so thin, what are you eating at that college?" Alyssa answered, "I'm fine, I'm eating lots of food" But, she ate the tub of baked ziti Antoinette made for Esther.

When she left us, we didn't get the usual hug from Alyssa but we got a Thank You. We hoped she'd keep our secret for the time being. Shortly after, we left. Black Marie and I made sure everything was the same, packed up the garbage and we took the empty tub with us. On the way out, Black Marie said, "I feel like I'm in a fuckin soap opera!" and we kissed and said goodbye.

George Cusimano came two more times the following week to give Esther physical therapy and then pronounced her ready for the outside world. One evening, Esther taught Antoinette how to do the Cha-Cha and Antoinette taught her how to do the Hustle. We had the usual Thursday evening meeting but, Black Marie and Irish Marie couldn't make it because Alyssa told Esther that she and her father were coming on Thursday instead of Friday. Antoinette sent them to Esther's with a tub of stuffed shells; Manny's favorite.

Antoinette and I were a little off kilter that Thursday evening; I told everyone I wasn't giving readings because I had a slight cold which wasn't true but, I was too distracted. Don't you know, that week I got the sniffles; never lie about having a cold! We asked Nancy Kochinski, who lived on 4th St and 3rd Ave, to give a lecture about crocheting decorative baby blankets using the diamond, shell and Afghan stitches. She crocheted some beautiful blankets and toilet paper holders and, she was a good teacher. For the rest who didn't crochet or weren't interested in learning, Theresa Guarino brought some of her handmade jewelry for sale. Antoinette made coffee that night and forgot to put the coffee in the basket so to our surprise only hot water came out. I told Antoinette to get the tea bags. Nobody cared as long as there was cake. Sylvia Cusimano took me aside and asked about Esther. I told her that her son was a miracle worker; Esther was up and about thanks to him. I told her to hold on for a second and I took an envelope out of the kitchen drawer and handed it to her. I said, "George wouldn't take any money but, a few of us pooled together a little something for him, tell him it's a tip. And tell your son we won't take NO for an answer and never bring it up again." Sylvia said, "You know I'd do anything for Esther; she and Murray helped me through some really rough times. If there's anything else I can do, call me." I kissed her and thanked her for what she and George did already!

Nancy told us after her lecture, tutorial, whatever you call it, a few people were offering to pay her to make baby blankets for them; baby showers were coming up in their family. Theresa sold a lot of earrings that night so she was happy. She stayed later because she was just as curious as me and Antoinette about how the Manny meeting turned out. Little Marie had to go home because she had her mother with her.

And we're waiting, waiting and pouring cups of hot water for tea because it was too late to make coffee and the agita is building in our stomachs. Around 9:15 we hear Esther's front door open so we run to the window. Out comes Manny and Alyssa; they didn't look angry but it was night and hard to see their faces behind the curtains. Manny got in his car with Alyssa and they drove off. About 15 minutes later, Black Marie and Irish Marie came out with the garbage bag; Irish Marie must have had to run because she kissed Marie and then got into her car.

Black Marie came in and immediately poured herself coffee and when just water came out, she said, "what the fuck?" We explained and I asked Antoinette to put on the 4-cup coffee pot I use during the week. When Antoinette came back in, Black Marie filled us in on what went down at Esther's.

She said, "Manny was a little surprised to see me and Irish Marie come through the door; Alyssa asked her father to take a good look at Bubbe and Esther got up and walked around the Living Room; she said nothing to him beforehand, good girl." And then Black Marie went on to say, "Well, the conversation had its surprises to be sure. I think Esther was both happy and sad after this meeting, it's still a shock to her." So, now she has us wondering. Good thing the coffee was perking and almost ready. Antoinette always knew when it was ready by the smell that whiffed through the house. If you smelled it in the Living Room, it was ready. We smelled it in the Living Room so Antoinette jumped up from her seat to bring Black Marie a cup. I wanted a cup, too.

Black Marie said that she laid out everything for Manny the same as she did with Alyssa; she showed him the bottle of Klonipin with his name on it. He said he never prescribed it for Gladys and wanted to know why it was in his mother's home. Marie told him Phyllis had the prescription filled in Gladys' name but, it was for Esther. He immediately came to the conclusion that we did about Phyllis taking a sheet from his prescription pad. "I told him Phyllis probably asked this new doctor from Great Neck but, he said no. As you can see, she doesn't need Klonipin. Look at how good she looks without it! I told him what Theresa Guarino did with the doctor and the CAT scan and the PT." Esther got up from her wheelchair and strutted her stuff around the Living Room, he was overjoyed." Manny asked, "how much Klonipin were they giving her?" And I told him, "At first, it was one a day but when your mother showed the doctor she could walk and was lucid, your wife upped the dosage to two pills, twice a day. Antoinette replaced the Klonipin with her iron pills but, we can only fool this new aid, Virginia, for so long." Manny said, "Antoinette did that?" Next, they went to the financials and Alyssa asked her father how her tuition was paid. Manny told her from the Microsoft stocks. So that confirmed for Alyssa that what her mother told her was a lie. Not something a daughter should have to mentally or emotionally confront but, it is what it is! Irish Marie told Alyssa not to be so hard on her mother, we all make mistakes and, you never know, we all go off the beaten path at times. But it was all bullshit, she just didn't want her to hate her mother. It's not our way to cause trouble in families, it's mala faccia, not a good thing. Yes, we all make mistakes but, sometimes the Fairy Comaras were able to nip it in the bud before it became a huge mistake, like this one.

Black Marie told us she went over the financials, line by line with him and she told him about Phyllis being the Executor, which he knew about but, did not know about the $10,000 fee she was collecting. She showed him the mutual fund transfer to the trust verified by Frankie Boy plus the new wire transfer number his wife gave the lawyer at Bernstein & York for future payments. She asked Manny if he changed banks recently. She asked him to check the routing number on his checking and savings accounts to see if it was the same routing number Phyllis gave Bornstein & York but, all of us knew it was not going to be the same.

So Black Marie says to us, "Now listen to this. Manny asked Esther if she remembered the doctor's name and she couldn't remember hearing it at first but then, later on, Esther remembered Phyllis calling him Joel. And then Manny said it was probably his friend, Dr. Joel Zimmerman, he played golf with him and was a regular at the house. He asked Esther what he looked like and it matched his friend. Me and Irish Marie said nothing about the alleged affair at that point and then, Alyssa interrupted, "Dad, are you and Mom getting along? I noticed that the both of you have been acting strange when I stay on the weekends; there's a tense-ness when I come through the door. Is everything alright?" And Manny said, "I think we need to have this conversation, just me and you".

And, with that, Esther gets up from her recliner and blew our socks off! "Phyllis is having an affair with the doctor that examined me. It shouldn't be me to tell you because I'm your mother but, I can't hold it in anymore. And, what's more, it's your friend Joel she's having the affair with, so I said it. You know I loved Phyllis like a daughter so there was never any bad blood between us. And, Alyssa, I know she's your mother but this is my son. There, I said it. I'm not happy that I said it but, I can't hold it in anymore. You want to be angry at me, be angry. I said my peace." We were not going to bring it up to Manny but, Esther was on a roll and only family gets involved in that drama.

Manny said, "Ma, calm down; no one is getting angry at anyone. I appreciate that you spoke up, I know it wasn't easy for you. It only confirms what I already knew. I knew she was having an affair but, I didn't know with whom so, you solved that piece of the puzzle. Alyssa, what Bubbe said is true but, I wanted to sit you down and talk to you about it after you finished your first year of college. Your mother and I didn't want to put that added stress on you in your first year. Between your mother's Zumba classes at night and spending a weekend with one of her girlfriends in Connecticut, I figured something was up. I went to her Zumba classes on two separate occasions and she wasn't there. I didn't follow her to her girlfriend's house in Connecticut; I couldn't stand finding out the truth. But I never knew about the money and the meds, I swear! I did confront your mother about the affair a couple of weeks ago. At first, she denied it and then she told me she did have an affair but it was all over. And she begged my forgiveness and, I forgave her. But nothing's changed between us; we're still as distant as ever. Other than you, we have nothing to talk about and I think we're both unhappy."

He then said, "What's she's trying to do with my mother, that's another thing and I'm going to take care of it." Marie said, "I asked him how?" He said, "I'll confront her and then I'll be the Executor." She said, "I told him to wait; I'll contact Joe Bernstein at Bernstein and York and find out what has to be done." Irish Marie chimed in, "Manny what first needs to be done is to get your mother examined by a local doctor around here on a steady basis. Theresa Guarino can take care of that; one of us can bring your mother. We think Phyllis is trying to sell the house, declare your mother to be unfit to be on her own and then put your mother in a home in Florida. She may or may not have a separate bank account but the trust is wiring the money to her. If the house sells, she'll have a pretty penny when she gets the additional commission as Executor. And, if you look on the bottle, this is her last refill on the Klonipin so lock up those prescription pads before you lose your license. You'll have to confront her about the prescription and fill her in on what jail time looks like; she may not be thinking of the trouble she is causing to both you or your friend, Joel. Manny either you or Alyssa need to find out if any realtors have been contacted about selling this house. We have to prove to the world that Esther is fit to live here!"

And then Manny had an idea. "Mom, next Sunday, me and Phyllis are going to a wedding. Dad's nephew, Seth, his daughter is getting married. Everybody on his side will be there. They included you through our invitation but Phyllis told Seth that you were in no condition to travel. You were not yourself when I visited you a couple of months ago. And, from what Phyllis was telling me about you, I thought it was the right decision. I didn't want them to see you so sick or as sick as I was made to believe. Why don't you go the wedding? But, not with me and Phyllis."

He turned to us, "Ladies, do you think you can get her to a wedding in Roslyn, NY in one week? I'll give you the date, time and place. Once everyone at the wedding sees how good she looks, they'll see she's not an invalid." Well, you didn't have to twist our arms to agree. The only day Virginia was not working was Sunday so that meant we had to get Esther's hair and nails done, put on her make up, get her an evening dress and shoes and then get her to the reception. No problem!

Antoinette was the first to volunteer. She'd drive Esther to Macy's on Thursday evening and buy an evening outfit and shoes. Black Marie said she will talk to Uncle Jimmy about getting a limo to take Esther. Irish Marie said she'll have the house cleaned from top to bottom while Esther is at the wedding. Seriously, the house was a mess, it needed a good cleaning. Manny said he will call with the wedding information tomorrow. Black Marie said that with all the jabbering and planning, we forgot about Esther in the room and so we all turn around, looked at her and asked, "Esther, do you want to go to the wedding?" and she said, "Does a bear shit in the woods? Of course! Some of these people I haven't seen in years and it will be like Murray's spirit is with me through his family. Who wants more coffee?" Manny had to leave and Alyssa bummed a ride with her father to her apartment. And so, the plot thickened. Black Marie was right, we were in a soap opera. Where were we going to find a beauty parlor open on Sunday?

Manny called my house the next evening and told me the wedding was the following Sunday, 5:00 PM at the Swan Club in Roslyn, NY. Ready, set, go. Black Marie went to Uncle Jimmy in the club. He was getting on in years and he was in semi, semi-retirement by now but, he could still call on a few favors. He was at the club maybe one or two days a week now; he'd visit the old gang who were sick or go out to lunch with his cronies. He was more into the grandchildren and he was home more; he did the husband thing and drove his wife to go food shopping and visit relatives.

But he was in the club that day. "What the fuck is going on in the world today! Excuse the language. There's no more respect anymore, what a desgraciado!" was all Uncle Jimmy could say after hearing the soap opera that Black Marie told him. The limo guy he knew retired, but, his son, Jimmy and the limo guy's son are friends so, he'll do the favor. Uncle Jimmy asked Marie to write down the pick-up time and place. And then, he took out a Christmas card from his drawer that contained a $100 Macy's gift certificate. He gave it to Marie and told her to buy Esther a nice evening dress. Well, that was an added blessing! Oh, the energy created when you get a bunch of women together….and Uncle Jimmy!

During the week, Antoinette would go to Esther's and do the exercises with her; when you have to sit down all day, you get rusty, so Esther had to walk around the house all night. The Thursday before the wedding, Antoinette drove Esther to Macy's in Kings Plaza to get a dress; she had the gift certificate. They went to the Estee Lauder counter first to get make up and the ladies did a demo of everything they bought. Then, on to the dress. Esther wanted a pantsuit rather than a dress but, Antoinette found a nice cobalt blue cocktail dress with silver sequins on the bodice. Esther tried it on and fell immediately in love with it and, it was on sale! The shoe department had a nice pair of silver wide width open toe shoes that were perfect for the dress. We had the make-up, the dress and the shoes.

On the drive home, Esther said, "Antoinette, I promise, I'll pay you back every penny that you spent tonight once this mess is all over. I'm so glad we're friends again." Antoinette told her it was a gift from Big Jimmy and Esther got misty. After a short pause, Antoinette said, "Esther, I decided to put the past behind me. I've learned to forgive and forget. I've accepted what happened with Manny and me; I know you wanted him to marry a Jewish girl. Life is short, I have to put the past behind me." Esther turned to look at her and replied, "Antoinette, I would have accepted you with open arms, Murray and I would have been so happy to have you in our family. Didn't you know? Your father ended it. He wanted no mixed religion marriage for his daughter. He squashed it." Antoinette was in shock; she was told it was Esther who was against the marriage. Her father would never lie to her! But it seems he did lie because when Antoinette called her brother Emil that night, he verified it, "Yeah, Manny was in the house when it happened and he told me. He was very angry at Pop; even I was pissed off but, those were different times, Antoinette. He thought he was being a good father, what can I say? You have to put the anger behind you. It is what it is. Manny has his life and you have yours and that's the way it is." And so, Antoinette told him everything about Esther and the wedding that Sunday. Emil said, "Boy, I'm going to hear an earful from Manny next month when we go midnight fishing on Sheepshead Bay!"

We stored Esther's wedding dress, shoes and make up in my house. Now, where were going to find a hairstylist who'll color and style her hair on a Sunday? Antoinette said she had a childhood friend, Thomas "Tommy" Costello, they were inseparable as children. She still gets together now and then although, it was some time since she spoke to him. "When we were little, he used to go to my house to play with my Barbies. He didn't like Ken dolls because they had no hair to brush; he loved styling Barbie's hair, though. He wasn't allowed any dolls at home." Back then, Italian mothers ignored things like that; they thought it was a phase; later on, however, when they became adults, there was no tolerance . Some gay men married, had children and had outside relationships but they were unhappy with the pretense and the guilt. Or worse, they contracted AIDS and passed away. Tommy did the brave thing in 1989 and came out of the closet. It was rough; his father kicked him out and he lived with a friend doing temp work for a little while; he also did a lot of drinking and drugs for about a year. His friend kicked him out into the street and, in despair, he decided to take a ride to the old neighborhood. This happened a little after Antoinette's father passed away. He happened to meet Carmela and Antoinette on 5th Ave; they heard his story and took him in to live with them. He lived there for about 18 months; during that time, he decided to enroll at the Robert Fiance Hairstyling School. He got his license and, according to Antoinette, he's was doing very well working in a salon in Manhattan; he lives with his boyfriend, Adam, in the Village. Although she hadn't spoken to him in a while, she still had his telephone number, so she gave him a call.

After the initial "how ar ya" and "how ya doin?" Antoinette gave him the condensed version of this drama and asked him if he could come over on Sunday morning or early afternoon and do his magic on Esther. "Antoinette, I'd do anything for you. Your mother, rest in peace, she took me in when I was a real cafone, a nothing. I owe my life to her. What she did for me, I'll never forget. She even spoke to my parents and reconnected us. God rest her soul. I've been meaning to call you but I've been so busy lately, I owe you a visit anyway. I will be there, what time?" Tommy knew Esther but, not as well; but, it didn't matter, Antoinette was asking. He asked if he could bring Adam with him and Antoinette said she would love to meet him; Esther was cool about gay men. Didn't I say Antoinette knew everybody?

Irish Marie had a knack for doing manicures so she said she'd drop Saturday night and do Esther's nails. It saved us a lot of time because Esther had to be ready by 4:00 PM the next day. She made Esther arroz con pollo for dinner and then she did the manicure.

Just so you know, Tommy and Adam did what should have been done long ago; they got married. Thank you, Supreme Court! We went to the wedding; gay men have the best weddings! I think it was about nine years ago. After the Esther episode, they became a fixture at Antoinette's place. They still live in the Village but, they're getting ready to move to the burbs. Tommy retired his scissors about 5 years ago, back problems, and Adam was already a retired nurse. Antoinette emails them Brewster listings every day; we'll be one big happy family in Brewster. I don't think she'll have to twist my arm to live there with Frankie Boy and God knows who else she convinces to move there!

Anyway, Sunday came; we took Esther to the Purity Diner for a big breakfast to hold her until the reception. Then Tommy and Adam came with the scissors, blow dryer and hair color; ready to color, cut and style. Hardest part for Esther was bending over the sink to wash the color out; she had a short torso, so they made her kneel with a cushion on the kitchen chair. Tommy brought the right color and he even did highlights! The color was really nice, a medium blonde, with blonde highlights around the sides and sections on top. She looked gorgeous! And then, we realized that Esther had no jewelry around the house. Esther said "Phyllis put all my good jewelry in a safe deposit box when Gladys started taking care of me." That was no problem, between me and Antoinette, we had enough jewelry for her.

Tommy and Adam were done and gone by around 2:30. We pulled out the cobalt blue dress and put it up against Esther; between the hair color and style, this dress matched perfectly! We put a napkin bib around her and Antoinette did her make-up just like the lady at Estee Lauder. Add those silver shoes and red nail polish and she was Va-Va-Va Voom! Antoinette took a lot of photos of us with Esther, Tommy and Adam with Esther and Esther all dolled up!

At 4:00 PM, a shiny black Cadillac pulled up and picked up Esther. Before she left, I told her that Little Marie was waiting for her at the Swan Club. "She'll help you out of the car and walk with you into the reception. Do you want Little Marie to escort you in?" And Esther said, "I want to do this all alone with my head held high" and we agreed. She kissed us. We told her no crying or it will ruin her make-up. We guided her down the stairs because she had new shoes on; you always have to break them in a little because they're stiff. And, away Esther went. The driver was friendly and, on the way going there, they were talking. He told her he knew both Antoinette and Black Marie because he was from around the neighborhood. He even knew her son, Manny! Small world.

When Esther finally arrived, she was nervous and the driver asked her if she needed help but, just at that moment, Little Marie Greco appeared and she walked Esther to the reception hall's entrance. Unfortunately, the wedding ceremony had just begun so Esther said to wait until it was over; she didn't want to take attention away from the bride and groom. Marie stayed with her until it was over; she took some more photos of Esther while they had the time. And then Little Marie gave her a hug and sent her off into the room.

When she walked into that reception, you could hear a pin drop on Murray's side of the family. When Phyllis and Manny turned around to see what was the matter, Phyllis was so shocked she missed her mouth and spilled wine on her dress. Manny got up so fast, he almost knocked his seat over. He walked over to Esther, "Mom, you look like a movie star!' and then, "I'm so proud to be your son right now!". Esther just said, "you have to look like a movie star in Roslyn!" He ordered another seat at his table. Seth came over and kissed his Aunt Esther. Murray's younger sister, Louise and her brother-in-law Stewart, their children and spouses all came around to kiss and hug her. The other two tables were also filled with cousins and their wives. They all came over to kiss her and gave Phyllis a quizzical look. Phyllis told them all that Esther was not doing good and was too sick to travel. Manny just let her run her mouth off and tell everyone in the family! All eyes were on Phyllis that night. The jig was up on her ever selling the house! Phyllis asked Esther, "Mom, you look great! How did you get here?" and Esther told her she has a friend who owns a limo service. Louise wanted to know who did her hair?

And from the corner of her mouth, Phyllis whispered to Manny, "How did she know about the wedding?" And Manny replied, "I told her and I told her I never prescribed Klonipin for her." I know about the prescription, Phyllis, and the Trust."

With that, Phyllis didn't speak a word through the entire reception but she did drink a lot. Manny got up and did a slow dance with Esther and the crowd all applauded, he said, "Mom, I promise you, I'll never let this happen again!" and Esther said, "And you never will as long as the Fairy Comaras are around!" he looked confused but they were having such a good time it flew over his head. After the dance, the bride and groom came over to hug her. Before they got to their table, Manny told her he was picking her up tomorrow morning to change the trust over to him and he would be taking care of everything from now on; no more macaroni and cheese dinners. He said, "Marie Greco called me up and she's sending a lady, three days a week, to help you with some chores. Out of the blue she called me, just like that!"

Esther got home around 11:00PM, and, of course, we were waiting for her! Little Marie gave us only the entrance story on the phone. Esther told us what Phyllis said to her, "Mom, I was only doing what I thought best for you" and Esther said, "well, you thought wrong and sadly, I was wrong about you". Esther told us she hadn't had this much fun since Murray was alive and it was so good to see his family. Black Marie told her that Joe Bernstein was expecting them with paperwork ready at 9:30 AM tomorrow.

Esther looked around and couldn't believe how clean the house looked and we told her Irish Marie scrubbed the whole house, did the laundry and shampooed the carpets while she was away. I told Esther, "And from now on, Irish Marie's crew will be cleaning your house once a week. Manny gave us the green light to do it with the trust's money. And, Antoinette will drive you to Key Food to do your food shopping, no charge." Virginia was let go and Little Marie Greco sent a young lady three days a week to help her out with laundry and special projects, like gardening and cleaning out the basement. The following Saturday, Esther took us out to dinner at Monte's to thank us all; Manny came, too! Esther became a regular at the Thursday evening meetings until she passed away in 2009.

Maybe about three months after the wedding, I saw Manny bringing in a few boxes to Esther's house. Esther told me that after Manny confronted Phyllis with the prescription, the Trust and lastly, the affair, they both agreed it was time to split. It was not a home to go home to any longer so he asked Esther if he could stay for the time being until the divorce was finalized. Alyssa stayed weekends with her mother for a year and then her mother told her the house had to be sold as part of the divorce. Bubbe had room in her house if she wanted to come on the weekends! Manny didn't want any of the money Phyllis took from the Trust which, after draining it for seven months came to a little over $100,000; for Alyssa's sake, he wasn't going to press charges. And Phyllis behaved and didn't ask for alimony. The divorce was finalized about 18 months later. Manny never moved out of his mother's house because….

Antoinette was there all the time! In addition to the Thursday meetings, Antoinette took Esther to bingo and all three of them went to the movies. She and Manny talked about the old neighborhood; even Emil, who was still living in Staten Island at the time, came over and spent some evenings with him. Needless to say, Antoinette was there most of the time. All of us knew she was in love with Manny since forever but, Antoinette was hesitant to jump right in because she didn't want to be a rebound victim. He was newly divorced; did he still have feelings for her or was this just a familiar face in an unsteady world?

Meanwhile, she was still having the Wednesday afternoons with Fred Manza but, after Manny came to live with Esther, let's just say, it wasn't the same and she wasn't always up to the "task." Actually, Fred Manza wasn't up to the task either; claimed his problems at home were getting more intense and he was actually contemplating divorce. He told her not to say anything on the phone when she spoke with his wife.

The next day was Thursday and we had an evening meeting; it was all readings that night coupled with gossip and Theresa's Guarino's handmade jewelry. This time, Antoinette asked me for a reading; in all the time she lived with me, she never asked for a reading. She believed in readings but never got one. She told me she had a problem that needed to be solved soon. I did her reading first before the majority of the ladies came so she could start serving the coffee and cake. Esther was coming, too; she made a bunt cake with icing. For the record, I don't usually give Tarot readings but, I was getting confusing signals from Antoinette from the start so I got the deck out of my drawer and told her to start shuffling as many times as she wanted. She placed the Sacred Heart funeral card on the table, sprinkled holy water on the Tarot deck and then I started placing the cards.

I'm not going to dissect every card that was thrown down on the table; it was a seven card draw and very lengthy. These days, I can't remember what I ate yesterday let alone what cards were drawn over 20 years ago. But the reading came out this way:

"Antoinette, I feel like you are in a relationship that is going nowhere. One of the cards I recall said "that the other party didn't have the same feelings for you as you have for him. Is this man involved in another relationship?" Antoinette, hesitantly said, "he could be in another relationship." She was very hedgy about it. Now, I'm saying to myself, Antoinette is home every fucking weekend, I've never seen her bring a man around, maybe this is a budding relationship and she wants me to say if it's good or bad? Is it Manny? I didn't know. So, after I psychically connected with the cards for a few seconds, I asked, "Antoinette, this guy married?" She put her head down and said yes. So, I asked, "Antoinette, you're asking about Manny? Because he's going to be divorced soon. Do you think that he has feelings for you now? So, she said, "well, it's not about Manny although it could be but, I am torn because there's another guy I know a long time who I have been seeing and I'm not sure if it could be something permanent." She said, "He also mentioned divorcing his wife to me."   And I said, "Antoinette since you've been living in my house, I've never seen you bring a man home or speak about this man or any man, not that it's any of my business. When do you date this guy? On your lunch hour?" She was sipping some water when I said this and she coughed; I had to pat her on the back! I was joking when I said it but, she told me yes, she did meet with him on her lunch hour.

And then she told me everything about her and Fred Manza's Wednesdays for almost 20 years and that he just told her he was thinking about getting a divorce. Did this mean she had a future with him? So, I threw out a few more cards and it came out that this was not her path; it didn't seem like this was going to happen. So, I said, "Maybe he was just saying this to you to keep the affair going? It's been 20 years, you know! Maybe he thought you were thinking of ending it?" In my mind, I'm thinking this guy was a real slime ball but, I had to be non-judgmental. "The cards say that what you think will happen, will not come to pass so, if you're thinking he's going to get a divorce and you will finally have a relationship with Fred, maybe it won't happen." And then I said, "you may be changing jobs" which she hadn't thought of but, she said she would think about it.

Fred Manza did get a divorce; Antoinette found out through his wife, Sue. She called one morning and Antoinette told her Fred was in a meeting but, he would be out in a few minutes. "I have to tell you something, Antoinette, and I know you're not going to be happy to hear this news but, Fred and I are getting a divorce." Antoinette said, "Sue, what are you saying? I can't believe it!"

Antoinette said she felt bad about lying like that and her right eye was starting to twitch; Fred hadn't said a word since the Wednesday they were together and after our reading, she thought Fred was just whining. And then Sue said, "he confessed he's been having an affair for some time." Antoinette's head wanted to explode! "We're still going to be living together until the divorce but, he stays at HER place on the weekends. Supposedly, she has an apartment on the East Side. To be honest, we haven't been close since our son graduated college and moved out; after that, we really had nothing to talk about. About six months ago, he started sleeping in our son's old bedroom. I'm glad in a way that he told me the truth. Please don't be angry at me but, at one time, I thought he was having an affair with you! I'm so sorry, don't be angry. Every time he came home, he would say, Antoinette did this, or Antoinette cooked me that and I thought it was you but, he told me I was crazy for thinking that and I'm sorry Antoinette for thinking that it was you. Don't tell Fred, I told you about the divorce. He probably wants to tell you himself."

Well, when Fred got out of the meeting, he did tell Antoinette but, it wasn't that he was getting a divorce. Fred told her he just got out of a strategy meeting; he was happy to tell her he got a promotion to Executive Vice President. He was moving up to the Executive Suites on the 22nd floor. Antoinette asked, "so, we're going up to 22?" But Fred said, "No, I'm going up to 22, you will be reporting to whomever takes my place from now on. They have a pool of Executive Assistants up there to handle senior management; I asked but, they said no." It turned out to be all bullshit because he was actually dating the Chief Operating Officer's daughter and he didn't want Antoinette around. After his divorce was finalized, they had a big engagement party for Fred and his fiancé, Sandra. Antoinette bowed out...for good. Antoinette worked for another manager for a couple of years but, it became uncomfortable. Every time she saw Fred; he would pretend he didn't see her. She finally left; not because her new boss was a bad boss but because of Fred and his lies.

Meanwhile, she and Manny were getting close. They started dating a few months after and, I mean really out in the open dating, when Manny's divorce was finalized. And, with Esther's blessing, they were married in 2003. We gave her a beautiful bridal shower in my house and the wedding was held at Prospect Hall; everybody came from all around. She made a beautiful bride; Bishop Giudice and Rabbi Schneider officiated the ceremony. Frankie Boy gave her away, Emil was Manny's Best Man and out of the Fairy Comaras, they chose me to be her Maid of Honor because I was the only one who was single. Esther gave them a cruise to Aruba as a wedding gift but Antoinette told her she'd only accept it if Esther came, too, so all three of them went. Antoinette told me Esther spent some considerable time on the cruise with a gentleman in the silver fox category and they all had a great time.

Antoinette and Manny decided to live with Esther and they took very good care of her. Antoinette got a job working for Bennie's Party Palace planning parties and weddings. It was her second calling! Little Marie Greco got a great home aid for Esther during the day and Irish Marie cleaned her house for the rest of Esther's life. Esther came to the Thursday evening meetings until she passed away in 2009. Antoinette, Manny, Alyssa and the Fairy Comaras were with her when she died.

Phyllis came to Esther's Shiva with her husband, Dr. Joel Zimmerman. For Alyssa's sake, her parents kept it cordial. Alyssa got married in 2007; Esther got to see her granddaughter get married and her first great grandchild before she died. Alyssa's husband is an electrician and after working for a company in Brooklyn, he saw an opportunity to start his own business upstate in Brewster, NY. By then, Manny was a grandfather twice to two boys.

Manny retired in 2016 and Antoinette retired three years ago after working at Bennie's Party Palace. They traveled back and forth to Brewster to see Alyssa and the crew and drove down to North Carolina, during the winter, to spend some time with Frankie Boy and Emil. They rented the downstairs apartment after Esther passed away; after a few years, the tenants moved out and they decided to leave it vacant. After we ended the Thursday evening meetings in 2010, some of the Fairy Comaras got together in my house or Antoinette's; sometimes she invited someone who needed our help. I gave readings in my home on an individual basis until my appointments dwindled to maybe one or two a year. And now, no one comes.

In 2017, Theresa Guarino was diagnosed with late-stage lung cancer; she never smoked but cancer ran in the family. We all took turns visiting her. Even though Little Marie Greco retired from Francone Senior Center, she still had some clout and found her a caregiver during the day; her two working daughters took over at night. By then, she was living in a condo in New Jersey near them. When she was nearing the end, Little Marie got Theresa hospice care. The day before she died, we had her pissing in her pants talking about all the crazy things we did; she coughed a lot laughing but her eyes were brightened with happy tears. She passed that night in her sleep and we all woke up the next morning knowing she had passed even before her daughters called us. It was at Theresa's wake that Antoinette started bugging me to tell our story or at the very least, some of it. When you get older you have more time but, you get distracted a lot and that's what happened to me so it took me until now to write it. And now, Antoinette is living in Brewster and I'm getting ready to move. To Brewster.

Our last Thursday evening meeting was Thursday, December 23, 2010. We had about 20-25 people that night: Me, Antoinette, Black Marie and her daughter, Annette, Little Marie Greco, Irish Marie, Marie from Long Island, Sylvia Cusimano, Ann Caracciolo and Theresa Guarino and her two daughters. Anyone who could make it that night was there. Antoinette made stuffed shells, I made chicken Parmigiana, Theresa Guarino made the daiquiris, Black Marie made her mother's famous linguini with clams and the guests brought cake and cookies. Manny came just to eat and then he left. Frankie Valdaro stopped by, too. Later on, Tommy Costello and Tony Slice dropped by to say hello and exchange Christmas gifts; they were sad to hear the Thursday evening meetings were ending. We all promised we'd see each other but, it was hard traveling so far and we weren't getting any younger. By 2013, it was only me and Antoinette still living on our block.

Antoinette suggested that we start a marketing campaign to create Fairy Comaras chapters; we're still waiting for the members to come.... maybe someday.

P.S. I did sell my house. I sold it to my Latino neighbors, the Beltranos, for a fraction of its market value. No realtor, Black Marie helped me with the legalese, just the bank for the mortgage and closing. The bank manager thought I needed a third party to intervene on my behalf because of the selling price. Why be greedy? I had the Microsoft stocks and my IRA. This could be my last act as a Fairy Comara.

Antoinette and I looked at a nice one story, no stairs, house in Brewster less than a mile away from her and Manny; I bought it. Frankie Boy bought a summer home in Brewster for his family; I knew Antoinette would convince him. And Emil and his family come up for the summer, too! Tommy Costello and Adam bought a house in Fishkill, NY and we see them at least once a week. Little Marie moved to Pennsylvania near her son and Black Marie and Sal Giordano live near their daughter, Annette, in Long Island. They stayed a week at my house this summer. Irish Marie sold the business two years ago, Brian retired, their kids are married and they have two grandchildren. They moved to one of those gated communities in Florida near her brother Hector. She promised us she'll visit this summer.

On summer evenings, we sit around in beach chairs, just like our mothers and laugh until our cheeks hurt. And though we've grown old and frail, we'll always be the Fairy Comaras.

THE End

Acknowledgments

Many thanks to Joseph Ricci for his design of the cover and book design, his invaluable research and support in getting this book published; and the patience to actually read this book! Special thanks to Joe Zwielich for his photographic talent in making me look good. And, thanks to Robert, my better half, for always giving me enough space and support to start writing this book. And last, but not least, thanks to all my friends who constantly asked me through the years, "when are you going to write that effin book!"

Made in United States
Orlando, FL
16 August 2022

21093650R00117